The Extremes

The Extremes

Christopher Priest

First published in Great Britain in 1998
by Simon & Schuster UK Ltd

This edition published in Great Britain
in 2005 by Gollancz
An imprint of the Orion Publishing Group
Orion House, 5 Upper St Martin's Lane,
London WC2H 9EA

3 5 7 9 10 8 6 4

A CIP catalogue record for this book
is available from the British Library

ISBN 978 05 7507578 8

Typeset at The Spartan Press Ltd,
Lymington, Hants

Printed in Great Britain by
Clays Ltd, St Ives plc

www.orionbooks.co.uk

For Leigh

CHAPTER 1

Her name is Teresa Ann Gravatt and she is seven years old: She has a mirror through which she can see into another world.

The real world is for Teresa a small and unexciting one, but she dreams of better things, of a world beyond the one she knows. She lives with her parents on a US Air Force base near Liverpool, in the north-west of England. Her father is a serving officer in the USAF; her mother is British, a local girl from Birkenhead. One day the family will move back to the USA when her father's tour of European duty is through. They will probably go to Richmond, Virginia, where Bob Gravatt originated, and where his own father has a franchise for distributing industrial paints. Bob often talks about what he will do when he leaves the Air Force, but it's plain to everyone that the Cold War is going to continue for many years to come, and that US military preparedness is not going to be relaxed.

Teresa has long curls of pale-brown hair, gradually darkening from the baby fairness that made her daddy call her his princess. Her mommy likes to brush it for her, although she doesn't seem to realize when the tangles get caught. Teresa can now read books by herself, write and draw by herself, play by herself. She is used to being alone, but likes playing with the other kids on the base. She rides her bicycle every day in the safety of the park near the living quarters, and it's then she plays with some of her friends. She's currently the only one with an English mother, but no one seems to notice. Every weekday her daddy drives her to and from the other side of the base, where the children of the serving men attend school.

Teresa looks and acts like a happy little girl; she is loved by her parents and liked by her friends at school. Nothing seems wrong in Teresa's life, because those who know her best live in the same secure world of the US Air Force. Her friends also lack a permanent home, and are moved at the will of the Defense Department from one Air Force camp to another. They too know the long weeks when their fathers are away on exercises, or training. They also understand the sudden disruption to their lives that follows when a posting comes through: to West Germany, to the Philippines, to Central America, to Japan.

Although she has never yet crossed the Atlantic, Teresa has spent almost all of her life on American territory, those pockets carved out of other people's countries that the US Government takes for its own bases. Teresa was born an American citizen, she is being educated in the American way, and in a few years' time, when her father finishes his military service, she will live out the rest of her life in the United States. Teresa knows none of this at the moment, and if she did she would probably not care. To her, the world she knows is one place, and the world she imagines is another. Daddy's world ends at the perimeter fence; hers goes on for ever.

Sometimes, when it rains, which in this part of England it seems to do almost every day, or when she most wants the company of other kids, or when she just feels like it, Teresa plays a game in her parents' bedroom that she has made up by herself.

Like all the best games it has been growing and changing for some time, and goes on getting more complicated week by week, but right from the start it has been built around the wooden door frame that stands at the mid-point of the bedroom wall. No actual door has apparently ever hung in the frame; perhaps no door was intended for it, for there is no sign in the smooth wood of where hinges might once have been.

Long ago, Teresa noticed that the window of the living room beyond is the same size, shape and appearance as the window of the bedroom, and that identical orange curtains hang in both. If she arranges these curtains just so, and then stands in a certain position a foot or two away from the door frame, and does not look to either side, it is possible for her to imagine that she is looking not through an open doorway but into a mirror. Then, what she sees ahead of her, through the frame, is no longer a part of the next room but actually a reflected view back into the room behind her.

The mirror world is where her private reality begins. Through there it is possible for her to run for ever, a place that is free of military bases, free of perimeter fences, a land where her dreams might come true.

That place begins with the identical room that stands on the other side of the frame. And in that room she sees another little girl, one who looks exactly like her.

A few weeks ago, while she stood before her make-believe mirror, Teresa had raised a hand, reaching out towards the little girl she could so easily imagine standing beyond her, in the next room, in the mirror world. Magically, the imagined friend raised her hand too, copying her every movement.

The little girl's name was Megan, and she became Teresa's opposite in every way. She was her identical twin, but also her reverse, her opposite.

Now whenever Teresa is left alone, or when her parents are busy elsewhere in the house, she comes to the mirror and plays her harmless fantasy games with Megan.

First she smiles and tweaks at her dress, then inclines her head. In the mirror the Megan-friend smiles and lifts the hem of her dress and lowers her head shyly. Hands stretch out, fingertips brush clumsily where the mirror glass would be. Teresa dances away, laughing back over her shoulder as Megan mirrors her movements. Everything the girls do has a reflection, an exact replica.

Sometimes the two little girls settle on the floor at the base of the mirror, and whisper about the world they each inhabit. Should an outsider ever be able to overhear what they are saying, it would not make sense in adult terms. It is a strange, erratic fantasy, endlessly absorbing and plausible to the children, but it would seem shapeless and random to an adult mind, because they make it up as they go along. For the two little girls, the nature of this contact is the rationale. Their lives and fantasies fit seamlessly together, because each is the complement to the other. They are so uncannily alike, so instinctively in touch, but their worlds are filled with different names.

So the pleasant dreams of childhood spin happily away. Days, weeks, months go by, and Teresa and Megan live out their innocent daydreams of other lands and deeds. It is a period of certainty and stability in their lives. They both have a constant friend, and they completely trust and understand each other.

Because Megan is always there, looking back at her from the other side of their mirror, Teresa draws strength from the friendship and begins to develop more ideas about herself and the world she lives in. She feels better able to see what's going on around her and live with what she finds, to understand what her dad is doing, and why he and her mommy had married, and what their lives would mean for her. Even her mother detects a difference in her, and often remarks that her little girl is growing up at last. Everyone can sense the growth.

In the mirror, Megan is changing too.

One day her mommy says to Teresa, 'Do you remember that I said we would be going to live in America?'

'Yes, I do.'

'It's going to happen soon. Really soon. Maybe in a couple of weeks or so. Would that make you happy?'

'Will Daddy be there with us?'

'He's the reason we're going.'

'And Megan?'

Her mother holds her against her chest more tightly.

'Of course Megan will be with us. Did you think we would leave her behind?'

'I guess not,' says Teresa, looking back over her mother's shoulder at the doorway, where the mirror usually stands. She can't see Megan from this angle, but knows she must be there, somewhere out of sight.

One day, while her parents are in another part of the apartment talking about the trip back to America, how close it's getting, all the things they have to do before they fly back, Teresa is alone in the bedroom. She has her toys spread out on the carpet, but she's bored with them. She looks across to the doorway, and sees that Megan is there, waiting for her. Her friend looks as cross and bored as she feels, and both little girls seem to realize that for once their shared fantasy world is not going to distract them from reality.

While Megan turns away, Teresa crosses the room to her parents' double bed, where the lightly padded quilt her mommy made last Christmas holiday lies in a show of muted colours across the sheets and blankets. Out of sight of Megan she bounces up and down a few times, but even this familiar physical activity is not enough to cheer her up. She's beginning to wonder if Megan really will be there, in the new house in America.

Teresa looks across at what she can see of the mirror, but because the bed is not visible she knows that Megan cannot be seen either. Already, her little world feels as if it is narrowing, that the perimeter fences are drawing in around her.

Later, after a meal, she returns to the bed, still worried and alarmed. Her daddy has been saying he will be flying out to Florida the day after tomorrow, and that she and Mommy will follow within a few days. At the mirror Megan is as unhappy as she is, fearing a final separation, and they soon move back from each other.

There's a low table beside the bed on her daddy's side, and facing into the room there's a shallow drawer which, once, long ago, her daddy had warned her never to open. Teresa has always known what lies inside, but until now she has never felt sufficiently curious to look.

Now she does, and lays her hand on the gun that lies within. She touches it once or twice, feeling the shape of it with her fingertips, then uses both hands to lift the weapon out. She knows how it should be held, because her daddy once showed her, but now she actually has a hold of it in her tiny hands her main preoccupation is how heavy the thing is. She can barely carry it before her.

It's the most exciting thing she has ever held, and the most frightening.

In the centre of the room, facing the mirror, she lays the gun on the seat of a chair, and looks across at Megan. She is standing there beside her own chair, still with the melancholy expression they have both been wearing for the last day or two.

There is no gun on Megan's chair.

'Look what I've got,' says Teresa, and as Megan strains to see she lifts it up and holds it out. She points it at her twin, across the narrow space that divides them. She is aware of movement in the room, a sudden intrusion, an adult size, and she moves swiftly in alarm. In that moment there is a shattering explosion, the gun flies out of Teresa's hands, twisting her wrists, and in the other part of the room, beyond the make-believe mirror, a small life of dreams has suddenly ended.

Thirty-five years pass.

Eight years after the family's return to the USA, Bob Gravatt, Teresa's father, dies in an automobile accident on Interstate 24 close to a USAF base in Kentucky. After the accident Teresa's mother Abigail moves to Richmond, Virginia, to stay with Bob's parents. It is an arrangement forced on them all, and it is difficult to make it work. Abigail starts drinking heavily, runs up debts, has a series of rows with Bob's parents, and eventually remarries. Teresa now has two new stepbrothers and a stepsister, but no one likes anyone. It's not a happy situation for Teresa, or even, finally, for her mother. The remainder of Teresa's teenage years are hard on everyone around her, and things do not look good for her.

As she grows into an adult, Teresa's emotional upheavals continue. She goes through heartbreaks, failed romances, relocations, alienation from her mother, also from her father's family; there's a long live-in relationship with a man who develops steadily into an alcoholic brimming with denial and violent repression; there is a short period living alone, then a longer one of sharing an apartment with another young woman, then finally arrives the good fortune of discovering a city scheme that funds mature students to take a degree course.

Here her adult life begins at last. After four years of intensive academic work, supporting herself with secretarial jobs, Teresa earns her BA in information studies, and with this lands a prize job with the federal government, in the Department of Justice.

Within a couple of years she is married to a fellow worker named Andy Simons, and it is on the whole a successful marriage. Andy and Teresa live contentedly together for several years, with few upsets. The marriage is childless, because they are both dedicated to their careers and sublimating all their energies into them, but it's the life they want to lead. With two government incomes they gradually become well off, take expensive foreign vacations, start collecting antiques and pictures, buy several cars, throw numerous parties, and wind up buying a large house in Woodbridge, Virginia, overlooking the Potomac river. Then one hot June day, while on an assignment in a small town in the Texas panhandle, Andy is shot dead by a gunman, and Teresa's happiness abruptly ends.

Eight months later, life is still in limbo. She knows only the misery of sudden widowhood, made infinitely worse by a deep resentment about the circumstances in which Andy was killed, and a lasting frustration at the failure of the Department of Justice to give her any substantive information about how his death occurred.

She is now forty-three. A third of a century has slipped by since the day Megan died, and in the cold light of hindsight the years telescope into what feels like a summary of a life, a prologue to something else she does not want. Everything that happened led only to the moment of bereavement. Teresa is left with the generous pay-outs from Andy's insurance policies, their three jointly owned cars, a large house echoing with unwanted acquisitions and treasured memories, and a career from which she has been granted the opportunity to take temporary leave on compassionate grounds.

In the dark of a February evening, Teresa finally takes up her section chief's offer of leave. She drives to John Foster Dulles Airport in Washington DC, deposits her car in the long-stay parking garage, and flies American Airways on the overnight plane to Britain.

As she looks eagerly from the window, while the aircraft circles down towards London Gatwick in the morning light, Teresa thinks the English countryside looks dark and rain-sodden. She doesn't know what she had been expecting, but the reality depresses her. As the plane touches down her view of the airport is briefly obscured by the flying spray thrown up from the runway by the wheels and the engine exhausts. February in England is not as cold as February in Washington, but as she crosses the airport's concrete concourse in search of her rental car, the weather feels to Teresa more damp and discouraging than she wanted or expected.

She drives away into England, fighting back these initial feelings of disappointment. She is nervous of the twitchy handling of the small car, a Ford Escort, uncomfortable too with the impatient speed with which the rest of the traffic moves, and the erratic and apparently illogical way the intersections have to be negotiated.

As she becomes more familiar with the car, she casts quick

glances away from the traffic and round at the countryside, looking with intense interest at the low hills, the winter-bare trees, the small houses and the muddy fields. This is her first trip back to England since she left as a child, and in spite of everything it begins at last to charm her.

She imagines a smaller, older, more tightly constructed place, different from the one she knows, spreading out, not in endless stretches of featureless country, as in the US, but in concentrated time: history reaching behind her, the future extending before her, meeting at this moment of the present. She's tired from the long flight, the lack of sleep, the wait at the UK Immigration desk, and so she's open to fanciful thoughts.

She stops in a small town somewhere, to walk around and look at the shops, but afterwards returns to the car and naps for a while in the cramped position behind the steering wheel. She wakes up suddenly, momentarily unsure of where she is, thinking desperately of Andy, how much she wishes he could see this with her. She came here to try to forget him, but in many ways she had been doing better so long as she stayed at home. She wants him here. She cries in the car, wondering whether to go back to Gatwick and take the first flight home, but in the end she knows she has to see this through.

The short afternoon is ending as she drives on south towards the Sussex coast, looking for a small seaside town called Bulverton. She keeps thinking, This is England, this is where I come from, this is what I really know. But she has no remaining family in Britain, no friends. She is in every way a stranger here. A year ago, eight months ago, what was for her a lifetime ago, she had never even heard of Bulverton on Sea.

Teresa arrives in Bulverton after night has fallen. The streets are narrow, the buildings are dark, the traffic pours through on the coastal road. She finds her hotel but sits outside in the car for a few minutes, bracing herself. At last, she collects together some of her stuff and climbs out.

A brilliant white light suddenly surrounds her.

CHAPTER 2

Her name was Amy Colwyn and she had a story to tell about what had happened to her one day last June. Like so many other people in Bulverton, she had no one to tell it to. No one around her could bear to hear it any more, and even Amy herself no longer wanted to say the words. How many times can you express grief, guilt, missed companionship, regrets, remembered love, lost chances? But failing to say the words did nothing to make them not thought.

Tonight, as so often, she sat alone behind the bar at the White Dragon with nothing much to distract her, and the story played maddeningly in her mind. It was always there, like music you can't get out of your mind.

'I'll be in the bar if you want me,' Nick Surtees had said to her earlier. He was the owner of the hotel, someone else perhaps with a story to tell.

'All right,' she said, because every evening he told her he was going into the bar, and every evening she replied that it would be all right.

'Are we expecting any visitors tonight?'

'I don't think so. Someone might turn up, I suppose.'

'I'll leave that to you, then. If no one checks in, would you mind coming in and helping out behind the bar?'

'No, Nick.'

Amy Colwyn was one of the many left-over victims of the massacre that had taken place in Bulverton the previous summer. She had not been in physical danger herself, but her life had been blighted none the less by the event. The horror of that day lived on. Business at the hotel was usually slow, allowing her too much time to dwell on what had happened to others, and what might have been her life now if the disaster had not happened.

Nick Surtees, another indirect victim of the shootings, was one of the matters of regret on which she frequently dwelt. There had been a time, not so long ago, when it would never have occurred to her that she would see Nick again, let alone be working, living and sleeping with him. Yet that had happened and they were all still happening, and she wasn't entirely sure how. Nick and she had found comfort in each other, and were still there holding on when that need had begun to retreat.

Bulverton was situated on the hilly edge of the Pevensey Levels between Bexhill and Eastbourne. Fifty years ago it had been a holiday resort, the type of seaside town traditionally preferred by families with young children. With the coming of cheap foreign holidays Bulverton had gone into rapid decline as a resort; most of the seafront hotels had been converted into blocks of flats or retirement homes. For the last two decades Bulverton had in a manner of speaking turned its back on the sea, and had concentrated on promoting the charms of its Old Town. This was a small network of attractive terraces and gardens, covering part of the river valley and one of the hills rising up beside it. If Bulverton could be said to have an industry now, it was in the shops that sold antiques or secondhand books, in a number of nursing homes in the high part of the town known as the Ridge, and in providing homes for the people who commuted to their jobs in Brighton, Eastbourne or Tunbridge Wells.

It was because of Nick that the White Dragon could not seem to make up its mind whether to be a pub or a seaside hotel. Keeping it as a pub suited him, because he spent most evenings in the saloon bar downstairs, drinking with a few of his pals.

The marginally more profitable hotel side, the bed and breakfast and the occasional half-board for a weekend, was Amy's domain, mainly through Nick's own lack of interest. In the days and weeks immediately after the shootings, when Bulverton was crammed with journalists and film crews, the hotel had been full. The work had offered itself as a welcome distraction from her own preoccupations, and she had thrown herself into it. Business had inevitably declined as the first shock of the catastrophe began to fade, and media interest receded; by the middle of July it was back to what Amy now knew was its normal level. So long as there were never too many people arriving at the same time, Amy, working alone, could comfortably keep the rooms clean and have the beds made up, provision the tiny restaurant with a reasonable choice of meals, and even keep the financial records up to date. None of these jobs interested Nick.

Amy often thought back to the times when she and some of her old schoolfriends would move across to Eastbourne every summer, from July to September, when there were always two or three major conferences taking place: trade unions, political parties, business or professional organizations. It had never been hard finding short-term but comparatively well paid jobs: chambermaids and bar staff were always needed in the big hotels. It had been a laugh as well, lots of young men on the loose, all with money to burn and no one taking too much notice of what was going on. She had met Jase then, also working the conference business, but as a wine waiter. That had been another laugh, because Jase, who was a roofer in real life, knew less about wine than did even Amy.

What Amy hadn't told Nick about was the feeling of letdown that had been growing in her all that day. It concerned a reservation made two weeks before from America. Amy had not mentioned the booking to Nick at the time it was made, and she had quietly slipped the deposit for the room into the bank. A woman called Teresa Simons had written to ask if she might reserve a room with en suite bathroom on an open-ended basis; she said she was making a long visit to Bulverton, and needed a base.

A pleasant daydream then swept over Amy, a vision of having one of the rooms permanently occupied throughout the slow months of late winter: it was a potentially lucrative booking, with meals and bar takings all boosted by the woman's stay. It was absurd to think that one semi-permanent guest could transform their fortunes, but for some reason Amy had felt convinced that she could. She faxed back promptly, confirming the room, and had even suggested a modest discount for a long stay. The booking and the deposit turned up not long afterwards. Nick still didn't know about it.

Today was the day Mrs Simons was due to arrive. According to her letter she would be flying into Gatwick in the morning, and Amy had been half expecting her to turn up from mid-morning onwards. By lunchtime there was no sign of her, and no message either. As the day crept by she still didn't arrive and Amy had been feeling a steadily growing sense of mishap. It was out of proportion to its importance – there were all sorts of reasons why the plane might have been delayed, and anyway why should the woman come straight to the hotel after getting off a plane? – and Amy realized this.

It made her aware yet again how much of herself she was pouring into this unpromising business. She had wanted to surprise Nick with Mrs Simons' arrival, tell him about what she assumed would be a welcome source of income for some time. It might even, she had briefly hoped, break him out of his seemingly permanent round of worry and silent brooding.

She knew that they were both in a cycle of misery, a long period of grief. They weren't alone in Bulverton: most of the people in the town were still grieving.

It was what Reverend Oliphant had said at the town's memorial service the week after the disaster – that one occasion in her life when Amy had wanted to go to church, and did. Kenneth Oliphant had said: grief is an experience like happiness or success or discovery or love. Grief has a shape and a duration, and it gives and takes away. Grief has to be endured, surrendered to, so that an escape from it lies beyond grief itself, on the other side, only attainable by passing through.

There was comfort in such words, but no solutions. Like so many others in the town, Amy and Nick were still passing through, with the other side nowhere in sight.

Sitting on a high stool behind the bar, staring vacantly across at the table where Nick and his pals were playing brag on a table lightly puddled with beer and under a pale-blue cloud of tobacco smoke, Amy heard a car.

It came to a halt in the street outside. Amy did not move her face or her eyes, but all her senses stretched out towards the sound of the idling engine. No car doors opened, and the engine continued to run. It was a sort of silence.

There was a metallic grinding of gears being engaged – lazily, incompetently, or tiredly? – and the car moved away again. Through the frosted lower panes of the bar windows Amy saw its rear brake lights brightening as the driver slowed at the archway entrance, then swung the car into the car park behind.

Amy's heightened senses followed it like a radar tracker. She heard the engine cut out at last.

She left the stool, raised the serving flap in the counter, and walked across the room to peer through the window at the street outside. If Nick noticed her movement he showed no sign that he had. The card game continued, and one of Nick's friends lit another cigarette.

Amy pressed her forehead to the cool, condensation-lined window, rubbed a wet aperture with her fingers, and looked across Eastbourne Road in the direction of the unseen sea. The main road outside was tracked with the shine of old rain and the drier strips where vehicle tyres had worn their paths. The orange light from the streetlamps reflected in distorted patches from the uneven road surface and from the windows of the shops and flats on the other side. Some of the shop windows were lit, but most of them were either covered by security panels or simply vacant.

Amy watched the passing traffic for a moment, wondering how it was possible that the sound of one car coming to a halt had stood out so noticeably against the continuous noise of all the others. It must mean that she had never relaxed, that the arrival of the American woman had assumed a personal significance of some kind.

She walked back to the area behind the bar, closed the hatch, then went into the corridor that ran behind the bar-room. At the other end of this was the part of the building in which she and Nick lived and slept. Immediately beyond the bar door was the small kitchen where they cooked and ate their own meals. She did not turn this way, though, but walked along to the fire exit. She pushed her way through the double doors. They opened into the hotel's car park at the rear of the building.

Amy switched on the main security light, drenching the area in light that seemed, suddenly, too white and intrusive. A rain-spotted car had been parked at an angle across two of the white-lined bays, and a woman was leaning through the open rear passenger door to reach something. Presently she moved backwards and straightened, and placed two small valises on the ground.

Amy went across to her as the woman opened the tailgate. Inside the car were several more cases, and large bags stuffed with belongings.

'Mrs Simons?' Amy said.

'I'll show you to your room,' Amy said, and started up the stairs. Mrs Simons had gone ahead, so Amy overtook her on the first half-landing. As she passed, she saw the woman flash her a grateful smile.

She looked younger than Amy had expected, but her expectation had been based on hardly any information at all: an American address, handwriting in blue ballpoint on a kind of notepaper Amy had never seen before, something about the phrasing she used. The careful formality of the letter had summoned a vague but now clearly baseless impression of a matronly woman, at or close to the age of retirement. This was not the case. Mrs Simons had that preserved attractiveness, apparently ageless, of some TV actresses. Amy felt as if she knew her already, and for a moment even wondered if she might have seen her on TV. Behind the well-made surface she looked and sounded tired, as you would expect from someone who had come in on a plane from the US, but even so she had a relaxed manner that made Amy feel at ease with her. She looked as if she would be different, a more interesting kind of guest than the weekending retired couples and the overnight business visitors they normally had in their rooms.

Amy took her to room 12 on the first floor, which she had prepared earlier by checking that the bed linen was fresh and that the heating was on. She went inside in front of Mrs Simons, switching on the central light, then opening the connecting door to the bathroom for inspection. Americans were supposed to be fastidious about hotel bathrooms.

'I'll go and see about the rest of your luggage,' she said, but there was no response. Mrs Simons had already passed through into the bathroom. Amy left, and closed the door.

Downstairs in the bar Amy informed Nick of Mrs Simons' arrival straight away, but by this time he had drunk more than he should – which was the same thing as his usual amount, which was always more than enough – and he simply shrugged.

'Would you help her bring her luggage in from the car?' Amy said.

'Yeah, in a minute,' Nick said, indicating his hand of cards. 'Who is this, anyway? I don't remember you saying anything about someone arriving tonight.'

'I thought it'd be a surprise.'

Nick played a card.

Suppressing her irritation with him, Amy went out to the car and picked up the remaining pieces of luggage herself. She struggled up to room 12 with them.

'You can leave them there,' Teresa Simons said, indicating the corner of the floor. 'Did you carry them up on your own?'

'It's no problem,' Amy said. 'I was coming to see you anyway. Would you like something to eat, a supper? We don't really keep hotel hours for meals so it wouldn't be any trouble to me.'

'I guess not, but thanks. I stopped somewhere along the way. One of those roadside restaurants back there. You have a bar here?'

'Yes.'

'I'm going to rest up for a while, then maybe I'll have a drink downstairs.'

When Amy returned to the bar, Nick had left the table and was behind the counter drawing another pint of best for himself.

'Why didn't you tell me about her?' he said, raising the glass to his lips, and sucking at the foam.

'I thought you'd look in the file.'

'I leave all that to you, love. How long is she likely to stay? One night? A week?'

'She's booked in for an indefinite stay.'

She had expected a surprised reaction, but he simply said, 'We'd better give her a bill every weekend, then. You can't be too careful.'

Amy frowned, and followed him out from behind the counter.

She went round the tables and collected the few used glasses she could find. She changed the ashtray on Nick's table. Back behind the bar she leant forward, her hair falling at the sides of her face. She washed the glasses under the pressure-tap then stacked them on the rubber tray that went into the drier.

She was thinking about Nick and his drinking, the aimless life

15

he had drifted into, and the way in which for him one day seemed to lead into the next with neither change nor improvement. Yet what was the alternative for him? Come to that, what was the alternative for her? Both her parents were dead, Jase was dead, many of her friends were away in Brighton or Dover or London, starting up again, anywhere that was not in Bulverton. A lot of people had forsaken the town since the summer. The same urge was strong in her.

Two weeks ago Amy had received an unexpected letter from a cousin called Gwyneth, who had flown to Australia on a working holiday ten years ago, had fallen in love with a young builder and stayed on after her visa expired. Now she was an Australian citizen, married, and had two small children. Amy and Gwyneth hadn't written to each other since last winter. Her letter was full of concern about the life she supposed Amy must be having to lead in Bulverton these days. She didn't mention the disaster in the town, like so many people who were outsiders, or who had become one. Gwyneth was urging her, not for the first time, to come to Australia for a holiday and give Sydney a try. She had a spare room and a spare bed, she said, and they were only half an hour from downtown Sydney, with the harbour and the surfing beaches just a tram-ride away . . .

'Hi.'

The American woman had returned. Amy looked up in surprise.

'I'm sorry,' she said. 'I was miles away. May I get you a drink?'

'Yeah. Do you have any bourbon?'

'Yes, we do. You want ice with it?'

'Please. Make it a double.'

Amy reached for a glass on the shelf behind her, and drew off a double.

When she turned back Mrs Simons had taken a seat on one of the bar stools and was leaning forward across the counter, resting her elbows on the curved edge of the bar. She cradled her drink in both hands, looking tired, but as if she was settling in.

'I thought I was ready to fall asleep,' she said, after a first sip. 'But you know, you find you're sitting there in a room a couple thousand miles from home and you realize sleep is the last thing that's going to happen. I'm still on that plane, I guess.'

'Is this your first visit to England?'

'I don't know whether that's a compliment or not!'

She made a wry grimace, then picked up the glass as if to drink more of the whiskey, but apparently thought better of it and put the glass down on the counter.

'My mother was English and I was born here. In that sense I'm English. My dad was a serviceman. I don't know what people here call it, but in the US they call people like me an Air Force brat. My ma married Dad while he was stationed here . . . there were a lot of our troops over here then. He was from Virginia. You ever hear of Richmond?'

'Yes, I have. Are your parents still alive?'

'No.' She added, with a shrewd look at Amy, 'It's been that way a long time. I still miss them, but you know . . .'

'Do you remember much about England?'

'I was only small when we left, and before that I always seemed to be on the base. You know how some Americans can be. They don't like being too cut off from familiar things. That was my dad. We lived on the base, we went shopping on the base, we ate burgers and ice cream on the base, we saw movies on the base, all my dad's friends were on the base. My ma sometimes took me to see my grandparents in Birkenhead, but I don't remember much about all that. I was too young. I grew up in the US. That's what I tell people, because that's where I feel like I'm really from.'

She had a mannerism when she spoke, perhaps exaggerated by fatigue: she often reached up and stroked her head behind her left ear, running the fingers down to her neck, gently touching something. She was wearing a silken scarf, so it was impossible to see what was there. Amy assumed the woman's neck was stiff after the journey, or that she had some kind of sore place.

She said, 'So are you on holiday?'

'No.' The whiskey glass was empty already, and she was turning it in her fingers. 'I'm here to work. May I buy you a drink?'

'No, thanks.'

'You sure? OK, then let me have another double, and after that I'm quitting. I was drinking on the plane, but you know it sort of flows through you and you don't feel anything. Not until you get up to go to the john, and then it seems as if the plane is moving all over the place. But that was hours ago.'

17

She took the newly filled glass of iced bourbon that Amy placed in front of her.

'Thanks a lot. I guess I'm talking too much. Just for to-night . . . I want to go to bed and sleep, and I can't do that after a journey unless I've had a couple of drinks.' She glanced around the almost deserted bar. Amy instantly looked at the back of the woman's neck, which was briefly exposed when she turned. 'So what's the main action in Bulverton?'

Amy said, 'Not much action, really. Some people come here to retire. If you go towards Bexhill you'll see a lot of big old houses, most of them converted into nursing homes. There aren't many jobs in the town.'

'Are there any places to see? You know, sights for tourists?'

'There's the Old Town. That used to be the big attraction. It's just round the corner from here. Where you parked the car, at the back, there's a road that leads away from the seafront, going up the hill. If you walk up there you'll see the market place. That's the heart of the Old Town.'

'You got a museum here in town?'

'A small one. There's another in Bexhill, and there are a couple in Hastings.'

'Local history, that sort of thing?'

'It's been a long time since I went to any of the museums, but I think that's what you'll find.'

'Is there a newspaper office here, where I can go talk to them?'

'The *Courier*, yes. There's a shop in the Old Town where they take bookings for classified ads. But the editorial office is in Hastings, I think. Or maybe Eastbourne. I'll try and find out for you in the morning.'

'So the newspaper doesn't just carry local news? I mean, about Bulverton only?'

'We're not big enough to have our own paper. Actually, the real name of the paper is the *Bexhill and Bulverton Courier*, but everyone calls it the *Courier*. It's the only one. It covers this stretch of coast, as far along as Pevensey Bay.'

'Right. Thank you . . . I don't know your name.'

'Amy. Amy Colwyn.'

'Nice to meet you, Amy. I'm Teresa.'

Teresa stood up, saying she was going to hit the sack; Amy

asked her again if everything in her room was satisfactory, and was told it was.

As she left, Teresa said, 'I hope you don't mind my asking. What kind of an accent is it you have?'

'Accent?' It was the first time anyone had commented on the way Amy spoke. 'I suppose . . . I mean, it must be the way we all speak around here. It's nothing special.'

'No, it's very attractive. OK, I guess I'll see you in the morning.'

CHAPTER 3

The first few times Teresa used the extreme experience scenarios she had played a witness. That was how the Bureau worked. You wired in and they did the stuff on you, and soon enough you found yourself in a situation that was about to go wrong.

The problem of being a witness, as they described it, was having to decide where to be before the action began. You had to *witness*, be close enough and see enough so you could write a report afterwards, but you also had to survive.

It was the Bureau's way not to explain too much in advance about what was going to happen, so before their first experience the only training Teresa and the others received was in how to abort a scenario.

Her instructor was Special Agent Dan Kazinsky, who said to her, 'You don't need to know how to get out. You only have to know that if you survive. But I'll show you anyway.'

He taught her one of those acronym mnemonics the instructors were so fond of: LIVER. Locate, Identify, Verify, Envision, Remove.

'But you aren't going to make it,' said Kazinsky. 'You might later on, but the first few times are tough.'

The first extreme experience lasted exactly seven seconds, and for all of that short time Teresa was overwhelmed and disoriented by a flood of sensations. Some were physical, some mental.

She shifted abruptly from the cool, underlit ExEx laboratory in the training facility in Quantico to brilliant sunshine in a city street at noon. She staggered as she entered the unaccustomed weight of another woman's body. The noise of traffic burst against her like an explosion. Heat stifled her. The tall buildings of the downtown area of a city crowded around and above her. The sidewalks were full of people. There was a siren wailing somewhere, construction workers clattering at something metal, car horns blowing. She stared around in amazement, astounded by the shock of this false reality.

Information rushed in at her. This was Cleveland, Ohio, on East 55th Street between Superior and Euclid. Date: July 3, 1962. Time: 12.17 p.m. Her name was Mary-Jo Clegg, age twenty-nine, address—

But the first five seconds were already up. Teresa remembered what she was here to do, braced herself against the risk of some violent event, and stepped into the cover of the first doorway she came to.

A man with a gun emerged through the door at the same moment, and he shot her in the face.

Entry into an extreme scenario was an almost instant process; withdrawal and recovery after virtual death were slow and traumatic. The day after her first session, Teresa had to report back to Agent Kazinsky to continue her training. She did so after only three hours' sleep, having spent much of the previous day and most of the night undergoing recovery therapy at the Quantico clinic. She was exhausted, terrified and demoralized, and convinced that she would never again venture into extreme experience.

She was obviously not the only one: two of the other trainees had not turned up at all, and were immediately dropped from the course. The remaining trainees looked as fatigued as Teresa felt, but no one had time to compare notes. Kazinsky announced they were all to return to the scenario and attempt to resolve it. Their only relief was that they would be more fully briefed about the details of the incident they were dealing with.

Instead of having to learn about the witness in the few seconds before the incident began, Teresa was now given a full character profile. She learned not only factual details about Mary-Jo Clegg, but something about her personality. She was also informed, significantly, that Mary-Jo had survived the incident. It was her description of the bank robber, and later her ability to pick him out in a line-up, that secured his conviction and, ultimately, his execution. Details of the gunman were also given. He was a man called Willie Santiago, age thirty-four, a repeat offender with a string of armed robberies behind him. At the moment of his encounter with Mary-Jo he was attempting to escape from the bank he had just held up. He had shot and killed one of the tellers, and was being pursued by the bank's security officers. The police had already been called, and were on their way to the scene of the crime.

Full of misgivings, and terrified of what she knew was almost certainly going to happen to her, Teresa re-entered the Clegg scenario later that day.

She arrived in Cleveland in circumstances identical to the first time. The same rush of impressions swooped in on her: heat, noise, crowded downtown. Additionally, though, she was in a state of blinding panic. She saw the door to the bank, and instantly knew not only what was about to happen but that she could do nothing to protect herself. She turned away from the door and ran as fast as she could. Santiago rushed out and ran up East 55th in the other direction, firing his gun at passers-by, wounding two of them. He was apprehended by the police a few minutes later. After another three hours Teresa was still in downtown Cleveland, wandering through the streets, unsure of what she was expected to do. She had forgotten all the training, the mnemonics and acronyms. She was overwhelmed by the sheer size of the simulation in which she found herself, its incredible attention to detail and its apparently limitless size, the thousands of real-looking people who populated it, the endless procession of traffic and events: she looked at newspapers, even found a bar where a TV was playing, and saw a news report of the Santiago hold-up. Her venture into this scenario had started in panic, and, after a short period of relief that Santiago had not actually harmed her this time, it ended in the same way: Teresa began to believe that she was permanently trapped, for ever stuck in the Cleveland of 1962, knowing no one, having nowhere to live, no money, no way back to the place and time she had left. It was terrifying to think this, and in her state of mental exhaustion she began to believe it. No thought of the LIVER mnemonic, nor how it could be used, entered her mind.

Finally, Special Agent Kazinsky took pity on her, and got the Quantico staff to pull her out before she became completely disoriented.

She reported back to the Academy the following day, in a worse physical and mental state than before, and with her resignation written down on a sheet of the Bureau's own memorandum paper.

Dan Kazinsky took it from her, read it slowly, then folded it and put it in his pocket.

'Agent Gravatt,' he said. 'I'm not concerned that you ran away, as taking evasive action is warranted. However, in the real event you are attempting to take control of, Miss Clegg obtained a witness description of the perpetrator that ensured his conviction and execution. You did not. You may take twenty-four hours' leave and report back here tomorrow at this time.'

'Thank you, sir,' Teresa said, and went home and called Andy. They were due to be married within two months. She told him what she had done, and what Kazinsky had said. Andy, who had already trained with extreme experience, was able to help her through this difficult time.

On her next visit to Cleveland, she did not run away but stood beside the door as Santiago rushed out, and tried to see his face clearly. He shot her.

Next time she tried to get a glimpse of Santiago, then threw herself face-down on the sidewalk. Not only did she fail to get the description, she was shot in the back of the head as she lay there.

Next time she tackled Santiago, hurling herself at him and trying to force him to the ground. She tried to use the disabling techniques in which she had been trained. There was a brief, violent scuffle, at the end of which she was shot again.

Each time the experience was worse, because although Teresa retained her own identity – she never believed she had actually become Mary-Jo Clegg – the fright, pain and trauma of being repeatedly shot and killed were almost impossible to handle. The hours of physical and mental recovery that followed the extreme experience were gradually extending to two days; this was not unusual for a trainee, but it used up expensive time. She knew she had to get this right or flunk the course.

On her next extreme, she did as Kazinsky had repeatedly advised, and tried to let Mary-Jo's own reactions control her behaviour. In the actual incident, which had really occurred as depicted, Mary-Jo of course had had no warning that an armed man was going to burst out of the bank, and she would not have reacted until something happened.

Teresa barely had time to adjust to the shift into Mary-Jo's identity. She took four steps along the street, then Santiago appeared in the doorway. Mary-Jo turned towards him in horror and surprise, saw the gun he was holding, and Teresa's instincts took over. She ducked away, and Santiago shot her. This time it took two bullets to kill her.

Teresa finally got it right on her seventh extreme. She allowed Mary-Jo to react as she would, turned in surprise as Santiago appeared, faced him, then raised an arm and stepped forward. Santiago fired at her, but because the instinctive attack by an unarmed passer-by took him by surprise, he missed. Teresa felt the heat of the discharge on her face, was stunned by the loud report of the gun, but the bullet went past her. At last she ducked, and as she fell to the ground she saw Santiago sprinting away in the brilliant sunshine. A few moments later two bank security guards appeared: one of them stooped to help her. Shortly after this the extreme experience scenario ended, and Teresa had survived with her description.

Over the next few weeks the extreme experience course continued, and Teresa was steadily progressed by Kazinsky and the other instructors from one type of event participant to the next: from witness to non-witnessing bystander, to victim, to security guard, to perpetrator, to police officer or federal agent. In one case she was a hostage; in another she had to negotiate.

The hardest cases to deal with were the ones in which the developing incident was not at all obvious, and the instructors set the scenario to run for a long time before the main event occurred. In one notable sequence Teresa was in the rôle of undercover police officer, staking out a bar in suburban San Antonio in 1981. She had to sit in wait for nearly two hours, knowing that the first chance would be the only one. When the gunman burst into the bar – he was a man from Houston called Charles Dayton Hunter, who was at the time one of the Bureau's Ten Most Wanted – Teresa got him with her first shot.

Later, she moved on to direct access with some of the surviving participants. For instance, she was taken to Cleveland to meet Mary-Jo Clegg a month after completing the Santiago extreme. Mary-Jo was by then in her late sixties, a retired city employee who clearly welcomed the opportunity to earn a few extra dollars working for the Bureau in this way. She appeared refreshingly untraumatized by her horrific experience back in 1962, and minimized her contribution to the arrest and execution of Willie Santiago, but Teresa found it disconcerting to have shared so intimately this woman's terror and, several times, death.

CHAPTER 4

Nick Surtees was living in London at the time of the Bulverton massacre. In the trauma of subsequent events he later found it difficult to remember what he had been doing during the actual day, except that he knew he would have been working as usual at his office near Marble Arch.

At the end of the afternoon he was driving home along the elevated section of Westway, part of the A40, heading out of London towards his house in Acton. It was a sweltering day in early June, and he drove with the car windows open and the cooling fan blasting at him. The radio was on, the volume adjusted as he preferred it, just below the level of perfect audibility. He liked to think when he was driving: not great or important thoughts, but a general state of reflectiveness, helping him wind down after the stresses of the day, half his mind turned inwards, the other half coping with the car and the traffic conditions. If the radio was loud it interfered with this, whether it was with music, the blathering of disc jockeys or the more urgent tones of newsreaders. So he had just enough sound on for a relevant word or a phrase to catch his attention: 'drivers in West London' and 'the elevated section of Westway' were common ones – anything that he was already mentally tuned into.

That evening one word came unexpectedly out of the background noise: 'Bulverton'.

He reached immediately across the dashboard to turn up the volume, but another telling phrase struck before he could do so: 'the quiet seaside town in Sussex has been devastated . . .'

Then he heard it at full volume: the newsreader said news was coming in that a gunman had gone berserk in the centre of town, shooting at anyone he saw, or at any vehicle that moved. The situation was still unclear: police had so far been unable to disarm the man, or prevent him from carrying on, and his present location was unknown. The death toll was thought to be high. The news was still breaking; more would be brought as soon as possible. Meanwhile, members of the public were warned to stay away from Bulverton.

Another presenter then launched into an obviously unscripted talk on the state of gun control in the country, the blanket prohibition on most types of gun, how sports shooters' lobby groups had failed to get the law changed, and the unsuccessful appeals that had been made to European courts. He was interrupted by a phoned-in report from a BBC reporter described as 'on the spot'. In reality she was phoning from Hastings, several miles away, and in spite of her compelling tone of voice had little to add. She said she thought the number of dead had reached double figures. Several policemen were believed to be amongst the casualties. The presenter asked her if any children were thought to be involved, and the reporter said she had no information on that.

A scheduled traffic report followed, but this too was dominated by the news from Bulverton. Drivers were warned to keep away from the A259 coast road between Hastings and Eastbourne, and generally to avoid the area until further notice. Bulverton was closed to traffic from all directions. More information, they said, would be made available soon.

All through this Nick continued to drive along in the slow-moving rush-hour traffic, his gaze fixed blankly on the back of the car in front of him. He was on a kind of emotional autopilot, suspending his feelings until he was convinced that what he was hearing was true. The programme switched to another topic, so he took the mobile phone from the glove compartment and punched in his parents' number. After a brief delay for cellular connection, the number rang and rang without answer.

He switched the phone off and on, then tried again in case he had keyed in the wrong number. There was still no answer.

He knew it could mean anything, and that their absence from the hotel could have a mundane explanation: they sometimes drove into Bexhill or Eastbourne during the afternoon to do a little shopping, and such expeditions were so much a part of their lives that he rarely phoned them before he arrived home from work. However, he also knew that it was unusual for them to stay out this late. Another explanation could be that they were simply outside the building. Or that he had in his anxiety dialled the wrong number; he had to wait for the traffic to halt for a few seconds, but then immediately punched the keys again, being extra-careful to get them right. No answer.

His mind started racing, imagining the worst. He thought of them hearing gunfire in the street outside, going to a window to investigate, or, worse, stepping outside the door, to be caught instantly in a fusillade of bullets. His father was an instinctive intervener: he never ran away from trouble.

Nick's dominant feeling continued to be disbelief. Terrible events reported in the news traditionally happen to other people, or are carried out in places you know of but are nowhere near, or they don't directly concern you at all. When all these self-imagined rules are broken, you find yourself emotionally exposed.

It was hard for Nick to believe that it had happened in the dull little place he knew, where he had grown up and which was full of people he knew. He couldn't take in the fact that it was happening now, that he was one of the people who were going to have to deal with it in some way, that he was already an indirect victim.

The radio programme was interrupted again, with another hastily arranged call from somewhere close to the incident. This was from a senior police officer, but again he was not on the spot, not there in Bulverton.

After this, it was clear that the shootings had become the main, the only, news story of that evening. Gradually, the BBC's news organization responded to the sudden incident, and information began to come through more coherently, and therefore more immediately and terrifyingly.

Nick switched stations, though, irrationally trying to find more news, or better news, some message that would cushion the shock. He discovered, of course, that all the London and national stations were concentrating on Bulverton. They seemed to be reporting at different stages of the incident. He retuned to the BBC, and continued to drive in a state of numbness and inattention. He was aware that drivers of the other cars around him would be listening to the news on their own radios, but to almost all of them it must have been as if it was happening to someone else, in a place they had only heard of. The other drivers' faces were neutral. Were they listening? Was he the only one? Unreality surged around him, coming and going.

At this time Nick was living alone in London, but he had a girlfriend called Jodie Quennell. He usually saw Jodie at weekends and on odd evenings in the week. That evening, that fateful day, he and Jodie had arranged as they often did to meet for a meal and a drink, but while he was in his car he had no way of contacting her. She too drove home from work at this time, but she had no mobile in her car. He would have to call her later. He distracted himself for a few seconds with an imagined conversation with her, but predominating were thoughts of the quiet and familiar streets of his home town and of people he probably knew being fired on in them.

At last he reached the Hangar Lane interchange, where the North Circular Road crossed the A40. He turned left, heading south, but was still heavily delayed by the slow-moving traffic. He was trying to think ahead, work out which would be the best route to the Bexhill region of the coast from this part of London, but all the time the radio was distracting him. He had driven this way dozens of times before, but usually timed his departure to miss the worst of the rush-hour traffic. He could easily imagine what the M25 would be like at this time of the early evening. He was in no mental condition to deal with that sort of stressful driving.

Nick had been born in Bulverton, the only child of James and Michaela Surtees. His parents lived and worked in the White Dragon for most of their adult lives, first as tenants of the large brewery chain that ran the place, then latterly, when the brewery started shedding its less prosperous sites, as the owners.

Bulverton had been in decline through all their years, but they had never given up trying to make the place profitable. What started out as a large white elephant of a pub on an unfashionable part of the coast had gradually been modernized and improved. When it was clear that Bulverton had no future as a holiday resort, his father took the difficult decision to move the White Dragon up-market and concentrate on the business and weekend markets. All the guest rooms were expensively refurbished, satellite and cable TV went into every room, the hotel installed fax, cellular phone and internet nodes, teleconferencing facilities, a small but well-equipped business conference suite. The rooms were centrally heated and air-conditioned, they had mini-bar facilities, the bathrooms had needle showers as well as pressure-jet tubs, and so on. For a time, James Surtees employed a gourmet chef, and he built up what he claimed was the finest small wine cellar on the South Coast.

All to only temporary avail. The economy of the area was not dynamic enough to support a hotel of that kind, and although there were good years the decline was measurable. At the same time, the public bar continued to be popular with the locals, and it would have been foolish to take away this core business. The White Dragon for years had a split personality, in the kinds of custom it sought.

None of this had been of much concern to Nick, although he knew better than anyone the amount of work, and the huge investment, that his parents put into making the place what it had become. He grew up taking it all for granted, as any child would. When he was old enough his father made it clear to him that the business would be his one day, but Nick was going through his own adolescent insecurities. Although he learnt the basics of the hotel trade, and helped out around the hotel in the evenings and at weekends, his heart was never in it.

Habitually lazy at school, at the age of sixteen Nick at last started to take his schooling a little more seriously. It was computers and programming that did it for him. After years of messing around with the school computers he suddenly became interested, and soon transformed himself into a typically obsessive computer freak. Programming came as naturally to him as French or German came to some of his friends, and within a few weeks it was clear where his career would lie. The only problem was that jobs were almost impossible to find locally.

He found the tasks around the hotel increasingly irksome, and tensions grew between him and his parents. A solution presented itself when Nick saw some computing jobs in London being advertised in the *Courier*; he applied, and within a few days was offered a full-time job as a software engineer.

The break from Bulverton, sought by so many other young people of his generation, had come quickly and unexpectedly.

Once he was established in London, Nick felt almost as if he had been reborn. His memories of his days in Sussex receded. At first he returned to Bulverton to see his parents on most weekends, but these visits gradually became less frequent, and shorter in duration. After three years he was promoted and became a department head. He later bought a small flat, then traded up to a small house, then a larger house. He married, and three years later he divorced. He changed jobs, started to make more money, and took on increasing responsibilities at work. He put on weight, lost some of his hair. He drank too much, spent too much money on food, wine, entertaining, went out too often, had too many women friends. He rarely thought of Bulverton.

But down in Bulverton his parents were getting older and less able to look after themselves. His mother's health gave special concern. They were beginning to talk about retirement, something that seemed inevitable to them but which worried Nick a great deal. The reality of the future of the White Dragon was getting closer to him every week. He knew that they had few savings, that all their wealth was tied up in the business, that neither of them could afford to stop working.

Unspoken pressure began to mount on him. He knew they wanted him to say he would move back to Bulverton and take over the running of the hotel, but by this time he was settled in his life in London and nothing could have been further from his wishes. As with many big decisions in families, nothing concrete was agreed on and the months and years slipped slowly by.

Then everything changed, that hot afternoon in June.

The news from Bulverton grew steadily more horrifying. The gunman was thought to be cornered, but then he somehow escaped. Now he had taken a hostage, but a few minutes later he shot her in the head and left her for the police to find. Witness reports were coming in from people who had managed to get away from him, but few details were confirmed: he was a young man, he was middle-aged, he wore combat gear, he was dressed in jeans and T-shirt, he carried one gun, he carried two guns, he carried several. One witness claimed the gunman was actually a woman. Another denied this, said it was a man from a village outside the town, someone he thought he recognized. All this was described disjointedly in a series of phoned-in reports. There was another BBC reporter on the scene by this time, and his descriptions, though incomplete, were graphic in detail.

After a period in which nothing seemed to happen, at least as reported on the radio, hard news came in again. Now the police had surrounded the gunman, but he managed to get into a church and again there was at least one hostage with him.

Nick knew from the rough description which church he was probably in. It would be St Stephen's, the parish church, a short way from the hotel along Eastbourne Road. It was not an especially ancient or beautiful church, but it was well-proportioned, solidly built and positioned attractively at the junction of the coast road and a residential street lined with good houses and many trees. It had been bombed during World War II, with some loss of life. Imagining the gunman there, brandishing his weapons, Nick started to drive faster. He was full of anxiety about his parents, but also for the town itself, for the people who lived there, for everyone. It was the worst thing that had ever happened in his life, and he hadn't even been there to experience it.

He headed for Eastbourne. On the outskirts of the town he turned off into the first of several narrow country roads that would take him past Pevensey and across the Levels. As he had guessed there was hardly any other traffic heading this way. By now he had by force of will put himself into a controlled state of mind, driving with super care, making acute anticipation of hazards ahead.

The radio told him that the known death toll in Bulverton had reached seventeen, most of them people who had been walking in the town or passing through in cars. Three policemen had been shot, and two had died. Three of the civilian victims were children, whose school bus had happened to stop just as the gunman rounded the corner. Many other children had been injured by stray bullets or flying fragments of glass.

As Nick passed Normans Bay, with Bulverton only a couple of miles ahead, the BBC reporter in the town revealed that several shots had been heard from inside the church, and police believed that one of them had been the gunman turning his weapon on himself.

Then, suddenly, the news bulletins ended. The BBC continuity announcer said that they were returning to the scheduled programmes and would bring regular updates on the incident whenever possible.

Nick switched channels again, finding South-East Sound, the local talk-based commercial station. It was covering the incident live, but in a style remarkably different from the BBC's. It had managed to get two of its reporters actually into the town, broadcasting their impressions live, and only interviewing people when they encountered them, in snatches of shouted questions. It was a crude, racy broadcasting technique that had become identified with the station, but until the massacre they had never really found a subject strong enough to do it justice. With the two young reporters alternating, both of them hoarse and sounding frightened, it was immediate, shocking and highly effective. Once you worked out what was going on it was impossible to tune away to another station. Nick was still listening to this channel when he reached the place where the narrow country road rejoined the A259, and he saw a police roadblock ahead. He drove slowly towards it.

He was immediately spotted by two armed policemen, who waved him to the side of the road. They were just outside the Old Town, a hundred yards from St Stephen's Church, twice that distance from the White Dragon. There was a curve in the road beyond the church, so he could see no further. He was so nearly home. The sergeant in charge took his name and address, told him to wait by his car but not to get back inside. Meekly, Nick complied.

Later, they allowed him to continue on foot, with a policewoman assigned to conduct him. He had to wait until she returned from some other mission. When she arrived she was pale and flustered, and would not look directly at him.

'Where did you say you lived?' she said.

'I told the sergeant. The White Dragon Hotel. It's not far from here.'

'I know where it is. Have they told you what's been happening?'

'Yes,' said Nick, but in fact they hadn't.

Until that moment, with the radio programme, the police

roadblock, the quietly spoken sergeant, there had been a veneer of unreality. Now it all became real. It was this young police-woman's expression, drained and too controlled, that finally convinced him. She muttered an informal warning that he would see distressing sights in the town, but her voice trailed off before she finished. She walked off down the streets he knew so well, keeping a couple of paces ahead of him.

The first sign was the broken glass. It was all over the place, scattered across both the road and the pavements. Much of it was the coarse granules of shattered car windows. They stepped over long smears of dark-brown stains on the pavements. Most of the windows they passed were broken. There were belongings scattered everywhere: shopping bags, children's toys, packages of food, satchels of school books, a pair of shoes. He saw several vehicles that had been abandoned in the middle of the road, their windows shot away and the panels of their doors pock-marked with bullet holes. He was astounded by the number of bullets that appeared to have been fired. How much ammunition could one man carry? How many weapons had he used?

The policewoman strode ahead of him, glancing back from time to time to make sure he had not fallen behind. By the time the White Dragon was in sight, he was no longer looking around at what they passed. He stared only at the back of her legs, clad in dark stockings, trying not to see, trying not to think.

At last they arrived at the White Dragon. It was at the epicentre of the violence that had spilled across the streets. Here at last Nick was forced not only to witness the results of the rampage, but to begin, ineptly, unwillingly, uncomprehendingly, the long process of facing up to what had happened to his parents that afternoon, the day they apparently decided against driving into Eastbourne to do a little late shopping.

CHAPTER 5

Dave Hartland, flattened uncomfortably on the bare and dusty floorboards below the window frame, inched forward on his stomach until his head was by the sill. His view of the street below was restricted and his heart was beating so fiercely that he could barely hold still. He glimpsed a number of policemen taking shelter behind a row of parked cars.

A bullet shattered the window pane and embedded itself in the ceiling. Glass and plaster showered down on the boards around him. In a reflex he rolled over, covering his head and neck as best he could.

Using his elbows for propulsion he wriggled backwards, scraping his limbs on the rough boards. Somewhere out there a helicopter was searching for him, and it was surely only a matter of time before it ventured within range. Once he had been picked up by the helicopter's heat-imager he would be effectively done for. He could hear the pulsating of the motor as an insistent rhythm beneath every movement, almost sub-audible, a throbbing pressure.

In the corridor outside he was able to stand. He looked to right and left, then raised his boot and kicked down the door opposite. He burst into the room, covering every corner of it with a sweep of the rifle muzzle. When he was satisfied it was clear, he crouched and moved across to the window. He looked down into a wide, straight road. A row of tall terraced houses stood on the opposite side.

Until this moment he could have been anywhere; now he knew that he could be anywhere except Bulverton. He had lived in Bulverton all his life. Nowhere in the town looked like this. Cars were parked on both sides of the street, and behind these he could make out, as before, several armed policemen crouching for shelter. One was only barely concealed; Dave Hartland raised his rifle and shot him.

In instant response, all the other police emerged from their positions, raised their rifles and fired back at him. Dozens of bullets smashed through the glass, thudded into the brickwork, or whined into the room behind him. Dave easily dodged them all.

He backed out of the room and ran to the window at the far end of the corridor. He could see the helicopter hovering, outlined against the snow-capped mountains in the distance.

Mountains?

An amplified voice suddenly burst around him.

'We know you're in there, Grove!' shouted the voice. 'Throw down your weapon or weapons, and come out with your hands up! Let the hostage go first! Lie on the ground face-down! Disarm your weapon or weapons! You can't escape! We know you're in there, Grove! Throw down your—'

The name Grove momentarily disoriented him. Until then Hartland had been suspecting he was in the wrong scenario. Now, briefly, he wondered again what was going on.

No time for thought! He hurried to the staircase, went down the steps two at a time and ran into the large room at the back of the house. This led through shattered french windows into a small yard protected by high walls. He dashed out, crossed the yard safely, and made it through a high wooden gate into an alley that ran along the back of the garden. He ran crouching along the alley until he reached a second gate. He vaulted over this and immediately took up a defensive position with the rifle, scanning from side to side.

He was in another wide road, this time a broad divided highway leading up to the suspension bridge that crossed the river by the downtown business section. Cars were streaming past in both directions, their drivers and passengers unidentified shapes behind the sky-reflecting windows. There were dozens of pedestrians, some walking or standing alone, others together in groups or couples. No one had a face with discernible features. Tall skyscrapers, glinting with gold, silver and blue mirror-glass, stretched up endlessly into the sky in dizzying perspectives.

Dave Hartland clicked on a new magazine, and opened fire.

Soon he was surrounded by bodies and wrecked cars, so he set off at a run towards the suspension bridge. He came more quickly than he expected to the row of toll booths. As he approached, numerous armed police emerged from their shelter behind the booths and began firing at him.

Dave threw himself to the ground while the police bullets cracked into the concrete road surface around him. He took aim and began picking off the cops one by one.

The helicopter moved in overhead, and again there came an amplified voice, screeching down at him from above:

'We know you're in there, Grove! Throw down your weapon or weapons, and come out with your hands up! Let the hostage—'

Dave rolled on his back, took aim, and pumped a dozen bullets into the belly of the helicopter. There was a mighty explosion. Shattered glass, engine housing and rotor blades flew in all directions.

He returned his attention to the police by the toll booths. Five of them were still alive, and continuing to fire at him.

He stood up, held his rifle by his hip, and walked towards them. Bullets scorched the air past his face.

The policemen did not move from their positions, but continued to fire an unending stream of bullets at him. Their faces were concealed by their silver helmets and mirrored sunglasses.

One was different: this was a woman wearing police uniform. She had removed her helmet and shades to reveal her face. She was gorgeous, with long flowing tresses of black hair. She regarded Hartland with a surprised expression.

He stood still, knowing that at this range the cops would not miss him. Moments later, the bullets struck him in the chest, throwing him backwards across the surface of the road. His last sight was of one of the tall suspension towers, coloured a glistening red, outlined against the frozen sky. An illuminated sign, strung between the girders, suddenly came to life.

An animated pig with an idiotic grin tottered into view, and settled at the top of the screen with a scattering of muddy droplets. A scroll it was carrying in its mouth unfurled. It carried these words:

Bullets continued to tear painfully into him.

The silence that followed neither lasted an eternity nor felt like one, because Hartland was brain-dead and unable to measure elapsed time. A few moments after the technician registered that his ExEx session had ended she activated the door-release and light flooded into the cubicle where Dave Hartland's body was lying.

The technician's name was Patricia Tarrant, and she was tall and intense-looking, with her brown hair stretched back tautly from her face. She coolly regarded the dead man lying there. He had thrown back both his arms – a not uncommon gesture amongst ExEx users. Patricia brought his arms down, then with some difficulty turned the man on his side. She brought forward the nano-syringe.

She laid it horizontally along the base of his neck, seeking the tiny valve that connected to the nerve cluster next to the spinal column. She slipped the point of the syringe into the opening of the valve, then twisted the plastic integument to seal it. With the syringe in place, she felt under the tiny flap and located the microswitch. She was supposed to use a special tool for this, but she had carried out the operation so many times that she now usually used the simple pressure of her fingertip. She flicked the microswitch, reactivating Hartland's life. He stirred immediately, grunting. One of his shoulder muscles twitched slightly and he drew a breath.

'OK, take it easy, Mr Hartland,' she muttered automatically, quietly. 'You'll be all right. Let me know if any of this hurts.'

He lay still, but she knew by the movements of his eyes behind the lids that he was either conscious or fractionally below the threshold of consciousness. To be on the safe side she reached over to the console above the trolley and sent a signal through to the medical team, giving them a green alert. This advised them that a resuscitation was in progress, with no complications expected at this stage.

With the life neurochip reactivated she extracted it into the syringe, then deftly transferred it to the phial placed beneath. Using the sensors she located the remaining nanochips and removed them from the valve with one steady suction of the syringe. When all the tiny modules had been removed, she took the phial to the ExEx cabinet.

What then followed was folly automated. The chips were checked electronically to make sure they were the same ones that had been administered at the beginning of the session, then they were moved to the ultrasonic autoclave and cleansed of any fluids or cells brought from Hartland's body. Each nanochip was then in turn deprogrammed, scanned, formatted and reprogrammed, and stored ready for the next use.

The ExEx cabinet, totally sealed not only against atmospheric and other pollution but also against interference from the user, performed all these operations within four and three-tenths seconds, of which by far the longest was the ultrasonic cleansing.

A total of six hundred and thirteen different neurochips had been injected into Hartland's nervous system for his session inside the ExEx equipment, and six hundred and thirteen of them were recovered from him, cleansed and reprogrammed.

After Patricia had completed her resuscitation work, she left the cubicle, leaving Dave Hartland to recover in his own time.

Soon Hartland was sitting up on the edge of the bed, glancing around the bare interior of the cubicle, feeling tired and listless, but as he reoriented, and remembered what had happened inside the scenario, he began to feel aggrieved. After a quarter of an hour, Patricia returned and asked him if he was ready. When he confirmed he was she gave him the releases to sign.

'I'm not prepared to sign anything, Pat,' he said, and thrust the sheaf of forms back at her. 'Not this time.'

'Any particular reason?' said Patricia, apparently unsurprised.

'Yeah. It was no good. It wasn't what I wanted.'

'Can you at least sign this one?' Patricia turned over the first three pages to expose the last one. 'You know what it is. It confirms I resuscitated you promptly and correctly.'

'I don't want to commit myself. I'm really pissed off with what happened.'

She continued to hold the page towards him, and after a

moment he took it from her. He read it through, and of course it was exactly what she had said it was.

When he had signed it, she said, 'Thanks. If you've got a complaint, you should see Mr Lacey. He's the administrator in charge of software policy here.'

'It's a pile of crap, Pat.'

'Which one was it?'

'The Gerry Grove one.'

'I was beginning to wonder if it might be. Quite a few people have complained about that.'

'I've been on the waiting list for more than three months. All the hype there was about it. Of all the scenarios I've tried, it's by far the most expensive—'

'Please . . . it's nothing to do with me. I know why you're unhappy, but I only make sure the equipment works properly.'

'All right, I'm sorry.'

She left the cubicle briefly, and went to her own desk. She returned with another sheet of paper.

'Look, fill out this form, and you can either leave it in reception, or if Mr Lacey's available you can possibly see him straight away.'

'What I want is a refund. I'm not going to pay all that money for—'

'You can probably get a refund, but it has to be authorized by Mr Lacey. I've put on the reference number of the scenario. All you have to do is explain why you weren't satisfied.'

He stared at the sheet of paper, which was headed *GunHo Corporation – Customer Services: Our contract of your guaranteed satisfaction.*

'All right. Thanks, Pat. I'm sorry to have a go at you.'

'I don't mind. But if you want your money back I'm the wrong person.'

'OK. Sorry.'

'How are you feeling? Ready to return to the real world?'

'I think so.'

Mr Lacey was not in the building that afternoon, so at the invitation of the young woman on the front desk Dave Hartland sat down in the reception area and filled out the complaint form.

He crossed out the first few pre-printed responses: equipment failure, staff error or neglect, impolite staff, incorrect selection of scenario software, interruption by power failure, and so on, and concentrated on the part of the form headed *OTHER?*. This had a large space where the customer could describe the complaint in his/her own words. Dave wanted to do this. After some thought he wrote the following:

1. This scenario was not set in Bulverton, because there are no mountains anywhere near Bulverton, there are no tall office buildings in Bulverton, traffic does not drive on the right, there is no suspension bridge, and no river either. The only reference to Gerry Grove is that his name is used.
2. This was an American-style police siege, not a gunman prowling the streets in search of his victims, whom my brother was one of, and I wanted to know how he might have died. This did not tell me.
3. I have been waiting several weeks to try the scenario, as advertised in the paper, and it costs a lot of money. I want a refund.

He handed the form to the receptionist, who read it quickly.

'I'll see Mr Lacey receives this tomorrow morning,' she said. 'They get many complaints about this one, and they've been talking about using a replacement. But there's still demand for it.'

'It's no bloody good. It's just a stupid game. My kids have that sort of thing on their console.'

'That's what people seem to want.'

'It could be anywhere! It's nothing to do with what happened here. Have you tried it?'

'No, I haven't.' She slipped the paper into a drawer. 'I don't think there's going to be a problem with a refund. Could you come back tomorrow afternoon, or call us?'

'Yeah. OK.'

He left, feeling disgruntled. Outside, in the cold evening, the wind was blowing sharply up from the sea. Dave Hartland turned up the collar on his coat and began the long walk down the hill towards his house on London Road.

CHAPTER 6

In the morning Teresa went in search of breakfast and found the hotel owner and the woman she'd spoken to in the bar apparently waiting for her in the tiny office by the downstairs corridor. The man stepped out to greet her as soon as she reached the bottom step.

'Mrs Simons?' he said. 'Good morning. I'm sorry we didn't meet properly last night. I'm Nicholas Surtees. Amy didn't tell me we were expecting a guest until after you had checked in.'

'She looked after me OK.'

'Is the room satisfactory?'

'It's fine,' Teresa said, instantly suppressing the irritated and perverse thoughts she had had as she dressed. She was full of contradictions: she realized she had been expecting something British and eccentric, not the familiar modernity you found in business hotels anywhere in the world. At the same time, she liked having satellite TV with CNN, she liked the mini-bar, she was impressed with having fax facilities in the room, the bathroom was modern and beautifully equipped. She guessed that what she had really deep-down wanted was an antiquated broom closet with a bowl and a jug of cold water, a lumpy bed, and a bathroom two hundred yards down the corridor.

'Would you like breakfast this morning?'

'I guess.'

He was indicating the room at the end of the corridor. She noticed that Amy was still standing behind him, watching and listening as this banal exchange took place. Teresa smiled politely, and walked past them both. She already felt uncomfortable. The great quietness that had descended on the building soon after she went to bed had convinced her she was the only guest in the place. It made her feel conspicuous, and she was already wishing she had paid a little more and found a larger, more impersonal hotel. Everything she did was going to be observed, remarked upon and perhaps questioned.

What she wanted . . . Well, she didn't know what she wanted here in Bulverton, except generally, and that general wish included a distinct need to be left alone. She wanted to keep a low profile, not look or act like whatever a typical American tourist looked like. Her dad would have been one of those, she guessed – Dad was the sort of American who went all around the world without leaving home. But she knew if she was going to be prominent there was nothing she could do about it. There was no point in coming to Bulverton at all unless she slept and lived in the centre of the town.

The White Dragon was supposedly the best hotel in town. She had located it almost by accident: an evening of web browsing found her a list of hotels in the UK, and thence to those in East Sussex. The White Dragon was the only one listed for Bulverton, but was recommended. With some misgivings she had airmailed her booking the next day, but she was surprised and pleased when she received a faxed acknowledgement and receipt a couple of days later.

The dining room was cold, although a large open log fire was burning. A side buffet table had been laid with a spread of cold breakfast foods: cereals, fruit, milk, juice. They seemed to be making an effort for her: if as she suspected she was the only guest, there was more food here than she could eat, and more choice than she wanted or needed. Just like the restaurants at home, dedicated to the cause of maintaining obesity in the American public.

When she had taken a bowl of mixed citrus fruits, and some muesli, she chose a place by the window. There were six tables, and all of them had been laid for four people. Her table looked out on a main road where traffic ground by at a funereal pace. There were few pedestrians.

Amy came through to take her main order.

Then came a long wait, and solitude. She wished now she had gone out of the hotel first and bought a newspaper. She had assumed there would be a row of newspaper vending machines outside the building, but her discovery that there was not had discouraged her. Her inability to throw off American assumptions

43

was adding to her self-consciousness about being an intruder here. She hated being on her own. It was something she doubted she would ever get used to. Now there was just the Andy-less void, the silence, the permanent absence. Much of the night had passed in that void: the aching for him never went away, and in her jetlagged wakefulness she could think only of what she had lost. She had listened to the town around her in the darkness: the immense silence, the uncanny quiet, and from this her imaginings had spread out, making her envision the whole place as a focus of grief. She was not the only widow in Bulverton, but that didn't help. Not at all.

With no sign yet of the food arriving, Teresa left her table and walked back along the corridor to the office, where Nick Surtees was sitting at a PC.

'Is there a newspaper I can buy?' she said.

'Yes, of course. I'll get it brought in to you. Which one would you like?'

Momentary blankness, because it was the *Washington Post* she was used to at home and she hadn't thought beyond that.

'How about *The Times*?' she said, that being the first one that came to mind.

'All right. Would you like me to order it for you every day?'

'Thank you.'

When she returned to her table a silver pot of coffee had been put out for her, presumably by Amy, together with several triangular pieces of toast, steepled in a silver holder. She took one of them, still warm, and spread it with low-fat yellow stuff from a tiny sachet. She looked around for the jelly, then remembered again which country she was in. She spread the marmalade, and liked it so much she wanted to ask what brand it was and where she could buy some for herself.

An hour later, bathed and dressed in warmer clothes, Teresa went downstairs and again sought Nick Surtees in his office. Although she had only recently woken she was tired again, and as she dressed she had felt the distracting mental fluttering of an incipient migraine. She had left her medication at home. She had thought the migraine attacks were a thing of the past, but she should have known better. Maybe the flight had brought this one on. She dreaded having to find a doctor here, and being given drugs she didn't know.

Nick Surtees was not in his office, but the computer was on, the screen shimmering with the glittering random shapes of a screen-saver program. It looked familiar, and it briefly amused her that the same software she saw being used all over the US was also popular here.

Amy was in the bar, vacuuming the carpet. Teresa found her there, having been drawn by the loud irregular humming of the machine. Amy switched off as soon as she saw her.

'May I help?'

'Yeah . . . Mr Surtees. Is he around?'

'He should be. Maybe down in the cellar?' To Teresa's surprise the young woman stamped three times with the heel of her shoe. 'He'll come up if he's there,' she said.

A few moments later Nick appeared at the door. He was carrying a large plastic crate filled with dark bottles of lager, their caps wreathed in shiny golden foil. He dumped the crate on the counter, and because Amy had turned the vacuum cleaner on again he led Teresa back to his office.

She said, 'I can't help noticing you're into computers.'

'Not really,' he said. 'Not as much as I used to be, anyway. I use that one for writing letters, and keeping the bar records. Amy does the hotel bookings on it as well.'

'I've been hoping you could help me with mine,' Teresa said. 'I've brought my laptop, but I'm not sure if I can use it while I'm in England. It's got rechargeable batteries, but I have to run them up from the mains and things are probably different here.'

'Did you notice the terminal connector in your room? That's compatible with most laptops.'

'No, I didn't see it.' Teresa realized that the strangeness of the hotel and the English accents were making her feel as if she was unable to look after herself. She had started acting what must seem to these people like the rôle of the helpless woman.

It was actually she who had bought the laptop in the first place, not Andy. He said he saw so many computers at work he didn't want to have to deal with them at home too. Teresa saw a lot of them at work too, but what that did for her was underline how useful a portable could be. These days she couldn't imagine how she could ever function without hers.

'There's something else,' Teresa said. 'There must be a pharmacy here somewhere?'

'There's a branch of Boots. And a couple of smaller places. Do you want me to tell you how to find them?'

'No, thanks, I thought I'd take a walk through the town.'

It was a cold, brisk day, but without rain. She left the hotel, wearing her quilted coat with the hood, and walked up the road at the side of the hotel. She left behind her the nondescript area of twentieth-century town houses and shops, and came almost at once into the Old Town area.

At one time Bulverton had sat astride an inlet of the sea, where there was a natural harbour. It had silted up and fallen into disuse many centuries ago, but all the houses in this part of town were built as if the harbour was still there, facing in from the declivities of the shallow hills around. Where Phoenician and Levantine trading ships had reputedly once docked was now a park, well covered for the most part with trees, and containing a small pond for boating and ducks, a bowling green and tennis courts. The houses had been built, replaced and rebuilt many times over the centuries, but apart from a few places of modern in-filling, presumably after German bombing during World War II, the houses were all pleasantly matured. Even the modern ones did not look too out of place.

Close to the park the buildings were mostly small cottages or houses, many of which had been turned into shops, restaurants or businesses, but above and behind them rose several terraces of larger white and pastel-coloured houses. Standing there, looking at the rows of attractive houses, Teresa felt a wave of recognition sweep over her. She knew she had been here before, in this park, in this gracious, resigned town. A sudden sickness rose in her: denying the unwelcome sensation, she snatched her head to one side, as if in an angry rejection of someone or something.

It worked, and she felt her head clearing. Her migraines were something she had always kept to herself, protecting her job. Anything that seemed to indicate chronic frailty was not a wise career move with the Bureau. Taking medication created another risk: all federal agents had to submit to random urine and blood tests, and you never knew what conclusions the testing teams would draw from the presence of certain chemicals in the body. A friend of Andy's had put her on to a psychotherapist in Washington, and he had taught her techniques to help ward off the onset of attacks. They worked once or twice. Later she had tried other methods.

Feeling a little better, Teresa walked through the centre of the park itself, enjoying the peaceful ambience in the cold air, with the surrounding houses constantly glimpsed through the shrouding branches of well-grown trees and shrubs. She could easily imagine how peaceful this park would be in summer. The noise of traffic was muted, even now, when most of the branches were bare.

She sauntered through slowly, half expecting to come across a hamburger franchise or sports store ruining the place, but there was none of that and the whole park gave off a sense of pleasant neglect. In fact, the only sign of sponsorship she could see anywhere was a number of wooden benches placed at various points, each with a small plaque, commemorating the lives of some of the residents of the town. Teresa was particularly touched by one: *To the Cherished Memory of Caroline Prodhoun (d. 1993) – She Loved this Park.*

Teresa walked as far as she could in the park, coming eventually through a gate into a residential street that ran across the top. She turned right along this, then followed the perimeter of the park and walked back down in the direction of the sea, pausing to glance in the windows of the small shops along the way. Here she discovered that appearances can be deceptive: many of the quietly prosperous-looking shops turned out, when you were actually standing in front of them, to be closed or – in some cases – closed and empty. Many of them were antiques shops or secondhand book stores, but almost without exception they were unstaffed and unlit. The antiques shops, in particular, looked as if they were used more for storage than for selling to the public. One or two had printed cards thumbtacked to the door, directing the delivery of packages to nearby alternative addresses.

Teresa peered through several of their windows, dreaming about being able to buy some of the chests, light-stands, tables, cases of books, dressers. They looked so solid, so well made, so old. Staring at the ancient pieces of furniture, Teresa felt the subliminal resonance of a different kind of culture from the one she was used to: the civilization of Europe, its history, long traditions, old families, deep-rooted customs. She was still enough of a Briton to recognize with a kind of longing the culture she had left behind when her father removed her to the US all those years ago, but also enough of an American to feel the urge to acquire some of it by purchase. None of the shops gave any indication of prices, though, and then there would always be the problem of shipping such heavy and bulky stuff back home.

Which made her remember again, in sudden acute anguish, the house standing empty in Woodbridge by the Potomac, and then think of Andy, and then of why she was here in England.

Halfway along the parade of closed shops Teresa turned to the left and walked up the hill to pass the larger houses. This was a residential zone, and from the look of it the people who lived here were fairly affluent. Although cars were parked at the sides of the road, the lanes that ran in front of each row of houses were obviously intended for pedestrians only. From this relative eminence she gained a wider view of the town, which continued to enchant her with its simple prettiness. She knew nowhere at home that had this kind of effect on her. Directly in front of her, on the other side of the park, was a large church with a square tower. A cluster of houses surrounded it, but behind those she could see taller buildings, longer roofs. Further towards the sea, on the same side of the park as the church, Teresa could see the coloured canopies of an outdoor market; again, there were large recently built buildings behind them. In the distance, inland, there was a ridge of higher land, crusted with modern houses.

She tried to imagine what this sleepy little town must have been like, that day Gerry Grove went walkabout with his semi-automatic rifle. The news reports from England had described how the quiet town had been shattered by the violence of the event, a rude awakening from its peaceful slumbers, and the rest of the clichés journalists loved so much. It wasn't a painting on the lid of a box of candy, or a still from a romantic movie. People lived and worked here, brought up their kids, grew their flowers. Some fell in love, some beat each other up, some tried to make a living, some tried to do something useful in the community . . . and one of them, a self-absorbed and lonely youth with a string of minor offences behind him, had a thing about guns.

Teresa, of course, came from a country where a lot of people had a thing about guns. She too had a thing about guns. There was nothing in the idea that was itself shocking, but for it to happen *here*, probably the last place you would expect it, was one step beyond the expectable.

Just as the tourists in Port Arthur, Tasmania, the school-children in Dunblane, the students in Austin, Texas, wouldn't have expected it. All were nice places, quiet and livable places, the sort of small towns that people moved to rather than from. There were dangerous cities, and all cities had areas where no one in their right mind would walk alone or after dark, but still there remained in most people a profound, instinctive belief that bad things only happened in bad places. Bulverton was the sort of place you searched for, so to speak, a kind of comforting ideal.

What was it? Staring down at the large area of the town she could see from this place, Teresa tried to isolate and identify what it was she was responding to. It was not just Englishness, nor prettiness, because England didn't have a monopoly on pretty places, and anyway Bulverton was too much of a muddle to be simply pretty. The area around her hotel was grim enough, and although grim in a particularly British way it was a quality of grimness that was commonplace to her. It could have been in almost any town anywhere. Maybe it was a sense of proportion: one building set against the rest, each one in its turn built to blend with the others. Scale came into it too: this was a town that had grown up in and around a small valley. American architects would have vied with each other to build the biggest, brashest place and grab the best view, but here the buildings seemed to work organically within a kind of consensus of what Bulverton meant to everyone who lived there.

It all made for a simple naturalness, and although she had been in the place for only a few hours – and had been trying to sleep for most of those – she already felt more deeply about the town than she ever had about Washington or Baltimore or even her agreeable dormitory town of Woodbridge.

She crossed the park again and headed for the church she had seen. It was called St Gabriel's, and was built on a low rise and fronted with a small churchyard. She tried to read some of the headstones but without exception they had been made illegible by erosion. The door of the church was locked and no one was around to open it for her.

Next to the church was a small garden, fenced and gated, but unlocked. A sign on the fence described its circumstance:

CROSS KEYS GARDEN. This is the Site of the Cross Keys Inn, Destroyed by a German Bomb at around 1.00 pm on 17th May, 1942. It being a Sunday Lunchtime the Inn was full and there were many Casualties. Eleven Residents of Bulverton died, and Twenty-Six more were injured, the worst Loss of Life in the Town in a Single Incident during the World War. The Names of the Dead are Inscribed on a Plaque at the rear of the Memorial Garden.

Teresa pushed open the gate and walked in. The garden had not been allowed to become overgrown, but it was obviously not given regular attention. The grass of the tiny lawn was in need of cutting, and long shoots drooped from the trees and shrubs. She found the commemorative plaque on the wall, and pushed aside a long thorny shoot from a rose bush that was growing across it. She regarded the names, trying to remember them for later, in case she came across anyone still living in the town who was related. Her memory was fallible, so she found her notebook and jotted down all the surnames.

Eleven dead; that was fewer than Gerry Grove's victims last year, but it had been a major disaster. It would have felt just as devastating in its day, even during a war, something so terrible it would never be surpassed.

Bulverton today was still in the aftershock of Gerry Grove's shooting spree, but in half a century would there be any more lasting memorial than this?

A sidestreet led away from the church and the memorial garden, and Teresa walked along it, emerging after a short distance into a broad shopping street. This was the High Street, a fact she elicited from a sign attached to a wall on one of the intersections. Many people were moving around, going about their shopping. She walked from one end of the street to the other, looking at everyone, feeling that although it was still only her first morning she had nevertheless been able to see many different facets of life in the town. She kept her notebook open, and while she walked along she wrote down the locations of the police station, the library, the Post Office, the banks, and so on, all places she would probably be needing in the days ahead.

At a newsagent's she bought a town map, and a copy of the local paper. She glanced quickly through the pages as she walked along, but if the massacre was still on people's minds that fact wasn't reflected in the local news.

Outside the council offices – a modern block, but built to blend unobtrusively with the rest of the town – she saw at last an explicit reminder of the massacre.

A large sign had been erected in the shape of a clock-face. The legend above it said: *Bulverton Disaster – Lord Mayor's Appeal.* Where twelve o'clock would normally be was the figure £5,000,000, and instead of two hands only one large one swept around, signifying what had been collected so far. It presently stood at about twenty-to, or at just over £3,000,000, and a red band had been painted in behind it.

Wreaths were laid on the ground beside the door to the building. Teresa stood a short distance from them, unsure of whether to go over and peer at the messages, feeling this would be intrusive, but at the same time she didn't want just to pass by, as if she had not noticed. It was beginning to seep into her at last: a constant background sense of the disaster. Not just the wreaths, the memorials, but the fact she was always thinking about it, looking for some sign of it.

She realized she had been seeking it in the expressions on the faces of passers-by, and bearing a hitherto unremarked surprise that there were no more physical scars on the town, or more specifically the fact that the people at the hotel hadn't said anything about it. But people hid pain behind calm expressions.

Teresa knew she too was acting like that. What she ought to do was get straight down to what she had planned. Find people, talk to them. Were you here in town on the day it happened? Did you see Grove? Were *you* hurt? Was anyone you know killed? She wanted to hear herself say it, wanted to hear the answers, wanted to release all the pain that was pent up in these people and in herself.

But it was of course none of her business. The disarmingly pleasant aspect of the town, the restrained conduct of the people in the streets, as well as the fact that she knew nobody well enough even to talk with them casually, underlined the fact that she didn't belong. She had wondered about this before she left home, knowing it would probably happen. How would she, an outsider, be treated? Would they welcome her, or would they shun her? Now she knew it would be neither. They left her alone presumably because they would anyway, but also perhaps because that is what they wanted her to do to them.

This was a town that had been bereaved, and she knew something about that. She was an expert, in fact. She thought about Andy again. Why could she never stop? However much time passed it never got better, never got easier. She forced her thoughts away from him, and almost at once a coincidence followed.

As she walked back in the general direction of the hotel, Teresa was thinking about Amy. She had been easy enough to strike up a conversation with, and Teresa wondered if she should start her enquiries with her. She must have been living in Bulverton last summer when the shooting happened, and would probably know a lot of local people. Working behind the bar in a small hotel had that effect.

As she was musing about this, Teresa reached a paved square where a dozen or so market stalls had been erected. People were shopping, wandering along between the stalls, and a pleasant hubbub of voices mingled with music coming from one or two radios placed at the back of the stalls. Many of the stalls were selling fruit, vegetables or meat, but there were other kinds too: secondhand books, videos and CDs, gardening tools, children's clothes, pine furniture, and so on. It was at one of these, which sold inexpensive household goods – plastic buckets, mops, laundry baskets, brooms – that Teresa saw Amy. She appeared to be arguing with the stallholder. He was a man no longer in the first flush of youth, his body apparently once developed but now going to fat; he had straggly hair and a full beard. He looked angry and was talking quickly to Amy, jabbing his forefinger at her. She was standing her ground, looking almost as irate as he was, her face jutting towards him. She looked pale and determined. At one point she pushed his prodding finger aside, but he brought it back threateningly.

Teresa was immobilized by the sight of the man, and stared at him in amazement. She knew him! But how, and where from?

Other shoppers, who had been walking behind her, were bumping into her and trying to get by, and she realized she was blocking the narrow passage between the stalls. She walked on as slowly as she dared.

As she approached she could see the man's face more clearly, and the certainty of recognition began to recede. His looks were undoubtedly familiar, but now she saw him close up she wondered if it was because he was a type she recognized, rather than an individual. His hair, moustache, high forehead, incipient pot belly, the dirty white T-shirt under the leather jacket, his thick shoulders and arms, were in themselves unremarkable enough, but there was something about his bearing, the aggressive way he confronted Amy, that reminded her unnervingly of many men she had had to deal with in the US. He looked like he belonged to one of the many armed militias that had formed in the last two decades in the rural USA, buried away on remote farmland, and hidden in woods. Teresa involuntarily cased his body with her eyes, looking for the bulge of a firearm, the linear indentation of a holster strap, or some other hint of a concealed weapon.

Then she checked herself: this was England, where firearms were banned entirely, where there were no armed militia groups that she had ever heard of, where you could not make the same assumptions based on someone's appearance. For all she knew, men who looked like that in England drove taxis, wrote poetry or sold household goods in street markets.

Even so that first flash of recognition had unnerved her, and as she drew closer she continued to feel wary of him.

Neither he nor Amy noticed her. Whatever they were talking about was nothing to do with her, but now she was so close she experienced another sense of intruding on the lives of others. She wanted to step right up to them to find out more about what was going on, but couldn't bring herself to do so.

She felt that to halt beside the stall would be to make her

interest obvious, so she kept going. Soon she had passed. She was briefly within earshot, and she was able to make out what they were saying. The man said, '. . . want you out of there. You don't belong, and you bloody know it. If Jase were here . . .'

But his words were lost in the general tumult of the place, even though she was only a few feet away from them. Amy made a reply, but it was inaudible.

Teresa walked on, trying not to be curious. Visitors always encroach on other people's lives. They can't help it. And they can't help being curious about the people they meet: strangers, but strangers with backgrounds and families and positions of some kind in the place where they are encountered.

Teresa was starting to feel hungry. It was still only the middle of the morning, but most of her was jetlagged back to Washington time. She looked around for a restaurant but there was nothing in the market square. Remembering she had seen a couple of places on the High Street she walked back that way, but when she found them she didn't like the look of them any more.

She decided to do what she would if she was at home, and headed for the big Safeway supermarket she had passed earlier. Inside, she went straight to the fresh food counters, thinking how much she would enjoy getting her own food ready, before remembering she was staying in a hotel room where there were no cooking facilities. She was still jetlagged, not thinking right. Or the sight of that man had rattled her more than she wanted to believe. Disappointed, and kicking herself for her momentary forgetfulness, she wandered round the store instead, experiencing the inquisitiveness she always had in someone else's supermarket. Everything was a fascinating mix of the familiar and the strange.

There was an in-store pharmacy, and she paused by the counter.

'Do you have anything I can take for migraine?' she said to the young man who was serving there.

'Do you have a prescription?'

'No . . . well, I'm visiting from the US. I do have prescription drugs there, but I didn't bring them with me and I was hoping . . .'

She let the words run out, disliking having to explain her life to a complete stranger. Actually, the real situation was more complicated than she wanted to say: she used the prescription drugs as little as possible. After the psychotherapist's methods had worked a few times, failed a few more times, she had consulted one of her neighbours, a homeopath. She had given Teresa ignatia, a remedy for migraine sufferers, and it had seemed to have some effect. The migraine attacks cleared up for a while, and one of her last decisions before leaving home had been not to bring the tiny tablets with her. She was already regretting this, but right now she didn't want to take the time to find a homeopath in this town and submit to the long diagnosis all over again. What she wanted was something to kill the headache.

The pharmacist had turned away as she spoke, and now he laid two packets on the counter before her. She picked them up, and read the instructions and ingredients on the backs. One product was based on paracetamol and codeine, the other on codeine alone. Both had an antihistamine ingredient. In one it was buclizine hydrochloride, which she recognized from medication she had taken in the US, so with nothing else to go on she selected that one, a product called Migraleve. She paid at the pharmacy counter, fumbling briefly with the unfamiliar British currency.

Before she was through in the supermarket she bought a triangular cellophane package of sandwiches and a can of Diet Coke from the lunch counter, and lined up at the main checkout to pay a second time. She nibbled one of the sandwiches as she headed down the High Street, again looking for Eastbourne Road and the hotel.

'Hello, Mrs Simons.'

Teresa turned in surprise, and found that Amy was walking along beside and slightly behind her. The tense expression she had worn during her confrontation in the market had vanished.

Teresa slowed. 'Hi, Amy!'

'I saw you back there, in the market square. Are you having a look round our town?'

'It's beautiful,' Teresa said. 'I love the way the houses sit on the hill, looking down across the park.'

Now she was speaking to someone, she realized that the

peaceful quality of the town was a bit of an illusion. They were both having to raise their voices against the noise of the traffic.

'I love it too,' Amy said. 'I do now, anyway. I didn't think much of it when I was at school.'

'Have you lived in Bulverton all your life?'

'I worked away for a while when I was younger, but I think I'm back for good now. There's nowhere else I really want to be.'

'You must know a lot of people here.'

'More of them seem to know me, though. Look, Mrs Simons, I've been worrying about the room we put you in. Is it OK?'

'It's charming. Why?'

'Well, I went to America once on a holiday, and everything seemed so modern over there.'

In the bland, silver-tinged daylight, Teresa saw that Amy was not as young as until now she had thought. Although she still had an attractive face, and she carried herself as if she was in her twenties, her hair had faint grey streaks and her body showed signs of thickness round the waist. Teresa wondered if she had ever tried working out, as she herself had done two or three years ago. The main benefit she had found was that while there was no obvious improvement to her figure, she *felt* she had been doing the best she could for herself. Unless you worked out for hours every week, exercise was essentially about morale, not looking good.

'Look, don't worry about the room,' Teresa said. 'When you were in the US, did you ever stay in one of our motels?'

'No.'

'I've been in motels all over the country. Let me tell you, after a few nights in one of those a place like the White Dragon feels as comfortable as home.'

They had now reached Eastbourne Road with its continual flow of slow-moving traffic in both directions. The noise had increased, and already the slightly eccentric feeling the Old Town had induced in her was slipping away.

Amy came to a halt, and said, 'I'd forgotten. I'll have to go back to the shops. I was on my way out to buy something.'

'That's my fault. Keeping you talking.'

'No, not your fault,' Amy said.

'The man I saw you with,' Teresa said. 'Who was he?'

'At the hotel, you mean?'

'No. Just now. In the market.'

Amy looked away, across the line of cars and vans, towards the sea. 'I'm not sure who you mean.'

'I thought I might know him,' Teresa said.

'How could you? You coming in last night, getting in late.'

'That's what I thought. Well, it doesn't matter.'

'No, I suppose not,' Amy said, her hair flailing across her eyes.

CHAPTER 7

Nick was already in bed and lounging around with that morning's newspaper when Amy came upstairs and went into the bathroom. He heard her brushing her teeth. A little later she walked into the bedroom and began undressing. He watched her as he always did. She was used to him lying there at night watching her, and didn't seem to mind. To him she still looked the same naked as she had always done. Everything that he had found attractive in the old days was unchanged by the years.

His parents and her husband had been cremated on the same day, less than a week after the massacre, and he and Amy had met at the crematorium. She had been waiting outside the chapel when he emerged, black-coated, dark-eyed, swathed in misery, alone, not supported by any of his friends. They had simply stared at each other. It was one more upheaval in a week of upheavals, a time of shock when nothing was a surprise. Afterwards they walked back down to the town, side by side, noticing other hearses moving up towards the cemetery on the Ridge, and the attendant camera lights and film crews, and the reporters.

He had no one left, and she was also alone. Subject to powerful feelings neither of them had tried to control, he took her back with him to the hotel in the afternoon, they were together that night, and had stayed together ever since.

That was still a time when people were able to speak about it. There were reporters everywhere, nowhere more than in the White Dragon, where many of them stayed, and telling the story of what Grove had done became a way of trying to deal with what happened.

Later, it was no longer like that. The survivors found that it was not after all a way, that it added somehow to the horror of what had occurred. Those enquiring faces and voices, sometimes polite, sometimes intrusive, the notepads and tape recorders and video cameras, led quickly to the headlines and pictures in the tabloids, the suffering translated into a series of clichés. At first it was a novelty for people in Bulverton to see the town and its people on television, but then it quickly sank in that what was being shown to the world was not what had actually happened. It was only an impression gained by outsiders.

Gradually a silence fell.

But five days after the shootings, when Amy and Nick came together again, was still in the time before anyone had learned media sophistication. People spoke from the need to explain, to try to make sense of the upheaval in which they were caught up.

That first night, still in distress after the funeral, Nick woke up into darkness and heard Amy sobbing. He turned on the light and tried to comfort her, but something unstoppable was flowing out of her. It was not long after midnight.

He sat up beside her in the bed, staring down at her naked back as she sobbed and groaned in her misery. Looking at her, unable to offer comfort, he remembered what she had been to him in the good times, when she was unpredictable, funny and sexy, and causing endless trouble between him and his parents. For a few weeks back then he had never been happier in his life, and that euphoria of being a young man with an attractive and sexually compliant girlfriend had borne him on for months after it had all started going wrong.

She said, her voice muffled by the pillow, 'Nick, if you want to make love again, we can do it. Then I'll leave.'

'No,' he replied. 'That's not it.'

'I'm cold. Please cover me.'

He loved to hear her voice, the familiar accent and intonation. He fussed around with the pillows and bedclothes, trying to make her comfortable and warm, then lay down once again beside her with his arm cradling her. A long time passed in silence.

Then Amy said, 'Your mum never liked me, did she?'

'Well, I wouldn't say—'

'You know she didn't. I wasn't good enough for her son. She actually said that to me once. It doesn't matter now, but it used to hurt me. She got her way in the end, and you went off to London.'

'We'd split up months before that.'

'Three months. It pleased her, anyway.'

'I don't think—'

'Listen, Nick, I'm trying to explain something.' When she breathed in he could still sometimes hear a sob in the sound, but her voice was steady. 'I started hanging around with Jase after that. You probably didn't know him, but your parents did. He often came in here with his mates, he liked a few drinks. Jase had his bad ways, and I never went along with those, but I saw the best of him. I didn't fall for him straight away, it took a couple of years, but he was always around, often had been even when I was going out with you. I'd been at school with him, but he wasn't in my crowd then. He was just one of the lads I knew from the village. Up the road, where you never went. You wouldn't understand someone like Jase, because all you'd notice about him would be the way he got drunk or drove his car with the stereo on loud or went berserk at football matches.

'We were both working over in Eastbourne, but after that he was offered some building work out at Battle. When he'd been doing it for a few weeks a new contract came up and he was offered a steady job as a charge hand. I quit the Metropole Hotel straight away, and we rented a flat in Sealand Place. You know, about half a mile from here. We decorated it, made it nice, and after we'd been living together for a while, we got married.

'I was pregnant within a few months, but I lost that one. The following year it happened again. Then we went three years without getting anywhere at all, until I fell for another baby and we lost that one as well. After that, the hospital told me I probably wasn't going to be able to have any more.

'That was when things started to go wrong. He went out drinking a lot more than he had, but he always came back and there was never anyone else. He always swore that was something I didn't need to worry about.

'One day, after we'd had one of our rows, he says to me, had I ever thought about going into the hotel business? You see it was this place, the White Dragon, that he used to come to with his mates when he wanted a few drinks. He'd got hold of the idea that your parents were going to sell the hotel and that he and I ought to buy it from them. We didn't have money like that, but

Jase said money was the least of the problems, because his brother Dave would come in with us. He talked big, and I believed him. We looked into it properly and went to the bank about it. They said no, and I think other people said no, because Jase dropped that idea. Instead, he said he was going to ask your dad for a job. There was an idea behind this, that if he worked hard and your dad grew to trust him, then one day, when he did retire, he might make Jase into a partner.

'Anyway, it came to nothing. Jase went along to see your dad one day, and he was out again almost quicker than he went in. I don't know what was actually said, but what it came down to was no again.

'This is where you come into it, Nick. He knew your parents hadn't liked you going out with me, and now he'd married me it was as if he had saved them from having to put up with me, a favour, like. Afterwards, when your dad turfed him out, Jase kept going on about how you must have spoken up against him. He blamed himself too, but in small ways. Kept saying he was a fool for even thinking of trying, he should have known people like you would keep him out. Bitter he was, and he never forgave you.'

When he first began talking to her earlier that day Nick had assumed, without thinking, that Amy's misery was the same as many people's: the unfocused sense of loss when a friend dies. No one had told him anything about the relationships between the people Grove had killed that day, because in a close community like Bulverton it was assumed that everyone would already know. Nick had never asked. All he had was the list of names, the one everyone in Bulverton now had and probably knew by heart. The twenty-three dead, of whom one was Jason Michael Hartland, aged thirty-six, of Sealand Place, Bulverton. Until Amy told him, as they walked down to the town after the funerals, he had not realized that Jason Hartland was her husband, that her bereavement was sharper, closer than most people's, including his. He was devastated by the deaths of his parents, and also by the way in which they had died, but how much more horrible was what had happened to Amy?

Grief comes unpredictably, out of control. Nick found himself weeping beside Amy that night, thinking of what had happened to Jase and all the others. Death brings innocence to the dead.

61

Whatever Jason Michael Hartland's failings in life had been – loutish behaviour, drunkenness, naïvety, running away – death wiped clean the slate and made the dead as children once again.

While Nick still lay close beside her, Amy continued with her story.

She said, 'Jase was the one the newspapers called "the man on the roof". He was helping a friend with some tiling, at the house next door to the Indian restaurant, out there by the church. When Grove came down the road Jase had nowhere to hide. He tried to get behind the chimney stack but Grove shot him. His body was thrown backwards by the impact of the bullets, and he slid down the roof on the far side, out of sight. Only a child saw this happen. He was in his parents' car, which had already been fired at and damaged by Grove. The little boy saw Jase being killed, and afterwards tried to tell one of the policemen. He was so upset that all he could say was "There was a man on the roof, a man on the roof." Because Jase had fallen back his body wasn't found until the next day.

'I had no idea where Jase was at the time. We'd had another row, and it felt like it was the last one. He left me. I hadn't seen him for two or three weeks. He could have been anywhere there was work: Hastings, Eastbourne, one of the villages outside, somewhere along the coast. He often went to see one of his mates when he was angry with me.

'After the massacre, the police listed him officially as a missing person, and put his name on the list with the other people who couldn't be found. All of them were actually dead, but for a few hours I had the devil of hope in me. More than anything I wanted to see Jase so I could tell him about the massacre. It was such an immense event, so shattering, it affected the whole town, it was on TV and the radio, and I just needed Jase with me so I could say sorry to him for the argument we'd had, and talk to him about what had gone on in the town. I suppose it was a way of coping, or burying my head in the sand. I was awake all that night, round at Dad's place, and in the morning the police told me they'd found him.'

Nick's own story seemed painless and unaffecting compared with hers, but she wanted to know it. Eventually he told her, ashamed of his weaknesses. She dried her eyes, sat up, listened.

They talked on through that long night, holding and touching each other, finding out what had happened, what, in fact, had brought them together again. Sometimes they lay still and in silence, but they never slept. He began to feel, perhaps wrongly, that only by being with Amy would he recover something of what he had lost.

Amy moved in to live with him the following day, arriving back at the hotel after midday, carrying a suitcase of clothes. Then, in the days and weeks that followed, she brought over more of her belongings and furniture from her flat in Sealand Place, as gradually she became a permanent part of his life.

They soon got over the surprise of their reunion, and settled into daily routines. When they talked about the past at all, the furthest back they went was to the Gerry Grove shooting, the only unfinished business that mattered.

That was then, this was now. While he watched over the top of his newspaper as Amy undressed, he noticed she was smiling. He loved the way maturity had filled out her body: strong and well-shaped legs, a long and handsome back, breasts that were much fuller than before but without any sign of sag, a strong face and a crown of dark hair. She was no longer pretty, but he could imagine no woman more attractive.

'What is it?' he said. 'What are you smiling at?'

'You, lying there looking at me.'

She was naked, and stood directly before him.

'I look at you every night. That's what you like, isn't it?'

'Shall I put on my nightie?'

'No . . . get straight in.'

He tossed the newspaper aside and took her in his arms as she climbed into the bed beside him. Her skin was cold, and when she turned her buttocks against him and pressed them into his groin she felt like a chill vastness. With the hand stretching under her body he cupped one of her breasts, with the other he reached around and pressed his hand against her sex, pushing that lovely chill vastness of buttocks harder against him. He loved to feel the soft weight, the hairy moistness, together.

They never hurried their lovemaking, and rarely fell asleep straight away afterwards. They liked to lie together, arms holding around, playing affectionately with each other's body. Sometimes it led to more lovemaking, but at other times they simply dozed together or talked inconsequentially about the day. That night Amy was not sleepy, and after a few minutes of cuddling she sat up, pulled on her nightie and switched on the bedside lamp.

'Are you going to read?' Nick said, blinking in the sudden glare.

'No. I want to ask you something. Do you think Mrs Simons is a reporter?'

'The American woman?'

'Yes.'

'I hadn't given it a thought.'

'Well, think about it now.'

'What's given you that idea?' he said. 'And what does it matter if she is?'

'I ran into Dave today. He said she was.'

'You know what Dave's like better than I do.'

'It doesn't matter, of course, not really. But I've been thinking. She hasn't said anything about it to us, and when the other reporters came around asking questions, they never made a secret of it. They weren't too popular and they knew it, but they didn't try to hide what they wanted.'

'Then she probably isn't,' Nick said. 'Not every stranger who comes to town is trying to get a story.'

'I wondered if, because she's an American, maybe she works differently.'

'Why don't you ask her?'

'All right.' Amy yawned, but showed no sign of being about to turn off the light and lie down. 'She told me she's British. Born over here, anyway. One of her parents was British.'

'Why are you interested in her?'

'I thought you might be.'

'I'd hardly noticed her,' he said, with complete truth.

'That wasn't the impression I got.'

Amy had an expression he had only recently learned to recognize, in which she smiled with her mouth but not with her eyes. It usually meant trouble for him, because of something he was thought to have done, or to have omitted doing. Now she was staring down into her lap, scooped into shape by her crossed legs. He reached out to touch her hand, but found it unyielding.

'What's up, Amy?'

'I saw you with her in your office, laughing and that.'

'What . . . ?' He could hardly remember it. 'When was that?'

'This morning. I saw her in there with you.'

'That's right,' Nick said, and glanced at an imaginary wrist-watch on his arm. 'I was setting myself up for a visit to her bedroom later this evening. Do you mind if I go to her now?'

'Shut up, Nick!'

'Look, just because a single woman checks into my hotel doesn't mean—' He couldn't bring himself to finish the sentence, so ludicrous was the idea.

'She's not single, she's married,' Amy said.

'Let's turn out the light,' he said. 'This is getting silly and pedantic.'

'Not to me it's not.'

'Suit yourself.'

He tried to make himself comfortable, bashing the pillow and pulling up his side of the bedclothes, but Amy sat in rigid anger beside him. Her lovemaking had given no clue of the mood she had been working herself into. He turned to and fro, trying to settle, and all the while Amy sat beside him, her eyes glinting, her mouth in a thin rictus of irritation. He fell asleep in the end.

CHAPTER 8

The next morning Teresa took her rental car for a drive around the Sussex countryside, but the sky was shrouded in low clouds, which were dark and fast-moving, bringing in squalls of heavy rain from the sea and obscuring the views she had come out to look at. She gained only the barest impression of the trees and hills and pretty villages she passed through. She was still ill at ease with driving on the left and before lunchtime she had done enough exploring to satisfy her curiosity.

She ate lunch in the bar of the White Dragon: Amy Colwyn served her in what seemed to be unfriendly silence, but on request microwaved a quiche for her and produced some boiled rice. Teresa sat at one of the tables closest to the fire, forking the stodgy food into her mouth with one hand and writing a letter to Joanna, Andy's mother, with the other. Amy meanwhile sat on a stool behind the counter, flicking through the pages of a magazine and not taking any notice of her. Teresa inevitably wondered what she might have said or done, but was not too concerned. A little later, when more customers came in from outside, the oppressively silent atmosphere in the room lifted noticeably.

After lunch she drove along the coast to Eastbourne, and found the editorial offices of the *Courier*. She saw this as a preliminary trip, expecting that a trawl through the back issues of the paper would take two or three days, but to her surprise the newspaper stored its archives digitally. In a small but comfortably appointed room set aside for the purpose she accessed the archive from the terminal she found there, and in under half an hour had identified and downloaded everything she wanted about Grove, including brief court reports of his earlier minor offences as well as detailed accounts of the day of the massacre, and the aftermath. On her way out she paid for the floppy disk she had used, thanked the woman on the reception desk, and by mid-afternoon she was back in Bulverton. If she had known, or had thought to enquire, she could have used the internet and downloaded the same information from home. Or perhaps even from the hotel, if there was a modem she could use.

She returned briefly to the hotel and put away the disk for future study. Consulting her town map she located Brampton Road. It was one small street amongst many others like it, on the north-eastern edge of the town. She worked out the simplest route that would take her there, then found her tape recorder. She slipped in the new batteries she had bought that morning and briefly tested the recording level. All seemed well.

Brampton Road was part of an ugly postwar housing estate, whose best feature was that its position on one of the hills surrounding the town gave it an impressive distant view of the English Channel. The thick clouds of the morning were starting to disperse, and the sea was brilliantly illuminated by shafts of silver sunlight. Otherwise, the estate itself was a bleak and dispiriting place.

The terraced houses and three- and four-storey apartment blocks were built in a uniform pale-brown brick, and had been positioned unimaginatively in parallel rows, reminding Teresa of the Air Force camps of her childhood. There were not many mature trees to soften the harsh outlines of the buildings, and gardens were few. Much of the ground appeared to be covered in concrete: paths, hard-standings, driveways, alleys. All the roads were lined by rows of vehicles parked with two wheels up on the kerbs. A short row of shops included a convenience store, a satellite-TV supplier, a betting shop, a video rental store and a pub. A main road ran along the crest of the hill, and through the line of trees up there she could glimpse the high sides of trucks moving quickly along. There was a smell of traffic everywhere.

When she had found a place to park her car, and had climbed out to walk the rest of the way, Teresa felt the sharp edge of the cold wind. It had not been too noticeable in the lower parts of the town; here the uneven dips in the rising land created natural funnels when the wind came in from the direction of the sea. From the angle at which some of the more exposed trees were growing, she presumed it must do so most of the time.

The house she was looking for was not difficult to find. In this most unappealing of neighbourhoods it presented an even harsher aspect than the others. It was clearly unoccupied: all the windows in the front were broken, and the ones at street level had been boarded up, as had the door. Remains of an orange police-line tape still straggled on the concrete step and round the corner into the alley alongside. The grass in front of the house had not been trimmed for several weeks or months, and in spite of the winter season it was long and untidy.

It was the end house of one of the long terraces. The number 24 on the visible part of the door confirmed that this was the house Gerry Grove had been living in during the weeks leading up to the massacre. Apart from its recent decrepitude – it had obviously been neglected since its moment of notoriety – there was little to distinguish the house from any of the others. Teresa found her compact camera in her shoulder-bag, and took photographs from a couple of angles. Two women, trudging wearily up the hill and leaning low over the child strollers they were pushing, paid no attention to her.

She worked her way round to the rear, but here an old wooden fence, several feet high, blocked her access. A garden door had been sealed with a wooden hasp nailed across it. She peered through the loose slats of the fence, and could see an overgrown garden and more boarded-up windows. If she had really wanted to she could have forced her way through the battered fence, but she wasn't sure of the rules. The police had once sealed this place; was it still protected by them from intruders? Why should anyone, other than the curious, like Teresa herself, want to look round this unexceptional house?

She stepped back and took some more photographs of the windows of the upper storey, wondering even as she did it why she was bothering. It was just one more lousy house in a street full of identically lousy houses; she might as well take pictures of any of them.

Except, of course, for the fact that this was the actual one.

Feeling depressed about the whole thing, Teresa put her camera away and again consulted her map. Taunton Avenue was two streets away, parallel to Brampton Road and higher up the hill. She left the car where she had parked it and walked up.

The women pushing their children were still ahead of her. It was not a steep hill, but it was a long one. When she paused for breath and turned to look back, Teresa could see the road trailing down and away towards the main part of the town for at least a mile. She could imagine all too easily what it must be like to slog up and down this long hill with small children to push, or when laden with shopping bags.

When she reached Taunton Avenue the two women ahead of her continued slowly upwards, and Teresa felt a guilty relief that she would not have to catch them up and perhaps speak to them. She was still acutely conscious of her status as an outsider in this shattered place, deserving nothing much from anyone. She was having enough difficulty explaining even to herself why she had made this expensive trip to England, and was not yet ready to explain herself to strangers.

Number 15 Taunton Avenue was a mid-terrace house, maintained to a reasonable standard of neatness with flowery curtains, a recently painted door and a tidy approach up the concrete path. She went to the door without glancing at the windows, as if to do so would give away the purpose of her visit, then rang the bell. After a wait the door was opened by a middle-aged, stoutly built woman wearing a clean but faded housecoat. She had a tired expression, and a fatalistic manner. She stared at Teresa without saying anything.

'Hi,' said Teresa, and immediately regretted the casual way she had brought with her from the US. 'Good afternoon. I'm looking for Mrs Ripon.'

'What do you want her for?' the woman said. A boy toddler came out from one of the rooms and lurched up to her. He clung to her legs, peering round them and up at Teresa. His face was filthy around the mouth, and his skin was pale. He sucked on a rubber comforter.

'Are you Mrs Ripon? Mrs Ellie Ripon?'

'What do you want?'

'I'm visiting England from the United States. I wondered if you would be willing to answer a few questions.'

'No, I wouldn't.'

Teresa said, 'Is this the house where Mr Steve Ripon lives?'

'Who wants to know?'

69

'I do,' Teresa said, knowing it was an inadequate and irritating answer and that she wasn't doing this well. She was out of her depth in this country, without the usual back-up. She was used to holding out the badge, and getting her way at once. Her name alone wouldn't mean anything to Steve Ripon himself, any more than to anyone else in the town. Come to that, neither would the badge. 'He won't know me, but—'

'Are you from the benefit office? He's out now.'

'Could you say when you think he'll be back?' Teresa said, knowing she was getting nowhere with this woman, who she was now certain was Steve's mother.

'He never says where he's going nor how long he'll be. What do you want? You still haven't said.'

'Just to talk to him.'

Something was cooking inside the house, and its smell was reaching her. Teresa found it appetizing and repellent, all at once. Home cooking, the sort of food she hadn't eaten in years, with all its implicit pluses and minuses if you were someone like her who had to watch what she ate.

'No you don't,' Mrs Ripon said. 'It's never just talking, what people want with Stevie. If you're not from the benefit office it's something to do with Gerry Grove, isn't it?'

'Yes.'

'He doesn't talk about that any more. And no one else does, see?'

'Well, I had hoped he might speak with me.' She could not help but be aware of the woman's deliberately blank expression, which had barely changed since she opened the door. 'All right. Would you tell Steve I called? My name is Mrs Simons, and I'm staying at the White Dragon, in Eastbourne Road—'

'Stevie knows where it is. You from a newspaper?'

'No, I'm not.'

'TV, then? All right, I'll tell him you were here. But don't expect him to talk to you about anything. He's all clammed up these days – and if you want my opinion, that's how it should be.'

'I know,' Teresa said. 'I feel that way too.'

'I don't know why you people can't leave him alone. He wasn't involved with the shooting.'

'I know,' Teresa said again.

She was suddenly taken by a tremendous compassion for this woman, imagining what she must have been through over the last few months. Steve Ripon was one of the last people to see Gerry Grove before the shooting began. At first he was assumed to be an accomplice, and had been arrested the day after the massacre, when he drove back into town in his battered old van. He claimed he had been visiting a friend in Brighton overnight. Although this alibi was checked out by the police, a search of his van and this house in Taunton Avenue had been ordered anyway. In the van they had found a small supply of the same ammunition Grove had used, but Ripon had vehemently denied knowledge of it. When it was forensically examined the only fingerprints found on the box or its contents were Grove's. By this time a sufficient number of eyewitness accounts had been assembled for it to be certain not only that Grove had acted alone but that any plans he might have made in advance had also been his alone. Steve Ripon had not been charged with an offence for having the bullets, but they got him anyway: for not having insurance or a test certificate for the van.

Throughout this period, the world's press had camped out in Taunton Avenue, trying to find out what anyone who lived there might have known about Steve's relationship with Grove, or indeed about Grove himself. This woman, Steve's mother, would have borne the brunt of all that.

Having been through something very like it herself back home, Teresa had only sympathy for her.

When she reached the end of the concrete path, she turned to glance back. Mrs Ripon was still standing at the door, watching to see that she left. Teresa felt an impulse to go back to her and try to explain, to say that what she was probably thinking wasn't true. But she had been trained never to explain unnecessarily, always to ask, wait for answers, evaluate carefully afterwards. Every situation with a member of the public had a procedure that had to be followed. Do it by the book.

The trouble was, the book was back home with everything else.

She returned to the hotel, and in her room she investigated the computer connection Nick Surtees had told her about. In fact it was simple and logical: her mains adaptor went straight in, and the battery-recharge light came on.

She worked for a while, concentrating on the newspaper material she had downloaded that afternoon, transferring it to her hard disk before loading it into her word processor so she could edit it and sort it out.

What she was trying to do was build up a detailed picture of the day of Grove's outburst: not only what he had done, but also where his victims had been, where the witnesses had seen him. From there she intended to use Bureau methodology, analysing backwards from the known facts into Grove's mental and emotional framework, to draw up a profile of his personality, psychology, motives, and so on. The newspaper reports were the bare bones of this. Next would come what police and video material was available, then the more interesting but infinitely more difficult work of interviewing witnesses.

She felt she hadn't done too well with Steve Ripon's mother. She opened a file for her, but it was as short and uninformative as the interview itself had been. She merely noted down the two main facts she had elicited: first, that Steve Ripon would probably not want to speak to her, and, second, that he was receiving money from the benefit office. Teresa was aware of how little she knew about the British welfare system, and therefore had no idea what this would mean, or how she could investigate it.

She had to decide what to do next. Probably the most urgent and important matter was to start her researches with the police. This was not a step to be lightly taken, because even with her FBI accreditation there would probably be limits on what she would be allowed access to, and she was too unfamiliar with the system to be able to bend the rules. Her network of insider contacts did not exist here, of course. And there were other difficulties. She knew for instance that there was no equivalent to the Freedom of Information legislation in Britain, which meant progress would probably be slow.

The remaining witnesses presented a different kind of obstacle, because after her unsuccessful interview with Mrs Ripon, Teresa was not eager to rush into another encounter for which she was unprepared.

She was tired; the jetlag was still affecting her. As she stared at the LCD screen of her laptop, she allowed her eyes to drift out of focus, and two images of the screen floated away from each other. She snapped her attention back, and the two images resolved into one, but the focus was gone. She felt that sense of being dazed by something, in such a way that you cannot tear your gaze away, even though you know it is simply a matter of deciding to do so. She stared at the screen, trying to will it back into focus; even moving her head to one side neither released her transfixed gaze nor brought back sharpness to what she was looking at.

Finally, she blinked and the spell was broken.

She glanced around the room. It was already looking familiar and homey, reminding her in its neat efficiency of a hundred hotel rooms she had used in the past. She only wished it could have been in a Holiday Inn or a Sheraton, something that was faceless outside as well as in. Everyone in town knew the White Dragon, and it wouldn't be long before everyone she met knew she was staying there.

Looking at the window, Teresa felt her gaze starting to lock again. This time she was too tired to resist it. The square of fading daylight, the four panes of glass, dominated her view. Nothing of interest could be seen beyond it: part of a wall, a grey sky. She knew if she walked across to the window she could look down to see on one side part of the hotel car park and on the other a glimpse of the main road, but she was in a state of mental passivity and she simply stayed where she was and stared at the window. She felt as if her mind had stopped, and her energy had leached away.

Gradually, the window began to look as if it was breaking up: crystals of bright light, primary colours and white, coruscating together so vividly that it was impossible to look at them, crept in across her view of the sky. The wall containing the window darkened in her vision, becoming merely an undefined frame for the square of light that was all she could see. But the unsteady, crystalline brilliance was eating up the image of the window, blinding her to it.

Nausea began to grow in her, and once again Teresa snapped out of the reverie. She realized at last what was happening, and in a state approaching panic she groped around to find her bag, and fumbled for her Migraleve tablets. They were in a foil shield, and she snapped two of them out and threw them straight into her mouth without pausing to wash them down with water. They stuck briefly in her throat, but she forced them down.

Leaving her computer, leaving the chair and table, turning away from the deadly window, she crawled across the floor, searching ahead of her for the bed. She crept up on top of it and fell across the covers, not caring how she was lying or where her head was. She lay still, waiting for the attack to pass. Hours went by, then at last she fell asleep.

CHAPTER 9

It was many years before.

Her name was Sammie Jessup. Sammie and her husband Rick were eating at a family restaurant called Al's Happy Burgabar, in a small town called Oak Springs along Highway 64 between Richmond and Charlottesville. It was 1958. Sammie and Rick had their three children with them.

The table was in a window booth, semicircular, with a central pedestal. The kids had piled in, noisily sliding into the centre of the padded couch seat, but Sammie knew from long experience that if Doug and Cameron sat next to each other they would end up fighting, and if Kelly sat between them she wouldn't eat anything, so she piled them all out again. She sat in the centre herself, wedged between Cameron and Kelly, with Doug next to Kelly on one end and Rick next to Cameron on the other.

They had eaten their burgers and fried chicken and salad and fries, and were waiting for the ice creams they had ordered, when a man carrying a semi-automatic rifle walked in quietly through the door.

He entered so quietly they hardly noticed him at first. Sammie realized something was wrong when she saw one of the waitresses running across the floor, tripping heavily as she collided with a table. The intruder, who was standing beside the cash register, stepped back nervously, jerking his weapon at anyone he saw. All the other people in the restaurant had noticed at the same time, but before anyone could move another man, dressed in the bright orange shirt worn by all Al's employees, appeared from behind the salad bar and fired a shot at the intruder. It missed.

People began screaming, trying to get up from their seats or duck down under the tables. Most of them were trapped by the narrow gap between the tables and the couches that ran round the booths. Sammie reached instinctively across to Kelly and

Cameron, attempting to pull them down towards her lap. Cameron, twelve years old and big for his age, resisted. He wanted to see what was going on. Sammie saw Rick rising in his seat, lifting a protective arm towards Doug.

The intruder's reaction to being shot at was instant and deadly. He fired a burst of shots in return, then moved across the floor of the restaurant, firing in all directions.

A bullet slammed into Doug's head, hurling the boy backwards and spraying the tabletop with blood. As Sammie sucked in her breath in horror and twisted frantically in her seat, another bullet tore through her neck and throat. She died not long afterwards.

'I hate this training,' Teresa said quietly to her friend Harriet Lupi, who was taking the same course. 'I was up sick all night.'

'You going to quit?' said Harriet.

'No.'

'Neither am I. But I sure thought about it yesterday.'

They were in the corridor with seventeen other trainees, waiting for Dan Kazinsky to arrive.

'Do you think it's a real incident?' Teresa said.

'Yeah. I looked it up.'

'Oh shit. They're the worst.'

'Yeah.'

It was many years before.

Her name was Sammie Jessup. Sammie and her husband Rick were eating at a family restaurant called Al's Happy Burgabar, in a small town called Oak Springs along Highway 64 between Richmond and Charlottesville. It was 1958. Sammie and Rick had their three children with them.

Teresa had time to look around, think back, think forward. Time to get frightened. She looked over her shoulder, out of the window, and saw a man with a rifle walking steadily across the parking lot.

They were in a semicircular window booth. The kids had piled in, noisily sliding into the centre of the padded couch seat, but she and Rick had piled them all out again. Now she was in the centre, wedged between Cameron and Kelly, with Doug next to Kelly on one end and Rick next to Cameron on the other.

They were waiting for the ice creams they had ordered when the man with the rifle walked in quietly through the door.

Teresa saw one of the waitresses running across the floor, tripping heavily as she collided with a table. The intruder, beside the cash register, stepped back nervously, jerking his weapon at anyone he saw. Everyone in the restaurant had noticed at the same time, but before anyone could move a staff member in a bright orange shirt appeared from behind the salad bar and fired a shot at the intruder. It missed.

People began screaming, trying to get up from their seats or duck down under the tables. Most of them were trapped by the narrow gap between the tables and the couches that ran round the booths. Teresa reached across to Kelly and Cameron, attempting to pull them down towards her lap. Cameron, twelve years old and big for his age, resisted. He wanted to see what was going on. Teresa saw Rick rising in his seat, lifting a protective arm towards Doug.

The intruder fired several shots at the man by the salad bar, then moved across the floor of the restaurant, firing in all directions.

Teresa sucked in her breath in horror and twisted frantically in her seat, snatching at Doug's jerkin to pull him down. The window shattered behind them. Teresa grabbed frenziedly at her children, sliding them under the hard, unyielding surface of the table. A bullet went past her neck and buried itself in the thick cushion behind her. Rick was thrown backwards by another bullet, and as Teresa turned towards him she too was struck in the back of the head.

Teresa sucked in her breath in horror and twisted frantically in her seat, snatching at Doug's jerkin to pull him down. The window shattered behind them. Rick was rising in his seat. Teresa leaped across at him, crushing Cameron down into the seat. The bullet went through the side of her head.

Teresa sucked in her breath in horror, and rose desperately from her seat, pressing down her children's heads with both hands. Rick was starting to get up too. A bullet went past her and the window shattered behind them. Doug spun round as another bullet went through him, spraying the tabletop with blood. She hurled herself across Cameron, crushing the boy down into the seat, and shoving Rick to the side. The bullet went past them both, and embedded itself in the brightly coloured painting of the clown on the wall behind them. She could hear Kelly screaming, and the man's gun fired again and again, a curious clicking, horribly rhythmic, surprisingly quiet.

Teresa and Rick were sprawling on the floor, and she rolled to one side, clawing her way upright by gripping the hard edge of the table. Her fingers slipped in the blood that now poured across it. As she forced herself up a bullet went through her chest, and she died not long afterwards.

Teresa sucked in her breath in horror, yelled at her kids to throw themselves flat. She stood up. A bullet went singing past Doug's head and smashed into the window behind them. Teresa forced herself up on to the hard surface of the table, then leapt across to the aisle. The man turned his rifle towards her, but she ducked down and ran crouching along the aisle. People were screaming, and the place was full of smoke. She briefly lost sight of the man, but when she came to a cross-aisle she realized he had moved swiftly to the side and was ready for her. Three bullets went straight into her.

Teresa sucked in her breath in horror, yelled at her kids to throw themselves flat. She stood up. A bullet went singing past Doug's head and smashed into the window behind them. Teresa forced herself up on to the hard surface of the table, then leapt across to the aisle. The man turned his rifle towards her, but she ducked down and crawled as fast as she could towards the salad bar.

The man who had fired at the intruder was lying there, face-down in a chaos of spilled ice and fruit.

Teresa snatched his gun, checked quickly that it was still loaded, then rolled into the shelter of a huge Coca-Cola vending machine.

People were screaming, and the place was full of smoke. When she looked she could no longer see the intruder. She changed position, presenting the weapon before her at every move. Her heart was pounding with fear.

When she saw the man again he had walked calmly to the table where she had been sitting with her family, and aimed his rifle at her cowering children. He began firing.

Teresa shot him, but not in time to save her family.

Teresa never did get the Oak Springs ExEx right.

On her last entry to the scenario she assumed the rôle of the gunman: he was a man with the name Sam McLeod, who had earlier in the day carried out an armed robbery on a gas station, shooting the clerk as he snatched the money. A month earlier he had crossed into West Virginia from the neighbouring state of Kentucky, where he was wanted for several other violent robberies. He had moved on into Virginia over the previous weekend. As a federal Most Wanted he had nothing to lose, and earlier in the day, before going to Al's Happy Burgabar, he had stolen several weapons from a gun dealer's store in Palmyra. These were in his pick-up truck parked outside the restaurant.

In McLeod's guise, Teresa entered the ExEx at the point when he was parking the pick-up truck. She loaded the semi-automatic with a fresh magazine, then climbed down from the pick-up, slammed the door, and walked round the back to gain a clear view of anything that might be moving in the parking lot. Traffic went by on the highway beyond the lot, but the restaurant was in a cleared patch of forest and thick trees rose in every direction.

Satisfied that there was no one observing her from outside, McLeod shouldered her way through the door of the restaurant. Full of ease, with her rifle resting casually on her shoulder, she surveyed the customers and staff. A waitress was by the door, writing something on a pad of paper next to the cash register.

'Open it up, and let me have it,' she said, bringing the rifle to bear.

The waitress glanced up, and immediately ran away from her, yelling incoherently. After a few steps she collided with one of the tables, which were heavy and made of metal and connected by a stout pillar to the floor. She sprawled across the floor. McLeod could have killed her then, but she had nothing against her.

She heard a shot, and turned in amazement towards the sound. Someone shooting at *her*? She strolled across the restaurant to see who it was, stepping over the waitress who had fallen. A man by the salad bar, in a stupid shirt, with a glove-compartment hand-gun. Salad Bar Man lost his chance to fire again, after McLeod started striding towards him.

In one of the semicircular booths by the window, a young family was crowded in together, empty plates and glasses and screwed-up paper napkins scattered on the table in front of them. The young woman, the mother, was getting to her feet, trying to press down the heads of her children as she did so, getting them below the surface of the table. McLeod paused in her progress across the room, to stare her down. She seemed unafraid of her, concerned only with her children.

Teresa loosed a casual burst in her direction, then continued across to the salad bar, where the man with the toy pistol was still standing, apparently paralysed by fear.

Teresa decided to spare them all any more concern on her account. She reached over, removed the handgun from Salad Bar Man, checked to see that it was still loaded, then shoved the muzzle in her own mouth and pulled the trigger. She died within seconds.

Later, Teresa was taken through video recordings of the ExEx scenarios about the Oak Springs shootings, shown where she had gone wrong in her decisions, how she could have acted, what further options were open to her.

[In July 1958, Sam Wilkins McLeod, a former inmate of Kentucky State Penitentiary, who had recently become a fugitive from the same institution, went berserk with a semi-automatic rifle in a hamburger bar on Route 64, killing seven people, including one child. A young woman on the scene called Samantha Karen Jessup tried to tackle him, but she was killed by one of McLeod's bullets. She was not related to the child who died.]

CHAPTER 10

When she had finished clearing up the restaurant and kitchen after breakfast, and Mrs Simons had gone upstairs to her room, Amy went through to the hotel office and discovered that a fax message had arrived overnight. She tore it off and read it.

Her first reaction was to run upstairs and show Nick, but he was still in bed asleep, and she knew he didn't like being woken early.

Instead, she decided to deal with it herself and let him see it later. Within half an hour she had drafted her reply. She faxed it to the number in Taiwan, confirming that the White Dragon Hotel in Bulverton had reserved four bedrooms with double beds for single occupancy half-board, from the Monday evening of the following week, for a minimum period of two weeks with an option to extend indefinitely. She quoted the prices. At the bottom of the letter she enquired as politely as she could as to their proposed manner of payment.

Thirty minutes later she was making a photocopy of the original fax for her files, and running the bookings software that Nick had installed – seriously under-used in recent months – when a faxed response came through.

It told her, in formal but roundabout English, that an account had been opened at the branch of Barclays Bank in Bulverton, where she could make arrangements for weekly direct transfer in sterling to the White Dragon's account. Receipted invoices were to be sent direct to the company's head office in Taipei. After a flurry of what read to her like exotic and oriental greetings, the fax message was signed by Mr A. Li, of Project Development Division, GunHo Corporation of Taipei.

At the bottom of the message were printed the names of the four GunHo executives on whose behalf the booking was being made. Amy stared at these for a moment, then went upstairs with the fax. Nick was still asleep.

The day went by, and although Nick did appear at midday he was obviously in another bad mood. Amy knew better than to try to get through to him.

In the afternoon she went for a brief walk, annoyed with herself for allowing him to control her with his moods, even, as things now stood, with her own anticipation of his moods. It wasn't as if the news was bad: it promised a sudden increase in business, with nearly half the hotel's rooms occupied, probably for the first time since the media circus had left town last summer. The further news, that the people from Taiwan would be staying half-board – which meant they would be in the hotel for dinner every evening – suggested that she and Nick could now afford to take on extra staff, at least on a temporary basis. As she walked through the Old Town park, Amy was already making calculations about how much help would be needed in the kitchen, in the restaurant, and also for servicing the rooms. She knew Nick would baulk at first at the idea of paying more staff, but the other side of the equation indicated that the hotel would be profitable for the next two weeks at least, and possibly afterwards.

When Amy returned to the hotel she noticed that Nick's car was missing from its parking place, so she was able to stay out of his way for the rest of the day. His moods still mystified her. She had seen many sides of him in the past, when they were younger, but this destructive moodiness had not been one of them.

That evening, after she had cooked and served Teresa Simons' dinner, Amy went down to the bar, where she knew she would find Nick. He was there, propped up on the stool behind the counter, a paperback novel on his knee. Half a dozen customers were drinking at one of the tables by the window. The jukebox was playing.

'I thought you'd like to see this,' she said, trying to make it sound casual. She gave him the original fax message on its curl of thermal paper, and then used one of the cloth towels to wipe down the counter needlessly, while he read the fax.

'Two weeks,' he said. 'That's good.'

'The hotel will be busy.'

'It'll be a lot of work. And what sort of food will Chinese guests expect?'

'That's mentioned.' She leaned over, and pointed out the sentence. 'They say they expect international cuisine.'

'That could be anything. Pity we don't have a chef.'

'We can manage, Nick! Come on . . . say you're pleased!'

'I'm pleased. I really am.' He twisted his hand round the back of her neck, and gently pulled down her face for a kiss. 'But do we have four rooms free with double beds? There are only ten rooms in the whole place, and six of those are singles or twin-bedded. Mrs Simons is in one of the doubles, isn't she?'

'That's something I wanted to ask you about,' Amy said. 'I was wondering what you would think if we asked her to change rooms?'

'Have you mentioned it to her?'

'Not yet. The booking only came through today. I thought until the people in Taiwan made it definite we shouldn't do anything.'

'But this is a firm booking.'

'Yes.'

'I don't think she likes this place,' Nick said. 'She never complains, but I'm certain she finds it uncomfortable. Just little things she lets slip.'

'That's what I think too. Maybe she would like to move out. This would give her an excuse.'

'Do you think she needs one?'

'I've no idea. She's so polite it's impossible to work out what she really means.'

Nick put the fax message on the counter, where the curl of its paper made it stand up like a shallow arch. Amy picked it up again.

'These don't sound like Chinese names to me,' she said. 'Kravitz, Mitchell, Wendell, Jensen.'

'GunHo Corporation,' Nick said. 'That doesn't sound Chinese either. A bit oriental, but who can tell any more, and does it matter anyway? If they pay, we let them in.'

'Did you notice? Two of these people are women?'

'Yes, I did notice,' Nick replied. 'What do you think, Amy? Can we manage on our own, or should we think about getting a couple of extra staff in?'

CHAPTER 11

Nick was in the bar, waiting for something or other to happen, with not much hope that it would. Dick Cooden and his girl-friend June were playing pool; three men who he knew worked in a garage in Bexhill were standing at the far end of the bar, putting away a lot of pints of bitter; one of the tables near the door had a group of five youngsters perilously close to the minimum legal age, but he didn't feel like checking. Other people had been in and out earlier, and there were always one or two who would straggle in shortly before closing time. Sitting in the bar was what he did, what he liked to do. Amy had gone to bed. He would close the bar in half an hour, once the Bexhill men had given up and gone home.

Then Teresa Simons came in and ordered a bourbon and ice. He put in a single measure, and reached down the counter for the ice. When he turned back she had drained the glass in one gulp without waiting for the ice. He hadn't known Americans would drink anything without ice.

'You people serve small shots,' she said. 'Let me have another.' He went to take the glass from her but she tightened her hold on it. 'Would you make me one the way I like it? Let me show you, and then after that whenever I ask for a bourbon, you can fix it that way.'

When he agreed she asked for a tall glass with several large chunks of ice, two shots of bourbon, and then some soda.

He wrote down the cost of this and the first drink on the account he was keeping beneath the counter.

'Are you finding what you want in the town?' he said, making barman's conversation.

'What makes you think I'm looking for something?'

'You're obviously not here on holiday, so I assumed you were on a business trip.'

'Kind of. Do people come to Bulverton on vacation?'

'Some do. Not as many now as in the past. They like the way the town looks.'

'The town's pretty enough, but it's kind of depressing.'

'Most local people think there's a good reason for that. You must know what happened last year.'

'Yeah . . . It's why I'm here, I guess.'

'Amy said she thought you might be a reporter.'

'What gave her that idea? My interest is . . . I guess you could say it's more personal.'

'I'm sorry,' he said, surprised, because Amy's suggestion had sounded right. 'I didn't realize. Did you have a relative here who was involved?'

'No, nothing like that.'

She turned away from him sharply, almost literally giving him the shoulder, and looked towards the window. The bottom halves of the bar windows were frosted; all that could be seen through them were the diffused and haloed lights of the passing traffic. The three men from Bexhill wanted another round of drinks, so Nick went to attend to them. When he returned, Teresa Simons was facing the counter again, resting her elbows on the top and cradling her now empty glass. She indicated she wanted a refill, which he poured her, using fresh ice and a clean glass.

'What about you, Nick? You don't mind me calling you Nick? Your parents were caught up in the shooting, weren't they?'

'They were both killed, yes.'

'Do you ever talk about it?'

'Not a lot. There isn't much to say, when you leave out all the obvious stuff.'

'This used to be their hotel, right?'

'Yes.'

'You really don't want to discuss it, do you?'

'There's nothing to talk about any more. They left me the hotel, and here I am. What I went through was less traumatic than some of the people here.'

'Tell me.'

He thought for a moment, trying to articulate feelings that had always remained undefined. He remembered how, when he had realized that he couldn't cope with the idea of what Gerry

Grove had done, he had begun to think in clichés. Soon, he heard other people spouting the same empty phrases: reporters on television, vicars in pulpits, leader-writers in newspapers, well-meaning visitors. He knew that those phrases, so quickly becoming familiar, simultaneously missed the true point and captured the essence of it. He learned the benefits of non-thought, non-articulation. Life went on and he joined in, because that way he was spared the need to think or to talk about it.

'There were all those people dead,' he said carefully. 'I didn't know them personally any more, because I'd been living away from the town, but I knew of them. Their names went on lists, their stories were told. All that grief, all those people being missed. The relatives, the parents, the children, the dead lovers, and a couple of strangers. At first nothing surprised me: of course the survivors were going to be shocked. That's what happens when other people get killed. But the more I thought about it, the more complicated it seemed. I couldn't understand anything. So I stopped trying to think.'

Teresa was looking away, twirling ice cubes as he spoke.

'But in a funny kind of way, you know, they were the ones who escaped, the people who were killed. They didn't have to live with it afterwards. In some ways surviving is worse than being dead. People feel guilty that they survived, when a friend or a husband or wife didn't. And then there are all those who were injured. Some recovered quickly, but there were others who didn't, who never will. One of those is a teenage girl.'

'Shelly Mercer,' said Teresa.

'You know about her?'

'Yes, I heard. How's she doing now?'

'She came out of the coma and she's out of hospital, but her parents can't look after her at home. They've had to put her in a special nursing home, in Eastbourne.'

He had been to visit Shelly one day, while she was still in intensive care in the Conquest Hospital in Hastings. He went with a small group of people from the town, all drawn to her by whatever it was that seemed to unite them. The feeling of guilt, he supposed.

The excuse was the radio and CD player that the people in the town had bought for her. She had been saving up to buy one like it before she was shot, and a collection was set up for her. They took it along to the hospital and there was a presentation while a photographer from the *Courier* took some pictures. Nick had been stricken by the sight of Shelly; she was just a kid, swathed in dressings, kept alive by drips and tubes, monitored constantly by electronics. He could hardly even see her face, and none of them knew if she was conscious or understood who they were and what they were doing. They left the CD player in its box, put down their cards and flowers, and they went away.

'What's your interest in all this?' he said to Teresa.

'Intense. How about yours?'

The swiftness of her response, and its fierceness, took him by surprise again. She was staring at him steadily, her eyes just a couple of feet away from his, an unsettling gaze. In the mix of different lights in the bar he could not tell the colour of her eyes, except that they were pale. He had never thought about them before. Now they momentarily eclipsed everything else in the room.

She picked up her glass and drank from it. He heard the cubes clinking as they shifted position in the long tube of the glass. The sound made him remember a bar in St Louis he'd been in while he was on holiday in the US a few years before. It was hot weather, deep summer. All around him, in the air-conditioned chill, Americans were clinking ice cubes in tall glasses. So much ice, every day and everywhere in that vast country, all that fossil energy being used up to freeze water to make drinks seem more cooling and refreshing. In the three days Teresa had been staying at the White Dragon they had got through twice as much ice as normal. Every day they put two extra ice-moulds in the freezer in case the American guest wanted ice. And here she was, clinking it around in her highball.

'Well?' she said, putting down the glass. After just a couple of drinks she had acquired that directness, almost aggression, that some people take on when drinking. 'What's your own interest in it?'

'Intense too, I suppose. I haven't really thought about it like that.'

'Getting over it?'

'Starting to, I think.'

'Look, if people ask what I'm doing here, tell them I'm a kind of historian.'

'Is that what you really are?'

'Kind of,' she said, but she looked introspective for a moment, turning away from him to glance at the men from Bexhill as they laughed loudly at some joke. 'I keep forgetting what you people went through. Did you ever hear of a place called Kingwood City, Texas?'

'No, I didn't, haven't.'

'I hadn't heard of Bulverton. I guess that's a kind of connection between us, if nothing else.'

'What happened in Kingwood, was that similar to this?'

'Kingwood City. The same.'

'A shooting? And you lost someone?'

'My husband. Andy. His name was Andy Simons, and he worked for the federal government, and he was shot in Kingwood City, Texas. That's why I'm here, in Bulverton, East Sussex, because some goddamned bastard killed the man I loved.'

She lowered her face, but her arm was stretched across the bar towards him, holding the glass. It was empty, apart from the barely melted ice cubes. She said nothing, but the drinker's body-language said it all; he poured her another double whiskey.

'Thanks,' she said.

She looked up at him again, but now her gaze was not so steady. Her eyes had the glazed look familiar to everyone who has ever worked behind a bar and waited for the release of closing time. She was getting drunk more quickly than Nick had expected. While she used the soda syphon with concentrated accuracy, he quietly added the price of the new drink to her slate beneath the counter.

'Do you want to talk about what happened?' he said. He was the sympathetic barman, member of the caring profession for the drunk and the disconsolate.

'No more than you did.'

The of-age kids rose from their table with much scraping of chairs, and headed in an unruly bunch for the door. They left their table littered with empty glasses and snack bags. An insistent column of smoke was rising from the ashtray. Nick went round, cleared up the table, then doused the smouldering paper and cigarette ends in the ashtray and started to wash everything in the sink underneath the bar. As he did so the door behind him opened and Amy appeared.

'Want me to take over for a while?' she said, with what he took to be a suspicious glance in the direction of Teresa Simons.

'No, it's OK. I'll be closing soon.' He straightened, and turned to face her. She beckoned him down to the far end of the bar.

'Is Mrs Simons all right?' Amy said, over the music that was still coming from the jukebox, something else the kids had left behind.

'She's drinking a lot of bourbon, but she doesn't have a long way to go home.'

'Are you going to carry her upstairs after she's passed out?'

'Come off it, Amy!' He gestured in irritation. 'I thought you had gone to bed.'

'I wasn't tired. I could hear you talking down here.'

'Look, I'm just the barkeep people tell their troubles to.'

'She has troubles, has she?'

'Don't we all?'

'She never seems to use the bar when I'm working in it.'

'Maybe she feels she can open up to men.'

'So what's she been opening up to you about?'

'Let's do this later, Amy. OK?'

'She can't hear us.'

'Even so. You're being a bit bloody obvious.'

'I don't get any choice.'

Her voice was rising, so Nick pushed past her and went out from behind the bar. He flicked the hidden switch at the back of the jukebox, ensuring the music would fall silent after the current record.

'If you're closing, the barrel for the draught Guinness needs changing,' Amy said.

'I'll do the cellar work in the morning.'

'I thought you always said Guinness was best left to sit overnight.'

'I'll do it in the morning, Amy.'

She shrugged, pushed past him and went through the door into the main part of the hotel. He dreaded what would be said, what might happen, when he eventually went upstairs to bed. He was still learning Amy, after all these years.

Teresa Simons had finished her drink again, but now she was sitting erect on her stool, her hands resting lightly on the counter.

'Did I hear you say you're about to close?' she said.

'Not to you. You're a resident. You can drink all night if you want.'

'No thanks, Mr Surtees. That's not my style.'

'Nick,' he said.

'Yeah, we agreed on that. Not my style, Nick. Hell, I don't even like bourbon much. That was Andy's drink, you know? I only started to drink it because of him, never had the guts to say I didn't much care for it. Before that I used to drink beer. You know all about American beer, right? Doesn't taste good, so you chill it right down so you can't taste anything at all. That's why people like Andy drink bourbon. Even he didn't drink too much of it. Said he had to keep a clear head, or he'd lose his badge.'

'His badge? Was he a cop?' Nick said.

'Sort of.'

'Sort of a cop like you're sort of a historian?'

She was standing now, and looked remarkably steady on her feet for someone who had drunk so much bourbon in so short a time.

'Hell, I guess it doesn't matter any more. Andy was a special agent, with the Bureau.'

'The FBI?'

'You got it.'

'And he was killed on duty?'

'You got it again. In Kingwood City, Texas. Little place no one ever heard of, even people in the USA. Even people in Texas, maybe. Just like Bulverton. In fact exactly like Bulverton, except it couldn't have been more different. You ever hear the name Aronwitz, John Luther Aronwitz?'

'I'm not sure, I—'

'Aronwitz lived in Kingwood City,' she went on, talking over him. 'No one knew him, he lived a quiet life. Stayed at home with his mother. People down the store saw him sometimes, but he had no friends anyone knew of. He had a few minor felonies on his record. Starting to sound familiar? Well, this was Texas so he drove around in an old pick-up, kept to himself, carried a couple of rifles in his gun-rack. Nothing unusual for Texas. Real quiet guy, a bit like Gerry Grove? Last year he went berserk, for no reason anyone could ever understand. Picked up his guns and started shooting. Killed and killed and killed. Men, women and children. Just like Grove. Didn't care who he shot, only that he shot them. Ended up holed up with a couple of hostages in some goddamned shopping mall, some half-empty place on the edge of town, out on Interstate 20. That's where Andy caught up with him and that's where Andy died. You got the picture, Nick?'

'Yes.'

'You ever hear of this, Nick? Because if you have, you're one of the few people in England who have.'

'I heard about it,' he said. 'The press tried to make something of it. I couldn't remember the name of the town. It's better known than—'

'Listen, OK, you're one of the few. Do you know when it happened?'

'Last year, you said. That's right . . . the same date.'

'June third last year. That's the day Andy died, and all because a hairball called Aronwitz picked up a gun and lost his mind.'

'The third of June was when—'

'Yeah, it was, wasn't it? That was when Gerry Grove flipped his lid. Same day, Nick. The same goddamned day. Quite a co-incidence, right?'

Later, when Mrs Simons had tottered off to her room, Nick closed the bar, locked the doors and turned out all the lights. Upstairs, the hotel was silent. He let himself into the bedroom. Amy was still awake, sitting up in bed and reading a magazine. Her mood had changed; yelling at him seemed to have vented some of the pressure.

Chapter 12

At the time of his death Andy Simons was forty-two years old and working, as he had worked for the previous eighteen years, as a Special Agent with the FBI. He specialized in offender psychology, with particular reference to outburst events, spree killings and relocatory serial killers.

Andy saw himself as a good Bureau man, believing in its methods and dedicated to its causes. He knew how to relax when away from the Bureau, but while he was on duty he kept his mind closed to anything but the immediate demands his work made upon him. Although he was still an active enforcement agent, in recent years his work had to a large extent moved off the streets and into the laboratory.

In the Offender Psychology Division attached to the Fredericksburg field office he and thirteen other federal agents were slowly and painstakingly constructing computer models of the psychoneural maps of the known or suspected mentality of disturbed spree killers. Their data had been drawn from the Bureau's own National Crime Information Center, police and ranger records of every state in the country, as well as from many countries in Europe, Latin America and Australasia. The psychopathological profiles they mapped – the basis of the computer models – extended not only to those of the killers, but also to those of their victims.

The theory under investigation was that in cases of crime traditionally considered to be motiveless – in which people became victims apparently only through the mischance of being in the wrong place at the wrong time – there was in reality a psychoneural connection between perpetrator and victim.

A psychological trigger appeared to be involved. It was not yet entirely clear what that might be, but in effect it was the last straw, the last step, which converted the socially maladjusted or psychopathically unstable from misfit to murderer. The apparently innocent victim was increasingly thought to make a contribution to the release of the trigger.

There were also the more conventional links of cause and effect, which were known and had been studied for most of the century. Resentment at long jail sentences was often cited by captured serial killers as the last straw, turning them on release into murderous sociopaths. However, the reliability of this was never absolute. It was obviously not the whole story, otherwise every released long-term prisoner would become a serial killer. Other more local or personal factors were thought relevant: a growing grievance against some institution, person or event, an increasing pattern of offending, which frequently included sexual offending, a reduction in socioeconomic status due to unemployment, relocation or domestic upheaval, and so on.

Andy Simons took a special interest in one case, which had become the starting point for the Division's research.

In 1968 an unemployed car worker in Detroit called Mack Sturmer had shot and killed three of his former workmates during their lunch break. Sturmer had been sacked by the Ford Motor Company management two days before the incident, the reason being that he had for the last six weeks been persistently late or non-attending at work. On the day of the shooting he had managed to gain entry to the Ford plant during the lunch hour, where it was likely he knew off-duty workers would be, even though, as the trial established, the actual victims were not known to him.

Sturmer was not a native of Detroit, having been born on the opposite side of Lake Erie in Lorain, Ohio, moving to Ann Arbor, Michigan, in 1962, or not long afterwards. After a series of increasingly violent crimes, including several of sexual harassment or abuse, Sturmer moved to Detroit, where he found employment. Although by this time he had a long police record, and had served several terms in the state penitentiary, Sturmer was given a job by Ford and for the first few months at least was an acceptable worker. He lived alone in a rooming house in the Melvindale area of the city, and did not mix socially with any of his workmates. At weekends he was a frequent visitor to bars and drinking clubs, where he sometimes bought favours from hostesses.

He was a collector of firearms, and at the time of his arrest was found to possess thirteen different pieces of varying sizes and power. The most formidable weapon he owned was the Iver Johnson M1 carbine he used on his victims, but he also possessed several handguns, one of which he also carried on the day of the crime.

It was relevant to Sturmer's case that the only thing he knew about his victims was that they too worked for Ford, because in this sense his victims were randomly selected. He shot seven of them; three died from their wounds, while the others eventually recovered after stays of different lengths in hospital. After the shooting Sturmer was overpowered by Ford security staff, and handed over to the police. Under interrogation, he said that one of the men had repeatedly made a sniffing noise whenever they were on the same shift, this being done deliberately to aggravate him. It was the only clue he ever gave about his motives.

Sturmer's case history was the first one Andy Simons post-investigated in detail when he began working for the Division. Because at the time he first looked at the records most of the people involved were still alive, he was able to re-interview them with modern hindsight, and use the experimental techniques then being developed to map the psychoneural connections between all the participants in the shooting.

For example, the wife of one of the victims had made a deposition that she had frequently seen Sturmer in a particular bar, where she happened to work as a waitress. This evidence was not admitted during the trial, because the District Attorney's office had not considered it relevant to the murders. There was no suggestion that Sturmer knew the woman or had even noticed her, or, if he had, that he would have been able to identify her as the wife of someone on the same Ford shift as his. However, from the hindsight view taken by the Offender Psychology Division it provided a mappable link between Sturmer and one of the men he had murdered.

From the same unfortunate woman, second and third links could be mapped to Sturmer: she also happened to be known to the woman who owned the lodging house in Melvindale where Sturmer lived.

Finally, she and her husband had, significantly, moved to

Detroit within twelve months of the time that Sturmer had also arrived in the city. Again, in traditional forensic investigations such a snippet of information would have no relevance to the eventual crime, but in psychoneural mapping terms it was of considerable importance. Relocation, by the perpetrator, the victims, or all of them, was a common circumstance in many spree killings.

In commonsense terms, a perpetrator would of course have dozens of links with people who did not ultimately become his victims. At first glance, these non-significant connections seemed to provide no clearer insight than any other forensic work. But Sturmer's case was paradigmatic, in the Division's terms: he had a past record of escalating seriousness, he had made a significant area relocation prior to the incident, he lived and worked in proximity to his victims and there had been a culminating spree event.

Several years of work ensued, in parallel with Andy Simons' regular duties with the Bureau.

The Division's purpose was no less than to produce an integrated database of violent crime in the USA, the emphasis being on what appeared to most civilians to be unpremeditated outbreaks, 'random' attacks on harmless victims, drive-by shootings, chance encounters with serial killers, outbursts of spree attacks in which passers-by were wounded or killed.

If patterns of violence emerged they did so unreliably, a fact that seemed constantly to undermine the Division's credibility within some other parts of the Bureau.

While no one involved with the work would ever accept that they were trying to predict such attacks, that was inevitably how it came to be seen. It became a tiresome habit that agents from other field offices around the country would think it funny to call in to Fredericksburg, with the news they had just cleared up one case and could they have directions to the next one? As with all predictable workplace jokes, the amusement content declined rapidly.

Agent Simons, part of whose job was to give briefings to authorized visitors to the Fredericksburg field office, described the ultimate purpose of the computer models as 'area anticipation'.

The Division would eventually be able to show trends, he said, based on geographical, economic and sociological data, in which the likelihood of an outbreak could be measured statistically. Many such results could already be determined from routine police and Bureau intelligence, which again tended to undermine the unique quality of their work, but the principal claim the Division made, using Bureauspeak, was that as data accreted so their anticipatory functions would be more sharply honed.

The reality, Andy had often admitted to Teresa, was that maybe within ten or fifteen years they would have a more accurate picture of the social and other conditions which gave rise to the phenomenon, but that no amount of computer modelling would ever be able to take into account the sheer unpredictability of human nature.

Events on a worldwide basis were also closely monitored by the Division, and where circumstances seemed relevant they made careful assessment of the evidence, followed by a first adumbration of psychoneural mapping. However, it was in the US, crime capital of the world, that most of their data was found.

It was this kind of work, unexciting, detailed, technical, with no immediate end in view, that Andy Simons was engaged in when an area of Texas to the west of Fort Worth and to the north of Abilene slowly grew into what the Division called psychoneural significance.

This part of the Texas panhandle had traditionally been a farming and ranching area, with high incomes for some and low incomes for most. In the 1950s it had been designated ILI – Industrial Low Intensity – with no state or federal incentives available for corporations. There were few exploitable oil resources. At the beginning of the 1980s, though, a number of computer and microchip manufacturers moved into the region, attracted by low land prices and taxes. An influx of middle-class population soon followed, which swelled through the middle of the decade, while the oil-price rise brought a new economic boom to what had always been a prosperous state.

From the Division's perspective, area relocation, the first step in creating the environment for outburst crime, had begun. Towards the end of the decade, when there was a slump in oil prices and the whole taxation and land macro-economy shifted in emphasis, the newly prosperous silicon industries entered a phase of downsizing and restructuring, with a consequent creation of a large new underclass. The second stage in the process had been reached.

Soon this region of north Texas was suffering a crime wave: aggravated assaults, rapes, armed robberies and homicides. By the beginning of the 1990s, the area had moved in the Division's terms from statistically negligible to statistically acute.

Andy Simons and his team started making trips to the Abilene area, liaising with the Bureau field office and the police department there. Andy kept himself and the rest of his team updated with information about policing numbers, crime statistics and patterns, gun ownership, court sentencing practices, state parole policies.

It was therefore not entirely a coincidence that Andy Simons should be in Abilene on June 3, a day when a man called John Luther Aronwitz decided to drive his pick-up truck to church, with his collection of firearms stashed in the back, ready for use.

CHAPTER 13

'Did you ever use a gun, Nick?'

He had been balancing a spirit bottle on the glass server, the thing that dished out those incredibly small British servings, but when she asked the question she saw him freeze momentarily. Then he finished, and turned towards her. She was on the bar stool again, her arms stretched out across the surface of the counter, her hands surrounding the highball glass without touching it.

'No,' he said. 'Why do you ask?'

'Did you ever want to?'

'No.'

'What about now?'

'It's an academic question. Guns have been outlawed in this country.'

'They've tried banning them in some places in the US. Never worked. People go across the county line, get what they want anyway.'

'You can't do anything like that here. They're illegal right throughout the country.'

'You could go across to France, couldn't you?'

'Some people do.'

'Then why don't you?'

Nick said, testily, 'Look, I'm not interested in guns! It would never occur to me to do that.'

'OK, calm down. I'm sorry.' She glanced around the room, which at this early hour of the evening was still empty. An early hour, but she had already drunk three large bourbons. She was bored with being in Bulverton, and in spite of all the work she had done she was beginning to feel she was wasting her time. 'I'm just making conversation.'

'Yes.' He picked up two empty beer-crates. 'I have to bring some stuff up from the cellar. Excuse me.'

He left the bar. She wished she had ordered another drink before he went, because her glass was nearly empty. She had come down to the bar this evening with only one thought in mind: to get wiped out as fast as she could, then fall into bed.

She was, though, still sober enough to realize how she must be sounding, and didn't like it. What on earth had possessed her to start in on him about guns? She clenched her left fist, digging the nails into the palm of her hand. All her life she'd been saying the wrong thing; all her life she had been resolving to be more careful with what she said. Here, of all places! Are you into guns, Nick? Oh yeah, ever since that maniac blew away my parents, and everyone else. Bigmouth American's in town. She felt her neck and face prickling with embarrassment, and she sat rigid, praying that Nick wouldn't return until she was back in control of herself.

She need not have worried. For whatever reason, he was staying down in the cellar longer than she expected, so she had plenty of time to sweat away her mortification.

She remembered a control technique she had sometimes used: make a list in your mind, straighten your thoughts.

What had she done in the town so far? Local newspaper accounts: done. National newspapers: some done, but the *Guardian* and *Independent* computer archives had been down when she tried to access the websites. She'd try again later. Police interviews: completed, but why had so many officers moved away to other towns since the massacre? Did they jump or were they pushed? Video footage: a lot viewed and a lot more on hand, but she found that most of it had already been shown on CNN and the other US networks.

Witnesses. Ellie Ripon's vagueness about where Steve could be found was explained: he was in Lewes Prison, remanded in custody on a charge of burglary. His lawyer had told Teresa she was hopeful she could get him out on bail when he was taken back to the magistrates the following week. Teresa hoped to interview him then. Her second attempt to talk to Ellie Ripon had been as unsuccessful as the first. She had interviewed Darren Naismith, Mark Edling and Keith Wilson; Grove had been drinking with them before the shooting began. Margaret Lee, the cashier at the Texaco filling station, would not agree to be interviewed, but Teresa had on video a long interview the young woman had given last year to a TV reporter, so that didn't matter too much. Tom and Jennie Mercer, the parents of the grievously injured young girl Shelly, had agreed to meet her the following day. She had located and interviewed about a dozen eyewitnesses of the shootings; again, many of them had been reluctant to speak, but Teresa had managed to piece together a fairly good descriptive account of what had happened in the streets. She was still trying to locate Jamie Connors, the little boy who had been trapped in his parents' damaged car, and had watched the last stages of Grove's spree in Eastbourne Road.

Locale: Teresa had covered all the ground of Grove's tragic adventure, from the seafront area of the town to the picnic site in the woods near Ninfield, to the Texaco filling station, and back through the streets of Bulverton itself. She had identified and timed every known incident. There were anomalies she had yet to resolve: there was an unexplained gap in the timing, and an apparent overlap, but she knew that more investigation would probably resolve these.

Amy walked through the bar on some errand or other, and gave Teresa a nod and a smile. It was the signal of being busy, or at least not wanting to be delayed. As Amy was about to pass out of sight Teresa called after her.

'Amy, may I have another drink?'

Without a word the other woman returned, went behind the counter and mixed her a bourbon highball.

'Will you be having a meal with us this evening?' Amy said.

'I haven't decided yet,' Teresa replied, swirling the glass between her fingers, and reflecting that in the Bureau some of the drinking men would say she was already halfway through the main course.

Amy wrote down the price of the drink on Teresa's account, then without saying anything continued with what she had been doing.

Teresa, left alone again, wondered what she had done to offend Amy. They both seemed to be avoiding her. She felt more and more like the loudmouth American, intruding, clumping around insensitively, offending everyone she spoke to. Maybe it was this kind of thing, the undercurrents of unsaid Britishness, that had made her leave England in the first place? No, it wasn't that. She was just a kid then. Wouldn't have known. She drank the whiskey, stopped when she was about halfway down the glass, and put it on the counter in front of her.

She wished she hadn't started drinking so early in the evening. She wished more customers would come into the bar. She wished she was somewhere else.

With the car lights slipping past the frosted panes in glistening blurs, the streaks of rain on the plain glass above highlighted by the streetlamps, and the bright central room light overhead, virtually unshaded, the bar felt bleak and lonely. Thinking that music might change things, she walked across to the jukebox and dropped in a coin, but nothing happened when she tried to make selections. She remembered Nick doing something to disable the instrument when he closed the bar at night, but when she peered behind the machine she could see no obvious switch.

The empty, silent bar was oppressing her, confusing her. She knew she had already drunk too much, and wondered if she should take this last drink to her room, and finish it there before sleeping everything off. Yet again. As she walked back to her seat, weaving between the chairs, she collided with one of the tables, knocking it to one side. She restored it to its position with careful, elaborate movements.

When she sat down she was startled by a sudden impression of brightness, flooding the room as if a stage light had been turned on. She twisted on her stool, and saw that the large windows all along the opposite wall were now lit up, as if by daylight. The impression was so vivid that for a moment Teresa wondered if she had passed out, slept uninterrupted for several hours, and woken up with no perceptible gap.

She put her weight on one leg, half sliding off the stool, ready to cross the room. A movement behind her startled her, and she became aware that a man must have come into the bar from the corridor behind, without her hearing. She turned sharply back towards him. He was tall, quite elderly, grey-haired, and had a face with fine bone structure. His blue eyes were staring past her towards one of the windows. He put down the cloth he was holding and stepped quickly sideways, along behind the counter, still looking anxiously towards the window.

He turned back, and she heard him shout through the door into the corridor: 'Mike! Are you there?'

There was apparently no answer. He lifted the bar flap and went through in a hurry, crossing the bar-room. The flap banged back down into place. He walked quickly between the tables, heading for the door that led out to Eastbourne Road.

It was then Teresa realized that several other customers were in the bar. She could see four people, all men. One was sitting at a table, with his beer glass pressed to his lips, but the others were standing, looking and peering, trying to see past and above the frosted panes, into the street outside. The jukebox was playing an old track by Elton John.

There was a series of sharp bangs from outside. The elderly man, almost at the door, ducked down.

He looked back towards the counter.

'Mike!' he shouted. 'There's someone out there with a gun!'

But strangely he went to the door, pulled it open, stepped outside. All four of the other men were at the windows now, stretching up on their toes to see through the clear glass.

In great consternation, her hold on reality abruptly uncertain, Teresa stood away from the bar stool, clinging on to the polished wooden surface of the counter.

The door to the corridor opened, and an elderly but still upright and good-looking woman came hurriedly into the bar area.

'Jim?' She looked directly at Teresa. 'Did Jim call me?'

'Is Jim the—?'

'He's outside!' one of the men yelled across the room from the window. 'There's some idiot out there with a gun!'

'Jim!'

The woman pushed her way through the bar flap at the same moment as one of the windows exploded into the room with a shattering crash, the glass flying in all directions. All four of the men fell back on to the floor, blood already flooding across the boards. The woman, obviously hit by flying glass, turned sharply away, buried her face in her hands and went down to a half-crouch, but then she continued towards the street door. Blood was pouring through her fingers. She leaned weakly against the door, and Teresa thought she was going to fall, but she managed

103

to hold on. Brilliant sunlight outlined her. A younger woman rushed into the bar from the road, thrusting her way past the drooping figure. Just then there was another series of shots, and the elderly woman was thrown backwards into the room by the impact of the bullets.

As suddenly as it had appeared the impression of daylight vanished, and Teresa found herself alone in the bar again. The overhead lightbulb, the darkened glass of the windows, the dreary emptiness, all as before. How long? A glimpse, a fleeting memory, a few seconds, a few minutes? How long had that gone on?

She was standing where she had been when the window exploded inwards: just a foot or two away from the bar stool, her hand still stretching back to steady herself against the counter.

The jukebox was silent, the bar flap still raised, as the grey-haired woman had left it as she passed through. Had it been open earlier, when Nick was tending the bar? It was normally closed.

She stared at her unfinished drink, trying not to think what it might be doing to her. And, now she thought about it, there was again that background sense of another migraine attack, looming somewhere, ready to swoop. The drink was her enemy: she couldn't take her tablets if she had been drinking. Not safely, anyway.

She sat down on the stool again, feeling drunk, feeling like a foolish drunk, a drunk who hallucinated, who was about to throw up.

But she held on, and was still sitting miserably at the counter when Nick returned. He was lugging two crates of beer bottles, one on top of the other. He dumped them heavily on the floor behind the counter.

'Are you OK, Mrs Simons?' he said.

'Teresa, call me Teresa. Am I OK? No, I guess I'm not. Don't call me Mrs Simons.'

'Can I get you anything, Teresa?'

'Not another drink. Never drink on an empty stomach. Look what happens.' She waved a hand vaguely to describe herself.

'I could make you a cup of coffee.'

'No, I'll be OK. Don't want any more whiskey. I'll finish this one.'

She didn't mean it though, and sat there staring at the glass while Nick went about stacking the bottles on the refrigerated shelves.

Presently, she said, 'That guy who comes in here sometimes, to help behind the bar?'

'You mean Jack?'

'Do I? Is that his name?'

'Jack Masters. He comes in on Saturdays, and some Fridays.'

'Jack. You got anyone who works here called Mike?'

He shook his head. 'Not lately, not while I've been here.'

'A guy called Mike.'

'No.'

'What about an elderly couple? Do they ever work in here, behind the bar? One of them would be called Jim.'

He straightened, and moved the top crate to one side, now it was empty.

'Are you talking about my parents? They used to own this place.'

'I don't think so.'

'My mother's name was Michaela. Dad sometimes called her Mike.'

'Oh shit,' said Teresa. 'Mike. She came in, I saw her. I'm sorry, I'm so drunk. It won't happen again. I'll forget all this. I'm going upstairs.'

She made it somehow, lurching from side to side on the stairs. The nausea of the migraine was rising in her now, and she no longer fought it. She threw up in the toilet bowl, as tidily as possible but with horrible retching sounds that she was convinced would be heard all over the building. She didn't have the energy to be prissy, to care what anyone thought. Afterwards, she washed her face, drank some water, took a Migraleve, then lay on the bed and gave way to everything.

CHAPTER 14

Kingwood City, Texas, was little different from any of the other satellite towns that were growing up around Abilene. Until the coming of the computer companies it had been a small farming town on the plains, but it had expanded rapidly through the 1980s. The original old centre of the town was now preserved and protected, and sometimes rented by the town council to TV or film companies. Craft shops and wholefood restaurants prospered there. Alongside was a small but intensively developed downtown area of banks, insurance companies, hotels, finance houses, despatch agents, convention complexes, public relations offices.

To the north of the town, stretching away towards the Texas panhandle, was a strip some five miles in length, lined with shopping malls, plazas, automobile dealerships, drive-thru hamburger bars, supermarkets and the mirror-glass industrial complexes that had brought the expansion to the town. In the same area were six newly constructed golf courses, an airfield for private planes and a marina built on the shore of Lake Hubbard. Extensive middle-class suburbs filled the rest, bulging east and west, and down towards Interstate 20 in a new grid pattern.

In winter, Kingwood City suffered under the chill of the northers, the icy winds from the mountains and plains, but during the long summers, from early May to the end of October, it sweltered night and day in the high 90s and low 100s, the outside air feeling as unbreathable as furnace fumes.

Andy was in Abilene on June 3, meeting with the section chief of the Bureau field office, Special Agent Dennis Barthel. This was a routine conference, one of many similar ones Andy held with section chiefs around the country, although in recent months the anticipatory demographics of the computer models had given his visits to Texas an extra edge.

While he was in Barthel's office, a message came through from the city police that there had been a hold-up and shooting at the Baptist church on North Ramsay Street. The gunman had taken a hostage and had driven with her to North Cross shopping mall, where he had shot several more people before the place could be made secure. He was currently cornered in the service bay of the mall, holding two hostages.

The FBI cannot automatically be called in to every crime: its remit is in theory restricted to fewer than three hundred categories of federal violation, although the details of these constantly change as a result of legislation and the process of events. A shooting alone would not normally cause the Bureau to be brought in. There had to be extra features to the offence: the involvement of organized crime, the market in narcotics, terrorism, foreign intelligence, or extreme violence and an interstate element to the perpetrator's relocation.

In this case, the gunman had been identified by witnesses at the church as John Luther Aronwitz, who was connected in some way with the church, perhaps as an attender or lay worker. The police computer meanwhile recorded that Aronwitz had gained a record of violent offences while he was living in the neighbouring state of Arkansas. Records of his crimes ceased when he moved to Texas, three years before.

Aronwitz was still at large when Andy Simons drove to Kingwood City, that sweltering afternoon in June. He went alone. His partner, Danny Schneider, who had been out of the field office when the call came through, was due to follow as soon as he could. Andy had not paused to call Teresa, apparently because all the signs were that the situation was already under control by the police.

The reality was different. Although Aronwitz was surrounded, the delivery area of the mall had large goods bays, connected at the rear by a long metal passageway, wide enough and high enough to take the fork-lift trucks that were now abandoned at a number of positions along its length. These, plus the steel doors that separated the bays, gave Aronwitz cover and several possible places of concealment.

When Andy arrived, the police SWAT team were trying to gain access to the delivery bays from inside the building, while

Aronwitz was held down by other police staked out in the service area. Two of the police had been shot during the operation; one was killed. One of the hostages was also now dead, and her body lay in full view of the long lenses of the TV cameras clustered behind the police lines. Aronwitz's score for the afternoon had already reached fourteen dead, and an as yet unknown number of injured.

Andy Simons was to become the fifteenth and last victim.

When his presence at the scene was known, the SWAT officer in charge briefed him on the situation. Andy pointed out that there was usually another way of gaining access to the delivery bay, from the service ducts below. After the feasibility of this had been established, a detachment of SWAT men went with a team from the mall administrator's department to get through to the delivery area that way. Shortly afterwards, Aronwitz was seen to open an inspection hatch behind one of the bays and drop down out of sight. Confident that this signalled an imminent end to the operation, the SWAT forces moved forward to arrest or deny. Andy followed. A few moments later Aronwitz emerged from another part of the basement area and opened fire on the police. He died as they returned fire, but not before Andy himself had been struck in the head by a bullet. He was dead within seconds.

CHAPTER 15

Teresa's first thought was, How do they get the cars looking so real? Do they have *old cars*? And the city! She whirled round in amazement, staring up at the buildings. Where do they find them, how do they build them? Who are all these people? Are they actors? Do they get paid for doing this?

But there was an armed man further along the street. His name was Howard Unruh, and she had to disarm and apprehend him.

She was in Camden, New Jersey, and it was midday on September 9, 1949. She was not in rôle: this was an ExEx training scenario where the subject brought his or her own identity into the simulation.

Teresa was distracted by the cars, the sound of traffic, the city noises. The street was filled with big saloons and sedans, mostly black or dark grey, some with a lot of chrome, some with running boards, all looking huge and cumbersome and slow. Trucks were upright and noisy. People in baggy clothes and old-fashioned hats thronged the sidewalks.

It's a movie! she thought. That's how they do it! They hire one of those companies that work out in Hollywood, renting period cars to the studios. They bring in extras from somewhere!

She heard the crack of another shot, sounding closer, but Teresa was still new to extreme experience, and the sheer physical detail of the simulations was a shock to her. She wanted to run into the street, force the traffic to stop, then lean down and talk to someone in one of the cars. Who are you? How much do you get paid for this? Do you have to give the car back at the end of the day? May I take a ride with you? Where are you going? Can we leave the city? What's beyond? Can you drive me to New York?

She knew everything that happened to her in the scenario was being monitored and recorded, so she began to walk along the street, past large stores and downtown office buildings. It was like the first few minutes in a foreign country: everything looked, sounded and smelled different. Her senses tingled. She heard old-fashioned honking car horns, engines that sounded untuned and rickety, a bell ringing somewhere, crowds of people, voices with the unmistakable New Jersey accent. The air smelled of coal smoke and engine oil and sweat. Every detail was authentic, painstakingly exact. The longer she was there, the more she noticed: women's make-up looked false and over-applied; people's clothes looked shapeless and unsuitable; advertisements were painted on walls, or stuck up as paper posters; not much neon anywhere, no backlit logos; no credit-card signs on doors.

It not only felt strange it felt unsafe, a place that existed on the edge of chaos. A reminder of this came with another outbreak of shooting.

Other people were noticing the gunfire. A crowd had gathered at the next intersection and were staring down the street. She wanted to stand with them, listen to what they said, hear their accents, find out what they knew.

Remembering at last why she was there, Teresa reached into the shoulder holster beneath her jacket and pulled her gun. She set off down the street, looking for Howard Unruh.

Twenty yards further along two cops drove by her, heading down the same way. One of them sat by the open window, holding a rifle in both hands, the barrel pointing out at the street. He saw Teresa, said something, and the car braked sharply to a halt. Teresa turned towards them, but the cop with the rifle aimed at her chest and killed her with his first shot.

Dan Kazinsky, her instructor at the FBI Academy in Quantico, said, 'You don't pull your gun till you need it. You don't run down the street with a gun in your hand. You *specially* don't run down a street with a gun in your hand when there's someone up there at the end of it firing, and when there are other agencies at the scene of crime trained in summary termination of the situation. Soon as you see a cop, show him your ID. It's his city, not yours. Keep your mind on your work, Agent Simons.'

'Yes, sir.'

'And quit rubbernecking.'

'Yes, sir.'

Teresa took it as calmly as she could. She replayed the video, made notes, put in more hours on the shooting range. She went again to the offender profile workshops from which she had already graduated. She wrote a paper on armed intercession. She tried again.

It's a movie! she thought. That's how they do it! They hire one of those companies that work out in Hollywood, renting period cars to the studios. They bring in extras from somewhere! She was amazed by the amount of trouble they had gone to in the cause of making it authentic.

There was the crack of another shot, sounding closer. She moved quickly to the intersection, where a crowd had gathered, staring down the street. She was briefly amazed by the men's baggy clothes, the women's garish lipstick.

She slipped a hand under her jacket, checked the weapon was ready for quick retrieval, then walked warily down the street towards the sound of the shooting. When another shot came, she realized Howard Unruh was positioned on the opposite side of the street, so she crossed quickly, darting between the bulky saloons and sedans, finding cover against the walls of the buildings.

A police patrol car went down the street. One of the cops sat by the open window, holding a rifle in both hands, the barrel pointing out at the street. He saw Teresa, said something to the driver, and the car braked sharply to a halt. Teresa pulled out her Bureau ID from its clip on her belt, held it aloft; the cops nodded their acknowledgement, and the car accelerated away.

Teresa saw the first body slumped against a garbage can at the street corner. One of the man's arms had hooked itself into the top of the can, holding him in place. His head lolled, and blood poured from wounds in his neck and back. A bullet flew past her, and Teresa threw herself on the ground behind the can. The shot had come from a window somewhere above her. The man's dead face looked blankly at her. She backed away in horror, scrambled back round the corner. She pulled her gun, cocked it, settled it comfortably in her hands, held it high in front of her.

She entered the building through the main doors, seeing more bodies lying in the lobby. Some people were still alive, and they called out to her for help as she passed through, the gun seeking before her at every obstruction, every corner. She was in a bank, she thought. All this marble, the big windows, the long counters.

There were police outside, shouting up with bullhorns to where Unruh must be hidden. Teresa paused, trying to remember the rule book. She could intercede, attempt the apprehension of the gunman alone or with any other members of the Bureau assigned to the incident. Or she could put herself at the disposal of the police, until Bureau reinforcements were sent in. She thought hard. This was not real; this was training. Would they send her into this only for her to throw in her lot with the city police?

She knew the answer, and dashed across the rest of the long lobby, pushing quickly but cautiously through double swing doors, to where there was a cage elevator built in the well of the staircase.

She took the steps two at a time, the gun always questing before her. She paused, listening, thinking, aiming ahead, at every corner. At the next level there was another pair of swing doors; Teresa trained her gun on them in case Unruh came through.

Then he did, pushing through with his back towards her. He was crouching, moving with great caution.

'FBI!' Teresa screamed. 'Freeze!'

Unruh turned in surprise towards her, holding his rifle. He worked the action without haste, but with deadly attention; she heard a mechanical process with loud clicks. Calmly he raised the weapon towards her, and squeezed the trigger.

'Oh shit,' Teresa said, and then his bullet struck her in the throat.

Agent Dan Kazinsky said, 'This is 1949. We don't shout "Freeze" to suspects.'

'I'm training for now, sir,' Teresa said.

'You got to be in rôle, Agent Simons,' said Kazinsky. 'None of this is made up. Howard Unruh was a real man, the event you're entering is a piece of Bureau history. Mr Unruh went through World War II in the US Army, in the Tank Corps. He came out in 1946 with a stolen service rifle, and in 1949 he used it to kill thirteen innocent people in Camden, New Jersey. He was apprehended by agents from the Bureau, and because he was judged insane spent the rest of his life in a federal pen.'

'Yes, sir,' said Teresa, who had researched the Unruh case before going into the ExEx the first time. 'How do they get all those details of the city right? The cars and all?'

'Beats me. Aren't they something? That authentic detail is there to help you. Next time look at yourself in a shop window, or a mirror if you can find one. Familiarize yourself with the clothes you're in, the way your hair is done, how you look. Feel the part. Your task is to apprehend Mr Unruh, either alone or with other members of a Bureau team, depending on how you read the situation on the ground. Are you ready to go in again?'

'I've got a medical note, sir,' said Teresa. 'I'm scheduled for another session next week, but I'm having trouble with the valve.'

She indicated the plastic seal on her neck, which was protected by a square of lint and some Band-Aids. The incision on her neck had gone septic after the latest entry to the Unruh ExEx, requiring it to be cleaned and the valve to be replaced, and delaying her training course by an extra three days.

She wasn't sure yet if she welcomed or resented the delay. More of this kind of training lay ahead, a great deal more, and so far it had not gone well. She was torn between trying to rush through it and get it over with, and backing off, preparing more thoroughly and getting it right. Andy had completed a similar course two years before her, and described it as a pushover. Maybe it had been a pushover for him, but Teresa knew that some of the other trainees were having as hard a time as she was. Not all, though. Harriet Lupi had also suffered a septic neck valve, but it had cleared up quickly and her training was already ahead of Teresa's.

The next day, the nursing sister in the medical wing told Teresa her neck infection was clearing up, and authorized her for ExEx duties again.

She was in a bank, she thought. All this marble, the big windows, the long counters. There were police outside, shouting up with bullhorns to where Unruh must be hidden. She dashed across the rest of the long lobby, pushing quickly but cautiously through double swing doors, to where there was a cage elevator built in the well of the staircase.

She took the steps two at a time, her gun always questing before her. She paused, listening, thinking, aiming ahead, at every corner. At the next level there was another pair of swing doors; Teresa trained her gun on them in case Unruh came through. She saw a shadow moving beyond, so she stepped across to them, kicked one of the doors open. Unruh was there, his rifle held ready. He turned towards her.

'Drop the gun!' Teresa shouted, but Unruh, with unhurried movements, worked the action; she heard a mechanical process with loud clicks. Calmly he raised the weapon towards her, and she fired. Her bullet caught him in his arm. He spun round and away from her, and the rifle clattered to the floor. Half crouching, he pulled an automatic from his belt and tried to aim it at her. Teresa moved swiftly behind him, her gun trained on his head.

'Drop the gun, and lie flat!' she yelled, and within a few moments Howard Unruh did exactly that.

'Harriet? It's Teresa.'

'Hi! How you doing?'

'I got him! I got Unruh!'

'You did? I never could. I managed to wound him, but I was out of ammunition. The city police came in and dragged him away. Dan Kazinsky flunked me, and moved me on. How did you do it?'

Later in the phone call, Teresa said, 'Harriet, have you ever been to Camden, New Jersey?'

'No, I haven't. Have you?'

'I feel as if I have. How the hell do they do that? All those cars and buildings! They're so real!'

'Have you ever been to Texas on a hot day?'

'No.'

'Then you haven't done Whitman yet. That right?'

'Yes.'

'Whitman's next. It's real tough. And it'll make you sick.'

It was noon on August 1, 1966, Austin, Texas. A former boy scout and Marine called Charles Joseph Whitman was on the observation deck of the University of Texas Tower, overlooking Guadalupe Street, 'the Drag'. In his possession was a 6mm

Remington Magnum rifle with four-power Leupold telescopic sight. He also had with him a rented handcart and a green duffel bag. In the bag, and spread around him, were packets of Planters Peanuts, sandwiches, cans of Spam and fruit cocktail, a box of raisins, two jerrycans, one containing water and the other three gallons of gasoline, rope, binoculars, canteens, a plastic bottle of Mennen spray deodorant, toilet paper, a machete, a Bowie knife, a hatchet, a .35-calibre Remington rifle, a .30-calibre carbine, a .357 Magnum Smith & Wesson pistol, a 9mm Luger automatic, a 12-gauge shotgun with sawn-off barrel and stock, a Galesi-Brescia handgun, some thirty-shot magazines, and over seven hundred rounds of ammunition.

During the previous night Whitman had murdered first his mother, then his wife. On his way into the UT Tower a few minutes earlier he had shot and killed a receptionist and a family of visitors. Now he was leaning on the parapet, peering through the telescopic sight at the crowds on the Drag below.

In the heat and humidity of the Texan midsummer, Teresa Simons, unaware of the sniper at the top of the tower, was looking at the handmade sandals on one of the craft stalls. The humid air smelt of cedarwood, hot road-tar and the incense that several stallholders were burning. On one of the other stalls the Beatles' new single 'Paperback Writer' was playing loudly. Teresa smiled and listened to the words; the song reminded her of a boy she'd known for a while, twenty years ago.

She moved on down, looking at the goods displayed on another stall: brightly coloured posters, tasselled leather shoulder-bags, embroidered muslin shirts and equipment for growing cannabis. She was Whitman's first victim, and died from a shot through her back.

The Austin Tower ExEx was one of the toughest assignments on the course, and Teresa was involved with the challenge it presented for most of a winter. But she got her man in the end.

CHAPTER 16

At lunchtime Teresa went to the hotel bar, where she knew she could order some sandwiches. Amy brought them to her, looking and sounding more friendly than at their last encounter, but after that she left Teresa alone in the bar. Teresa drank a glass of chilled mineral water, feeling virtuous, and a small cup of coffee afterwards. The bar remained solidly normal. Nick and Amy appeared at intervals, going about their business, serving the handful of other customers who appeared.

Back in her room she again consulted her street map of Bulverton. She located Welton Road: it was in a small grid of streets close to the Ridge, the ring road that followed the line of hills to the north of the town, forming an effective boundary with the countryside.

She drove up to Welton Road and found that it was part of a recently built industrial estate. A number of large, undistinguished buildings, constructed of prefabricated concrete with brick facing, lined the streets. Most of the businesses appeared to be light industry: she saw signs for computer software companies, packaging suppliers, manufacturers of electronic components, package couriers. In this environment the extreme experience building blended effortlessly. She drove past it twice before she located it. All it had was a discreet white sign next to the door announcing: GunHo ExEx. The place had few windows, and only one entrance area; in front of the building there was a wide parking lot. Teresa drove in, but could find no spaces left and had to move to a place on the side of the road a couple of hundred yards away.

She was locking the car when she became aware that someone was leaving the building. She instantly recognized him: it was the man she had seen talking aggressively to Amy in the Old Town market. Teresa moved at once to the rear of the car and opened the hatch door. Using the raised door as cover she looked up the road through the tilted glass of the window. The man walked briskly from the main entrance, strode through the parking lot and went to a car parked not far from her own. He did not appear to notice her, nor should there be any reason why he would.

She waited until he had driven away, not fully understanding why she felt the need to stay out of his sight. She closed and locked her car, then walked across to the building. A pair of double glass doors led into a conventional reception area, where a young woman sat behind a large desk.

There seemed to be people everywhere. Five people were sitting in a waiting area opposite the reception desk, and there were two others already in a line in front of her at the desk. The young receptionist was speaking on the telephone, and writing on a pad of paper with her free hand. To one side of her desk there was a pile of wrapped packages, apparently awaiting collection or delivery.

Beyond the waiting area, on the side, there was a door with a glass panel, and as it appeared she was going to have to wait for several minutes Teresa sauntered across to it and peered through. Above the door was a large sign, the lettering drawn in a brilliant emulation of the kind of spray-paint graffiti you saw everywhere: CYBERVILLE UK. It was a long, windowless room, not brightly lit, equipped with at least a dozen PCs. Each computer was in use, with someone staring raptly at the screen. Teresa realized that the place was an internet café: website graphics were constantly loading and wiping, as the endless search for data went on. At the far end of the room were some arcade games machines, but these were not being used. Most of the computer users looked remarkably young.

She returned to the reception desk, and waited her turn. At last, the young woman, identified on her lapel badge as Paula Willson of Customer Services Dept., was free.

'May I help you?' she said.

'I'd like to make use of the ExEx equipment here.'

'Yes, we have that facility. Are you a member?'

'No. Do I have to be?'

'Yes, unless you're already a member of one of our associate clubs.'

'I've used ExEx in the States,' Teresa said. 'But not on public equipment. It was . . . training equipment.'

Paula Willson passed her a form from a large pile on her desk.

'If you would fill this in,' she said, 'we can enrol you straight away. Were you planning on using the equipment today?'

'Yes, I was. If that's possible.'

'We're always booked up, but there are a few slots free this afternoon. Weekdays are better than weekends.' She had turned the form round on the desk, and was indicating it with a finger. 'All we need from you is some form of identification, and we do require a membership fee when you enrol. We accept all major credit cards.'

'When I've filled this out, I give it back to you?'

'Yes. May I help you?'

She had turned to the two people standing behind Teresa, who had come in from outside while they were talking. Teresa picked up the form and took it across to the waiting area. She found a space on one of the black leather sofas, and leaned forward to lay the form on the glass-topped table in front of her. The page was headed *GunHo Corporation – Extreme Experience and Internet Access.*

It was a low-intensity form compared with some of the ones she had had to complete in the US; there were the usual questions concerning identity, status, finances and occupation, none of which bothered her. She hesitated over the questions about her job, wondering how she should describe it. There was no official Bureau policy on this, although when answering similar form questions in the US she and other agents usually named their employer in vague terms, such as 'US Government' or 'Dept. of Justice', and their job as 'civil servant' or 'federal employee'. For the time being she left this box blank, and turned over the page.

Here she found a list of questions about her intended use of the equipment, ranging from e-mail, internet conferencing and access to website browsing, to use of extreme experience scenarios – general and specific uses, with a long list of the latter – and training modules. She glanced through the list, remarking to herself on the extent of what was on offer.

She confined herself to two choices: the general scenario option, because she was unclear about what was available and this seemed to open the way to the rest, and from the training modules *'Target Practice: Handgun'*. A note to this one said that applicants were required to produce accreditation or licence, and a police or employer's reference also had to be produced.

She ringed it anyway, then returned to the front of the form. In the box enquiring about her employer, she wrote *'US Dept. of Justice – FBI'*, she described herself as *'federal agent'*, and in the Number of Years Employed box she wrote '16'.

After another wait at the reception desk Teresa handed in her form, and waited while Paula Willson checked through it.

'Thank you,' she said after a moment. 'May I have some identification, Mrs Simons, and your credit card?'

Teresa handed over her Baltimore First National Visa, and her Bureau ID. The young woman ran the card through the electronic swipe, and while waiting for a response she glanced at the ID. She handed it back without comment, then typed a few entries on the keyboard in front of her.

Finally she said, 'I'm afraid I'm not able to assign handgun target-practice authorization myself. Would you mind waiting for a few minutes, and I'll ask our duty manager to see you?'

'No, of course not. You said there were some slots free this afternoon. Assuming I get the go-ahead, can I book one of them now?'

Paula Willson looked surprised, but she typed at the keyboard, and in a moment said, 'Well, we have target range software free at three-thirty, in just under an hour. And there's another slot at five. Or would you prefer to use the general scenarios?'

'I'll take the three-thirty slot, for target practice.' The words came out quickly. Teresa was still apprehensive about the full scenarios, the extraordinary onslaught of physical sensations, the dislocation from reality. On the other hand, she knew what ExEx target ranges were like and they were regularly used by the Bureau. But she asked, 'What about the other scenarios?'

'We have nothing free today. There are a couple of hours available tomorrow.'

Teresa considered, not having expected there would be a delay. She had thought it would be something she could just walk into, as she had done at the Academy.

'Are you always as busy as this?' she said.

'Pretty much. ExEx has recently become much more popular than it was even a year ago. The problem's worse at some of the bigger centres. There's a four-month waiting list for membership at our centre in Maidstone, for instance. In London and some of the other big cities you have to wait nearly a year. They're planning to close membership here soon. We're running at capacity, just about.'

'I hadn't realized ExEx had grown as big as this.'

'It's big.' The young woman's eyes flicked towards the screen. 'What shall I do? Book you in provisionally for the three-thirty slot?'

'Yes. Thanks. After that, I'll book some other time ahead.'

A printer built into the body of the desk emitted a familiar muted screech, and a curl of paper came jerkily into view. Paula Willson ripped it off, and passed it to Teresa for her signature. It was a credit-card charge slip.

'I'd better let you have our current price list,' the receptionist said, and gave Teresa a folded brochure printed on glossy paper. 'We'll send the membership folder to you in due course.'

'You assume they're going to let me in,' Teresa said.

'I don't expect there'll be a problem,' said Paula Willson. 'I think you're the first FBI agent they've had in this centre.'

CHAPTER 17

'May I speak with Ms Amy Colwyn, please?' It was a determined American voice: male, making an effort to be polite.

'This is she,' Amy said, but then corrected herself. 'Speaking.'

'Ms Colwyn, this is to advise you that we will be checking in at your hotel this evening.'

'Who is that, please?'

'This is Ken Mitchell, of the GunHo Corporation. We have some reservations with you, made by our head office in Taiwan?' His voice rose, as if asking a question, but it was unmistakably a statement. 'Is this the White Dragon Hotel?'

'Yes, sir. We are expecting you this evening.'

'OK. We've just landed at London Heathrow and I've picked up a file copy of the reservation, and I want to advise you that our company always makes it a condition of reservation that in a small hotel like yours we expect to have sole occupation. I see you have not confirmed this in your letter, although you would have been advised of the condition when the reservation was made.'

'Sole occupation?' Amy said.

'Yeah, I know this would have been discussed. We like the place to ourselves.'

'I confirmed the reservation myself. I don't remember this coming up. But all our rooms are completely private—'

'I'm not getting this across to you, am I? No other people in the place. You got that?'

'Yes, Mr Mitchell.'

'OK, we'll be with you directly.'

'Do you know how to find the hotel, sir? I can arrange to have someone pick you up from the station—'

'We don't go anywhere by train,' said Mr Ken Mitchell from Taiwan, and put down the phone.

*

121

A little later, Amy looked into the bar. Nick was sitting there alone, a newspaper propped up on his knee and spreading untidily across the counter.

'Have you seen Mrs Simons this afternoon?' she asked him.

'No.' He didn't look up. 'I think she went out somewhere. Not in her room?'

'I've had those American people from Taiwan on the phone. They say they don't want anyone else staying here at the same time as them.'

'That's bad luck.' He put down the newspaper, and took a sip from the glass at his side. 'Not much we can do about it.'

'I didn't like the sound of it,' Amy said. 'He seemed pretty certain of what he wanted.'

'Maybe somewhere else could take them in.'

'Are you serious? Do you realize how much money these people could make us?'

'Well, maybe Mrs Simons would like to move to another hotel. You said she wasn't happy about something.'

'No, I did ask her,' Amy said. 'She told me she had no complaints, and wanted to stay.'

'Then what are you asking me?'

'It's your hotel, Nick! These people from Taiwan are determined to have the place to themselves, or sounded like it. What's the law? Can they insist on us throwing out another guest?'

'The only person who can do that is me. And I'm not about to.'

His eyes kept straying towards the newspaper, and Amy felt herself getting irritated with him. She left him there, and went to be by herself in the tiny office.

She sat down behind the desk, staring blankly and distractedly at the mess of papers before noticing the bills that had come in during the last week. Nick had tossed them in a heap on the desk. She leafed through them, then looked around for their latest bank statement. She switched on the computer and after it had booted she put up on the screen the spreadsheet file where she kept the list of cheques they had paid. She looked over them, noted a few differences, and within a few minutes was contentedly occupied by the familiar drudgery of checking her own book-keeping.

'I'm going upstairs for a bath,' Nick said from the doorway, and tossed in the newspaper. It landed on the desk, dislodging pieces of paper she had only just sorted out.

'Anyone in the bar?' she called after him.

'Not at the moment.'

She glared after him, then surrendered once again to the familiar sensation of being trapped in this hotel. She still hadn't completely worked out her feelings about Nick, or even about why she had moved back in with him. Running the hotel was displacement activity of a sort, a postponement of decisions about her own life.

A day never passed when she did not think to herself how easy it would be to leave. But inevitably there was another thought that always followed: leave, yes, but in which direction? There was nowhere in Bulverton for her, nowhere in Eastbourne or any of the other resort towns along the coast. She had done all that when she was younger, and she was uncomfortably aware of how long ago that now was. Everything had changed. Jase dead, of course, but all her old friends were married, or had left town. They wouldn't be a solution, anyway: the discontent was inside herself. If she really wanted to improve her life she would have to make a clean break, head away from Bulverton and Sussex. London, of course, was the obvious place, but that didn't appeal. Or somewhere abroad? Once again she dreamed of having the guts to take up Gwyneth's invitation, and give the life in Sydney a try.

But there, or wherever she went, in the end there would be another Nick Surtees.

Nothing appealed. There was only this: a list of cheques recorded in a computer, which she had just about made to agree with the bank statement. They were more broke than she had thought, or maybe remembered. The overdraft was appreciably larger, while takings were continuing to drift down. Only the prospect of guests staying in the hotel gave any hope: the income was erratic, but even when only one person was staying, like Teresa Simons, the place could operate profitably.

Did Nick know this? If he knew, did he care? She remembered his disagreeable expression when he went upstairs, and she listened to the knocking in the plumbing as he ran the water for his bath, as if it were a drumming refrain of why she now regretted her life.

What on earth had brought her back to him? By the time she had realized what she was letting herself in for, she was in for it. She knew you should never blow over old coals; she remembered her mother mystifying her with this saying when she was a child, but it had a meaning after all. It reminded her of how many times her parents had split up after rows, then blown noisily over their own old coals as they tried to put everything right again. But now there was Nick. Their relationship hadn't worked properly when they were in their teens, and after the recent months with him she knew it probably never would.

Even so, she was trapped by past events. All this would continue.

She heard the outside door to the car park open and close, so she trundled her wheeled office chair back from the desk, and craned her neck so she could see along the corridor. Teresa was heading for the staircase, with a heavy shoulder-bag weighing her down to one side.

'Mrs Simons! Teresa!'

The American paused, then walked down the corridor towards her.

'Hi,' she said, looking tired but cheerful.

'I was wondering if you planned to be in the hotel for dinner tonight?'

'I guess I don't know yet. Yeah, why not? What do you have in mind?'

'Anything you like.' Amy pulled down the menu from the top of the filing cabinet and passed it to her. 'We've got most of what's there in the freezer, but if you would like to decide now, or you want something else, I've still got time to buy it fresh for you.'

Teresa scanned the menu, but quickly, obviously with her mind on something else.

'Maybe I'll decide later,' she said in the end and passed the card back. 'I'm not hungry yet.'

Amy wished she hadn't brought up the subject. She had really intended to ask Teresa as gently as possible how she would feel about moving to another hotel, but when it came to it she hadn't been able to find the words. Or even the wish to find the words.

She stared up at Teresa, again putting off the evil moment and wishing Nick was there to do it instead. She wondered what time these Taiwanese with American names and accents were likely to arrive, but also she was wondering how she could find out the law on hotel licensing. Could one guest, or one set of guests, *really* demand that they be the only people allowed in the building as guests? She supposed film stars, or visiting politicians, might do this sometimes, but she suspected that that would be better or more delicately organized. Anyway film stars would never stay in a place like the White Dragon, so it wouldn't arise. Maybe money was the way it was done: people who wanted solitude paid for every available room in the hotel and used only the ones they wanted. But what would they do about people who were already staying there?

Teresa said, 'I've got work I need to do upstairs. I'll be down for a drink a little later.'

'All right. I think Nick would like to talk to you about something.'

'Any idea what?' Teresa said. Amy shook her head, still evading an issue she saw increasingly as Nick's, not her own. 'OK, I'll see you later.'

She lifted and eased the heavy shoulder-bag, then swung round. In a moment, Amy heard her footsteps as she went up the stairs.

Amy took down the bookings ledger, and found the thin file of faxes she had exchanged with Mr A. Li in Taiwan. She carefully checked through what had been written on every scrap of paper she had received. In essence this was that the GunHo Corporation of Taipei required separate rooms with double beds for four adult guests, two men, two women, surnames Kravitz, Mitchell, Wendell and Jensen. All expenses run up by the guests were to be allocated to the corporate account, and at the end of each week one of the four named guests would check and sign the account, after which it should be faxed to Mr Li in the Taipei office. A draft in US dollars or UK pounds, based on this amount, would then be available from the Barclays Bank in Bulverton, and would be paid to them on demand. The booking was confirmed initially for two weeks only, but there was an option to extend the arrangement indefinitely. All enquiries would be dealt with by Mr Li.

Amy could not see any mention anywhere of them requiring exclusive use of the hotel.

She glanced at her wristwatch and mentally calculated how long it would take to drive to Bulverton from Heathrow. She reckoned the earliest they could arrive would be within the next hour, but they would certainly be here by the evening. Still she had done nothing.

She went upstairs to find Nick. He was lying on the bed, naked, and smoking a cigarette.

'It's the middle of the day, and there's nothing doing,' he said. 'Want to come to bed for a while?'

Her first instinct was to turn round and walk out of the room. She still enjoyed all that with Nick, but these days he seemed to want to spend most afternoons in bed. Instead, she decided to shrug it off.

'There's something I need to know,' she said. 'It's pretty urgent. Is that true what you said? That you're the only one who can make a guest leave the hotel?'

'What's bothering you, Amy?'

'I was trying to tell you earlier.'

'Don't worry about it.'

She sat down on the edge of the bed, and in spite of herself she laid a hand on his chest. His skin felt clean and smooth and warm.

'I don't want us to lose the money,' she said. 'This booking could solve a lot of financial problems for us. Well, for you, but that means me too.'

'Leave it to me. I've brought in an extra double bed for them, and that'll keep them happy. When are they arriving?'

'Any minute now. They called from Heathrow an hour or two ago, and said they were going to drive down.'

'It always takes longer than people think,' Nick said, rolling towards her. 'Come on, get your clothes off.'

'No, I want to stay downstairs in case they arrive.'

He said no more but began pulling determinedly at the buttons down the front of her dress. In his haste he fumbled them, so she pulled away from him and slipped the dress off. She lay down next to him, enjoying the sensation, as always, of him slipping his hands beneath her undies and sliding them down her skin.

Later, they were still lying against each other when they heard the sound of a heavy-engined vehicle pulling into the car park beneath their window. They could hear the gears clanging in and out, as the driver eased to and fro in the confined space.

'That's them!' Amy said. 'I know it'll be the Americans.'

She rolled away from Nick and he turned over on to his side in simulated disgust; in fact, Amy knew only too well that once they finished lovemaking during the afternoons he was usually quick to move away from her and either take a short nap or get back to reading his newspaper.

She hurried naked from the bed. Crouching down by the window she peeked into the yard and saw a long truck, painted an unobtrusive dark green, being manoeuvred into the parking bay next to Teresa Simons' rented car. It had what appeared to be a collapsible satellite dish folded down into a special cavity built into the roof. The number 14 was next to this, painted in a lighter shade of green. Amy wondered briefly why anyone should want to paint an identifying number on the roof of a van, where only a few people would ever be able to see it.

A young woman with short, pale-brown hair climbed down from the passenger door, and went to the back of the van to help guide the driver into the parking bay. She glanced up at Amy's window, and for a moment their eyes met.

Even though she knew only her head could be seen from the low angle from the yard, Amy backed away and rushed over to retrieve her clothes from the floor beside the bed.

'They're here!' Amy said to Nick. She wrapped her bra round her with the cups at the back, hooked it together beneath her breasts, then twisted it round and pulled the straps into place. She stepped into her pants, and looked around for her dress. Nick had rolled on to his side and was either reading, or pretending to read, yesterday's copy of the newspaper. 'It's all right, Nick,' she said. 'I can manage downstairs on my own.'

'I knew you would.'

But he grinned affably at her, threw the newspaper on the floor by the side of the bed, and after a quick and furtive glance into the car park began to put on his clothes. She was finished before him, but he grabbed her and gave her a quick kiss.

'I'll cook dinner tonight, if you like,' he said. 'And do the bar.'

'You don't have to.'

'Maybe I do. It's been long enough.'

'Has something happened to you? Good news or something?'

'No . . . but I'll cook the meals tonight anyway. I feel like it.'

She returned his kiss, then pushed him away with both hands flat against his chest.

'These people will want to check in,' she said.

Amy was downstairs in the reception area before any of the Americans appeared, and had time to compose herself, making it look as if she had been busy with paperwork for some time. A few seconds later the door from the car park opened and Amy, without looking up, was aware of two figures entering.

'Good afternoon, ma'am,' said a polite American voice.

She stood up and turned to the counter. It was a man in his middle thirties, and the young woman she had seen from the upstairs window.

'Good afternoon,' she said.

'We'd like to register, if we may?' The rising inflection again.

Amy pushed forward the pad of registration cards.

'If you would fill out four of those, please,' she said. 'And may I see your passports?'

'Of course.'

The formalities went ahead without a hitch. The remaining two people came in behind, and took their turn at filling out the cards.

'Your reservation was for four single rooms, each with a double bed?'

'Right.'

'OK, but we don't have many rooms in the hotel, and so we have had to split you up. There are two rooms next to each other on the first floor, and two more on the floor above. That's what you call the second and third floor, I think. Anyway, the rooms are separated only by a staircase.'

They were nodding. Amy spread the electronically coded room key-cards across the top of the counter, deliberately making a clattering noise with them. She wondered how the Americans would allocate the rooms: would the women take the two adjacent ones? The two on the top floor, tucked under the eaves of the old roof, were smaller than the others, but they had a distant view of the sea.

'I guess that'll be OK,' said the man who Amy now knew from his registration card was called Dennis Kravitz. He glanced around at the others. They all nodded or shrugged. One of the women – Acie Jensen, according to her card – had taken down a handful of leaflets from the tourist noticeboard, and was looking through them. 'Listen, we have a van out there with some expensive equipment,' Kravitz said. 'I noticed you don't have a gate on your parking lot. Is there any way we can secure it at night?'

'There's an intruder light over the yard. If you wish we can put up a parking bar in front of the vehicle to stop someone trying to drive it away.'

Dennis Kravitz frowned.

'It's not the vehicle we're too concerned about,' he said, pronouncing it vee-hicle. 'But the equipment we've got inside. If the yard isn't gated, how can we be sure no one's going to take a look?'

'I'm sure it'll be all right,' Amy said. 'There isn't much crime in Bulverton.'

'That isn't what we heard,' said Acie Jensen from across the room, not looking up from a leaflet about Bodiam Castle.

'Not that sort of crime,' Amy said stoutly.

'Suit yourself,' the woman said, losing interest. She crossed the room and spoke quietly to the others. They picked up their key-cards and all went towards the rooms without any further re-marks. If they'd asked, Amy could have offered to arrange for Nick to help carry up some of their baggage, but they seemed uninterested in having assistance.

For a while the four Americans moved to and fro in the re-ception area, picking up suitcases and other baggage from the van in the yard and carrying it in, but before long the hotel had quietened down again.

True to his promise Nick came down not much later, glanced through some of the paperwork on the desk in the office and then went to the kitchen. Amy stayed on in the reception area, listen-ing to the sounds she could now hear in the building: footsteps on the ancient floors above her head, water moving through the almost equally old plumbing, Nick clattering around in the kitchen. Amy realized that this was the first time the hotel had had more than one or two overnight guests since the few days that followed the massacre. Maybe life in the end really was capable of returning to a semblance of normality.

Half an hour later Teresa Simons came in again from outside through the main door, gave Amy a friendly smile, then headed off upstairs to her room.

CHAPTER 18

Teresa returned to the ExEx building the following morning. She used the two hours of scenario time she had, after all, decided to book, after she had made her timid venture into the shallows of virtual target practice.

She was however still nervous of plunging fully into unknown worlds of virtuality, and once she was inside the simulations suite she asked the technician to help her.

'Are you a new user?' the young man said. His lapel badge identified him as Angus Jackson, Customer Liaison.

'I've trained with ExEx in the US,' Teresa said. 'Interdiction scenarios.'

'Were those terminal, or non-terminal?'

'They were both.' Believing that there was no longer any point blurring the truth about her job, Teresa described the kind of scenarios she had used.

'OK,' said Angus Jackson. 'We have plenty of those. Now I assume you know how to abort a scenario?'

'Yeah. LIVER is what we use in the Bureau.'

'I don't know it.'

Teresa explained the acronym, and at once he nodded his understanding. They had a different mnemonic, but it had the same effect. He left her for a couple of minutes, then returned with the familiar sealed phial of nanochips.

'Let me explain what I've done,' he said. 'We do anthology packages for new users, and this one is a randomized selection of the kind of scenarios that many law-enforcement agencies are currently using. You will possibly recognize some of them. It's a real mixture, drawn from a library of about nine hundred different situations. You've booked two hours, so either you can surf through the selection until your time's up, when you'll be pulled out automatically, or you can abort when you've had enough.'

'Are we talking terminal or non-terminal?' Teresa asked.

'These are all non-terminal. Is that OK?'

'I prefer that. Yes.'

Teresa roamed around the familiar world of outburst violence, tackling each problem as it was presented to her, using whatever weapons were supplied by the writers of the software.

In São Paulo, Brazil, 1995, there was a knife fight in a salsa club; this was tricky because of the darkness inside the club, but it took only a single disabling shot to bring the dispute to an end. LIVER. In Sydney, Australia, 1989, a young drug addict had run amok with a handgun; this had a fairly straightforward interdict-and-arrest resolution, but one which she found physically demanding. LIVER. In Kansas City, Missouri, 1967, and still out of breath from the last scenario, Teresa found herself in the McLaughlin siege, one on which she had trained with the Bureau. An ex-cop called Joe McLaughlin had barricaded himself in the house of the wife from whom he was separated, and was shooting at anyone who went near. Because of her familiarity with the scenario, and because she wanted to move on to the next, Teresa went impatiently to the side of the house, forced an entry into the basement and shot McLaughlin on the stairs. Had she been undergoing training Dan Kazinsky would have made her go back and get it right (McLaughlin had only to be arrested), but she wanted to try scenarios she hadn't used before. LIVER.

The next scenario was a more complex one, new to her, and it absorbed her from the moment she entered it.

San Diego, California, 1950: William Cook was on the run from the police, having already abducted and murdered a family of five in Missouri, and with another man as a hostage had driven to San Diego in the car he had stolen from the family.

Teresa entered the ExEx scenario at the point when Cook's stolen Pontiac was spotted on Route 8; rather than try a dangerous interception on the road, the police and federal agents had decided to allow Cook to enter the outskirts of San Diego, and either stop him there or arrest him when he tried to leave the car. His progress was being monitored by unmarked police cars.

It was another scenario in which the sheer quality of the

detailed background, and the authenticating details, took the breath away. This was often a feature of the older incidents, Teresa had found. Dan Kazinsky said the explanation lay in the quality of memory. Moments of traumatic experience survive more completely and vividly in long-term memory. Teresa and the other trainees had noticed that ExEx scenarios about relatively recent events were sometimes blurred, as if parts of them had been mentally blocked by those recalling them.

She entered the Cook scenario on a blisteringly hot day, a sea wind bending the palm trees, making the dust fly at the street intersections, puffing the canopies of shops and swinging the overhead traffic signals precariously. The sky was cloudless, but there was grit from the sandy shore in the burning wind. Clothes pressed against bodies, and hair blew. Shiny, rounded cars moved in leisurely fashion through the streets. A DC-3 of Pan American circled overhead, moving down towards the airfield; the brilliant sunshine glinted off the unpainted wings and engine cowlings. Men in Navy uniforms loitered round a military truck parked in a lot beside an equipment office, where the Stars and Stripes was flying.

Teresa had no time to take in any more. The scenario was in progress.

She had a key in her hand, and as she entered the action she was hurrying towards a row of cars parked diagonally against the sidewalk. She was out of breath, and her back and legs were hurting. She reeled mentally, perhaps physically too, at the impact of the sensory overload from the collectively remembered scenario. She was too hot, the wind took her breath away, something in the air flew into her eye. She turned away, blinking hard, needing to concentrate instead on the unfolding of the scenario. She wanted to maintain her own individuality, her own reactions. With the grit out of her eye, she turned back quickly enough to see one of the buildings beside her – some kind of motor-spares or tool store – flicker into solidity as her vision persisted in that direction. It happened so quickly that she might have imagined it, but it was a breakdown in the extreme reality and she found it perversely comforting; even this dazzling technology was not yet one hundred per cent.

She was moving towards a silver-and-blue Chevrolet station

wagon, but again she resisted the scenario and went instead to a green Ford saloon parked alongside. The driver's door was locked, and the key she was holding would not even slide in. Her hand burned on the sun-hot metal of the door. She gave up and went to the Chevrolet instead. The door of this was unlocked, and after she had slid on to the bench seat, comfortably spreading her large body, she got the key into the ignition at the first try. She wound down the window on the driver's side.

A few moments later she was driving north along 30th Street, and at the intersection with University she moved across into the turn lane and took a right.

It was the first time she had driven a car in an ExEx, and it was exhilarating. Two impressions predominated. The first was a feeling of complete safety: the car could not crash, she could not be hurt, because she could not act alone and could not make her own decisions. The scenario was laid out for her to follow. She had taken the right into University because that was the way she had to go; she shortly came to the large intersection with Wabash Boulevard, and here she took a left, driving on to the highway and accelerating to keep up with the rest of the traffic. The sun was shafting in through the driver's window, making her arm and face tingle. She wound up the window, and pulled the visor over to help shade herself.

This action, this decision, was part of the second and contradictory impression: that she could defy the scenario and act independently of it. She could put her foot down on the gas pedal and just drive, keep on going, head east or north out of the town, drive for ever across the great virtual America that lay out there, just beyond her immediate view of the simulation, letting it piece itself together, shaping seamlessly about her, unfolding endlessly for her.

Instead, she reached into the glove compartment and took out the automatic pistol that was there.

While she drove she checked it was loaded, then laid it on the seat beside her. She switched on the radio: the Duke Ellington Orchestra was playing an instrumental number called 'Newport Up'. How did she know that? She'd never listened closely to Duke Ellington in her life, and would hardly be able to identify the sound of the orchestra let alone any individual tracks.

She stretched back in the seat, drove with her arms straight and her head lying back on the rest, the radio on, the sun blazing in on her, and the wonderful rumbling slow traffic of 1950 gliding past and around her.

Moments later she saw diversion lights ahead, and a police roadblock. Most of the traffic was peeling off to the left, going around the diversion, but she slowed and signalled to the right, heading straight for the police line. She came to a halt, and pulled on the parking brake with long, solid vibration from the ratchet. An officer walked towards her, leaning down to see into the car.

Suddenly, she was no longer sure of what she was doing. Had she decided of her own will to drive up to the police line? Or was this what the woman driving the car would have done? The police officer was just a few feet away from the car, a hand extended to indicate she should not drive off again.

Teresa made an instant judgement: that she had decided on her own initiative not to follow the diversion. She was in control. From long habit she fished into her pocket for her Bureau ID, but it was missing!

She looked down at herself, realizing for the first time that she was wearing some other woman's clothes. She was fat! She was wearing terrible clothes! She had runs in her stockings! She grappled at her belt, where she kept her badge, but down there, under the copious folds of her overweight body, sagging down into her lap, there was just a thin plastic belt.

She glanced up into the rear-view mirror, leaning across to see herself; an elderly black woman's face, full of mild concern, looked back at her.

'Ma'am, this is a restricted area,' said the cop, now leaning down by the window. Teresa noticed that it had re-opened itself somehow, while she was driving, while she was distracted from the simulation. 'Would you reverse up, please, and rejoin the main flow of traffic.'

'I'm Federal Agent Simons, attached to Richmond station,' Teresa said, but by now the cop had seen the automatic lying on the seat beside her.

He said, 'Ma'am, would you raise both your hands slowly and leave the car—'

But then, maddeningly, the ExEx ended, and Teresa's mind's

eye was filled with white crystalline light, and her ears roared with static.

Teresa returned to her own semblance of reality: a small, cool room, painted white, with an overhead strip light. She was lying on a narrow bench, on a cream-coloured paper sheet which rustled as she stirred. There was a distant murmur of air-conditioning, the voices of other people close by in another room or corridor. From the moment she left the scenario Teresa was aware of her surroundings and what she had been doing; this was a major improvement on the traumatic period of recovery that followed a terminal event in the FBI's training scenarios.

A technician was standing by the open door to the cubicle. As soon as she saw Teresa stirring, she came fully into the cubicle and stood next to her.

'How are you feeling, Mrs Simons?' she said, her gaze flicking professionally over her.

'I'm fine.'

'No problems, then?'

She helped Teresa sit up straight, and immediately attended to the nanochip valve on the back of her neck. Teresa, who had rarely been conscious for this procedure, tried to see what the woman was doing. The angle was wrong: she glimpsed a syringe-like instrument being deployed, felt a significant pressure on her neck, a twinge of pain, then a slight and not unpleasant vibration. The technician's name badge was just about all she could see: her name was Patricia Tarrant, Customer Liaison. As Ms Tarrant removed the syringe, Teresa felt the valve move against a sore spot, somewhere there, under the skin or around the valve itself. She put a hand up, and touched it gingerly.

Teresa watched as the contents of the syringe – the nanochips suspended in a pale liquid – were transferred to a glass tube, which Patricia Tarrant then placed inside a cabinet at the foot of the bench. She activated some mechanism, and warning lights briefly showed.

'Fine. When you're ready, if you'd like to come outside we can complete the paperwork.'

Teresa's mind was still swimming with the images of San Diego, the hot wind, the open road. Before the technician could leave the cubicle she said to her, 'That Cook scenario. I'd never come across it before.'

'Cook?'

'William Cook,' Teresa said, trying to remember. Images of extreme reality still dazzled her memory, tending to confuse false memory with real. '1950, San Diego. Something about a fugitive with a hostage.'

'I don't know it,' Patricia said. 'Were you on a random-access package?'

'Yeah, that's it. Random non-terminal. Anthology scenarios.' She followed Ms Tarrant out of the cubicle, to a nearby work station with a large computer monitor and a huge number of ring-binder manuals. 'I wasn't sure what software you had available, and one of your colleagues suggested I use one of the packages. I was just trying it out.'

'I can look up the scenario for you,' Patricia Tarrant said, turning to her computer. She began tapping keys, watching the monitor.

While information began to scroll on the screen Teresa said, as if to help the technician pin down the scenario, 'I wasn't in there as myself, but I could remember who I was and what I was doing. I've only ever used FBI scenarios before—'

'Yeah, here we are. William Cook, 1950. We've got quite a library of stuff on him. Do you know which scenario it was?'

'I was in the body of an elderly woman,' Teresa said. 'She was overweight, out of breath, had a silver-blue station wagon. A Chevy.'

'It must be this one,' Patricia said, pointing at the screen. 'That's the only scenario that's been accessed this week. That would be you, just now. Elsa Jane Durdle was the witness; age sixty-nine, lived at 2213 North Sea Road, San Diego. I wonder how they found her?'

'They?'

'The people who wrote the software. It's shareware. You don't often get witness scenarios from shareware producers. Maybe they happened to know her? No, she must be dead by now. I wonder how they did it?'

'She was a witness? But she had a gun.'

'She did? I suppose that's possible. I mean, in this sort of interdiction scenario you have to have a gun to use, isn't that right? The witness might have owned one anyway, and if she didn't the programmer could have put it in.'

Teresa sat back, surprised by all this. She fingered the sore place in her neck again. The pain was not wearing off.

'I didn't know you would be using shareware,' she said.

'We take stuff from all over. Someone here always checks it out. Or in our head office. If you didn't want shareware on the roll-through, you could have specified that before we started.'

'It doesn't matter,' Teresa said. 'It was interesting. In fact, I'd never been in an ExEx that felt so convincing. I'd like to use it again.'

Patricia found some Post-it notes, and wrote down the reference number on the top slip. She peeled it off and gave it to Teresa.

'How long is it since you last used ExEx equipment?' she said.

'I was here yesterday. One of your colleagues supervised me. I can't remember who it was.' Patricia nodded. 'I used the range for target practice, and was only in there for an hour. Apart from that, it's been maybe a year or two. But back then I was using the Bureau's own ExEx equipment, so I always assumed the software was the best available. And the training was closely supervised. You can probably imagine how the Bureau operates. I had no idea there were all these other scenarios.'

Patricia indicated a pile of cartons stacked against one of the walls across the room.

'You should see some of the software that comes in these days,' she said. 'That lot arrived this week alone. The problem isn't getting hold of the programs, but selecting what we can safely use. A government organization like the FBI wouldn't have time to check everything that's released, so they'd just buy in the commercial programs. You're safe with those, but they aren't always the most interesting. The cutting edge has been deregulated.'

'So is there any difference in practice?' Teresa said. 'You mentioned safety. Is it dangerous to use shareware?'

'No, there's no physical risk, of course. But the commercial programs are always documented, and they have back-up.'

'I don't follow.'

'Back-up means their scenarios are based on witness statements, hypnotic regressions, character evaluations, historical documents. They use film or TV footage wherever it's available, and always go back to the scene of the original incident. As far as possible a commercial scenario is an actual re-creation of the event. Also, when the software arrives it comes with masses of hard-copy documentation: you can check just about everything. We do a lot of scenarios in-house. GunHo, the company that owns this building, started out as a software producer. With shareware, you have to take it on an as-is basis. We do all the checking we can, and some of the shareware companies are well known to us, but there's no way you can check the authenticity of the scenarios. Some of them are brilliant: they come up with character evaluations or regressions that were completely missed by the big companies, and so they genuinely add something to what is already known.'

'I've used shareware on my PC,' Teresa said. 'There's usually something wrong with it. It always feels a bit unfinished.'

'Yes, and that's the other problem. From our point of view as a provider, we can never take for granted how good the programming has been. You get a lot of sloppy stuff, mostly from kids: they patch in routines from other scenarios, or they use the public-domain footage libraries, or they simply don't bother with backgrounds. Others go the other way: you see some scenarios that are almost fanatically detailed and real-seeming. I sometimes wonder how they do it.'

While she spoke, Patricia was scrolling idly through the database, and Teresa watched the screen. She noticed that the William Cook case had at least twenty different scenarios attached to it.

'Can I try some of those others?' she said.

'If you're interested in the Cook case, you probably should. We've got the FBI scenario here, as well as police ones. Those are the most historically accurate. The rest are probably all shareware.'

'I don't have a special interest in the case,' Teresa said. 'But maybe it would be interesting to study it from different angles.'

'Then you should talk to Mr Lacey. Have you met him?'

'Was he the duty manager yesterday?'

'Yes.'

'I met him.'

'Ted Lacey runs the education modules here. We have an affiliation to the University of Sussex, and there's a whole range of study aids and courses. Do you want to sign up for one of those?'

'No,' Teresa said quickly. 'Not just yet. But I wouldn't mind using Elsa Durdle's scenario again.'

'No problem. You want to go back in now? We've had a couple of cancellations today, so there's machine time available.'

Teresa considered for a moment, feeling another twinge of pain from the valve in her neck. 'I don't think so. Not today. But would you mind looking up a couple of other cases for me?'

'OK.'

'You got anything on Charles Joseph Whitman?'

'I think so,' Patricia said, starting to type. 'That was Texas, 1966, wasn't it?'

'That's right.'

'Yeah, we've got a huge number of them. Let's see . . .'

Teresa saw the name **Whitman** running down the left side of the screen, all the way through, as Patricia repeatedly touched one of the keys. Finally, she said, 'We have two hundred and twenty-seven main scenarios for Whitman. With hyperlinked associate software, you're talking about maybe twenty thousand access points. The Whitman case is one of the biggest we have. Not the actual largest, though.'

'Which one is that?'

'The Kennedy assassination, of course.'

'Of course,' Teresa said, wondering why she hadn't thought of that herself. 'Are the Whitman scenarios shareware?' she said.

'Many of them, but Whitman also generated a lot of commercial programs.' She pointed at the summary box which had appeared at the bottom of the screen. 'The FBI have sixty, but those aren't publicly available. You could probably get access to them, I imagine. The ones we can run for anyone are from Travis County Police Department, Austin City Police, Texas Rangers, University of Texas Humanities Research Center, Fox 2000, Paramount, MTV, the Playboy Channel, CNN – CNN have a huge library on Whitman – and our own in-house compilations. You want to try a few?'

'Not right now. Would you look up Aronwitz for me?'

'How do you spell that?'

Teresa spelled it, hearing her voice unexpectedly slur.

'OK,' said Patricia, 'Kingwood City, Texas. Let's see. Texas Rangers again, Abilene City Police. The FBI have fifteen scenarios, not publicly available, Kingwood County Police, we have three of our own. CNN again, Fox News Network, NBC, a few of the religious networks. The rest are all shareware. Not many of them, but most of the source names are ones I've seen before. Pretty good material, I imagine. You want me to check them out for you, for next time?'

'I'm not sure yet,' Teresa said.

'Are you OK, Mrs Simons?' Patricia was looking at her, affecting concern.

'I guess so. Why?'

'Is the valve giving you trouble?'

'It's been a while since I used it. Maybe the connectors you use in this country are a different size or something.'

'Should be standard,' Patricia said. She had picked up her internal telephone. 'I'll get the nurse to check you over. It won't take more than a couple of minutes. Hello?'

Teresa sat still, holding the valve against her neck, as if not to do so would allow it to rip away. She was drifting mentally in and out of the San Diego simulation, the shock of it, feeling that hot wind and the grit in her eye, remembering what it was to drive a 1940s model Chevy on a wide road, the smell of the leather seats, the soft, bouncing suspension, the gearshift sticking out from the side of the steering-wheel shaft, the parking-brake handle prodding out from beneath the dash. The memories were like . . . memories. Her own memories, real memories, things that had happened to her.

Yet only this place was real: the commercial facility building with its computers and functional furniture, the cubicles, the piles of unopened software, the painful valve in her neck.

Patricia said, 'The nurse will be along in a moment. It's always as well to check these things. You don't want it to get infected.'

'You're right.'

'While you're waiting, would you mind signing this?' She passed Teresa a plastic-covered clipboard with a sheaf of papers attached. On the top was a disclaimer form, and a printed invoice with a credit-card authorization on a tear-off slip below. Teresa signed woozily, and passed back the clipboard.

The woman checked the signatures, then tore off the top copies of everything and gave them to Teresa.

'How's the neck feeling now?' she said.

'Not too good.'

'The nurse won't be long.'

'Look, I'm grateful for everything you've done,' Teresa said.

'That's my job. I'm paid to help the customers.'

'No, I mean, telling me about the shareware, and all that.'

'It's OK.'

Teresa was feeling as if she was about to faint. She stared at the computer screen, which was still showing the list of Aronwitz's scenarios. She knew that somewhere in there, perhaps everywhere in there, would be living images of Andy. If she went into any of those scenarios she could see him again, talk with him again . . .

The poignant longing overwhelmed her, and she closed her eyes, trying to control herself.

She knew she could have seen him while she was still in the US. Her section chief had offered her free access to the Bureau files, when the ExEx scenarios started becoming available a few weeks after the actual shooting. She had turned down the offer then, and knew she would have to again. It would be unbearable to be there, knowing he was about to die. All over again.

Waiting for the nurse, trying to distract herself, Teresa said, 'Do you have scenarios about Gerry Grove?'

'Not at present. We had shareware that's about to be replaced. It's not too good. They're working on a couple of new ones at the moment, and they should be here in a few days. One before, one after. You know.'

'No I don't,' Teresa said. 'What do you mean?'

Patricia picked up her phone again. 'Are you feeling OK, Mrs Simons?'

'Yeah, I'm fine. Before or after what?'

But her hold on the conversation was no longer so certain. In the last couple of minutes the nausea had increased unpleasantly, a huge distraction. She wanted to find out more from this efficient young woman, but at the same time she could no longer focus her eyes. She sat helplessly at the side of the desk, from where she had been watching the monitor, unable even to turn her head. Patricia was speaking on her phone again, but Teresa could not hear the words.

Presently, a tall, youngish man in a long blue nursing jacket appeared, introduced himself as the duty nurse, and apologized for the delay. He helped her stand up, then supported her as he took her along to the treatment room, at the far end of the building, well away from the ExEx equipment. Teresa managed to hold back until she was there, but threw up as he closed the door.

An hour later he drove her back to the hotel. She went straight to bed.

CHAPTER 19

There had been American voices around her at breakfast in the hotel, or at least they spoke so loudly that they had seemed to be all around her. They were the worst kind of Americans, Teresa thought unfairly: young, ambitious, crude, loudmouthed, superficial. She despised their expensive but tasteless clothes, their bland Midwest accents, the gaucheness of their responses to things British. They made her feel like a snob.

Why does any of that make them worse as Americans? Or as people? She didn't know, but she couldn't suppress the thoughts, and disliked the feelings they aroused in her.

Normally she liked most of the people she met, a trusting kind of liking, just in case. But being nice was the last thing she felt like at present. After two quiet days, spent mostly in private misery in her hotel room, the dressing on her neck was ready to be removed and the sickness had passed. She was still on antibiotics. She found a weighing machine in the public toilet next to the bar, and if the thing was registering accurately it looked as if she had lost five pounds since arriving in England. She liked that news: in the miserable months after Andy's death, she had given up caring about her figure and her clothes had started feeling tight. On the plane to England she had unbuttoned the top of her skirt, making the excuse that you always swelled up a little on a long flight, but knowing the truth was more prosaic. Now, though, things were definitely improving.

But she couldn't ignore the Americans who had moved into the hotel. As soon as she was feeling better, and able to move around the hotel again, they seemed to be everywhere she went. They exerted a deadly fascination over her. They radiated insincerity and ambition, seemed to dislike or misunderstand everyone they met, even themselves, but suppressed their sourness unenthusiastically, keeping it deliberately unspoken, and thus underlining it.

She admired the calm way Amy had served them at their table, smiling and chatting with them, not letting her face or body-language reveal anything other than a cheery pleasure at seeing them there for breakfast. Yet she knew Amy must be feeling much as she did.

Teresa had spent the days dreaming of America, an older America, one where a hot wind blew and there was a sense of ever-unfolding space. She was stimulated by the idea of exploration, of pushing at the edges of reality, of moving beyond the limits of the scenario. She felt drawn by a mystifying kinship with the large, elderly form of Elsa Durdle, the woman with the big car and the gun in the glove compartment, and her drive along the wide highways of southern California.

She had phoned the ExEx medical room the previous afternoon, and arranged to call in this morning to have her dressing removed. If the infection had cleared up she would start exploring the scenarios straight away. The extremes were an allure to her, like the ultimate narcotic.

When Teresa left her room a few minutes later, to go to her car, one of the young men she had seen at breakfast was waiting in the corridor. She glanced at him, then let the hint of a polite smile rest on her face and went to walk past him.

But he said, 'Excuse me, ma'am? I'd like to say hello. I'm Ken Mitchell, and I'm visiting from the USA.'

'Hello.' Teresa tried to make the word sound as non-American as possible, not wanting to be drawn into a conversation. She added, out of politeness, 'Good to know you. I'm Teresa Simons.'

'I'm pleased to meet you, Ms Simons. May I ask if you are staying in this hotel?'

'Yes.'

'OK, that's what we thought.' He glanced towards the door of the room she had just left, as if having established a significant proof. 'Are you here in England with your family, your partner?'

'No, I'm staying by myself.'

Who the hell was he to ask? Why did she answer? She stepped

forward. He sidestepped as if casually, but none the less temporarily blocked her way.

'Ms Simons, are you planning on checking out real soon?'

'No, I'm not.'

She said it with as much of a British accent as she could muster, but he was clearly uninterested in anything about her, other than the fact of her presence.

'Right, ma'am. We'll see to that.'

'Thank you.'

It was the only thing she could think of saying, but however inappropriate it was it gave her an exit line.

She pushed past him, picking up a faint whiff of scented soap. His skin was so clear, healthy, repellent. She went down the stairs and through the hotel to the car park. She was bristling with irritation, a familiar kind. It seemed to her that she had known people like him all her life, though she hadn't expected to run into any of them here in England. Maybe they were everywhere, these Americans whom America had once kept to itself but was apparently now exporting. They promoted a distorted version of the American way of life, one of clean, groomed, highly paid, quietly spoken and superficially polite young men and women, narrowly pursuing their careers, completely self-absorbed and uncaring of anything or anyone else around them.

Her rental car was virtually concealed behind the bulk of the huge van in which the young Americans had arrived. One of the women was sitting in the front passenger seat with the door open, looking at a road map of south-east England spread on her lap. If she looked up as Teresa went past the gesture went unnoticed, as Teresa was intent only on getting out of the hotel as soon as possible.

She started her car, and after squeezing narrowly out from behind the van she drove it from the parking lot with a minimum of delay. She turned on to the Eastbourne Road, heading west, and almost at once found herself held up in the slow-moving crawl of traffic that seemed permanently to clog the roads during the early part of the mornings. After half a mile she took a right at a traffic signal, and headed up towards the industrial estate overlooking the town. She parked in a space at the front of what she now knew as the GunHo building.

Half an hour later, with her neck dressing replaced by a simple Band-Aid, she was sitting in the driver's seat of the car and looking through the road map of Sussex. She had been told she should not use the ExEx simulations for another two days, until she had finished the antibiotics and the infection on the valve incision had cleared up. Once again she had time on her hands.

The road map she had found in the rental car intrigued her. English roads spread out illogically, following no discernible pattern. The map showed features you would never see on its equivalent in America: churches, abbeys, vineyards, even individual houses. Clergy House, Old Mint House, Ashburnam House – did people still live in these places? Was the fact they were marked on the map an invitation to go visit?

There was for her something solid and real about the English landscape, unlike the sensuous glimpse she had had of the California of 1950 when she briefly took over Elsa Durdle's identity. Then she had been haunted by the sense of an infinite unfolding of virtuality: nothing existed beyond her immediate awareness, but she had only to turn her head, or drive towards it, for it to spring suddenly into existence.

This English map was another intriguing code, like a programming language, a series of symbols depicting a landscape that for her was mostly imaginary, mostly unseen. The codes would turn to reality as she went towards them, the ancient England of her dreams would be there to be discovered, an endlessly unfolding panorama.

She left Bulverton on the coast road, crossed the Pevensey Levels, and after driving through several tiny villages reached the main highway between Eastbourne and London. Here she turned north towards London and let the car build up speed. She closed her window and put on a CD by Oasis, one of several records she had found in the car. She had heard of the band, but had never listened to their music. She turned the volume up loud.

Driving had always helped her think, and all the decisions she remembered having taken were made in a car. Not all were the right decisions, of course, but they were none the less memorable for that.

She and Andy had decided to get married, one day in a car

going through the flat countryside of southern New Jersey while they were looking for a motel for the night. She had not only decided to apply to join the Bureau one day while driving, but had also decided to take leave of absence, again in a car, although that particular car had been parked in the drive outside her empty house in Woodbridge, where the windows were dark and the memories were uselessly and frustratingly of Andy alive and living there with her.

Her eyes misted as she drove, while she remembered that day and the violent events which had led up to it. They had become the basis of everything, the rationale of all her actions, or so she had supposed. That dread feeling of blankness, spreading out and around her, swamping everything but replacing nothing.

Life became a series of clichés, some of them mouthed by the people around her who loved her, many more of them forming unbidden in her own mind. Bereavement turned out to be beset with comforting formulae for the bereaved, no doubt springing from the shared unconscious mind, used by every generation that had preceded her and who had lost someone close to them. As much as anything else, it was trying to escape from these easy platitudes that had helped her conceive the idea of the trip. Bulverton, East Sussex, England, a town so appallingly twinned with Kingwood City that it became an irresistible lure.

At that time the coincidence had beckoned her: she could not find what she needed at home, so maybe it would be there in the English seaside town few people in the US had ever heard of. The vagueness of this attraction made one part of her suspicious, but the pull it exerted on the other half was undeniable. It was not even the unfamiliar, alien quality of Bulverton, as she had imagined it before she got here, because Kingwood City had been just as much an unknown quantity for her before the massacre; if foreignness was the only characteristic pulling at her she might as well have been drawn to that soulless place on Interstate 20 near Abilene. It would have been easier for her to get to, and cheaper too, but Bulverton was where she knew she had to be.

Now Bulverton's vagueness had become a specific: it was just a dull, tired, unhappy seaside town, full of the wrong memories and with no conception of its future. The real Bulverton was undermining her resolve, making her think about Andy more than she wanted or needed. Being able to glimpse the losses some of the people had suffered did not help at all. She was not comforted by them, and the stark uselessness of everything that had happened, the pointless waste of lives, the tragic, unintelligent nihilism of the gunman, only underlined her personal tragedy.

Worse, being here was driving her back to the gun. The ExEx scenarios pandered to that fascination.

She could not stop thinking about Elsa Durdle. What she thought out loud, so to speak, was her reaction to the hyperreality of the shareware scenario: the wind, the heat, the lovely old car, the sense of an endless landscape. But deeper feelings, ones she had suppressed until now, were more visceral.

She kept remembering the moment when she opened Elsa Durdle's glove compartment, found the weapon and took it in her hand. The weight of it, the coldness, the feel of it there. For a few moments she had been reminded of how it felt to be driving to an imminent spree event, with no idea of how it would resolve, but with a loaded gun at her side.

She drove past a sign that told her she was in Ashdown Forest, and on an impulse she turned into a narrow side road. It led windingly through open, well-wooded countryside. She drove more slowly. The Oasis record was beginning to intrude on her thoughts, so she flicked it off. She wound down the window, relishing the sweet smell of the woodland, the sound of the tyres on the road, the flow of cold air around her. She slowed the car to a crawl.

Something kept changing her mind about what she wanted to do, where she wanted to go: she told herself it was the old familiar scents of a wet-floored English winter landscape, mild sunshine on grass and branches and pine needles, things rotting away, mould and fungus and moss.

Teresa saw a cleared space for cars at the side of the road, so she stopped and switched off the ignition. She climbed out and stood for a few minutes on the grassy verge.

Sometimes driving made her think even when she didn't want to.

She had been born into the world of guns: even before she was taken to the USA by her parents she was used to the sight and feel of weapons.

Her father was obsessive about guns; there was no other word for it. He collected guns as other people collected old coins or books. He talked guns, cleaned guns, disassembled and reassembled guns, fired guns, carried guns, subscribed to gun magazines, sent off for gun catalogues, made friends only with those who shared his obsession with guns. There was at least one loaded gun in every room of the house; more than that, probably. There were two in her parents' bedroom, both adapted with hair triggers, one on each side of the bed, ready for use the night the supposed intruder came. There were two more in the kitchen, one attached to the wall next to the door, in case someone tried to break in that way, one concealed in a drawer in case the intrusion came from somewhere else. (But who in their right mind would force an entry into a house where a gun fanatic lived?) There were even two loaded guns stored in a locked drawer in the closet of her own bedroom.

Down in the basement there were more weapons than she had ever been able to count, many of them in pieces, while her dad slowly restored them or cleaned them or customized them in some way. He never went anywhere without a gun either in the car or carried on his belt or under his shirt, ready for use. He belonged to gun clubs and training squads, and four times a year went up into the mountains with a group of his friends, armed to the teeth.

Teresa was target training by the age of ten, and was recognized as an above-average shot by the time she was eleven. Her dad enrolled her into the junior section of his club, made her show what she could do, entered her for every competition. She won and won; shooting came naturally to her. At fourteen she could out-shoot her older cousins, most of the men at the training camps she went to during the summer vacations, and even her father. It was the thing she did of which he was the proudest.

Her accuracy with a weapon thrilled her. She recognized as natural the weight of the weapon in her hand, the way it balanced there, and the jolt of adrenaline that flowed when the recoil kicked at her arm and shoulder, and because these were exciting to her, the condition of gun ownership and use was integral to her personality and identity. Every time she pulled the trigger she felt total power, fulfilment, certainty.

Standing there by the side of the woodland road, thinking of guns, feeling gorged with her family memories, Teresa was tempted for the first time since her arrival in England to pack her bags and go home. She had friends in Woodbridge, a career in the Bureau, a house, the remains of a life, a certain place in a culture she understood. England was full of mysteries she didn't want to have to deal with right now. She had made the trip in an attempt to move forward, away from her old itinerant father-dominated past, yet immersion in the quiet sorrows of Bulverton was stirring up too many memories of what she had wanted to leave.

She knew if Andy could have been there with her he would have gone into one of his sessions of criticizing her – their marriage, though happy overall, had had its tensions – and brought up a dozen similar incidents when she had dithered helplessly about which direction she should take. She deserved it, because making her mind up had always been hard.

She kicked loose pebbles against the wheel of the car, and she thought, This is silly. Why do guns still exert their fascination?

Her love of guns, the hold they had over her, had reversed in the instant she received the news of Andy's death. It was as if she had suddenly been able to see her life from a different direction: her life was the same, but her view changed. From right to left, from looking down to looking up, whatever it was.

That skill she had with guns, the facility, the deadly accuracy, suddenly became a curse to her. In her hand was the object that ultimately had killed the person she loved most in all the world.

She hated the way her father's personality had changed when his gun friends were around, or when he was practising with his weapons: it was as if he grew several inches in all directions, taller, broader, rounder, thicker. His voice was louder, he moved with more energy. His physical stance became threatening or confrontational, became that of someone who could only cope with the complexities of the world by putting out a challenge to it. And she had hated the way her own skill converted to the dark side: a deadly efficiency, the side of her that gave pain, the unyielding side of her.

Also in the long moment of the news of Andy's dying she had thought, for the first time in many years, about Megan.

That shocking instant of childhood had been effectively cam-ouflaged over the years. It was so long ago she could barely remember it, and whenever she did try to remember it she could not find the truth. She had never really disentangled what had actually happened from the lies and evasions her parents told her.

They said she had dreamed the whole thing; Megan was an imaginary friend; all little girls had imaginary friends. But surely she had been born a twin? said Teresa, prodding for the truth, knowing this at least was so. Yes, there had been a twin sister; yes, and her name was Megan. But Megan had died at birth, so frail, so small, such a tragedy. You wouldn't remember Megan, they said. What she thought she remembered was untrue, unreliable.

If it had happened the way she remembered, and not the way they told it, how could they have covered up such a death? A small child, killed by gunshot? Even if they had found a way, why had they done so? It was surely an accident? But they never admitted anything. What Teresa remembered as a shattering mirror-image of herself, a dying friend, a gun whose recoil had twisted her arm so painfully it had hurt on and off for more than a year, was changed by them into a tragic delusion, a persisting error.

Then decades later Andy died, and in her moment of penetrat-ing grief and understanding, Teresa had known at last what must be the truth about Megan's death.

Her father's house was full of guns, in every room in any place they lived. The guns were always loaded, always ready for this chimera of expert self-defence. She, like any other child, explored and tested, and did what she was told she must not do. The greater the warnings of danger, the more attractive were the temptations of ignoring them.

From this, the greater truth: the more there were people who owned guns, who made themselves expert with guns, who pre-pared to defend themselves with guns, who went on hunting trips with guns, who mouthed slogans about freedom and rights being dependent on guns, the more those guns were likely to be abused and to fall into the wrong hands.

Just once, that time when she was seven, her little hands had been the wrong ones.

So, finally, Andy was dead, and that had been hard enough, but it was not entirely unexpected. The risks went with the FBI territory.

She grieved, she mourned, she was prescribed medication, she took a vacation to see friends in Oregon, she joined self-help groups, she underwent counselling. She was a widow, but life eventually began to cohere once more around her. What she was unready for, though, was the other consequence of Andy's death: the profound reversal of her trust in guns.

All her life until this point seemed to be a deceit. Everything she had grown up with, and all the work and training she had done as an adult, she now turned against.

During this period a word, a name, a place, kept circling somewhere on the fringe of her awareness. Bulverton, England.

What did it mean? Andy's death had swamped everything, and for weeks she had stayed away from newspapers and TV news. For a day or two she herself had been the news. Media celebrity distracts, no matter what the reason. Even so, the name of Bulverton crept into her consciousness, and although from the start she had known on some buried, unarticulated level what the link was, what the coincidence was, she could not take it in.

Denial, her bereavement counsellor told her. You are blocking everything to do with your husband's death.

Even this puzzled her: how was Bulverton linked with Andy's death? What am I supposed to be denying? What is being assumed that I am unaware of?

Finally, the grief and confusion lifted sufficiently for her to be able to think for herself once more, and soon afterwards she began to ask her colleagues, she looked up Bulverton on the web, she searched the newspaper files for the story.

There the coincidence was laid before her: Bulverton, Kingwood City. Two massacres by outburst gunmen. Same day of the year, same time of the day.

The parallels were not exact: twenty-three people died in Bulverton, only fifteen in Kingwood City. (Fifteen? Is that not enough, when one of them was Andy?) The general circumstances were different: Aronwitz was obsessed with God, while Grove was apparently not. (But Aronwitz's spree began in a church and ended in a shopping mall; Grove's began when he stole a car from outside a shop and ended inside a church.)

Fifty-eight other people were wounded in Kingwood City, and fifty-eight were wounded in Bulverton. The same number of law-enforcement officers were killed or injured in both places. The guns carried and used by the killers were the same make, although different models. The same number of cars were damaged, or so it was said; did they count and include the two police units that accidentally scraped bumpers on the way to North Cross mall? And more coincidences: someone with the surname Perkins was killed in both places; someone with the given name Francesca was killed in both places; both gunmen had previous convictions for robbery, but not for firearm abuse.

Coincidences make good headlines for newspapers, they feed the suspicious minds of conspiracy theorists, they open up debates for philosophers about time, perception, consciousness and reality. But to most ordinary people they are only remarked upon, thought about or discussed briefly, then forgotten.

There were superficial coincidences between the assassinations of Presidents Lincoln and Kennedy. Were they significant? How could they be, except on some cosmic or metaphysical level of no concern to most people?

In a more general arena, criminal lawyers are aware of the surprising coincidences that crop up regularly in even the most straightforward of cases: the two men destined to collaborate in a major crime who come together only by chance; the killer and his victim whose lives are almost exact parallels until the day they meet; the innocent bystanders and the guilty perpetrators who happen to look amazingly alike. None of these coincidences, nor hundreds of others like them, is significant in any way.

They signify only that coincidences occur all the time in ordinary life, but only when one's attention is focused by something like a crime do they become apparent.

How could the series of coincidences between Kingwood City and Bulverton be explained away, or disregarded, once everyone had remarked upon them? To Teresa, they seemed to have been placed for her to find.

As the immediate loss of Andy began to recede, the need to make sense of what had happened became increasingly important.

The trail ultimately led to here, and to now, to this levelled space by the side of a minor road, the winter-shorn trees of Ashdown Forest around her, the lightly drifting rain, the traffic rushing by in a flurry of tyre noise and road spray.

Teresa breathed the air, relished the chill dampness of the woods, and spread her hands on the highly polished paintwork of the car, feeling the standing droplets of rain running out from beneath her fingers.

It was impossible to accept the metaphysics of coincidence in an ordered universe, because only by believing that the emergence of killers like Aronwitz and Grove were random events could you ever come to terms with what they had done.

You could only accept their murders by believing in the harmony of chance, believing that the tragedies they inflicted were so to speak unique, unlikely to be repeated.

To think they were part of some pattern that could be understood and interpreted, and therefore predicted, made reality less real.

Yet that was what Andy had been trying to show, before Aronwitz ended everything for him. Andy ultimately believed in predestiny, even if he had not put it that way himself; she had to overturn that belief to be able to get through the rest of her life.

CHAPTER 20

She arrived in San Diego on a blisteringly hot day, a sea wind bending the palm trees, making the dust fly at the street intersections, puffing the canopies of shops and swinging the overhead traffic signals precariously. Shiny, rounded cars moved in a leisurely fashion through the streets. A DC3 of Pan American circled overhead, moving down towards the airfield; the brilliant sunshine glinted off the unpainted wings and engine cowlings.

She had a key in her hand, and she was hurrying towards a row of cars parked diagonally against the sidewalk. She was out of breath, and her back and legs were hurting. She reeled mentally, perhaps physically too, at the impact of the sensory overload from the collectively remembered scenario. She was too hot, the wind took her breath away, something in the air flew into her eye. She wanted to maintain her own individuality, her own reactions, and turned back quickly enough to see one of the buildings beside her flicker into solidity as her vision persisted in that direction.

She was moving towards a silver-and-blue Chevrolet station wagon, but again she resisted and went instead to the green Ford saloon parked alongside. The driver's door was locked, and the key she was holding would not even slide in. She gave up and went to the Chevrolet instead. The door of this was unlocked, and after she had slid on to the bench seat, comfortably spreading her large body, she got the key into the ignition at the first try.

A few moments later she was driving north along 30th Street, and at the intersection with University she took a right. Shortly afterwards she came to the large intersection with Wabash Boulevard, and here she took a left, driving on to the highway and accelerating to keep up with the rest of the traffic. The sun was shafting in through the driver's window, making her arm and face tingle. She wound up the window, and pulled the visor over to help shade herself.

She reached into the glove compartment and took out the automatic pistol that was there. While she drove she checked it was loaded, then laid it on the seat beside her. She switched on the radio: the Duke Ellington Orchestra was playing 'Newport Up'.

She stretched back in the seat, drove with her arms straight and her head lying back on the rest, the radio on, the sun blazing in on her, and the wonderful rumbling slow traffic of 1950 gliding past and around her.

Moments later she saw diversion lights ahead, and a police roadblock. Most of the traffic was peeling off to the left, going around the diversion, but she slowed and signalled to the right, heading straight for the police line. Teresa resisted. She wrenched the steering wheel to the left and swerved across the traffic lanes and away from the roadblock. One of the cops, who had stepped towards her car as soon as she signalled right, raised his arm and shouted something after her.

Teresa accelerated away, seeing hills ahead, yellow and brown and dotted with dark trees, shimmering in the hot day. In moments, the police diversion was behind her. She kept her foot down, letting the large, quiet-engined car pick up speed at its own pace.

She looked down at herself, realizing that she was wearing some other woman's clothes. She was fat! She was wearing terrible clothes! She had runs in her stockings! She glanced up into the rear-view mirror, leaning across to see herself; an elderly black woman's face, full of mild concern, looked back at her.

'Hi, Elsa!' Teresa said aloud, smiling at her own reflection.

The road became straight. There were no buildings on either side of it, and flat, featureless ground, dotted with scrub, stretched away on both sides.

She drove for several minutes, peering ahead with interest to see how the landscape would develop, but now she was away from the edge of the city there was little to look at. There was no other traffic. On either side of the road the gravelly ground and the grey-green scrub sped by in a blur. In the distance she saw mountains and white clouds. The sun beat down on her, so high that it seemed to throw no shadows.

Eventually Teresa realized that there was no more landscape for her to find.

She swung the steering wheel to the right, trying to skid off the road, but the car merely moved a few feet to the side. It spun along as smoothly as ever, the tyres apparently moving across the rough ground without touching.

In her rear-view mirror, Teresa could see the buildings of San Diego clustered against the shoreline. She remembered the meaning of the acronym LIVER.

She arrived in San Diego on a blisteringly hot day, and went to the silver-and-blue Chevrolet parked diagonally against the sidewalk. She got the key into the ignition at the first try.

A few moments later she was driving north along 30th Street, and at the intersection with University she took a left. The car had already moved into the right-turn lane, but Teresa swung it across the traffic, forcing it to go the other way. Horns blared around her. The sun was now in front of her, and she lowered the visor to reduce the dazzle in her eyes.

She reached into the glove compartment and took out the automatic pistol that was there. While she drove she checked it was loaded, then laid it on the seat beside her. She switched on the radio: the Duke Ellington Orchestra was playing 'Newport Up'.

She glanced up into the rear-view mirror, straining to see herself; an elderly black woman's face, full of mild concern, looked back at her.

'Hi, Elsa!' Teresa said aloud, smiling at her own reflection.

Apartment blocks had been built on both sides of the road, partially screened by rows of tall palm trees, and these flashed by uniformly. Ahead was the ocean, placidly shimmering. After several minutes of driving, in which the ocean came no closer, she remembered the acronym LIVER.

Teresa spent the rest of the day learning to use the computerized catalogue of available ExEx titles. The first useful information she gleaned was that the Elsa Durdle shareware had been written by an outfit called SplatterInc, based in a town called Raymond, Oregon. She asked Patricia if she knew anything about them.

'More likely to be one person than a business,' Patricia said. 'Some kid working out of a back room, perhaps, who downloaded the imaging software from the internet? Anyone can do it, if they're packing enough computer memory.'

'And there's no way of telling where the scenario images came from?'

'Not from the information we have here. I suppose you could call them, or write to them. Is there an e-mail address?'

'Just a Post Office box in Raymond.'

'Have you tried running a web search on them? They'll have a site.'

'Not yet.'

Teresa went back to the scenario database, and keyed in the search parameters. A moment later, SplatterInc's list of titles scrolled down the screen. Teresa read through it.

She located the Elsa Durdle scenario, and from this logged the group and category in which it was filed: **Interactive/Police/ Murder/Guns/William Cook/Elsa Jane Durdle.**

Learning as she went, Teresa worked backwards through the hierarchy of sub-categories. Alternatives to **Guns** were **Automobiles, Bombs, Clubs, Hands** and **Knives** and from each of these there were hyperlinks, presumably to other software producers.

Alternatives to **Murder** were **Arson, Hostage Taking, Mugging, Rape** and **Sniper.** Again there were hyperlinks.

Police was in a long list of categories, which flooded the screen: the alternative offerings from SplatterInc included **Arts, Aviation, Movies, Sex, Space, Sport, Travel, War.**

Idly she clicked on **Sex,** and was astonished at the number of options, all hyperlinked, that unfurled rapidly before her: **Amateur, Anal, Astral, Audient, Backsides All, Backsides Big, Backsides Close-up, Backsides Small, Bestial, Bondage, Breasts All, Breasts Big** . . . and so on, for dozens of screens.

She clicked it away, and glanced furtively across the room to see if Patricia was watching her. She was working with another customer on the far side of the room.

Teresa moved up a level to **Interactive,** and here found the list of main options: **Active, Collective, Interactive, Intruder, Nonactive, Observer, Passive, Perpetrator** and **Victim.**

Teresa browsed through the various levels, quietly amazed at the extent of what was there to be found. All of it the product of a single outfit called SplatterInc, from Raymond, Oregon. Where the hell was Raymond, Oregon, and what else went on in that small town?

She waited until Patricia looked over in her direction, then asked her to come and advise.

'You still with SplatterInc?' Patricia said, obviously amused.

'I'm trying to see what they've made available,' Teresa said. 'It's incredible how much there is.'

Patricia glanced at the screen.

'Yeah, they keep busy,' she said. 'But they're just a medium-small. You should see the catalogues put out by some of the co-op groups in California or New York.'

'These headings – are they just used by these people, or are they general?'

'Everyone uses them. You can download the complete index, if you want to see the extent of it.'

'And it's all shareware?'

'The SplatterInc programs are,' Patricia said. 'Are you specially interested in those people? Or are you interested in shareware generally?'

'I don't know,' Teresa said. 'I'm just browsing at the moment. Trying to find what you have.'

'It's a lot.'

'I'm learning.'

'You know, you might do better to stay away from shareware. It gets expensive, because nearly all of what you pay us for is machine time. What most people do is buy into one of the commercial packages, then use shareware as a supplement. You know, what I was showing you the other day. One of the TV networks, or the big software companies, or our own modules, of course. Or do what you did the other day, choose a category then randomize on an anthology basis. We've got a whole catalogue of sampler scenarios.'

Teresa turned away from the screen. 'The truth is, I don't know where to begin. It's confusing.'

'Maybe you should take home some of our brochures? There's a pile of them out at the back there.'

'I'm wasting your time,' Teresa said. 'Is that what you're trying to tell me?'

'No . . . but I only deal with what the customers select, and want to use, and make sure the equipment functions properly. I see a bit of what they are interested in, but I don't see the whole picture. You need Mr Lacey or one of his assistants to talk you through some of the sales packages we have on offer. Most people don't really know what they're looking for until they find it.'

'I'm beginning to see why.'

'I thought you were interested in guns. We get a lot of people who are.'

'Mine's a professional interest.'

'Then why don't you buy the comprehensive shooting course? That includes target-practice use, interdiction and arrest scenarios, you can choose terminal or non-terminal, and you get full access to the scenarios. That sort of use is our bread-and-butter business.'

'And for that I would have to talk to Mr Lacey?'

Patricia said with a smile, 'I'll arrange it for you.'

'OK. Thanks.' Teresa looked back at the screen, with its almost obsessively detailed arrays of scenario subjects. 'Do you mind if I go on browsing?'

'Help yourself.'

CHAPTER 21

Nick was serving behind the bar when Teresa came in halfway through the evening. She asked him for a club soda. He passed her a glass with ice cubes, and the syphon. She sloshed the water into the glass, then gave him a direct look. He wondered what was coming; when Amy looked at him like that he was usually in trouble. He thankfully noticed another customer approaching the counter, so moved adroitly away to serve him. Teresa obviously got the message, because by the time he finished she had taken her drink to one of the tables. Sitting alone, she read the book she had been carrying.

The bar gradually emptied, and half an hour before closing time there was hardly anyone left. He collected glasses and empties, washed them, wiped the bar counter. Teresa saw this, and came back and settled on her stool. There was no avoiding her any more.

'Do you mind if I ask you something, Nick?' she said.

'Do I have a choice?'

'I guess not. Why don't you or anyone else ever talk about the Grove shootings?'

'What is there to say?'

'Not a whole lot, it seems. It's like it never happened. OK, I know.' She took a sip of her drink. 'I'm a brash American and I've no right to ask any questions at all, but most people here have nothing to say.'

'I'm another of them,' he said.

'But why, Nick?'

'In my case, I wasn't actually in town when it happened. I was—'

'No, you told me that before. It's just an excuse, and you know it. You might not have been physically present in the town when it happened, but the fact you stayed on afterwards suggests that you're a part of it, just as much as if you'd been living here.'

'If you say so.'

'No, dammit. If you think that, why don't you get out?'

Nick said, thinking how often he had gone through this in his own mind, as well as with Amy, 'Because this was my parents' business, and I owe it to them to keep it going, and this town was my home—'

'And you dated Amy when you were kids, and she's here for the same reason, and you can't leave because something's holding you back.'

Nick stared at her, reluctant to admit that she might be getting close to it, and wondering how she knew.

'That's right, isn't it, Nick?' she said.

'Sort of.'

'Look, just once, can I ask you some questions about what happened that day? As you know it.'

He said again, 'I wasn't here. I didn't see anything.'

'No one saw it all,' Teresa said. 'Many of the people who did were killed. Even those who survived, they only saw their bit of it. Everyone's got the same excuse: I didn't see much. A lot of the surviving witnesses have left town. But everyone who's still here knows exactly what happened.'

'There you go then.'

'No,' she said. 'I've got a reason for this. I'm trying to work something out, because there's a big inconsistency somewhere. I've analysed, timed and placed everything that Grove is supposed to have done, and it doesn't add up. Can I run it by you, compare it with what you know?'

'It sounds as if you already know more than anyone else.'

'I need to straighten this thing out.'

Nick could feel himself backing away from her in his mind. Why should that be? It was true that for him the Grove shootings would always have a third-hand quality, but that obviously wasn't everything. He had been profoundly shocked by the way his parents died, and the depth and extent of his tormented feelings had been a revelation to him. He had lived away in London long enough to start believing he might no longer feel close to his parents, but that had turned out not to be so.

And there was a darker psychological level, one he rarely touched. That was something to do with the collective trauma in the town, the sharing of a shock that made everyone bury the memories they could cope with least well.

He plunged around in his mind, trying to find the words.

'Amy's out this evening,' he said. 'I'm on my own in the bar.' He indicated the rest of the room vaguely with his hand.

Teresa glanced around; the only other customers were a couple sitting at one of the corner tables, and two young lads playing pool. She gave him another direct look.

'We can break off if you have to serve someone. Anyway, it's not going to take long.'

He moved to the beer pumps, and drew himself a pint of best. He made a production of filling it carefully to the brim, not spilling any, aware all the time that Teresa was watching him. He went back and placed it on the counter between them.

'I've established what Grove was doing that day before he started shooting,' Teresa said. 'In fact, I can trace his movements right up to mid-afternoon, when he drove away from the Texaco filling station. He left there at twenty-three minutes to three. That's an exact time because I've been through the police log, and that was when the police received the emergency call from the cashier. I can also trace him from the moment he began shooting. According to the police, and one of the eyewitnesses, he fired the first shots in London Road at four minutes to five. So the first thing I want to know is, what was he doing for those two hours in between?'

'But you surely know where he was?'

'I know where he was for part of the time,' said Teresa. 'He went to the ExEx building in Welton Road. Is that where you meant?'

'Yes.'

'He was only there a few minutes. They keep a record of everyone coming and going, and the police have a copy and I've seen it. Grove was in the ExEx building for less than fifteen minutes. Then he left and he walked down the hill into the Old Town. I've done the same walk myself: even going slowly, it took me less than half an hour. Grove was carrying his guns, but even if they were heavy, and he had to rest for a bit, it still wouldn't add up to two hours.'

Two customers came into the bar from the street, and Nick broke away to serve them. When he went back to her he refreshed her ice, and she put another long shot of soda water into her glass.

'I gather you've been up at the ExEx place yourself,' he said to her.

She nodded, but looked surprised, 'How do you know that?'

He said, 'Small town. People notice these things. Virtual reality is still a novelty. Someone visiting the town who uses it is worth gossiping about, I assume.' In fact, Amy's brother-in-law Dave Hartland had mentioned the other day that he had seen Teresa there, but Nick had no reason to suppose that she would know the man.

'It's not that much of a novelty any more, is it? There are ExEx facilities in most cities in America. One of the bookstore chains over there was starting to sell franchises when I left. And they're opening all over the place in this country.'

'Maybe, but ExEx is still new,' Nick said. 'Most people don't appear to understand what it's used for. I'm not even completely sure myself. You presumably are?' Teresa's expression gave nothing away. 'Since the branch here has become associated with Grove, some of the locals say it should be closed down.'

'If he'd been renting X-rated videos they'd say the same.'

'I know.'

'OK,' Teresa said. 'Let's get back to Gerry Grove. Do you know what the police were doing during this time?'

'Presumably looking for the killer of Mrs Williams and her little boy, and the man who shot up the filling station.'

'That's the second thing I don't understand. The police say they reacted promptly and efficiently, taking all the problems into account. I interviewed the station superintendent last week, and he maintained the police operation had been cleared by the enquiry. That's broadly true, and I've read the enquiry report. But I think they really screwed up. They weren't anywhere around. They had more than two hours to figure out there was a gunman on the loose, and yet when Grove started shooting it took them completely by surprise. A patrol car had gone out to the Texaco station but until emergency calls came through from the town there were no extra police on duty. Just the local force, and most of them were on normal duties around the town. Since last June most of the officers involved in the shooting have transferred to other divisions. For a body that's been given a clear, they're sure acting like they want to cover something up.'

'A lot of people have left town since last year,' Nick said.

'Yes, but the police are different. Or should be.'

'The police in this county are moved around all the time. Some would have applied to go to another division, others would have been due for a transfer anyway. Do I have to explain that?'

'No, I'm sorry. What I want to do is talk. I keep going over this in my mind, and I want to hear myself saying the words.'

'And I'm handy for it.'

'Yeah . . . but you also know a lot about what went on.'

'Less than you may think,' Nick said.

'Even so. Let me finish this, because there's a third thing I don't understand. Grove only possessed two guns, the ones he used that day. This has been established beyond doubt. The girl he knew, Debbie—'

'Debra,' Nick said.

'Right. Debra. See what I mean about you knowing things? OK, Debra says Grove only ever had those two guns, and he was obsessed with them, always cleaning them and oiling them. But they were the only ones he had.'

'No one's ever disputed that.'

'Listen, because someone's about to. As far as I can tell he had four guns, not two. There were the two he used in the streets, and two more were found in the luggage compartment of the car he stole.'

'Is this relevant?'

'I don't know about relevant, but it mystifies me. The guns he used were a handgun and a semi-automatic rifle. The handgun was called a Colt All-American: it's well known in the US. The rifle was an M16 carbine, the great American rifle. Set aside the problem of how he got hold of them in this country in the first place – I guess there are ways if you want them bad enough. Why should he have two of each?'

'But did he?'

'The police found an M16 and a Colt in the back of the stolen car; they found an M16 and a Colt with his body.'

'Exactly the same?'

'Same makes, yes. Same models, probably. I can't get it any more exact than that.'

'I'm sorry, I don't think it's much of a mystery,' Nick said. 'They're probably the same ones, and somebody made a mistake.'

'Grove's car was found in Welton Road, about a hundred yards from the GunHo building. It was unlocked. Grove's fingerprints were all over it. They found the rifle and the handgun inside, and his prints were on them too. I've seen the scene-of-crime officer's report. There's no mistake on this. Anyway, the forensic and ballistic reports prove that the handgun was the one used on Mrs Williams and her boy, and the M16 was the rifle he fired at the cashier in the filling station. Right, so far so good. But the problem is, identical weapons were found at the end of the massacre.'

'With the same forensic evidence?'

'Yes.'

'So did he have four guns or two?'

'The police say he had four.'

'Have you looked at them yourself?'

'They're not in town any more. The police said they'd try to find out for me where they are now, but they didn't sound too interested.'

'So what's your point? Surely the only thing that matters is that he had guns from somewhere?'

'OK,' Teresa said. 'Let me ask you something else. Did you know Gerry Grove?'

'No, I never met him, even when I lived here.'

'Do you know anyone who did know him?'

'Yes, a lot of people. Some of them come in here.' Nick nodded towards the pool table, where the two young men were still playing. 'Those lads were at school with Grove. Amy also knew him, I think. He was one of the locals. Most people only knew him by sight, though. He didn't have many friends. After the massacre, when it was known who had done it, there was a feeling of shock. You don't expect someone you've seen around town for half your life to go mad with a gun in his hand.'

'So you think no one could have predicted what happened?' Teresa said.

'How could they? Grove was typical of a lot of young people who come off the estate up there on the hill: he was unemployed, he was often in trouble with the police, but never anything really serious, he did drugs when he had a bit of spare cash, he liked a drink or two. But he was quiet. Afterwards, everyone said how quiet he was. He was an only child, he stayed at home a lot, always looked a bit lonely and distracted when you saw him, never had much to say for himself. A bit of an obsessive, someone said. Always collecting things and making lists. When the police searched his house they found a pile of notebooks, full of numbers he had written down. He never threw away magazines, and the house was full of them.'

Nick paused, staring down at his glass of beer.

'That's not a lot,' Teresa said. 'What it amounts to is it basically lets the police off the hook. They got away with a crappy investigation.'

'What do you mean?'

'Isn't it obvious? For starters, which guns did Grove actually use while he was killing people? Which guns did he pick up from his house, which ones did he leave in the car when he went into the ExEx building, and which ones did he use afterwards in the town? Was the rifle he used at the filling station the same one he used here? And the handgun, in the woods, was that the same one he used later? If not, where did he get them from? Which ones did he leave in the car? How can two sets of guns give identical ballistic test results? Then you've got the lousy police response to explain. When there was a shooting at the filling station, why didn't they put up roadblocks and haul him in straight away? When he started shooting in the town, why didn't they have armed marksmen out on the streets within five or ten minutes?'

'We don't do that sort of thing over here, I suppose,' Nick said, hearing the primness in his voice even as he spoke. 'Not straight away, at least.'

'Right, and so Gerry Grove gets away with it because you're a bunch of tight-assed Brits.'

Nick said, defensively, 'People get away with it in America too.'

'Sometimes.'

At last he realized what he had been getting at, if only sub-

168

consciously. He said, 'That's how your husband was killed, wasn't it?'

She turned away, looked across the almost empty bar to where the kids were playing pool.

'Yes,' she said. 'You're right.'

'I'm sorry,' Nick said. 'I didn't think. I'd forgotten that, for a moment.'

'I deserved it.'

There was a long silence between them, while the jukebox played and the pool balls clacked intermittently. Nick was ashamed, not just of what he had said, but of having said it in the dowdy bar in the old hotel he ran, where people came for a couple of hours to be less bored than they were at home, but still bored. Ashamed of being still here in Bulverton. Of doing what he did, of the drinks he got through, of holding on to Amy, of being frightened of the future.

Finally, Teresa said, 'May I have that bourbon now?'

'OK.'

'No, I don't want it.' Then she pushed her glass across to him. 'Yes, I do, but only one.'

CHAPTER 22

It was a blisteringly hot day, and the Duke Ellington Orchestra was on the radio playing 'Newport Up'. Teresa backed the car away from the sidewalk, did a U-turn and drove south along 30th Street. She eased herself more comfortably on the wide bench seat, and glanced up into the rear-view mirror, straining to see herself; an elderly black woman's face, full of mild concern, looked back at her.

'Hi, Elsa!' Teresa said aloud, smiling at her own reflection. 'Let's go to Mexico!'

She followed signs across town towards the Montgomery Freeway, Highway 5, and turned south again. The sea was on her right, glimpsed through palm trees and apartment blocks. A new track came on: Artie Shaw playing 'I'm Coming Virginia'. The Mexican border was not far ahead. She drove until the rest of the traffic had disappeared, and the buildings of San Diego were static in her rear-view mirror.

The sea remained out of reach, far away, glistening out to the horizon, still and tranquil.

When she was sure she could go no further, Teresa returned the gun to the glove compartment. She waited until the Artie Shaw record ended.

LIVER.

Teresa was a man, sweating in the heat, jacket off, cap on, dark glasses on her eyes, gun on her belt, gum in her mouth, itch in her crotch. Her name was Officer Joe Cordle, San Diego City Police. Officer Rico Patresse stood beside her, his pistol resting on the white-painted hood of the car. They were on duty at a roadblock across Route 8, three miles east of downtown San Diego. Another police unit was parked at a similar angle on the opposite side of the highway. Two officers stood at the ready there. In case there was an attempted getaway, back-up units were parked at other strategic points on the road, most of them hidden from view.

Traffic moving towards San Diego was being monitored by a team of four other armed officers standing at the roadside. They gave each vehicle a quick look-over before waving it through. The car they were interested in was a dark-blue '47 Pontiac being driven by a single white male: William Cook. A second man, Cook's hostage, identity still unknown, was tied up and lying on the rear seat. The Pontiac had been identified earlier, heading in the direction of San Diego. It had been decided to carry out the intercept well away from the built-up area of the city, but close enough to city limits to allow rapid access to hospital if that became necessary.

A radio message came through that Cook's car had been spotted in the vicinity and was still approaching. It was expected to reach the roadblock in the next few minutes. Teresa removed the safety catch, and placed her gun next to Patresse's on the hot paintwork of the police car. She wiped her brow with the back of a sleeve, and they both spat into the dust at the side of the road.

Teresa stepped back from the car. She gazed at the surrounding scenery: the low hills, the small trees, the sagebrush, the telegraph poles alongside the highway, the buildings of San Diego behind, and a distant glimpse of the sea. Teresa knew that this was a finality, that there was nothing beyond or behind what she could see, but that everything within sight and touch was flawless, seamless, a self-enclosed reality.

She stretched her hands and arms down behind her back, linking the fingers, then tensing them until the knuckles popped. Her barrel chest and protruding belly swelled out before her. She brought her hands back, and flexed the fingers in the sunlight, turning her hands to and fro. There was a tattoo of a blue heart inscribed with the name 'Tammy' visible beneath the forest of black hairs on her right hand. Her palms were sweating, so she wiped them on the seat of her pants. She picked up her gun, crouched down, rested her left forearm along the hot metal of the car, and sighted the weapon towards one of the cars currently slowing down to pass through the roadblock.

Beside her, Rico Patresse was doing the same. He was talking football: the Aztecs game upcoming at the weekend was going to be a tough one, so long as they fielded the same side from last week. What they needed to do—

A blue Pontiac appeared at the corner, following two other cars. Teresa and Rico hunched down, trigger fingers relaxed but ready to fire.

'You wanna bet he won't stop?' said Patresse.

'Nah, he'll stop,' Teresa said, and recoiled mentally from the sound of her own voice, redolent of too much old beer and stale smoke. 'They always haveter stop in the end.'

They both laughed. She shifted the gum to her cheek and wadded it behind her teeth, so as to concentrate on her aim.

She heard a car approaching from behind their position, and broke her concentration long enough to glance quickly over her shoulder. A silver-and-blue Chevrolet station wagon was driving slowly towards the roadblock. An overweight, elderly black woman was at the wheel, peering anxiously ahead.

'Who let that goddamn car through?' Teresa shouted, even as she realized who the driver must be.

'Get back, lady!' Officer Patresse shouted, without shifting his position. He and Teresa both waved their arms. The station wagon kept on coming. It steered between the two police cars, and drove uncertainly on. For a few seconds the car was in their line of fire, blocking most of their view.

Beyond it, just in sight around it, Teresa could see the Pontiac, still driving towards them. Finally, the Chevrolet lumbered out of the way, and in the same instant the driver of the blue car must have seen the roadblock. The Pontiac's nose suddenly dipped down and the rear end skidded round. There was the sound of tyres, and a cloud of dust rose in the air.

The driver's door opened, and a figure half fell, half scrambled out. He pulled open the rear passenger door, and dragged out a man with his hands tied behind his back. The hostage collapsed on the surface of the highway. The driver crouched down beside him, and pulled a rifle out of the car. He moved swiftly, and handled the weapon with appalling skill and exactness of motion.

The Chevrolet was alongside him at this moment, and Teresa could see the woman driver looking in horror at what was happening beside her. She braked suddenly, throwing up more dust. It was getting difficult to see clearly.

'Take him out, Joe!' said Patresse.

Teresa fired, and a spurt of dust flew up beneath the trunk of Cook's car. The man immediately swung the rifle towards her, and fired twice in quick succession. The first bullet buried itself somewhere in the body of the police car, the second screeched along the metal hood and snatched at Teresa's non-firing arm. Pain flashed through her.

'*Shit!*' she yelled in her bar-room voice, turned hoarse with agony.

'You hit bad, Joe?'

Her hand was still working, her aim was steady. She dashed to one side, crouching low, and threw herself on the rocky ground behind the police car. She had a clear line of fire. She took aim on Cook, but things had changed again.

The driver of the Chevy had climbed out of her car and was holding a gun, levelling it at Cook.

'Hey, Joe!' Rico shouted. 'The witness has a handgun! You want me to shoot her?'

'Hell, no! Leave it to me!'

She still had a clear line to Cook, so she fired. Then again, and again. Her third bullet struck him and he was thrown to the ground. Beside him, the hostage was struggling to get away. Cook sat upright slowly, got hold of his rifle, took aim at her, fired. He fell back.

Gravel and grit flew up in front of Teresa's face, spitting into her mouth, eyes and hair. She ducked down, waiting for the next shot, but after a few seconds of silence she chanced another look.

Her last bullet must have struck him decisively. Cook was again lying on his back in the road. He was still gripping the rifle, which was standing on its stock, pointing at the sky. As Teresa watched him his grip relaxed, and the rifle clattered to the ground.

She got to her feet, and with her gun aimed steadily at Cook's body she returned to the shelter of the police car.

'What you think, Rico?' she said to Patresse, and discovered she could hardly speak, so short of breath was she.

'He's dead. You got him. You gonna be all right, Joe?'

'Yeah.'

They moved forward cautiously, levelling their guns, ready to fire at the first movement. The other cops were moving in too. A dozen pointing gun muzzles staked the man's body. The driver of the Chevrolet threw her gun down on the ground, and covered her face with her hands. Teresa could hear her wailing with fright and misery.

They all advanced slowly, but William Cook was not going anywhere. His head was tilted back at a horrible angle, and a rictus of pain distorted his face. His eyes stared into inverted distance. Teresa kicked his rifle away from him, just in case, and it skittered across the dusty road.

Her arm was bleeding badly.

'I guess that's it,' said Patresse. 'You wanna get that arm looked at, Joe?'

'In a while,' she snarled, and kicked the body of William Cook in the gut, with just enough force to be finally sure he was dead. 'You OK there, ma'am?' she growled at the witness.

'Sure, honey.'

'You carryin' a licence for that gun, ma'am?'

Then Teresa stood back and looked around again at the static scenery, glowing in the windless heat of the day.

She Located, Identified, Verified, Envisioned, Removed.

LIVER.

The words stayed visible for a few seconds, then faded slowly and smoothly. There was no music.

CHAPTER 23

Teresa ate alone in the hotel dining room that evening. She used her elbow to hold open the paperback beside her, while she forked in the food with one hand. She was glad there was no one else around. Amy served her, coming and going with the dishes, not saying anything unnecessary, but nevertheless seeming friendly. There was no sign of the four young Americans, and when Amy brought coffee Teresa asked if they had checked out.

'No. They said they wanted to eat out this evening. I think they went to Eastbourne.'

'Do you think they're going to find the sort of food they like in Eastbourne?'

'You know about the food, do you?'

'Nick has dropped a few hints. I gather they're picky.'

Amy said nothing, but smiled and moved away from her table.

Teresa dawdled over her meal, because a long unoccupied evening loomed ahead, and she wanted to resist the easy temptation of the bar as long as possible. She had a few practical matters to attend to; notably, she needed to sort out her credit-card accounts. Every use of the ExEx equipment ran up a large bill. Although in theory the bills would be comfortably within her credit limits, the accounts, she had belatedly realized, would be sent for settlement to her home address. As there was no one there to forward mail nothing would be paid until after she went home. She had noticed 24-hour emergency phone numbers printed on the backs of the cards, and she was planning to call them this evening to try to straighten out the problem.

She was tired after her long and physically demanding sessions on the ExEx equipment, and in similar circumstances at home she would have killed the evening mindlessly: watching TV, catching up with letters or housework, calling friends. None of these appealed or was possible while she was stuck in her hotel room, and the thought of running up more transatlantic phone charges from a hotel line was discouraging. The time differences anyway meant most of her friends would still be at work.

So she continued to read the paperback while she sipped her coffee at the table. When she realized Amy was waiting for her to finish up, she reluctantly closed the book and went upstairs, thinking vaguely about what to say to the credit-card company, and how to say it in the shortest way.

As she walked down the short hallway towards her room, card-key ready in her hand, she became aware that someone was standing in the shadows at the far end. A disagreeable sensation of fear passed through her. The man stepped forward. He went as far as the door to her room, then halted. He stood there, waiting for her.

She recognized him immediately as Ken Mitchell, the young man who had spoken to her before, and the fear dissolved into irritation. She recalled that the last time they had met he had also been in wait for her outside her room.

'Hi there, ma'am,' he said, with his falsely friendly smile.

'Good evening.'

She raised the key-card, and looked ahead to the door lock, trying to disregard him. He stood right beside her door, in such a way that if she wanted to go ahead and open it she would have to press past him. She could smell something expensively and subtly aromatic: a tonic lotion, a hair dressing, a body oil. He was wearing a suit, but it was cut in a casual style and made of light-coloured fabric, for informal wear. His tie was straight, knotted neatly, and with a restrained pattern. His hair was short and tidy. He had white, regular teeth, and his body looked fit. He made her crave to ruin him violently in some way.

'I've been trying to find you, Mrs Simons. We need to speak together.'

'Excuse me, I'm tired.'

'We know who you are, Agent Simons.'

'So what?'

'So we have to make you a proposition. We find your presence here in the hotel disruptive. We've made enquiries with your section chief in DC and have established that you are not here on official business.'

'I'm on vacation,' Teresa said, instantly wondering what had been said between these people and her office. 'Would you please let me pass through into my room?'

'Yeah, but you're not really on vacation, because you're kind of running a private investigation into the Gerry Grove case. The FBI say they know nothing about it, and haven't authorized you in any way. You're outside your jurisdiction, ma'am. Isn't that so?'

'It's none of your goddamn business, and it's none of the Bureau's business either. I'm on leave of absence.'

'As I understand the situation, the Bureau remains interested in whatever you do so long as you carry the badge. Anyway, we consider it to be our business. We checked into this hotel on the basis that the place would be otherwise vacant—'

'That's between you and the hotel,' Teresa said, already grappling with a feeling of paranoia about what this young man or his associates might have been saying to her office. The last thing she needed right now was trouble at work. 'It's nothing to do with me.'

'I think you'll find we have ways to get you out of here.'

'Go ahead,' said Teresa, with some private amusement. 'Not many Americans feel like messing with the FBI.'

'What makes you think I'm a US citizen?'

'Sorry, my mistake,' said Teresa. 'Now would you excuse me?'

'We need this hotel to ourselves,' said Ken Mitchell again. 'For that reason we have arranged an alternative room for you at the Grand Hotel in Eastbourne. Our company is prepared to pay the costs of relocation, and we request you to vacate your room by tomorrow. We also require you to quit making use of our corporate facilities in Welton Road.'

'What is it with you?' Teresa said. 'Don't you ever listen, or what?'

'I listen, sure enough. But do you? We want you out, lady.'

'Tell me why and I might even consider it.'

'In this case we require the hotel for our sole use. We have a contract with the management—'

'Not as far as they are concerned.'

'They are in error, which will turn out expensive for them if they are in breach of contract. In the meantime, either you leave of your own accord or we will take out a removal injunction against you. It's your choice.'

He hadn't shifted his position, looming unpleasantly close to her door. She was deeply reluctant to make physical contact with him, which she would have to do to open her door, but she reached forward with her key-card to see if he would budge. Apparently, he would not. She withdrew, and stood again a few feet from him, disliking and fearing him in almost equal measure.

'There are other ExEx providers,' she said. 'There's a place in Brighton. You can't stop me going there.'

'Suit yourself. We're only concerned with our own corporate facility.'

'Why do you want me out?'

'You're disrupting our plans. We operate under a software creation licence drawn up within the draft Valencia Treaty, the European agreement to regulate freedom of electronic access. In the US we'd be operating under federal licence: the McStephens Act. You know what that is?'

'Yes, of course.' Something clicked in memory then; a training session last year; a subject she hadn't followed too well; areas designated sanitaire for software development; the right to serve notice to quit.

Mitchell said, 'US federal laws have no effect here, so we work under the European equivalent. The Valencia protocols don't have the same legislative muscle, but applied with full force they amount to the same.'

'Can I see your licence?'

It snapped into his fingers as if by sleight of hand. She bent forward to read it, and he held it still for her to do so.

'All right,' she said. 'Why didn't you say that at first?'

'Why didn't you say you were a fed?'

'What about the hotel staff?' Teresa said. 'Are you getting them to move out too?'

'No, we need them.'

'Why them and not me?'

'Because they were here on the day of the Grove shootings, and you were not. They have memories of what happened, and you don't. We're interested in what they remember, and we're not interested in your theories.'

'I don't have theories.'

'Sure you do. Theories are what you're into. That's what we don't want. Your presence is disruptive.'

Teresa gestured in exasperation.

'You can't empty hotels any place you want to stay,' she said. 'Just because you feel like it.'

'You want to bet on that, Agent Simons?'

'All right, but under McStephens you've got to serve notice. Seven days. What's it with Valencia?'

'You're sharp, aren't you? The same. Eight days, in actual fact.'

He was putting away the licence, more slowly than he had produced it. Teresa watched the precise way in which he folded it, before slipping the slim leather wallet into his rear pocket. He reminded her of an agent she had known in Richmond, a friend of Andy's. Calvin Devore, his name was. Cal. Amusing guy was Cal, with a big face and big hands, but astonishingly dainty movements. What had become of Cal? Nice guy.

'OK, then,' she said. 'I'll work the eight days' notice. Back off me, you hear?'

But she was looking past Mitchell towards the light at the end of the corridor, thinking maybe she would call up Cal when she was home.

'Give me a break, Mrs Simons,' Mitchell said. 'Eight days—'

'I might leave before, anyway. Just lay off me until then. OK?'

'All right.' He glanced away with an irritated expression, but Teresa knew she had scored the point.

'What's the big deal?' she said. 'Why does it matter so much?'

'We don't need to use exclusion powers every place we go, but crossover doesn't occur in most places. You've got an interest in the Grove scenario that conflicts with ours. You're into reactional crossover, and we're into proveniential integrity and linear coherence. The bottom line is, we're licensed to be here and you're not.'

'What's reactional crossover?' Teresa said, having re-focused on what he was saying, but struggling to keep up with his flow of jargon.

'It's the way you trained. What the Bureau uses ExEx for. They operate interdiction training scenarios. You go in there repeatedly, entering the scenarios from different points of view, and that introduces neural crossover. Successive experiences of the scenario alter your perception next time you go in. To us that means crossover, and if it happens while we're programming it screws the code. What people like you do after we've compiled doesn't matter a damn to us, because that's what ExEx is all about, but while we're coding the regressions and memorative accounts we don't want crossover. It corrupts linear coherence.'

'What was the other thing you said you were into?'

'Proveniential integrity. Provenience is—'

'I know. Or I thought I did.'

'OK, but when we first build the parameters of a scenario, what we seek is a re-creation of the integral whole. We're talking iterative purity here. We want the past event as it really was, or as it is remembered by the main players. It's the same thing, in algorithmic terms, as your basic what-the-hell symbolic adumbration. We can fast-track the code from either point, but until then we keep the provenience integral, and at the waterline. You got that? We don't want false memory syndromics, we don't want anecdotal reportage, we don't want *post hoc* invention or narration, and we sure as hell don't want people like you coming in and trying to put an interpretive spin on the events.'

'You're incredible,' Teresa said. 'You know that?'

'Yeah,' Mitchell said. 'I'm paid for incredible.'

'Did that actually mean something to you? What you just said?'

'It's the thing we do.'

He had barely shifted position while they spoke, and he still bore the same expression of neutral stubbornness, but his undercurrent of menace was dispersing. Teresa thought how young he looked, and tried to estimate his age: he could be – what? – twenty or more years younger than she was? Is this what young people do now? she wondered. In her day if you got an education you left college and went into business, or law, or you joined a government agency, but now you learnt to speak code-babble, relocated to Taiwan, changed your nationality and wrote software for virtual-reality providers. What would she think of him if she were twenty years younger?

'All right,' she said. 'But I don't see how my staying in the same place as you—'

'Have you been talking to the manager while you've been here? Or that woman who works for him?'

'Amy? Yes, of course.'

'And you've been asking them about Grove.'

'I don't see what's wrong with that,' Teresa said. 'It's what people think about in this town, because they lived it.'

'That's what *you* talk about in this town, Mrs Simons. And it's why we don't want you here. We know you've been talking with Steve Ripon's mother, the police, the newspapers, the Mercer family, and God knows who else. Also, you've been up at our facility running shareware. To build this scenario we need these people's memories of what happened, and we want them uncontaminated. And everyone else's too. What you're doing is all fast-lane crossover, lady, and we don't want you in town even, until we've finished.'

'You've made a contract with the town? You going to sue them as well if I don't leave?'

He stared at her with his unchanged level expression, but moments later he actually smiled, though briefly. His face was transformed when he smiled. She wondered what he would do if she asked to see his licence a second time; she wanted to see his hands work that way again.

She said, 'Let me ask you something. I was up at the ExEx building the other day, and I asked if there were any Grove scenarios. It was like I'd blundered into something. The technician said something about before or after. Then she clammed up.'

'That's right.' He was cold and incredible again.

'What do you mean, that's right?'

'That's right she wouldn't tell you. Who was she?'

'No way. You'll make trouble for her.'

'Sounds like you've already done it. I can work out who she was.'

'I'll bet you can. Look, just tell me what she meant. Before or after what?'

'She was asking you, do you want to see the scenario of Grove before he started shooting, or the one after he started shooting?'

'Why should there be two?'

'We're working on it right now. This technician was speaking out of turn.'

'Why should there be two?' Teresa said again.

'Because halfway through his outburst event Grove went to our facility and ran an ExEx scenario. It was aberrant behaviour, coherence-wise, but we've got to patch that in to the new scenario. It makes linearity fade like yesterday. It has mega-potential for looping. For the first time ever we've got a scenario where someone runs a scenario. You think of the coding that will have to go into that!'

'Where was Grove before he started shooting, and after he left the ExEx building?'

'That was the original question, wasn't it?' said Mitchell. 'Before or after? You're carrying a lot of theories, and they're fast-lane crossover. We don't want to hear them.'

Teresa waved her arm in exasperation.

'You never give up, do you?' she said.

'Not until I've got what I want.'

'Well, what I want, and what I'm going to do, is to go into my room,' she said.

Mitchell made no move; she was still barred from her room unless she pushed past him. Since he showed no sign of getting out of the way, she decided that pushing past him was what she would have to do.

She moved forward, stretching out her hand and turning her wrist at an angle, to slip the card into the swipe-lock. Mitchell stayed put, leaning against the upright jamb of the door. His face was only inches away from hers; once again she smelt his lotion. It summoned an image of him standing before a mirror, moving an aerosol spray across his torso, staring into a condensation-blurred mirror.

It stirred something in her.

His face moved closer.

'What do you do in this hotel, Mrs Simons, all on your own?' he said softly, almost directly into her ear.

Teresa felt the quiet words impacting on her, as if they had coned on to a patch of her skin, somewhere beneath her ear, across her neck, a gentle tactile intrusion with almost musical rhythm. The nerve-ends across her shoulders prickled, and she felt her face burning. She turned her head to look at him, and his face was right there. Nine inches away, twelve, staring steadily at her. He was so young; it was years since—

She concentrated again on the lock, not wanting him to judge her as someone who couldn't cope with modern electronic technology. She knew the card had to go in at exactly the right angle, otherwise it relocked the door and she had to start over.

Mitchell spoke again, this time barely breathing the words.

'What's the story, lady?' he said. 'How do you like it done to you?'

She gave up with the key, took a step back and faced Mitchell again.

'What did you say?' she said, flustered.

'Why are you here on your own, Agent Simons? You want it, you can have it with me.'

She said nothing.

A long silence followed, while he continued to stare at her and she had to look away. All she was aware of was his lean, masculine shape, his clean and well-fitting clothes, his neat hair, his firm body, his distracting smell of expensive lotion, his quiet voice, his grey eyes, his smoothly shaved chin, his precise hands, his youth, his slender height, his closeness and his total unwillingness to back down. He held up one hand, palm outwards, at the same level as her mouth.

'You know what I can do with this?' he whispered.

She replied, quietly, 'Will you come in for a while?'

At last he stepped aside to allow her to operate the lock, and she swiped the key-card efficiently, getting it right with the first try, glad not to have to redo it while he was watching, not to have to delay and give herself time to think about what she was doing.

The door opened to a room in semi-darkness, light from the streetlamps coming in through the opened curtains, and she went inside with Mitchell following close behind her. He kicked the door closed. She threw aside her bag, the paperback book, the key-card and its plastic case, heard them all scatter on the floor. Already she was turning towards him, yearning for him, eager for his body. In their haste their faces collided, cheekbones knocked, lips crushed against each other, teeth grated momentarily. She thrust her tongue greedily into his mouth: he tasted sweet, cool and clean, as if he had just eaten an apple. She tore open the front of her blouse, and pulled his hard young body against her breasts, grappling her hands possessively across his straight back, his narrow waist, his small tight buttocks.

The fingers of one of his hands rested on the tiny valve in the back of her neck, teasing at it with a precise, dainty lightness of touch. The other hand settled on her breast, as gentle as the mist of an aerosol spray.

Mitchell left her an hour later. She remained on her bed with the scattered sheets, her clothes, the pillows and covers, heaped around her. She lay on her side, still naked, her hand stretched out and resting lazily where his body had lain just a few minutes before. She thought contentedly of what they had done together, how it had felt, what it had been, the shocking flood of relief it had brought her. She was wide awake, physically rested.

His maddening masculine fragrance lingered around her: on her skin, on the sheets, on her lips, under her nails, in her hair.

Later she began to feel cold, so she dragged on her robe and found her hairbrush where it had fallen on the carpet. She sat on the side of the bed pulling the brush idly through the tangles and curls, staring at the wall, dissatisfied with herself, thinking about Ken Mitchell, remembering Andy.

The two men existed with equal prominence in her consciousness, unfairly but undeniably. For the first time since Andy's death, her feelings about him had been changed by meeting someone else.

Progress towards the rest of her life had begun.

But as she went back to bed, and lay down under the covers, she felt a terrible sense of misery, and a belated but real betrayal of the man she had loved innocently and truly for so many years.

'Sorry, Andy,' she muttered. 'But I needed that. Shit, I needed it.'

CHAPTER 24

They had parked their satellite van next to her car again, and it loomed massively over it.

Teresa paused at the hotel door, trying to see if the van was in use. She knew that although Ken Mitchell and his colleagues sometimes drove the van away, more often than not they used it as a mobile office where it stood. Today Teresa saw the satellite dish was in position, aligned on somewhere in the sky. At once she ducked back inside the building. Her efforts to extricate her car would inevitably draw her to their attention.

She decided instead to walk up to the ExEx building on the Ridge; the weather was fair, which gave her enough of an excuse, and it would be a chance to see some more of the town at ground level. Anyway, she had had something in mind for a couple of days and this would be a good opportunity to try it out.

She walked down Eastbourne Road towards St Stephen's Church. On this crisply cold morning, with the usual traffic edging noisily past, the shops open and a few pedestrians going about their business, it was easy to imagine the chaos that Grove's outburst must have caused on that afternoon. The traffic here would have been brought to a halt by the vehicles that had piled up in the vicinity of the hotel, but the people in the cars would probably not yet have found out what was causing the delay. Teresa could visualize them sitting with their engines idling, waiting for what they must have thought was a temporary traffic hold-up ahead to be cleared. Those people would have presented easy targets to Grove. Six people had actually died inside cars in this short stretch of Eastbourne Road, but many more were wounded. The rest managed to scramble out of their cars, or found cover until Grove had passed.

Teresa reached St Stephen's Church, which was on the corner of a road called Hyde Avenue. This was one of the alternative traffic routes up to the Ridge, bypassing the narrow streets of the Old Town, and Teresa herself had already driven along it several times on her journeys to and from the GunHo ExEx building. Next to the church Hyde Avenue was an attractive road, with good houses and numerous trees, but further up it was lined with estate houses and a few industrial sites. Near where it joined the Ridge, the elevation afforded glimpses of the view across the town, and out to sea, but there were better vantage points and better panoramas in other parts of the town.

Looking at her town map Teresa had noticed that a series of footpaths and alleyways ran between the houses in this part of Bulverton; they were known locally as twittens. With a few road-crossings taken into account, the twittens provided a continuous network of paths behind the houses. Teresa had worked out that she could probably walk most of the way up to Welton Road and the ExEx building by this route.

She crossed Hyde Avenue. On the opposite corner was a tandoori take-out restaurant, and between it and the adjacent building was a narrow alley that led to one of the twittens. The alley was bounded by the walls of the buildings on either side, and overhead by the floor of an upper-storey extension of one of them. The alleyway floor was made of stone flags; as she walked through the metal-tipped heels of her shoes set up a clacking that echoed around her. The traffic noise from behind was quietened by the enclosed space.

Almost at once, in the half-light of the alley, she began to feel giddy. An all-too-familiar display of brilliant but unseeable flashes began in the corner of her eye, and she paused, overtaken by a rush of familiar despair. She should have known that this was a day when a migraine attack was more than possible: she had hardly slept during the night.

She paused, resting one hand on the wall at her side, looking down at the uneven stone floor, trying to rid herself of the nausea. She wondered whether she should give up her plans for the day, return to the hotel for one of her pills and try to sleep.

While she stood there, undecided, a series of shots rang out in the street behind her.

The sound was so close she instinctively ducked. Between shots she could clearly hear the quick, efficient clicking of the mechanism of a semi-automatic rifle, a sound that in spite of everything continued to fascinate her.

Teresa looked back: she could see a stationary car framed in the rectangle of daylight. A wild imagining came into her mind: cars were already backed up along Eastbourne Road while a new gunman prowled, firing at will.

She hurried back towards the road, scraping herself for cover against the rough bricks of the alley wall. Momentarily dazzled by her return to the bright cold sunlight, Teresa put her hand up to shield her eyes, and tried to see what was going on. She stood in the entrance to the alley, careful not to step out into the open. Vehicles coming down from the Ridge along Hyde Avenue were passing through a green light at the junction with Eastbourne Road, and turning left or right. Their engines and tyres made the usual loud noise as they accelerated away along this narrow, built-up street. There was no sign of panic, or of anyone carrying or using a rifle.

While she watched, the lights at the intersection changed, and traffic began moving off in the other directions. The car Teresa had first seen framed in the entrance to the alley moved away with the others, the driver glancing back at her with a puzzled expression, no doubt wondering why she had been staring at him so intently.

Still on her guard for the presence of a gunman, or more alarmingly a sniper, Teresa stood warily in the entrance to the alley, watching as the cars and trucks went by. The incident profoundly puzzled her: she was obviously mistaken, in the sense that no one appeared to have been firing a weapon in the street, but the sounds she had heard were so close at hand, and so familiar and distinctive, that she knew she had not imagined them.

When a couple more minutes had gone by she decided to continue with her walk, but the incident had made her nervous. As she came out from between the two buildings the path continued with wire fencing on either side – she looked from side to side in case her imagined gunman had moved round so that he was behind these houses and able to see her. Where the twitten turned right-and-left between a junction of gardens, Teresa looked back. The path through the alley was clear, and she could glimpse the traffic on the main road still moving past normally.

Then she looked up.

There was a man on the roof of the house next to the restaurant.

Teresa immediately ducked down and moved into cover, even as she realized that he was no threat to her. She looked back. He had fallen, and was lying head down across the sloping tiles. His foot had been caught by a joint between two scaffolding poles, and was preventing him from sliding any further. He had been shot several times. A stain of dark blood spread out from his head and chest, down the tiles and over some of the planks on the scaffolding.

Teresa felt her pulse racing, her head thumping, her hands trembling. Conflicting instincts ran through her: to call out to the man, to scream aloud, to run away, to shout for help, to dash across to the scaffolding and try to find some way to climb up and reach him.

She did none of these. She simply stood at the junction of the path, trembling with fear, looking up at the dead man on the roof.

The sirens of emergency vehicles were approaching, and Teresa could hear a man's voice amplified and distorted by a bullhorn. A helicopter was weaving overhead, about half a mile away towards the Old Town. There was another rattle of gunfire, more muffled than before.

Teresa hurried back down the path, and ran through the covered alley. Moving traffic was framed in the sunlight ahead. As she emerged into Eastbourne Road she saw a woman walking towards her, pushing a stroller with two small children inside.

'A man!' Teresa shouted, but incoherently, because she was short of breath and she found it difficult to form words. 'On the roof! Back there! A man on the roof!'

Her voice was rasping, and she had to cough.

The woman looked at her as if she was mad and pushed past her, continuing on her way. Teresa wheeled round, looking anxiously for someone else who could help her.

The traffic was rolling by as normal. There were no emergency sirens, and no helicopter moved overhead. She looked left and right: in one direction the road curved away towards the railway bridge, in the other it became indistinguishable as it wove through the clustering of old red-brick terraced houses and concrete commercial buildings on either side.

She looked again at the roof of the house where she had seen the man.

From this position at the front there was no sign of him, and none either of the scaffolding. That was another mystery: from where she had first looked, the scaffolding was built as high as the chimney stack, spreading across to the front of the building. It should be visible from here. She went back through the alley, hurried along to the place where it turned, and looked back.

The man lay at his steep angle, trapped by the scaffolding.

Close at hand, swelling terrifyingly around her: gunfire, sirens, amplified voices. In the square of daylight, glimpsed through the alley, nothing moved.

Teresa put her hand up to her neck, feeling for the valve.

CHAPTER 25

Teresa had by this time browsed through the catalogue of scenarios often enough to be able to find her way around quickly, but the sheer extent of the range of software, and the complexity of the database itself, still daunted her.

The sense of unfolding endlessness lent her a wonderful feeling of freedom, spoiling her for choice. Each time she clicked on a new selection a range of apparently limitless options appeared; every one of those itself opened up innumerable further choices; each of those led to further levels of choice, endlessly detailed and varied; and each of those choices was a remarkably complete world in itself, full of noise, colour, movement, incident, danger, travel, physical sensations. Most of the scenarios were cross-referenced or hyperlinked to others. Entry into any scenario gave her a magical sense of infinitude, of the ability to roam and explore, away from the constraints of the main incident.

Extreme reality was a landscape of forking paths, endlessly crossing and recrossing, leading somewhere new, towards but never finding the edge of reality.

Today she made her selections, trying to calculate how much real time each of them would use up, and how long in total she could remain inside the simulations. She had learned, although reluctantly, that she should be sparing with her time. Too much ExEx in one day exhausted her.

She confined herself to three unrelated scenarios, and selected the option for repeated entry as required. Two of the scenarios were the sort of interdiction set-ups she was used to from her Bureau training, but which for all their sensory engagement were beginning to bore her. However, she was already thinking ahead to her return to the office, knowing that Ken Mitchell had probably made trouble for her. Some interdiction experience while on leave might count a little to her advantage, if advantage were needed. But her growing feeling of tedium was real, so for her third ExEx she decided to try an experiment: a short scenario which depicted a major traffic accident, the point being that the user had to learn to anticipate and avoid the accident.

After she had made this last choice Teresa continued to browse through the catalogue. She wanted something different, something that carried no risks, no responsibility, no censure. Gun incidents and traffic accidents were not the sum of life's experiences, she decided. There were other affairs of the mind and body she would like to experience vicariously, especially those of the body.

She was in a foreign country, alone, largely unknown by the people around her. She wanted a little fun.

She had no hesitation in going to the material she wanted to try, but she did have misgivings about the staff here knowing she was using it. The thought of doing it made her throat feel dry with anticipation; the thought of being observed or noticed doing it terrified her.

Before making her selection she therefore turned to the *User's Operating Manual* lying on the bench next to the computer, and looked for the chapter on security.

The manual had been written by a technophile genius, not a human being, and like many works of its kind it was difficult to read and follow. However, with determination she gleaned the reassurance she wanted: the user's choice of scenario was coded and identified. This was primarily intended for the programming of the nanochips. By default it was information that was available to the technical operator, but the user could alter it if privacy was required.

To activate security measures, the user should select the following option . . .

Teresa selected the following option, then made her final choice of scenario. The fact that it was shareware, as she realized at the last minute, gave her an extra edge of anticipation.

She waited while the ExEx nanochips were programmed. Half a minute later a sealed plastic phial was delivered to the desk by the peripheral, and she took this through to the ExEx facility, eager to begin.

*

Teresa was a gendarme on night patrol in the immigrant quarter of the city of Lyon; it was January 10, 1959.

Her name was Pierre Montaigne, she had a wife called Agnès, and two children aged seven and five. A steady rain made the cobbles gleam; doorways to clubs and restaurants were lit with a single bulb over the lintels; the streets were a noisy chaos of fast-moving traffic. Teresa was trying to think in French, a language she did not know. With an effort and a flaring of panic, she forced herself back to English. Everything was in black and white.

From the start, she recognized a difference: she had more choice, more control, in this scenario. Indeed, as she joined it Pierre Montaigne came to a sudden halt, practically falling forward. Her partner, André Lepasse, was obliged to turn and wait for her. Teresa immediately relaxed her influence over the man, and the two gendarmes continued their patrol.

They reached a small, unpretentious cous-cous restaurant. It had an unpainted door and a large plate-glass window steamed up with condensation. Over the door, a hand-painted sign said: *La Chèvre Algérienne*. Montaigne and Lepasse were about to walk on, when someone inside the restaurant must have noticed them. The door was thrust open, and an exchange of shouts took place with two men, one of whom appeared to be the proprietor.

Teresa and her partner pushed their way roughly into the restaurant, where a man had taken a young woman hostage and was threatening her with a long-bladed knife. Everyone was yelling at once, including Lepasse. Pierre Montaigne did not know what to do, because she could not speak French.

Teresa remembered LIVER.

Berkshire, England, August 19, 1987. She was Sergeant Geoffrey Verrick, a uniformed traffic policeman, passenger in a fast-pursuit patrol car on the M4 motorway, fifty miles west of London.

A call came through from Reading police headquarters saying that a shooting incident had taken place in the Berkshire village of Hungerford. All units were to proceed there directly. Maximum caution was advised. Officer in charge would be . . .

Teresa said to the driver, Constable Trevor Nunthorpe, 'Hear that, Trev? Next exit, Junction 14.'

Trev put on the blue strobe, headlights and two-tone siren, and traffic ahead of them began to clear out of their way. The Hungerford turn-off was the next one along, and five minutes after the first call had come in their car was speeding down the slip road towards the roundabout at the bottom.

Teresa said, 'Give the Hungerford road a miss, Trev. Go right round.'

'I thought we had to go into Hungerford, Sarge.'

'Go round,' Teresa said. 'Take the Wantage exit.'

Leaning the car over on its nearside tyres, Trev swung it through three-quarters of the roundabout, then followed the A338 north towards Wantage. As a result they were heading directly away from Hungerford. The traffic again swerved out of their way, or slowed down and pulled over to the verge.

Another message came through, urging all available units to get to Hungerford as quickly as possible: the gunman had killed more than a dozen people, and was still at large, shooting at everyone in sight. Teresa acknowledged, and confirmed they were responding.

'What's the idea, Geoff?' said Trevor as they drove at high speed the wrong way through the scenario. Fields and hedgerows and gated drives flashed past. 'This isn't the way to Hungerford.'

Teresa said nothing, watching the landscape through the window at her side, blocking out the intrusive banshee whine of the siren, looking out at the sky, the trees, the endless vista of summertime England. It unfolded around them as they sped along, urging her on to the edges of reality.

Then there was a jolt, and reality was tested to the point of destruction.

As the scenario lurched back, Trev abruptly jammed on the brakes and the car slowed awkwardly, nosing down and sliding at an angle across the dusty road. They had arrived in an instant at the Bear Hotel at the bottom of Hungerford High Street, where a police line had been thrown across the road.

They parked their patrol car, then walked round to the luggage compartment at the back, where the bulletproof jackets were stored. Teresa and Trev pulled them on, then went to work in Hungerford.

Teresa, disappointed, remembered LIVER.

There was an electronic buzzing until the words faded. No music, though.

Teresa was driving the curves of Highway 2, north of Los Angeles, through the mountains; it was May 15, 1972. The sun shone down into her open-top, the radio played the Mothers of Invention, she had her girl curled up affectionately beside her.

As they rounded one of the steeper bends a truck on the other side of the road did not take the grade and it tipped to one side, crashing down and skidding towards them, crushing their car with devastating effect.

Teresa was driving the curves of Highway 2, north of Los Angeles, through the mountains; it was May 15, 1972. She braked, hauled the car over to the side of the road and did a U-turn. Grit and dust flew up behind them, and hovered in the sunlight after they had accelerated away down the hill.

After driving ten miles back towards the city, she took a left on the freeway heading east towards Las Vegas, and settled down for the long drive. The radio was playing the Mothers of Invention, and her girlfriend was rolling a joint. When they came to the desert the road became a blur, the car's engine note steadied, and there was nothing more to do or see.

Teresa waited until she was certain, then recalled the LIVER acronym.

Teresa was instantly aware of heat, bright lights and clothes that were too tight for comfort. She blinked, and tried to see what was going on around her, but her eyes had not yet adjusted. There were people standing further back, beyond a ring of lights, not paying the least attention to her.

A woman came up to her, and brusquely patted her forehead and nose with powder. 'Hold still a while longer, Shan,' she said impersonally, then moved back behind the lights.

Shan, Teresa thought. My name is Shan. Shouldn't I have known that from the start?

Full of curiosity, Teresa looked down at herself and discovered that she was dressed as a cowgirl. She raised a hand to touch her hair: she had some kind of cowboy hat on her head, making her scalp feel glossy with sweat, and the strings dangled beside her face. She peered down at her chest and found that she was wearing a shirt made out of a cheerful check material. With one finger, she eased forward the V above the top button, and glimpsed a tiny under-wired bra made of black lace. She had breasts that swelled wonderfully above the cups, in a way she had always dreamt of. The leather mini-skirt she was wearing exposed most of her legs, which she could see were clad in sheer silk stockings. She touched them sensually. Her fingers discovered what felt like a suspender belt under the skirt. She knew she had panties on, but they were far too tight and they were cutting into her flesh. Her boots were made of white calf, and came up to her knees. They pinched the sides of her feet.

* * * SENSH * * *

She turned to see where she was, feeling the clothes twist uncomfortably against her body and tightening under her armpits. She discovered she was sitting precariously on a high bar stool, next to a wooden counter with a polished surface. Behind this was the space where the barman would work, and on the wall behind that was a tall mirror with an ornate gilt surround. Teresa could see her reflection in the mirror, and she looked at herself with immense interest and amusement.

Her face had been made up with lavish and exaggerated features: black-outlined purple eyeshadow and heavy mascara, white foundation cream, too much blusher, and lip gloss that glistened wetly, like red plastic. The woman's efforts to dull the sheen of perspiration on her brow and nose had been only partly successful. Long auburn curls tumbled from beneath her hat.

Teresa straightened, and by shrugging her shoulders and pulling at the seams of the clothes attempted to make herself more comfortable. She tried unsuccessfully to pull down the hem of the mini-skirt.

There was a man standing next to her, also dressed in cowboy clothes. He had a long drooping moustache and a beard, both apparently false, and he leaned back on the counter with one elbow, showing no interest in her. He was holding a tabloid newspaper in his free hand, and was reading the sports page. She

195

thought she should know his name, but apparently that information was also not a part of the package.

* * * SENSH * * *

She looked into the main part of the room, but the bright lights still made it difficult to see the other people clearly. There were at least four men there, as well as the woman who had spoken to her. One of the men was also dressed in cowboy clothes. It was hard to make out the area beyond them, but Teresa gained an impression of unused space and that this small set, the bar of a western saloon, was the only part in use.

A large video camera stood on a tripod. Another slightly smaller one was being held by one of the men, who was making some adjustment to a battery pack he wore around his waist.

After a few more moments of consultation, one of the men stepped forward to where Teresa could see him. He was short and bald, and was wearing a filthy T-shirt with a cannabis leaf drawn on the front. He raised his voice. To her surprise Teresa discovered he had a British accent.

'All right, everybody, we'll do another take. Quiet please! Everyone in their places. Are you ready, Shandy and Luke?' Teresa said she was, and the man with the big false whiskers put his newspaper out of sight somewhere behind the counter. 'OK, we'll start now.'

Shandy and Luke. Teresa glanced at Luke, who gave her a wink.

* * * SENSH * * *

Teresa had been expecting the director to shout 'Action!', but apparently this was not necessary. Both cameras came into use, indicated by tiny red LEDs that glinted at the front.

Luke at once moved towards her roughly and began grappling with her, his arms round her back, trying to kiss her. At first, Teresa instinctively resisted, but after a few seconds she forced herself to relax and not to try to control the events of this scenario. She felt the areas of her mind and body that were Shandy's also resisting Luke's advances, but with less conviction. After a few seconds of half-hearted wrestling, Luke took the front of her shirt in both hands and tore it open. Teresa heard the familiar screech of velcro, and realized that the buttons were fake. Her exaggerated breasts were revealed.

Shandy turned away and picked up a bottle from the counter.

Holding it by the neck, she brought it down on the crown of Luke's head. It shattered instantly with an unconvincing noise that sounded more like plastic apparatus dismantling than glass breaking. Luke reared up, shook his head, then came back for more.

* * * SENSH * * *

This time he snatched at her bra, hooking his fingers under the scrap of cloth that connected the half-cups. He pulled at it roughly. The bra tore apart as easily as the shirt had done, and fell away from her body instantly. Tossing it aside, Luke sank his face between her breasts, cupping them in his hands and pressing them against his cheeks. Teresa felt the stiff bristles of his moustache scratching against her. She groaned in ecstasy. The man with the hand-held camera moved in closer.

She allowed Luke to nuzzle her breasts for several more seconds, but then there was an interruption. The man in the cowboy suit who had been standing behind the lights stepped forward.

He grabbed Luke by the collar, pulled his head back and away from her body, then took a mighty swing with his fist. To Teresa he appeared to miss by several inches, but Luke's head jerked backwards, and he staggered away from her, his arms windmilling. He collapsed into a table and two chairs, which smashed at once. Both cameras briefly recorded this, then returned to their main focus of interest.

Her rescuer was now sizing her up with over-acted relish, standing before her and stroking one of her naked breasts with his fingers. Shandy licked her lips, and her nipples became erect. She stroked her hand across the front of his jeans; Teresa was startled to realize that there was already an immense bulge inside them. His hips were gyrating slowly. This went on for some time.

* * * SENSH * * *

Behind them, the director's voice cut in.

'Come on, Shan!' he shouted. 'Get on with it!'

Shandy deliberately delayed a little longer, letting her tongue play temptingly across her lips, but after another annoyed shout from the director she reached across to the zipper of the man's jeans and slowly slid it down.

Teresa was undeniably impressed by what she saw come

197

prodding out of there, and was intensely interested in what Shandy and the man did for the next uncounted minutes. She stayed to the end of the action, thinking how little she had previously known about certain kinds of sexual performance, how well and enthusiastically Shandy could perform them, how much quick pleasure they brought, but how few of them were ultimately worth knowing.

Finally it was all over. With not much more likely to happen Teresa recalled the LIVER mnemonic. Shandy was walking towards a shower cubicle, clutching the tiny costume against the front of her body.

```
* * *          You have been flying SENSH Y'ALL          * * *
* * *              Fantasys from the Old West            * * *
* * * Copyroody everywhere – doan even THINK about it!! * * *
```

A piece of inane music, synthesized somehow with a drumming beat and an endlessly repeated sequence of three chords, jangled deafeningly around Teresa as she returned, not entirely willingly, to reality.

Later that evening, alone in her room and stirring restlessly with her memories of the day, Teresa took her notepad from her bag and found an unused page. She regarded it for a long time.

Finally, in careful handwriting, she put down the words:

Dear Andy – I didn't need that. I'm sorry, and it will never, ever happen again. I enjoyed it, though. I think. It was interesting, anyway.

That wasn't what she had meant to say, wasn't even what she thought. It hadn't been so interesting. Size wasn't everything. Neither was stamina.

She didn't sign the page, but instead stared at the inadequate words, trying to summon memories of her times with Andy, the long and happy years becoming so increasingly difficult to recall. The caprice of writing down the flippant words had instantly died, to be replaced by a familiar longing.

He was slipping ineluctably away from her, ceasing to be the person she remembered, becoming instead simply the bearer of a name, the man who had had a past rôle in her life, someone she recalled as a lover but not as someone making love, except in fragments of memory, incidents that had with time lost their passion. A man, a figure, a lover, a friend, a husband, he had been all of these, but he was becoming more remote from her. He would never know this reality of the years beyond his death in which she had to live without him. How could he ever have known them? She would never have flown to England for this trip, never have stayed in Bulverton. This had become her life, and it would always be without him. She knew she was ceasing to grieve, that she was therefore losing him, not because he had changed but because she had: she could not prevent herself changing and moving on. She still had no idea what she would do in her life without him, where eventually she would go, but she knew that this was the way, ultimately, that Andy would have to die.

She left the notebook open while she showered, but before she went to bed she tore out the page and crumpled it up. She threw it in the wastebin next to the door. Before she fell asleep she changed her mind again. She climbed out of bed, retrieved the page from the bin, then tore it into shreds.

CHAPTER 26

Nick Surtees stared in silent disbelief at the contract that had just been handed to him by Acie Jensen. What had started out as an ordinary-seeming morning in the hotel, with familiar chores lined up ahead, had been abruptly swept away by visions of virtually unlimited wealth. This cataclysmic event had occurred a few minutes earlier, during a remarkable interview with Ms Jensen inside the large van parked behind the hotel.

The contract itself was a boilerplate, but Jensen said she would let him have this copy so he could familiarize himself with the wording ahead of time. She seemed to assume Nick would want to retain an attorney. There was a blank line on page 17, where the amount of money he would be paid would be inscribed when the deal was agreed. Ms Jensen had until now appeared to Nick to be a dissatisfied guest, but this morning she had been amiable and relaxed and seemed even to take pleasure in the amounts of money being bandied around. At one point she had drawn Nick's attention to how large the space in the contract was, to accommodate the generous sums available.

The contract itself was a mass of impenetrable legalese, finely printed compact text which filled more than thirty large sheets of paper.

The first page was a summary. This was written in relatively straightforward language, and outlined the intent and effect of the agreement. For most people offered the contract, it was obviously assumed that this would be the only page they would read. It explained that in return for payment for full disclosure of 'relevant memorative information' as held by the licensor, the GunHo Corporation of Taipei, Republic of China, the licensee, would have complete and unlimited rights of 'electronic creation, adaptation, development, retrieval and replay'.

Significantly, the most prominent passage occupied the bottom third of the page. It was printed in large characters and was enclosed in a thick red border. It said:

YOUR RIGHTS. This contract is valid throughout the member states of the European Union as presently constituted, and is written in all official languages of the countries in the Union; this version is in English. Similar validity operates within the USA, but an attorney should be consulted. The contract describes an agreement concerning electronic creative rights to psychoneural memories. All such agreements within the European Union are protected by the protocols of the Treaty of Valencia. Before signing the contract, or accepting payment for your memories, YOU ARE STRONGLY RECOMMENDED TO SEEK COMPETENT LEGAL ADVICE.

Nick was in a state of mild shock: everything in his life was now centred on those thirty-odd pages of closely printed words. The prospect of suddenly receiving a substantial fortune had the capacity to change a life for ever. It was impossible to pretend away such a sum of money; it couldn't be ignored. No matter what, things were about to change.

For Nick, money had always been something that came in and went out at more or less the same rate, leaving him never rich, never poor, but more the latter than the former. Now, within the last thirty minutes, he had been told that he was on the point of becoming a rich man. Seriously rich. For the rest of his life.

There was no hurry: Acie Jensen had advised him to take his time, to read the contract carefully.

This must be how it felt to win a lottery. Or to be left a fortune by a relative you hardly knew. Possibilities opened up in all directions, dominated by the petty concerns of the immediate present. In the short term he knew he could at last settle his bills, pay off his overdraft (a strenuously worded demand from the bank had arrived only that morning), clear his credit-card debts. Then the luxuries would become instantly available: a new car, a new house, new clothes, a long holiday. And still there would be millions left over. Investments, dividends, property, endless financial freedom . . .

Nick had come up to the bedroom alone, closing the door

behind him. His first instinct had been to rejoice, to find Amy and grab her, dance down the street with her and share the incredible news with her. But an inner darkness had loomed.

It was not that he wanted to keep the money to himself, but within the first few moments he knew that it signalled the end of his relationship with Amy. The windfall was his ticket out of Bulverton, away from the hotel, and inevitably away from Amy. They were held together only by pressure of past events.

The money transformed everything, and it would release them both, a violent throwing open of the gates. He was trying to cope with an onrush of thoughts: it wasn't the money, because he could and would give half of it to her and still be wealthy beyond his dreams, but its impact on them both.

He felt a tremendous dread and misery rise within him, but not predominating, somewhere out on the edge of his consciousness. It had to be confronted, though, because it was rushing towards the centre. This windfall had come too suddenly: where he and Amy were headed was no secret to either of them, but he didn't want it precipitated by a sleazy get-rich deal. Which was exactly what this was.

He went down to the bar and poured himself a large Scotch. There was no sign of Amy, who earlier had been working in the kitchen. He returned quietly to the privacy of the bedroom.

He felt he was going mad: his thoughts were whirling around. Plans, relief, excitement, guilt, dreams, freedom, places to go and things to buy and ambitions at last to fulfil. Then the darker side: a raging guilt about Amy, a fear that all this money would evaporate as quickly as it had materialized, that there was some unannounced drawback, some evil catch that Ms Jensen had not warned him about. He looked at the contract lying on the bed beside him, and again read the warning on the first page.

He decided to follow its advice, and after searching around for his address book he put through a call to an old friend of his who practised in London as a solicitor.

John Wellesley was in a meeting when Nick telephoned, but returned his call a few minutes later. By a massive effort of will Nick had still only sipped his whisky once or twice. Every familiar instinct and habit urged him to drink himself into a horizontal position, but a harder centre warned that he needed to keep his wits about him.

He gave Wellesley a brief if slightly hysterical description of what had been offered to him. Until he began speaking he had no real idea of the effect the news had had on him. He heard the words tumbling out, and he could hear that his voice was pitched several tones higher than normal. It took a conscious effort to stop himself babbling.

Wellesley listened in silence, then said calmly, 'Is it a Valencia contract?'

Nick took a breath, feeling giddy. 'I think so, yes. There's something about that on the front.'

'Is it thirty-two pages in length?'

'Yes,' Nick said, riffling the sheets and looking at the number on the last one.

'I have to be sure about something, Nick. I know it sounds like an irrelevance, but I have to know. Are you asking me for informal advice on this contract, or do you want me to negotiate it on your behalf?'

'Both, really. Advice first, I think.'

'Would you like to go away and calm down before I say any more?'

'Do I sound that bad, John?'

'I can't say I blame you. I've done several of these deals before, and they always seem to have the same effect.'

'All right. I'll try to stop gibbering.' Nick swigged the rest of his whisky, tried to concentrate on what Wellesley was saying.

'I'll make it easy for you. The bottom line is that it would be safe for you to sign the contract in the form in which they've handed it to you. There are international treaties that govern these deals. Are you prepared to submit to the electronic scanning – did they describe that to you?'

'Yes.'

Acie Jensen had told him about it, but Nick had still been reeling from the news about the money. At times like that you tend not to pay close attention to the rest of what someone is saying.

'OK, so long as you know what's involved. I gather it's no more unpleasant than having your blood pressure tested, but I haven't done it myself so I can't be certain. I believe there's no physical risk, but the Valencia Treaty allows you to get medical advice without prejudicing the agreement.'

'I'm not too bothered about that.'

'OK. As for the money: which company is it?'

'They say they're Chinese, from Taiwan.'

'Not the GunHo Corporation?' said Wellesley.

'Yes.'

'Congratulations. They're one of the biggest virtual-reality players. You're home and dry, Nick. Their contract is always the standard one, so far as I know. From your description it sounds as if they're still using it. If they are, it's been tested in all the senior courts: the Supreme Court in the USA, the Appeal Court here, the European courts in The Hague and Strasbourg.'

'You seem to know a lot about it,' Nick said, impressed.

'As I said, I've worked on several ExEx contracts in the last couple of years. How much are they offering you?'

Nick told him.

'Not bad. In terms of the going rate, that's medium to high. What's it for?'

'The Gerry Grove shootings in Bulverton. My parents were killed.'

'Of course! I should have realized. Bulverton is just about the hottest ticket in town at the moment.'

'I wasn't even here when it happened,' said Nick. 'I keep wondering if they've made a mistake. It makes me nervous, in case it's all going to fall through when they find out.'

'That might have been a risk once. Until last year they only wanted people who actually took part in the events, or who were eyewitnesses. But they've been making big improvements in the software. If there are plenty of hearsay accounts, that's apparently good enough. The results wouldn't stand up in a court, but hell, this is rock 'n' roll, this is showbiz. You're living in your parents' house, aren't you?'

'They ran a hotel, which I've taken over.'

'What happened to your parents is probably why they want you. As I understand it, the problem with Bulverton is that many of the best witnesses were killed on the day. It's partly why the virtual-reality people have taken so long to get around to it. Look, we've gone over the ground, as far as I'm allowed. The Law Society rules say I can't promise you anything in advance, but would you like me to act for you?'

'Er, don't get me wrong,' Nick said, 'but if the contract's as safe as you say, would there be any point in that?'

'Depends if you want more money or not,' said Wellesley.

'Well . . .'

'You've got something GunHo are obviously prepared to pay for, and in corporate terms they're leaking cash from every pore. Have you any idea of the expected global take from extreme experience this year?'

'No. Until recently I was only barely aware it existed.'

'People used to say that about the internet. A pal of mine in the City puts it this way: if ExEx was a country, it would currently be the second largest economy in the world. It already has more paying customers every day than all the major soft drinks companies combined. And they charge substantially more than the price of a Coke.'

'Are you saying you can get me *more* money for this? It already seems like a ludicrous amount.'

'I can't offer you that as an inducement to retain me. I'm a lawyer, Nick. We operate under rules.'

'What would you say if you weren't a solicitor?'

'Well . . . since it's you. Doubling the principal sum would be the easy bit. With that out of the way I could fight them for residuals like TV and movie rights, as well as royalties and translations. I can probably get most of them. The important ones, anyway. What about dependants? Have you married that girl you were living with?'

'Amy? No.'

'So there aren't any children?'

'No.'

'That's a pity. There are tax breaks if you have a family.'

'At this exact moment, tax is the last thing I'm worrying about.'

'You won't be saying that a year from now.'

They talked for a few more minutes. Nick needed time to think and talk, a necessary part of the process of adjustment going on in his head. By the time they hung up, John Wellesley was formally acting for him. Wellesley said he expected that negotiations with GunHo would take about a week to complete, but that he should be able to obtain an upfront payment more or less straight away.

'By the way, I shall have to charge you for this phone call,' Wellesley said.

'How much?'

Wellesley told him, laughing.

'That's an outrage!' Nick said.

'Yes, isn't it? But in the time we've been talking you've made approximately fifty times as much as that in interest. You've become my cash cow, Nick. You can't blame me for taking advantage of you.'

Reeling slightly from the shock of it all, Nick went downstairs, knowing that he must talk to Amy as soon as possible. She was still nowhere to be found, so he assumed she must have gone into the town on an errand.

He sat in the bar, the empty whisky glass on the counter in front of him. The temptation to have another drink swept over him, but he resisted it. To put space between him and the temptation, he left the bar again and went to see if he could find Amy. She had become the priority. Nothing more could be thought about, dreamed about, planned for, without her. Suddenly, everything had changed.

He met her coming into the hotel through the door at the rear. She was flushed and hectic, and she was holding a draft contract that looked identical to his.

Amy left the hotel for the rest of the day. After she had gone, Nick found her contract lying on the chair in the bedroom where she usually placed her clothes overnight. He phoned Jack Masters and asked him if he would come in and serve behind the bar that evening, and then he went through to the dining room to prepare for the guests' dinners. They were all there, sitting, as usual, at two tables at opposite ends of the room. Teresa Simons sat with her back to the other four. Nick wondered if Acie Jensen would mention the contract to him, but she said nothing.

Nick cooked the meals as quickly as he could, thinking, The

second thing I'm going to do is sell the hotel, but before that the first thing I'm going to do is employ a chef.

There was still no sign of Amy, and by the time he and Jack closed the bar at the end of the evening Nick had convinced himself that she had gone for good. He stayed up until after one o'clock, still restless, wide awake and possessed by the circling thoughts about the prospect of imminent wealth. It was the most distracting thing that had happened to him in his life, even including those terrible hours after the Grove massacre.

Amy finally returned. She came quietly up the stairs, saw him lying awake in bed, and went through to the bathroom. He waited while she showered, wondering if this would be the last night they would have together, ever.

She said nothing, but climbed in beside him, snuggled up as affectionately as always, and soon they were making love. It was not the wildest, most exhilarating session they had ever had, and afterwards Nick was preoccupied and sad.

Amy said, 'You've always wanted to get out of this place. Is that what you're going to do now?'

'Why should I?' he said, prevaricating.

'You've got the money, or you will have. There's nothing to stop you any more. Here's your chance.'

'I haven't decided yet.'

'That means you're probably going to, but don't want to say.' She moved around restlessly in the bed, throwing back the covers, sitting up. He could see her body in the darkness, outlined against night light from the uncurtained window. He sat up too, and then could see the high curve of the top of the satellite dish on the van. 'Well, I've been making plans of my own for weeks. I want out, Nick, I never want to see Bulverton again, as long as I live.'

'All right. That's more or less how I feel.'

'I was going to leave you,' she said. 'As soon as I could get away. I've never felt so trapped in all my life. You and Jase, the hotel, all that. But this . . . everything's changed. It's not the money. It's what the money will let us do. No pressure, no worries about how to make a living. I know money isn't the answer to everything, but it does give us a way out of this. Couldn't you come with me? If you don't want to make any promises now, that's OK, but let's do whatever we have to do with those people, then get out of town.'

'Did you say you want me with you?' Nick said, amazed. 'Did I hear right?'

'Yes.'

He laughed. 'Say "please".'

'Yes please, Nick. But what about you? Don't you want to go off on your own?'

'Oh no,' he said, meaning it as never before. 'Not now.'

In the morning, after a sleepless night of plans, decisions, fantasies expressed aloud, they went downstairs to prepare the breakfasts for their guests.

Nick said, 'I never want to do hotel work ever again. Of all the underpaid, unappreciated, unsocial, unrewarding jobs . . .'

'Do you realize,' Amy said, as she cleaned out the coffee percolator, and took from the fridge the low-caffeine, low-sodium, high-zinc, economically sustainable non-exploitative coffee grounds they had expensively obtained from an independent shipper in West London, 'do you realize that this might be the last time in your life you will have to do this?'

'Nothing ever changes that quickly,' he said.

'Remind me you said that in three hours' time,' she said. 'At nine o'clock.'

'What's going to happen at nine o'clock?'

'Something I spent all day yesterday setting up for you.'

'What is it?'

'Wait.'

Half an hour later, with the guests' breakfast preparations complete, they sat together in the kitchen and drank some of their own instant coffee from the jar: high in caffeine, high, probably, in sodium, and zinc content unknown.

Amy said, 'We shouldn't trust these people an inch. You should get yourself a lawyer.'

'I already have,' said Nick. 'So should you.'

'That's something else I did yesterday.'

Chapter 27

Teresa was starting to feel self-conscious whenever she went to the ExEx building; she had become a familiar figure to the staff. She was not used to that. She had been trained to be unobtrusive, to function but to stay low. The knowledge that she lay unconscious in the tiny cubicle, while she roamed the inner worlds of ExEx, made her feel more vulnerable than anything else in her adult life. Perhaps it was this, by reversal, that made her feel so at home exploring the actual scenarios. She was the secret intrusive presence in these fragments of drama, the undetected mind, the will that could be exerted to override the programming and yet remain undetected.

She was learning how to push at the limits of the scenarios. There was a freedom involved. At first it had seemed to be one of landscape: distant mountains, roads leading away, endless vistas and promises of an ever-unfolding terrain. She had tested the limits of landscape, though, with results that were usually disappointing, and at best only ambiguous.

At last she was realizing there were other landscapes, other highways, the inner world of the consciousness, the one she touched directly the moment she entered a scenario.

This was a terrain that could be explored, this was a landscape that had only tenuous limits. She remembered the way she had felt herself become Elsa Durdle, and liked doing so; how even without speaking his language she had managed to influence Gendarme Montaigne's movements; even further back, the old FBI training scenarios, when she briefly influenced events, or failed in trying.

Two days after her first visit to the cowgirl skin-flick scenario Teresa again exercised the privacy option, and returned to the makeshift film set.

*

Luke, the actor in the false whiskers, was waiting on the set beside her, reading the sports page of the tabloid newspaper. In Shandy's guileless persona Teresa tried starting a conversation with him, hoping to move the scenario in a different direction, but nothing she could do or say would divert him from his newspaper until they began filming.

When Willem, the magnificently endowed young Dutchman who played the cowboy, came leaping in on cue to throw a false blow at Luke's jaw, Shandy ducked away from him and deliberately went after Luke. But Luke had become inert again, simply lying in the wreckage of the prop furniture he had fallen against.

While the director yelled at her in fury to get back to the action, Teresa withdrew from Shandy, and, with a quick incantation of the LIVER mnemonic, she aborted the scenario.

* * *   **You have been flying SENSH Y'ALL**   * * *
* * *   **Fantasys from the Old West**   * * *
* * * **Copyroody everywhere – doan even THINK about it!!** * * *

The moronic music jangled at her again, seeming interminable.

It was the next day. She returned to being a cowgirl.

This time, Teresa waited passively at the back of Shandy's mind, while the young woman went with remarkably spontaneous excitement through the explicit but now predictable motions of making the video.

When the cameras had stopped, and Shandy and Willem were collecting the various pieces of their discarded costumes, Teresa deliberately moved forward in Shandy's consciousness. She spoke to Willem, and tried setting up a date with him. Willem spoke only a little English, but Teresa/Shandy pestered him until he agreed to meet her outside for a drink.

Shandy walked naked towards the shower cubicle in the corridor behind the set, clutching the tiny costume against herself. Teresa loved the way the young woman's body felt from inside: she seemed to glow with healthy relish from the series of convulsing orgasms she had gone through, and she walked with an easy grace. A couple of the men who worked behind the cameras grinned at her as she went by.

Once she was inside the shower cubicle with the door closed, her demeanour changed. She spat dramatically on the floor of the shower, growling in her throat, clearing herself out. She put her lips to the cold-water tap, drank a quantity of the water, then swilled some of it around her mouth. She gargled three or four times. When she was showering she washed herself thoroughly, using soapy fingers to clean the parts of her body Willem had penetrated, and lathering herself energetically where he had jetted his seed on to her skin.

* * * SENSH * * *

She took her street clothes from a locker outside the shower, and dressed quickly. She put on light make-up: a little eye-liner, a touch of blush, no lipstick. After a final look in a mirror she went to meet Willem.

Outside, Teresa found they were in London. She was immediately struck by the details: especially the noise, the crowds, the traffic, the red buses, the advertising signs, the dismal weather, the overall sense of minutiae beyond the strictly essential.

Willem led her to a pub in nearby Rupert Street, and sat by himself at an unoccupied table while she went to the bar to order drinks. He had asked for a Dutch imported beer called Oranjeboom, which for some reason made Shandy laugh. She softly hummed a jingle while she waited to be served. The barman knew her and obviously liked her, and between serving other customers chatted to her about someone they both knew; Shandy apparently had a number of jobs around the West End, working for clubs and escort agencies, and in hotels.

Teresa, fascinated by this glimpse into the young woman's life, lost interest in Willem and listened instead to Shandy talking about the people who owed her money, the man (boyfriend? pimp?) who seemed to control her, the hardships she sometimes had to endure, the late nights, the harassment she received from the police, and most of all the problem of her elderly mother, who lived in the Midlands. Her mother was having trouble with a disability allowance that was being reduced by some interpretation of the rules, and which might mean she would have to move to London to live with her daughter. Shandy's apartment wasn't big enough for two, so she would have to move.

* * * SENSH * * *

Teresa thought, This is real! This is Shandy's life! I could stay here in her mind, follow her around, see how she lives, what she eats, where she sleeps.

She glanced back at Willem, who was still sitting at the table, waiting for her to return with the drinks, apparently stranded by her lack of interest in him.

The barman slipped Shandy a scrap of paper with a phone number written on it, and she took out her bag, found a diary and placed the piece of paper between its pages. Just as Shandy was about to return the diary to her bag, Teresa decided to have a look at it, and laid it on the counter. She flipped through the pages.

Shandy's real name was Jennifer Rosemary Tayler, Teresa discovered from the first page, where the young woman had filled in her personal details in disarmingly childish handwriting. She had an apartment in London NW10. The entries in the diary – the year was 1990, which Teresa wouldn't have known otherwise – were mostly phone numbers and amounts of money; on a whim, Teresa led Shandy across to the call box on the wall by the entrance to the toilets, and dialled one of the numbers.

* * * SENSH * * *

A man with a foreign accent answered, and Shandy said, reasserting herself, 'Is that Hossein? Hi, it's Shan . . . Listen, I'm at the Plume of Feathers in Rupert Street. Know where I mean? I wondered if you'd got anything for me?' A long silence followed, before Hossein said, 'You call me back at ten. I work something out.' Shandy said, 'OK,' and hung up. She went back to the counter, and wrote the time in her diary.

Willem was still at the table, patiently waiting. Teresa decided to leave him there, and left the pub. She walked back down Rupert Street to where it joined Coventry Street.

To one side was an open space bounded by large buildings, full of trees and pedestrians: Leicester Square, she dredged up from Shandy's mind. In the other direction was Piccadilly Circus, which Teresa had not realized was so close. With all the curiosity of a tourist Teresa walked down that way, gawping at the sights. She stared at the statue of Eros for a few moments, then decided she would like to see where Shandy lived, so she walked across to the nearest entrance to the Underground station. She ran down the stairs, Shandy's steel-tipped stiletto heels clattering on the metal steps. At the bottom of the stairs was a brick wall. Shandy stared at it for a moment, then returned to street level.

Another entrance to the station was on the corner of Lower Regent Street and Piccadilly, so Shandy negotiated the crossing through the traffic, and tripped quickly down the steps. Another brick wall. Determined not to be beaten by this Teresa led the way back to the pub, where Willem was still waiting for her.

* * * SENSH * * *

She sat down next to him.

'Tell me where you come from, Willem,' she said. 'How do you live? What is the name of the place where you were born?'

'Ah,' he said, staring with habitual eyes at her cleavage. 'I from Amstelveen, which is a little way from Amsterdam to the south, on the polder. You know polder? I have two sister, who are both more old as me. My mother and father—'

'Excuse me, honey,' said Shandy. 'I got to go.'

She left him there again, and returned to the street.

London spread around her, noisy and crowded. How did they do this? Teresa wondered. We were making a lousy skin-flick, budget of zilch, and I walk through a door and out here is a whole imagined virtual city of millions of people, crammed with things going on and places to go.

No Underground station, though. Maybe they didn't get around to programming that.

* * * SENSH * * *

As she stood there a double-decker bus roared by, heading for Kilburn. It said so on the front: Kilburn High Road. Teresa thought, I could get on that bus, see what happens in Kilburn. People who have lives, share apartments, go bankrupt, fall in love, travel abroad, hold down jobs, get thrown into jail, make skin-flicks. Is this scenario unlimited? From Kilburn, another bus-ride to the edge of London, and from there into the country? What after that? Another blank wall at the edge of reality? Or the rest of England, out into Europe, then the world? The awareness of unlimited space dizzied her.

She caught the next bus that came along (it said on the front it was going to Edgware), but for an hour it drove around the West End, repeatedly passing the same buildings and stopping in the same places.

Willem was still waiting in the pub when she went back.

'Did I get that drink for you?' Shandy said.

'No, but is OK. I wait OK.'

She left Willem again, and returned to the street: the weather was as damp and cool as before, and the crowds continued to press past her. Shandy had a way of walking that made her skirt tighten against her thighs with every step. Admiring male glances were flashed at her from many quarters.

* * * SENSH * * *

'Doesn't that drive you crazy, Shan?' Teresa said on an impulse, thinking inwardly to her own mind.

'Doesn't what drive me crazy?' Shandy replied, calmly. 'The guys staring at my tits? That's my job, love. One of them's always the next meal ticket.'

'Not that. The goddamn computer logo that appears every minute or two. And the electronic music that goes with it!'

'You get used to it.' Shandy mentally played the jingle at her.

'Where's it coming from?'

'I think it's Vic. He's like that.'

'Who's Vic?' said Teresa. 'Is that the director? Mister Bad Breath and Zero Personality?'

'No, *Vic*! You know Vic, don't you? He's the mate of Luke's who does the script, right? Luke's the one who—'

'I know Luke. Carry on about Vic. I'm interested.'

'Vic does the script. He's one of those computer geeks with a weirdo sense of humour. Thinks everything he does is funny. That's how Luke gets in, you see. He likes being in the movies, but he isn't, you know, like Willem. Willie with the big willie.'

'I know who you mean.'

* * * SENSH * * *

'Course you do. Well, Luke likes a bit of the physical stuff with me, and I never mind, so Vic writes him in before the action starts. Always a small part, a warm-up for the punters. Luke's been in all the videos I've done for Vic, and he enjoys a good old grope, but he can't, you know, get it up enough. He's a mate of mine, really. We always have a bit of a laugh about it. You've got an American accent. Is that where you're from?'

'Yes,' said Teresa.

'So's Vic. I don't know what he's doing in England, but he's into computers and that.'

'So how does he do all this?'

'Do all what?'

Teresa gestured with Shandy's hand.

'London! All these people! The noise, the rain, the crowds.'

'I dunno. You'd have to ask him. You can get cities for computers now, can't you?'

'Cities? What do you mean, you get them for computers?'

* * * SENSH * * *

'On disk, I think. Or you can download them, if you know how to do it. You get the whole thing, and just use it. Add it on, somehow. I mean, Vic's got all sorts of places he uses as locations. He's into cowboys and that, and so a lot of the programs he does take place out there in the West. You know that set we were just filming in? Well, if you go out the other way, the door at the back, it isn't London at all! It's somewhere in America . . . you know, you've seen it on the movies. Where they filmed all those westerns. A lot of desert, and all them rocky mountains with flat tops sticking straight up.'

'Not Monument Valley?'

'Yeah, that's it!' said Shandy. 'Arizona, someplace. He's barmy, is Vic. He just bolts on bits of software as he feels like it. Like, there's one he's got which is Finland. I mean, the whole of Finland! I play an air hostess on an aircraft, and me and the guy get down to it in a row of seats. Not very comfortable, but we put the arm-rests up. Anyway, if you look out of the window there's hundreds of miles of trees and lakes. You can make the plane go anywhere you like, but it's always flying over Finland. Can't see the point, myself, because the people who come in, they just want to join in with the shagging, and they're not interested in where we're doing it, right? But Vic must have bootlegged the software from somewhere, so that's what he uses. There's another one he's got, in—'

* * * SENSH * * *

'Shandy, do you mind if we go somewhere to talk?' They had been walking along Coventry Street, weaving their way through the crowds, but even in this state of acknowledged unreality, Teresa was acutely conscious of the way she must appear to be talking to herself. 'Could we go to your apartment?'

'No, can't do that.' Teresa felt an awkward resistance rising in the young woman's mind. 'I'm only supposed to be in the West End, and that.'

'But you must go home sometimes.'

'Yeah.'

'Then can't we go now?'

'No. I don't think so.'

Shandy started fretting with the strap of her shoulder-bag.

Teresa realized that there must be a limiting wall in Shandy's mind, like one at the bottom of a flight of steps that should lead to the Underground.

'Is there somewhere else we could go?'

'No, we have to stay around here. Or we could go back to where we were filming. Would you like to go back to the studio and see Monument Valley? I'll take you for a drive. That's another of my jobs. We go to some great places—'

* * * SENSH * * *

'Where's the studio from here?'

'Back there.' Shandy indicated a narrow sidestreet called Shaver's Place.

'And that's all there is?' Teresa asked.

'Well . . . there's the whole of London! You can do a lot in London. I could take you to the clubs I know. I do a live show in one of them. You could help me out in that, now you know what to do. One of the guys is a bit . . . you know, but the other's a real good mate of mine. He's better at it than Willem, not as big, but he really knows how to get me going! And there's another girl, Janey. You'd like Janey. I do a lesbian act with her. She went to America last year on her holiday, and told me all about it.'

'No, I don't think so.'

Teresa retreated from the forefront of Shandy's mind, allowing the young woman to assert her own life, so to speak. Shandy promptly changed direction, and walked back towards the pub where they had left Willem. She said hello to several men they passed in the street. She seemed to know everyone around here.

Teresa decided to retreat again, further, abort the scenario at last, but before she did so she reached up awkwardly and felt the back of Shandy's neck. As she expected, there was no ExEx valve in place.

This was 1990. ExEx hadn't been available. There was only software set in that period. Teresa recalled the LIVER mnemonic.

* * *   **You have been flying SENSH Y'ALL**   * * *
* * *   **Fanta—**

She snapped it off before she had to listen to the music again.

Later, as she checked out at the ExEx reception desk, Teresa was presented with a charge to her credit card that was so huge it momentarily dazed her. She was about to protest, when she noticed that her real-time usage had been carefully logged. She glanced at the clock on the wall. She had spent nearly the whole day in virtual reality, and as a result had been charged for six and a half hours of premium time. Night had fallen while she was there.

Teresa signed, thinking of the slug of insurance money she had received after Andy's death, which had remained more or less untouched until her trip to Britain. Her phone calls to the credit-card hotlines in the US had sorted out her billing problems, and increased the credit limit at the same time, but even so she made a mental resolve to use her ExEx time more carefully.

Walking back down through Bulverton's rows of postwar council-built houses, Teresa kept her gaze low, avoiding the dreary sights around her. The dazzle of ExEx was her preferred reality.

She was remembering the way she had experienced Shandy's walk, with her tiny leather mini-skirt constraining her thighs and her stiletto heels clacking dismissively on the paving. Teresa put her hands in her coat pocket, and dragged the garment round her, tightening it in front of her legs to make a tiny reminder of how it had felt to wear that skirt.

She thought about being young and pretty again, of having the sort of legs men admired in the street, the kind of high, prominent breasts that looked good no matter what she wore, and for which wearing a bra was an option. She relished the memory of how Shandy's body had felt from the inside: supple and agile and much used to pleasure. She even loved Shandy's attitude to everyone around her; it was years since she had felt free not to care what other people thought.

In the cold winter's evening, with the sea wind moist in her face and the lights of the depressing housing estate glinting around her, Teresa could not help fantasizing about lovemaking. She imagined she was in a large airliner, flying slow and low, the engines a subdued roar. She would stretch with her lover across the cushions of a row of seats, the armrests raised erect to make room; she would be sating her body, naked and languorous, dreaming of buttes in Arizona, while below her the unending lakes and forests of Finland would be slipping deliriously by.

CHAPTER 28

Teresa was in a car, parked on the seafront at Bulverton. Brilliant sunlight poured in on her from the direction of the sea. She was tightening the hot-wired connection she had made earlier beneath the dash, stretching forward with her hands, her cheek pressed against the boss of the steering wheel.

A figure stopped beside the car, shading the flood of sunlight. Without looking up at him Teresa straightened and wound down the window.

'You Gerry?' the man said.

'Yeah.'

The man outside pushed his hand through, palm up. Teresa laid six ten-pound notes on the hand, and watched as he crumpled them up and withdrew. Moments later, a small plastic bag was thrown in; it flew past her face, bounced on the passenger seat beside her and ended up on the floor.

'Fuck you,' she said automatically, and reached over to pick up the bag. The man was already moving quickly away, weaving through the cars parked along the front. He was tall and thin, and his long black hair was tied back in a pony-tail. He wore a dirty pale-brown jacket and faded jeans. He hurried across the main road without looking back, then disappeared down a side-street.

Teresa weighed the bag in her hand; it felt about right, but she had probably been undersold, as always. She could see the white powder through the polythene, and it ground with the right feeling when she squeezed it lightly between her fingers. She slipped the bag into her jacket pocket.

As she drove away she saw Fraser Johnson hanging around outside the amusements arcade. He waved to her urgently, but she drove on. She owed Fraser a bit of cash, not a lot, but because of the deal she had just done she wasn't going to be able to settle up with him for a while. Anyway, she would probably see him that evening, and by then things would be different.

She drove towards home, thinking about Debra, the titless bitch, the bleeding bitch with the spotty fucking face, and that lad called Mark who'd turned up with her from somewhere and crashed at her place the night before. In fact, all of them had been at her place overnight, because Mark's mates came along too. They'd gone through her stuff, looking at her lists, asking her stupid bloody questions about what she wrote down.

Because of this she was ready for more aggravation from them, but halfway up the long hill of Hyde Avenue the engine coughed and she pulled over to the side. She left the car where it stopped, the driver's door open. It was a pile of crap, anyway. It took her ten minutes to walk up to the house where she was staying, the one the Housing Benefit woman had found her a couple of weeks back. The lads had gone. She looked for food, but if there had been any they had stolen it. She did a line of the coke, then put away the rest for later.

She walked round the damaged interior of the house, angry with everything and everyone. Someone had had a piss on her stuff. Why did people always do this to her? There was another broken window downstairs; it must have happened during the night, because the bits of broken glass were still lying around on the floorboards. There was one of the lads, a kid from Eastbourne called Darren, who'd really wound her up over that window. She couldn't remember why, now. Probably something to do with Debra, because he was the one who'd run off with her that morning, wasn't it? She couldn't remember exactly. Her finger-nails curled into the palms of her hands, and she wished she'd smacked him in the fucking face, like he deserved.

Outside, she saw another mate of hers, Steve Ripon, driving down towards the front, and she grabbed a ride with him. Steve dropped her outside the Bulver Arms, saying he might call in for a pint later. She didn't want to know. Steve usually got on her nerves. She saw a couple of the lads in the bar, playing pool, so she hung around with them for a while, hoping for a game. They pretended they hadn't seen her, and made jokes about her as if she wasn't there, the sort she'd heard before. Fuckers. One of them said he'd buy her a pint but in the end didn't, and made the others laugh at her again, and she had to buy her own. She was hungry, but didn't fancy any of the food. Couldn't afford it.

'I'm going home,' she said, but they didn't seem to hear.

She set off in the direction of Hastings, but it meant walking along the seafront and there was no shade from the sun. She was already feeling light in the head, and the sun only made it worse. She turned off the coast road at the first big junction, and started walking up Battle Road.

Steve Ripon drove past again, and slowed down. She didn't want another lift from him, so she pretended not to notice.

Through the driver's window, Steve shouted, 'Oi, Gerry! That Debra of yours told Darren all about you.'

'Piss off, Steve!' she yelled back.

'She reckons you can't get it up. That right?'

'Piss off,' she said again, but under her breath. She cut away down an alley, where Steve couldn't follow. After a hundred yards she came out in Fearley Road, which she knew well. A mate of hers had turned over the off-licence there a couple of years ago, and got done with community service. She was getting fed up with all this walking about and feeling dizzy, so now she was keeping a sharp eye open for something she could drive away in.

On an impulse she went up to the car park built on the flat roof of the AllNights Market, and started trying the car doors. She wanted a car that was fairly new, not an old heap, but most of the really new cars were difficult to hot-wire, unless you knew what you were doing. The last car she was going to try before giving up turned out to be the easiest one to take: a dark-red J-reg Austin Montego. There was a wallet in the glove compartment (with forty quid and a Barclaycard), a stereo system and a full tank of petrol. Two minutes later she was driving up Battle Road with music playing, heading back to the house.

Debra came out of the house as she parked. Teresa leapt out of the Montego and broke into a run as soon as she saw her, but Debra dodged away. She was carrying an armful of her clothes, and a Sainsbury's plastic bag stuffed with something.

'Here, I want you!' Teresa shouted.

'You fucking leave me alone, you fucking weirdo!' Debra yelled back.

'Get in the fucking car!'

'I've had enough of all that! Fuck off, Gerry!'

She tore away down the hill, dropping garments and stumbling on the uneven ground.

'I'll fucking get you!'

Teresa broke off the chase, and ran into the house. Someone had been in and shat on the floor. She ran up the stairs, kicked open the door of the cupboard, and grabbed her guns and ammunition. It took her two trips to get everything outside and into the Montego, but as soon as she was ready she drove down the hill in search of Debra. The rifle was hidden in the luggage compartment at the back, but she had put the handgun on the seat beside her.

She knew where Debra would be going: her mum had a house lower down on the estate. Teresa stopped the car with two wheels up on the pavement and shoved the gun under her jacket. She ran to the door of the house, kicking and pummelling it with her fist.

'They saw you coming, they did!' said a woman, leaning over the wall from next door. 'They've done a runner! Good thing too, you little dickhead!'

Teresa was tempted to blow a sodding great hole in her face, grinning at her over the wall, but instead she whipped out her cock and tried to piss all over the door, but she had dried up. The woman yelled something, and disappeared. Teresa looked around: she knew Debra's mum's car, and like the neighbour had said it wasn't in sight.

She went back to the Montego, screeched it round in the narrow road and headed away.

She drove fast until she had crossed the Ridge and was going out into the countryside around Ninfield. The sun beat maddeningly down. A police car went past in the opposite direction, blue strobe lights flashing; Teresa instinctively hunched down in the seat a little, but they were obviously going after someone else, and neither of the two cops even glanced in her direction.

The right-hand side of the road was thickly forested: Teresa had only a dim memory of having driven along here before, but after a while she saw a sign for a Forestry Commission picnic site next to a lay-by. She was driving too fast to stop, but she went down to the next farm entrance, did a turn, and went back.

She realized that neither of the guns was loaded; bleeding right! She'd gone after Debra like that!

She skidded into the parking area in a cloud of dust, and angrily picked up the handgun. She slammed in a magazine of bullets.

A path led off through the trees, and ahead of her she glimpsed the bright colours of summer clothes.

She came into a clearing in the trees, where three long wooden tables had been set up. Huge logs lying beside them were used as seats. A young woman was sitting at one of the tables, with plastic cups and plates, scraps of food, and several toys spread all about: a ball, a train, a scribble pad, dozens of coloured bricks. The woman was laughing, and her boy was running around on the grass, pretending to do some stupid thing or other.

Teresa felt sick at the sight of them, stupid middle-class bastards with too much money and spare time. With a deliberate movement she brought the gun out from her jacket with a wide swinging motion of her hand. She had seen that in a movie somewhere. She cocked the gun. That wonderful sound of efficient machinery, ready for action. She worked the mechanism three or four more times, relishing it.

The noise had made the woman turn towards her. The fucking stupid child just kept on running about, but the woman was calling to it, holding out her arms protectively.

As Grove advanced on them, his gun levelled, Teresa thought, I can't take any more of this!

She Located, Identified . . . retreated instantly from the scenario and from the mind of Gerry Grove.

A silent darkness fell. Teresa walked home miserably to the hotel afterwards, sick at heart.

Chapter 29

Although the feeling of being conspicuous never left her, Teresa found that one advantage of her frequent visits to the ExEx building was that the staff began to take her presence for granted. They would let her use the computer terminals more or less whenever she felt like it, and they usually left her alone to browse.

The database itself was becoming increasingly interesting to her. All complex computer programs seem at first sight to be an impenetrable maze of options, assumptions and usage conventions, and the catalogue of ExEx scenarios was a gigantic example of this.

The program was always running, always on-line, and was presumably in a constant state of being updated and reprogrammed somewhere in the further reaches of the web. The amount of data it held was clearly beyond the memory capacity of any single industrial computer, and must have been stored in networked sites in different parts of the world. But however large it seemed, it was only a single, closed program. Copyright notices infested it, and warnings about restrictions on usage appeared with monotonous frequency.

Finding the information it contained, provided you had mastered the syntax of the search engine, was surprisingly fast and efficient. The result of any search – usually a single screen with the information that had been requested – appeared so quickly that it gave the illusion that what you wanted had been placed near the top of the pile so that it might be easily found.

The simplicity was deceptive, though. When Teresa set the command to browse, and merely scrolled through some of the data in sequence, the sheer scale, detail and extent of what was held in memory were a source of constant amazement to her.

Again, she sensed limitless horizons. But Teresa was starting to learn that the scenarios were not as she had thought at first.

A scenario always turned out to have a measurable edge; reality came to an end when memory ran out. No matter how well the programmer disguised it, or fudged it, you could not take a car and drive it away, out of virtuality into reality. You could fly over the whole of Finland, you could cross and re-cross, you could tour the periphery, you could circle for ever over one chosen lake or stream, or you could dart and weave with unexpected turns . . . and still Finland would calmly and interminably unfold beneath you. But it was always Finland; it was not for ever.

Where the true unlimited was to be found was, so to speak, in the headings of the scenarios, in the indexes to them. The limitless lay in hyperlinks, cross-references, hyperreality.

All scenarios ultimately touched, their edges were contiguous. You could approach the same incident from a number of different viewpoints. But the contiguity lay in the fourth dimension: you could not cross the margin from one scenario to the next, unless one was bolted on, London's West End or Arizona's Monument Valley bolted on to a film-set of a cowboy saloon, and that counted only as expansion. It made the scenario seem more complex, while in fact it only made it larger.

The real nature of contiguity lay in the adjacency of memory, hyperlinked by character or situation or point of view. Contiguity was psychological, and it was related to memory, not conscious planning.

In one scenario a character would be memoratively significant: it might be the elderly woman named Elsa Durdle who drove a Chevy with a gun in the glove compartment.

That scenario existed for a number of possible reasons. Someone involved with the William Cook case must have remembered Elsa, or had heard her story somehow, or had met and interviewed her after the incident. It could even be so remote a contact as someone who had merely read about her. Whatever the reason, there was enough of her, enough about her, to place her centre-stage in one scenario. Another person, witness to the same central event, or participant in it, might know Elsa Durdle only peripherally: she could be the unnamed driver of the car that drove past police lines, momentarily blocked a policeman's view.

Both were true accounts, both were limited by their viewpoint, yet through contiguity they tended towards a concurrence, an agreement on basic facts and images.

Placed against these two scenarios might be a third one, contiguous to either or both of them, which knew nothing at all of Elsa in person, yet admitted the presence of her car driving through, or past, or in the distance.

Next to that scenario would be another, and beyond that more. Each contiguous scenario was a step on the way towards the margins of Elsa Durdle's reality.

Here, in the on-line computer, with its endless scrolling index headings, each with its own subheadings, and each of those with further subheadings, uncountable generational levels unfolding below, and all of them cross-referenced and linked to one another, virtuality was taken towards its edge and beyond.

There was no end, only another scenario contiguous to the last.

Sitting alone in a side office, with the computer terminal to herself, with no one on the staff apparently taking any interest in what she was doing, Teresa eventually found her way to the database of Memorative Principals.

Guessing what that meant, and reading the screen menus, she entered the name 'Tayler' and the subset 'Jennifer Rosemary'. At the prompt for physical location, to narrow the search parameters, she entered 'London' and 'NW10'.

Within a few seconds an abstract of scenarios in which Shandy appeared poured across the screen.

Each scenario was identified by a title, a long code number, a synoptic description, and a tiny video icon. Noticing that there was an option to display the videos, Teresa clicked on the menu, and at once all the video icons changed into tiny frozen-frame images from the opening of each scenario.

Teresa clicked on one, and a five-second teaser extract ran in the tiny box. The image was so small it was hard to see what was going on, but it was clear that Shandy was ready for action.

The list of Shandy's scenarios was long; worryingly long, when you bore in mind the abandon with which she took part in them. Teresa moved the information to and fro, top to bottom, estimating how many Shandy scenarios there were. She roughed a guess at nearly eighty, and then she noticed that the database had a facility for counting successful finds and that the true number of Shandy scenarios presently available was eighty-four.

Each index heading carried a dozen optional hyperlinks from Shandy: to other people involved with her, to the video clips previewing her scenarios, to adjacent subjects, to library material, to biographical material, to available slots for additional or supplementary scenarios. Information about Shandy's ExEx world was exploding about her, as her contiguity was revealed.

Teresa ran a hyperlink search on the list, using the name 'Willem', and immediately discovered that Shandy and Willem had appeared in fourteen scenarios together, including the one called *Brawl in Wild West saloon – for adults XXX.*

She learnt from this listing that Willem's real name was actually not Willem but Erik. He was Dutch, though, and he had, as he had told her, been born in the small town of Amstelveen.

Willem's own listing as a memorative principal, which Teresa accessed next, was even more alarming than Shandy's: in addition to the fourteen scenarios he had made with her, he had been involved in a further ninety-seven. Teresa noticed that many of these skin-flicks (as she assumed they were) had been made with a young woman named Joyhanne, herself a memorative principal.

Teresa ran a search on Joyhanne. She had been born in The Hague, worked for a while as a telephonist (hyperlink to Holland Telecom), but appeared to have been making videos since the age of fourteen. Attached to Joyhanne's name was another long abstract of porno scenarios (she assumed from their titles). Dozens more options scattered in all directions from Joyhanne's indexed activities: virtuality was spreading out and away, the known limits of events accelerating to the horizon in every direction.

For instance, Joyhanne had another regular co-star; this man, a German, had made more than fifty porno (Teresa assumed) videos, but in addition he had made a couple of appearances in real films, both of which were mentioned in reference books (three hundred and fifteen hyperlinks); the author of one of the film books worked in the Humanities Department of the University of Göttingen, which offered more than two hundred and fifty educational scenarios on developmental studies; one of these, which Teresa chose at random, dealt with soft-drug culture in the USA, 1968–75; this single scenario had more than fifteen hundred hyperlinks to other scenarios . . .

It was impossible to keep a mental hold on everything.

Teresa paused, dizzied by the endless choices. She was side-tracking, and getting away from what she had set out to do.

She returned through the hierarchy to Shandy's main listing, and used the program's memo feature to store three coded references, selected more or less at random. One day she might like to visit Shandy at work again: two of the titles she chose were *Heat and Dust in the Arizona Desert* and *Open Top – X-Rated Drive Through Monument Valley*.

Now Teresa selected the hyperlink option, and from this picked out **Remote Link**.

From **Remote Link** came yet more new options: **Copy, Date, Edit, Gender, Motive, Name, Place, Significant Objects, Weapon**, and many others. Each of these had sub-options: Teresa clicked on **Place**, and saw a huge list of subsidiary choices: **Continent, Country, State, County, City, Street, Building, Room**, was just one sequence.

Again feeling sidetracked, she went back to the entry point of the hyperlink, and picked out **Name**. At the prompt she typed 'Elsa Jane Durdle', added 'San Diego' as a locater, and clicked on it.

Please Wait.

Teresa was so used by now to the apparently instant response of the program that the appearance of that message made her feel almost smug. Her search criteria were complex enough to slow the computer perceptibly.

Not long later, in fact in under a minute, the screen cleared and a message appeared:

248 hyperlink(s) connect 'Jennifer Rosemary Tayler' to 'Elsa Jane Durdle'. Display? Yes/No.

Teresa clicked on **Yes**, and almost at once a long list of the codes of contiguous scenarios began to scroll quickly down the screen. Each had its tiny still video image attached to it. The first scenario took place in part of a mocked-up saloon in an improvised film studio in 1990 in the West End of London, and the last on a hot windy day in San Diego in 1950. Events connected them.

Two hundred and forty-eight scenarios were linked in collective memory. The realities were contiguous; there was no edge.

The road of extreme virtuality ran on beyond the horizon, as far as the mountains, through the desert, across the seas, on and on for ever.

She downloaded the codes of the two hundred and forty-eight contiguous scenarios, and waited a few seconds while the printer turned them out. One day, when she had time and credit enough, she might start exploring the links that were said to exist between Elsa and Shandy.

Teresa next entered the name 'Teresa Ann Simons' as a memorative principal, added 'Woodbridge' and 'Bulverton' as defining physical locations, and waited to see what would happen.

The computer did not pause. With almost dismissive instantaneity, a screen appeared with her name at the top. A single scenario was noted below. There were no hyperlinks, no connections to the rest of virtuality.

Surprised at this result, and actually rather disappointed, Teresa clicked on the video icon.

Her curiosity was satisfied and dampened all at once: such as it was, her only scenario in the whole of ExEx was of the day she had first visited this range, and spent an hour or so on target practice with a handgun.

She squinted at the allocated few seconds' preview of herself, noticing mostly the fact that from the rear view her backside looked considerably larger than she had realized. When asked if she wanted access to the entire video, or to enter the scenario itself, she declined.

With her own information still on the screen, Teresa tried to establish hyperlinks first with Elsa Durdle, then with Shandy, but at both attempts the program curtly informed her:

No hyperlinks established from this site.

CHAPTER 30

Teresa travelled up to London by train. She wanted to be a tourist, take a few photographs and buy some presents to take home to her friends. She knew her visit to England was coming to an end. One day soon she would have to return to her job; although her section chief had granted her 'extended' compassionate leave, with no firm date by which she had to report back, she knew that the Bureau did not allow indefinite leave to anyone. Her time was almost up.

The train took her to Charing Cross Station in the heart of London. From there it was a short walk to Trafalgar Square, Whitehall, the Houses of Parliament and, eventually, Buckingham Palace. After an hour or two of dutiful trudging around, Teresa had had enough of playing tourist. She took a taxi to Piccadilly Circus, and went in search of Shandy.

She walked along Coventry Street as far as the point where it became a pedestrian precinct, then walked back again on the other side of the road. While it remained recognizably the same street, many of the details seemed to have changed. Could this be explained by the fact that Shandy's scenario was set back in 1990, and there had been rebuilding since? Or by the fact that what she had seen was simply a computer emulation of the real place, full of approximations? She wished she had been able to take more notice of her surroundings while there, but as so often happened while inside a scenario, the sheer sensory impact had been extremely distracting.

She found Shaver's Place, a short, narrow alleyway leading off to the south, but there was nowhere along it that looked as if it could be used as a studio for making skin-flicks. On the other side of the road, Rupert Street led north towards Shaftesbury Avenue. Halfway along Rupert Street on one side there was, exactly as she recalled, a pub called the Plume of Feathers. Teresa walked in, but as soon as she was inside she knew it was not the same place. Everything about it was different. She looked all around, but there was no one there who looked remotely like Shandy, or even what Shandy might look like after the passage of a few years.

She retraced her steps, remembering the day she had walked along this street, or one like it, feeling the sexy tightness of Shandy's thigh-constricting mini-skirt, talking about Arizona and Finland. They had left Willem waiting in the pub, and for a while walked to and fro along Coventry Street. Teresa walked as far as the statue of Eros, then went down the steps of one of the station entrances and found that where the virtual London had ended in a brick wall was now the bustling concourse of a busy Underground station.

She returned to street level, then went back to Rupert Street. Suppressing the temptation to look inside the Plume of Feathers once again, Teresa walked up to the intersection with Shaftesbury Avenue and crossed over, following Rupert Street into Soho.

The streets here were much narrower. After a few hundred yards she noticed a doorway ornamented on each side by tall illuminated pink plastic panels, obviously portable, into each of which was set a large photograph of several naked and near-naked women. A man, whose face was masked by a clumsy virtual-reality headset, was drawn groping lasciviously towards them. A hand-lettered sign said: *Extreme Thrills – Imported – Downstairs NOW – ADULTS ONLY!*

A doorman stood just inside the entrance: he was a youth with short spiky hair and tattooed tears angling down from the corner of one eye, and was incongruously wearing a dark suit with collar and tie.

Teresa, realizing that this place was selling a version of ExEx, was brought up short by a shocking thought. She knew what was available in ExEx, so it was likely that at least a few of Shandy's scenarios would be available somewhere in this dive . . . maybe they even had the cowgirl scenario where Teresa had first found her.

Teresa's thoughts instantly raced off towards the edge of reality: she imagined herself venturing into the cellar below this unprepossessing doorway, paying over a sum of money to the youth, entering the scenario in which Shandy played a cowgirl who was enthusiastically screwing a Dutch-accented cowboy, then afterwards leaving again with Shandy, occupying her body and mind, feeling the sexy constraints of her don't-care clothes, heading out of the studio into these streets around Piccadilly and Leicester Square, then walking north across Shaftesbury Avenue to this spot, to the entrance to this ExEx club, where she and Shandy would venture inside, enter the extremes of unreality . . .

'What you want, lady? You want inside?'

'No,' said Teresa, startled by his sudden voice.

'Good prices for ladies. Big discount. Come, I show you.'

'No . . . I don't want in. Did you ever hear of a girl called Shandy?'

For a moment the youth looked disconcerted, a look that was exaggerated by the needle-drawn tears, but then he reached into the back pocket of his pants and produced a small wad of business cards.

'Yeah, Shandy. She here. You want Shandy, you have her OK. We got plenty Shandy. What you want, you like girl-girl with Shandy, or you wanna watch?'

'Do you know who I mean?' Teresa said. 'Her real name's Jennifer. She works around here, in joints like this.'

'Yeah, yeah.' He held the business cards in surprisingly long and delicate fingers, and with a clean fingernail peeled back the top one. Teresa thought he was about to pass the card to her, with no doubt detailed but unwanted information inscribed, but he gripped it lightly between his thumb and forefinger and scraped at the gap between two of his yellowed front teeth. 'Shandy. She give big discount for girl-girl. We have plenty Shandy.'

'OK, I get the picture.'

Teresa turned away, irritated with herself for letting the boy drag her into the exchange, and still preoccupied by what she had been thinking about when he spoke to her.

What *would* happen? Inside a scenario, suppose she found a GunHo facility or a dive bar or somewhere else with ExEx equipment, then used it to enter a second scenario?

What then of virtuality? Would the realities be no longer contiguous, but intersecting?

'Hey, lady!'

She continued walking away from him.

'Lady!' The young man had left his pitch in the doorway, and he laid a hand on her arm.

She snatched it away from him.

'Quit that!' she said loudly. 'I'm not interested!'

'You lady, you one of us? You Shandy?'

His tone was no longer flat and automated, the voice of the shill. An earnestness gripped him. He was pointing at her neck. Teresa saw how young he was, hardly more than in his middle teens. He turned his head away, and laid a finger against the base of his own neck.

There was a nanochip valve embedded there. It was obvious what it was, but it was unlike any other Teresa had seen. It was larger than hers, and was made of bright purple plastic: it was set in a mount made of some silvery material, probably plastic again but glossed up brilliantly. The valve looked like a cheap stone in a gaudy setting.

Teresa had always been self-conscious about her embedded valve, thinking that to anyone who didn't know what it was it must look like something left over from an operation. She usually wore a high collar or scarf in an attempt to conceal it. By contrast, the youth's nanochip valve was almost flagrantly exposed, a startling flash of colour on the back of his neck, like body-piercing, a fashion statement, a tribal declaration.

'You know ExEx, lady? You real thing! Big, big discount for real ExEx! We find you Shandy, you bet!'

'No,' she said yet again, but less assertively than before. 'Look, I know what ExEx is. I was just surprised to find it. Open to the public.'

'Members only. You join! You no come in? Special deal before evenings.'

Realizing she was wasting her time, and had been doing so from the first exchange of words, Teresa backed away. The youth tried again to lure her inside, but she turned her back on him and strode off in what she hoped looked like a determined way. She soon reached the junction with Shaftesbury Avenue, and had to wait for a break in the traffic before she could cross. She glanced back: there was no sign of the young man.

She walked to Charing Cross Road, and spent nearly an hour

trying to distract herself in one of the big bookstores; after this she returned to the Leicester Square area and went to see a movie. She caught the last train back to Bulverton with minutes to spare; she had not looked at the timetable in advance, and discovered she was lucky to have caught it. An hour later, as the train left Tunbridge Wells and moved into the almost unbroken darkness of the Sussex countryside, Teresa, alone in the carriage, closed her eyes and tried to doze. She was body-tired from all the walking she had done in London, but stimulated and alive mentally.

She had barely been able to keep her mind on the film, in spite of the intrusively loud music and explosive special effects. Something had unexpectedly become clear to her. At the beginning of the show, as she sat in the auditorium waiting for the lights to go down, she had remembered the conversation in the hotel corridor with Ken Mitchell, and the seemingly impenetrable objections he had raised to her presence in the hotel.

His talk of linear coherence and iterative purity had sounded at the time like code-babble to her, the natural language of the computer geek. But the Shandy scenario had undermined everything. That thought she had had, outside the ExEx dive, about the way reality might be made to intersect, made her think she understood at last what Mitchell had been driving at.

An ExEx scenario already represented a sort of intersection. It stood at the interface between human variables and digital logic.

The programmers took people's memories of certain events, their feelings about the events, the stories they told about them afterwards, the imagination surrounding them, and even their guesses at what the events had actually been, they took all of these and coded them into a form of objectified experience, and made them seem real, or virtually so. Thus were the scenarios derived.

Mitchell had spoken of what he called reactional crossover: the fact that the ExEx user will inadvertently affect the shape of the scenario, so that on second and subsequent visits the scenario will seem to have modified itself to take account of the previous visit or visits.

From the start she had been all too aware of the interactive nature of ExEx. The only difference since then was her growing understanding of how interactivity was a way of testing the limits of the scenarios.

Why she should be a perceived threat to the programmers was a mystery to her.

But that wild thought of the afternoon: entering Shandy's scenario, moving around within it, testing its extremities, going with ExEx Shandy to the ExEx dive off Shaftesbury Avenue, then entering another ExEx scenario, a simulation within a simulation . . .

It couldn't happen then. Then was 1990, before ExEx had been made publicly available, probably before it had even been developed. The simulation of London that was Shandy's home would not include the ExEx dive.

Things had changed since 1990. Sitting in the cinema, as the film began, Teresa had recalled the logical problems that Gerry Grove presented. The guns, and the unexplained passage of time during his final afternoon of life.

It was known that Grove had been to the Bulverton ExEx building between his first murders, the killing of the mother and her child picnicking in the woods near Ninfield, and his final explosive spree. It was not known what he had done while he was in there.

When she had asked the staff in the building about this, expecting them to remember, they were vague and contradictory about details. The Grove shooting was probably the single most disruptive event in Bulverton since the upheavals of World War II, but the crucial moment within it was misremembered by those who witnessed it.

From the point of view of Ken Mitchell and his colleagues, any attempt to recreate the events of Grove's day had to take account of that visit. Mitchell had said as much.

Had Grove already intersected two realities on the day of his massacre? Had he entered Extreme Experience?

Would that explain the mystery of the guns found stashed in the back of his stolen car? It was known what guns Grove possessed, and that he had taken both of them with him on the day. None was found afterwards at the house. Two were found in the car, two were the ones he used. They intersected: they seemed to be the same ones.

Most of the official reports and media coverage dwelt on the guns Grove had carried and used that day. Some others referred to the guns later found in his stolen car. But none drew these two elements together. There was apparent vagueness, a blurring, a resistance to the idea that there might be conflict between the two sets of objectively checkable facts.

Nodding off on the almost deserted train, in spite of the draughty carriage and the uncomfortable swaying, Teresa felt that the problem, and also any potential solution to it, was constantly slipping from her grasp. She understood so little.

The train stopped for a long time at Robertsbridge station. There was no explanation from the guard, or anyone else. The cold night enveloped the train. Two railway workers walked slowly along the platform carrying torches which they pointed approximately at the wheels. There was a conversation up ahead, presumably with the driver. Teresa could hear the voices, but not what they were saying. Train doors slammed. A generator started up beneath the carriage floor. Teresa huddled lower in her seat, dreading an announcement that the train had broken down or was being taken out of service. It was already after 1.00 a.m., and she was desperate to get to her bed. The day had been too long already. Finally, to her great relief, the train continued on its way.

She could not stop thinking about Grove, especially since she herself had ventured into the scenario of the day of the shooting.

It was impossible to forget what it had been like to enter his mind. His thoughts, which had come at her like the hot, unwanted breath of an intrusive stranger, had felt as if they were too close to her face. How do you recoil from someone inside whose head you are lurking? It had been a descent, if not into the evil that many people said had possessed Grove, then into a profoundly unhappy and deficient mind, one tangled up with petty fears and motives and revenges. He was clearly sane, but also sick: Grove was mean, dangerous, unreasonable, socially inadequate, violently disposed, unpredictable, riddled with hatred, unloved by anyone around him, unloving to anyone he knew.

His mind was so blankly unprotected, so obsessed with ferocious irrelevance, that any intrusion would affect it. She could have caused reactional crossover within that scenario, simply by entering it and residing briefly within his mind.

When Mitchell had talked to her in the corridor outside her

room he spoke as if she had already caused the crossover. In reality she couldn't possibly have done so.

'In reality' . . .

The phrase kept recurring. But reality was an assumption that was no longer viable.

Teresa already knew that some realities were contiguous, she had sensed that others could intersect, and now she was beginning to believe that Gerry Grove must have caused an intersection, a crossover.

Today, in the aftermath of Grove, in which of these realities were they anyway living? The one in which Grove had left his guns in the back of the stolen car, or the one in which he went back to the car, collected the guns, and took them to the town centre?

The answer was both, hinted at in the blurring of memory. The crossover Mitchell was concerned with had already occurred. But had Grove caused it, or had she?

In her tiredness her thoughts were circling on themselves. It was too late in the day to try to think about a slippery subject like this. She kept recoiling from the consequences of her own thoughts.

At long last, twenty-five minutes after the scheduled time, the train drew in to Bulverton. Teresa wearily left her seat, the only passenger to alight, alone on the dimly lit concourse, with no staff in the station. She walked back to the hotel as quickly as she could, her mind focused on one simple intent: getting to bed as soon as possible.

She crept into the hotel, using the master key Amy had lent her a few days earlier, and walked quietly through the darkened building. The stairs creaked as she climbed them. When she reached her bedroom and closed the door, she did so with a feeling of errant lateness she had not had since her teenage years.

Chapter 31

In the morning, on her way down to breakfast, Teresa felt that something about the hotel had changed. As she passed the office she realized what it was: on most mornings the radio was playing in the office, and today it was not. This tiny alteration to her temporary routine made her uneasy.

In the dining room, the four young American programmers were sitting at their table in the furthest corner, and as usual did not acknowledge her arrival. One of the two young women was reading a copy of *Investors Chronicle*, and was rhythmically pumping an arm-muscle exerciser with her free hand; the other was dressed in a track suit and elasticated sweatband, and had a towel draped around her neck. Ken Mitchell was speaking to someone on his mobile phone, and the other man was typing something on a palmtop computer. They all had in front of them their customary breakfast of high-fibre, organically grown, non-fertilized, non-antibiotically treated oriental pulses (which Amy had told her she had had to buy in expensively by mail order from Holland), but none of them was eating.

Teresa sat down at her own usual table. Whenever she saw Ken Mitchell she could not suppress her curiosity and irritation about him. He never seemed to notice her – today, for instance, he was sitting with his back to her table – and although she absolutely did not intend to have anything more to do with him, she wanted him to find out she was still there without, so to speak, her having to remind him.

She had picked up her newspaper from the table in the corridor, and was glancing at it when someone came across to her table.

Assuming it would be Amy, Teresa looked up with a smile. It was not Amy: a heavily built man with a close-shaved head was standing there, holding an order pad and a ballpoint.

'May I take your order for breakfast, please?' he said.

'Yes.' Surprised, Teresa reached automatically for the printed menu. In her three weeks in this place she had grown used to confirming to Amy simply that she wanted the same as she always had: fruit juice, coffee, a lot of toast made with wheat bread. She placed her order. The man wrote it down, and walked off towards the kitchen.

Teresa had the feeling that she had seen him before, but couldn't think where. She assumed it must have been somewhere around the town, because she had no memory of seeing him in the hotel. She wished she had taken a better look at him.

While she was waiting for him to return, the four programmers left their table and walked out of the room. None of them appeared to notice her, and Ken Mitchell was pressing the keys of his mobile phone for another call.

She sat alone in the silent dining room, waiting.

After a short delay, the man with the shaved head returned and put down a silver pot of coffee and a large glass of orange juice.

'I didn't realize you would be wanting wheat bread,' he said. 'I've had to send out for some. It'll only be a few minutes. The bakery's just round the corner from here.'

'It doesn't matter much. White bread would have been OK.' Teresa saw herself through this man's eyes: another damned American picky about obscure food. Although, hell, wheat bread was on the menu! 'Amy knows I usually like wheat bread, and gets it in for me.'

He had straightened and was standing across the table from her, holding the tray against his chest.

'Amy's not here any more,' he said.

Teresa reacted to the news with a little start of surprise, but the truth was that ever since she had come downstairs she had been expecting news of change.

'What's happened?' she said. 'Is she OK?'

'Yeah, she's fine. She just wanted a break.'

'So you've taken over from her?'

'I've taken over everything. I'm running the hotel now.'

'You're managing it?'

'Well, I'm managing it, yes. But I'm the new owner.'

'Has Nick Surtees gone too?'

'It all happened yesterday. I've wanted to run this place for a long time, and I heard Nick wanted to sell up, so we did a deal.'

'Just like that? They were here yesterday, and didn't say anything about it.'

'I think they've been planning it for a while.' Teresa was looking blankly at him. He said, 'My wife will have brought the bread by now. Excuse me.'

She stared after him, as the service door swung closed behind him. The news, trivial though it probably was, went round and round in her mind. She knew that managers of hotels didn't regularly consult their guests about business matters, but both Nick and Amy had seemed so open and willing to talk that she was surprised neither of them had said anything to her. 'Goodbye' would have been pleasant.

She poured her coffee and sipped the orange juice, while she waited for the toast. A few minutes later the man returned.

As he put down the toast – racked in the British manner, to ensure more or less instant cooling – she said, 'I've seen you somewhere before. Don't I know you?'

'Maybe you've seen me around the hotel. I used to come into the bar from time to time.' He rubbed his chin. 'I used to have a beard. I'm Amy's brother-in-law. David Hartland.'

Then she remembered that day, in the market, this man talking to Amy. There had been something aggressive about his behaviour, but it had been unimportant at the time. And another time, she had seen him leaving the ExEx building.

'So you're the brother of . . . ?

'Jason's older brother. That's right. You probably know what happened to Jase?'

'Amy told me.' And her own personal memory of Jase, lying dead on the roof of the house in Eastbourne Road.

'Jase and I wanted to take over this hotel, long ago, when Nick's parents were running it. Nothing came of it back then, but when I heard Nick was selling up I didn't want to miss a second chance.' He had stepped away from her while he spoke, and was standing by the service table. He opened one of the drawers and took out a handful of knives and forks, which he wrapped in a cloth he had brought with him. 'Things are changing in Bulverton. Maybe you've heard. There's a lot of new money coming into the town.' He glanced in the direction of the table recently vacated by the four Americans, though Teresa couldn't immediately see the connection. 'People's lives are going to be transformed, and the town will follow. Ten years from now Bulverton will be a different place.'

'So you bought the hotel – just yesterday?'

'We haven't done the legal stuff yet, the paperwork, but we shook hands on a deal. Nick's using a lawyer in London. I've got my own. You know how long lawyers take. In the meantime, Nick and Amy wanted to get going straight away, so they left yesterday evening. Most of their stuff's still upstairs, but we're storing it for them until they want it.'

'Do you know where they've gone?'

'They didn't tell me,' he said, but in a way that Teresa knew meant that they actually had. 'I think it's like a honeymoon, you know.'

She laughed then, but more because this news needed some kind of release than because she found it amusing.

'So am I likely to see them again?' she said. 'I was starting to get on well with Amy.'

'I wouldn't know. Maybe if you're still here in a month or so? But the way they were talking yesterday, it didn't sound like they were planning to return to Bulverton. A lot of unhappy memories here. For them, and for a lot of people.'

'Yes, I know.'

There didn't seem to be anything more to say to that.

Dave Hartland headed back towards the kitchen with his bundle of cutlery, and Teresa started on her rapidly cooling toast. She was upset by the suddenness of the changes in the hotel; it felt almost like a personal affront, that she had offended Nick or Amy in some way. Of course it couldn't be anything like that – or so she hoped.

Teresa had often tried to put herself in the minds of the people in this small town, the sharers of collective grief. She knew too well how it felt to suffer an individual loss, but had no idea of how different it would feel to be one of many who survived a massacre. Did it provide more comfort or less, to know you weren't alone? The upheaval, the shock, the sense of betrayal, the guilty feelings of the survivors, the intrusion of the press . . . all these were elements of crisis aftermath that were known about and studied by psychologists, but none of their research could explain how it actually felt to be amongst those involved. Before she came to Bulverton, Teresa had thought she might identify with the people here, because of Andy, but the truth was that the only thing they seemed to share was the emotional stasis that had followed. The paralysis of feelings, of ambitions, of movement, of hopes, consumed everything. You simply tried to continue as before, letting the grief roll over you, knowing that nothing could be worse than what had happened, but also knowing that it could never get better.

In fact, it never did get better. Andy was a permanent loss; all that had happened since his death was that she had slowly, painfully, started to face up to the fact that she would never see him again.

While she was finishing her coffee, Hartland walked through the dining room without looking in her direction, put back the cutlery he had taken from the drawer and removed some more. He returned to the kitchen.

Teresa picked up her newspaper and walked through to his office. He was not there, so she knocked on the connecting door and looked into the kitchen. Hartland was there with a woman, presumably his wife, but he made no introduction. They were both wearing aprons and had the cutlery spread across a newspaper on the table.

'Mr Hartland,' Teresa said. 'I'm sorry to do this to you so soon after you've taken over the hotel, but I will need to check out in a day or two.'

'That's no problem. Do you know exactly when it will be?'

'No, not yet. I need to fix up a flight, and there are a couple more things I want to do here in town. It won't be today, at least, but I'll check out maybe tomorrow or the next day.'

He had removed his apron while she was speaking, and now moved across to the door on the far side of the kitchen, which Teresa knew led to the tiny reception area in the main entrance hall. This had been only rarely used by Nick and Amy. He held the door open for her, and indicated she should go through ahead of him.

He switched on the computer terminal on the desk, and they

both waited while it booted up. He fumbled around at the keyboard, apparently trying to find the hotel records.

He said, 'I haven't had a chance to check your bill until now. There was so much other detail to get through yesterday.'

'You want to sort it out, and talk to me later?'

'Let me see if I can find your account.' Teresa had seen Nick and Amy working on the program several times, but she didn't think she should offer to help. 'Don't worry about walking out on us the first day we're in business,' said Hartland. 'After you and the others have left, my wife and I are not planning to take in any more guests.'

'You're just going to run it as a pub?'

'Well, yes. But we've got plans for the place. I have to put in a planning application to the council, because we want to convert the building into a sort of multimedia pub. You ever hear of that before? We've been to a couple in London, and a large one opened in Brighton two months ago. There's so much unused space in this building, and the car park is empty most of the time. With the position on the main road it's ideal. I don't suppose you have that sort of thing in America?'

'We have multimedia. But pubs?'

'It's what people call them. A multimedia pub is a kind of multiple entertainment complex all under one roof. The heart of it all, and where we'll start, is a large bar and brasserie extending the whole length of the front of the building, with a terrace for the summer. After that, we'll convert the other floors. We're going to have a disco in the cellar, there'll be a family room and restaurant at the back, and an internet café in one of the function rooms upstairs. We're going to make the whole of the top floor into boutiques and craft studios. We want people to bring their kids, so we're going to build an indoor adventure playground, with a gallery where the parents can watch their children and have a few drinks. We're even thinking of putting in a gym, so people can work out before they come in for a drink or a meal. You know the old barn at the back that Nick and Amy used for storage? We'll convert that. And we're probably going to have an extreme experience facility here as well. I was talking to those friends of yours from America. Their company will be franchising ExEx in this country soon, and if I move fast we'll be the first private facility on the south coast.'

'You certainly do move fast,' Teresa said, impressed by the man's ambition.

'I've spent all my life in the town, watching this place run slowly into the ground. You know what it's like upstairs: the whole place needs clearing out and starting from scratch. Well, Jean and I know how to make the place profitable, and we aren't getting any younger, so we're putting everything we've got into this.'

'I guess so.'

Teresa couldn't imagine how much it would cost to undertake a full-scale conversion along the lines he had described, but it must run into millions. Hadn't she seen him running a market stall in the Old Town? That was hardly the sort of enterprise which would develop enough spare capital for an expansion along these lines.

She waited a few minutes longer, but it was clear he couldn't find the hotel records on the computer. It made her impatient, watching him fumble around with simple software, and she knew she wasn't helping by standing over him. She suggested again they could sort out the account later. He seemed relieved to agree.

CHAPTER 32

Thinking about crossover and how to avoid it, Teresa came into a clearing in the trees, where three long wooden tables had been set up. A young woman was sitting at one of the tables, with plastic cups and plates, scraps of food, and several toys spread all about. She was laughing, and her child was running around on the grass, wrapped up in his game.

Teresa retreated as far as she was able, back and back into the recesses of Grove's mind. How could she use his eyes, yet look away?

Grove brought out his handgun from the concealment of his jacket with a deliberate, wide swinging motion of his hand. He cocked the gun, working the mechanism three or four more times, relishing the sound.

The noise made the woman turn towards him. She saw the gun levelled at her, and panicked. She shouted in terror to her child, trying to twist round on the heavy log, to get across to the little boy, but she seemed paralysed by her fear. The boy, thinking it was still a game, dashed away from her. The woman's voice became a hoarse roar, then, after she had sucked in her breath, she was incapable of further sound.

Teresa thought, Grove has never handled this gun before!

He was holding it one-handed, like an untrained beginner. She corrected him instinctively. She steadied his gun-hand by gripping his wrist with his free hand, she forced him to aim a little low, to allow for the recoil, and she made him relax his trigger finger, made him squeeze the trigger, not jerk it.

As the woman at last scrambled away from the log, Grove shot her in the head, then turned his gun on the child.

She was back in the stolen car, with the gun hot on the seat beside her. Teresa's mind was racing defensively: It's only a scenario! It was real but it's not real now, it happened before, the woman knew nothing, there was nothing I could do to stop it, I must not interfere, Grove must continue, that woman and her child were not hurt, it's all imaginary. They were dead months before I came to England; Grove killed them without my assistance.

Yet she knew Grove would almost certainly not have killed them without her intervention.

'Shut that fucking noise!'

In her distress she allowed herself to spread forward in Grove's mind, so she could ride in the forefront of his thoughts, to witness his actions without interference. If she went too far forward she became as one with him, jointly responsible; too far back and she became detached from his raw motives, and so became capable of influencing him. How to strike a balance between the two?

As Grove drove towards Bulverton, Teresa repeatedly shifted mental position, trying to find the place where she could observe most closely without feeling the pressure against her of that hot breath of banal cruelty.

When she was forward, what appalled her most was his lack of reaction to what he had just done. She was still squirming in horror at what she had witnessed, but Grove was complaining to himself: he'd stolen the wrong car, a pile of shit, fucking exhaust making a lot of fucking noise, the only money he had was the forty quid he'd nicked but he didn't want to spend that because he was going to celebrate later. Where's that bitch Debra? Bet that Mark shafted her last night, the bastard, need more money, should have looked through that woman's bag . . .

Teresa was still trying to settle somewhere in his mind when he slowed the car and swung it on to the forecourt of a Texaco filling station. Another car was leaving, waiting with its nose out in the main road, indicating left. The driver glanced up at Grove as he passed.

Grove stopped the Montego at an angle across the pumps, making it difficult for any other car to drive in from that direction, then picked up the handgun and walked across to the shop.

A young woman with dark hair – Margaret Lee, who had refused to be interviewed by Teresa – was sitting alone at the till, skimming through a magazine spread on the counter in front of her. She looked up as Grove strode towards her between the racks of magazines and bars of chocolate, and saw the gun at once.

After a moment of uncertainty, she leapt back from the counter, one arm flailing in the air. In the same instant, a grey metal security barrier came rattling noisily down from the ceiling and crashed on to the surface of the counter. Several small items stacked there – display cards with special offers, air-mile vouchers, a box of ballpoints – scattered across the floor as they were dislodged.

Teresa felt Grove's anger rising, and he fired the gun several times at the barrier. The bullets made visible dents, lodging in the mesh surface without penetrating. Grove raced across to the barrier and bashed it with his elbow. It hardly budged.

There was a large notice printed in the centre of the barrier, which Grove scarcely glanced at, but which Teresa could read:

This security barrier is bulletproof,
fireproof and soundproof
IT CANNOT BE REOPENED BY THE STAFF
Do not attempt to force it
An automatic alarm message has been sent
to emergency services

Grove uselessly fired two more bullets at the barrier, then looked around for something to steal. There was a tall refrigerator cabinet filled with drinks, so he shattered its glass door with a couple of rounds. He reached inside and took out two cans of Coke. He kicked at one of the heavy display stands, but succeeded only in shoving it a short distance across the floor. He grabbed some magazines, and thrust them under the arm of his gun-hand.

He walked unhurriedly across the forecourt to the Montego, and opened the front passenger door. He threw the stuff he had stolen inside, then laid the handgun on the floor of the car, between the front seats.

He opened the luggage compartment and took out the rifle. Holding it with the muzzle aloft, he made a show of snapping the ammunition clip into place, and cocking the weapon. Traffic went by on the main road, only a few yards away, the people inside the vehicles apparently noticing nothing.

Teresa, in Grove's mind, seated immovably behind his eyes, saw everything.

She eased forward to try to enter his mind, but shrank away. His mind was blank, insofar as any mind can be free of thought. All she found was an almost wordless blur of images: Girl kill find hit fucking stupid door window run get car . . .

Once again, risking intercession in the scenario, Teresa retreated as far as she dared. Grove was now stepping across the forecourt, heading for the side of the building where a night-cash window was situated. He came to a halt directly in front of it, raised his rifle and took a steady aim at the glass. Although there was a light on in the room behind, there was no sign of Margaret Lee.

Grove maintained his stance, and a few seconds later was rewarded when the young woman slowly stood up. She turned to face the night-cash window, and immediately saw Grove pointing the rifle at her.

He fired. The recoil punched against his shoulder, and the strengthened glass shattered into opacity. He fired twice more, both bullets hitting the glass but apparently not penetrating.

Grove went quickly to the window, but the crazing was so fine that it was impossible to see through into the room beyond.

Grove turned and walked back to the car. He slung the rifle on to the back seat, then climbed in and started the engine. Without another look back he stepped hard on the pedal, screeching the tyres, and noisily clouting one of the pumps. He continued to accelerate as he reached the road, swinging on to the carriageway without regard for traffic. He drove frantically towards Bulverton, flashing the headlamps at anyone who was in front of him, and overtaking recklessly.

Inside Grove's mind Teresa felt herself relaxing. Normally, any other person's fast driving, apart from Andy's, struck fear into her heart and numbness into her thoughts, but she knew Grove could not hurt her. Even if he drove head-on into an oncoming car she would not be physically hurt. Anyway, she knew no accident was about to happen, because no accident *had* happened.

Grove was forced to slow when an empty coach pulled out from a side road, and lumbered heavily along towards Bulverton.

Grove braked the Montego sharply, followed the coach, then pulled out to overtake. Two police cars were approaching, their headlamps on full beam and their electric-blue strobe lights flickering. The wailing sirens were a deafening chorus. Grove ducked back behind the coach, but as soon as the police cars had passed he pulled out again.

It was not far to Bulverton. Within a few minutes of leaving the Texaco station they had reached the intersection at the top of the town; straight on led down through residential areas to the town centre, a left or a right took the road along the Ridge. Grove barely slowed for the junction, but skidded round and took the Ridge to the left. The traffic was heavier here, forcing Grove to slow a little, but still he wove dangerously round the other vehicles, overtaking when he could. Teresa was almost enjoying the sensation of unsafe speed; it was like the thrill of watching a car chase in a movie, knowing that it was all unreal, that there was no danger to her.

She waited for him to take the side road to the industrial estate, where the ExEx building was situated, knowing that this was where he had parked the car and therefore where he must be heading now. As the turning approached she braced herself, knowing that he was going too fast to take it safely. But he was still weaving, and the Montego went past the side road at high speed. He braked a short distance further on, and took the sharply angled turn into Hereford Avenue, the road that ran through the heart of the housing estate. Teresa had a glimpse of the distant sea, light clouds on the horizon, heat-haze resting over the town, before the car was wrenched round again into a sidestreet. Teresa recognized the bleak terrace of houses where Grove had been living. The car braked hard to a halt, with two wheels up on the paving stones at the side.

Grove held his hand down on the horn, staring aggressively at the house. Nothing appeared to move within.

'Fucking hell!' he said aloud, and pulled himself out of the car with a violent motion. He wrenched open the rear passenger door, and grabbed the rifle. He went quickly towards the house, making no attempt to hide the weapon, or, for that matter, to conceal himself behind any available cover. At the back of his mind, Teresa could not forget her Bureau training on approaching a building where the command situation was unknown: all available means of cover were to be sought.

As soon as she thought this Grove ducked swiftly to one side, and instead of approaching the house as he had been, going straight up the concrete path towards the door, he crouched down on the far side of the wooden fence, and proceeded more cautiously.

Teresa thought, I'm still influencing him!

She made herself move forward, but the sheer blast of anger and unreason swilling through Grove's mind repelled her.

Holding the rifle aloft, Grove kicked at the wooden door at the rear of the house: it was flimsily made, and it opened without resistance. Grove dashed in. Debra was standing in the main room at the back, cradling a small cat in her arms. She looked pale, undernourished, pathetic and terrified. She was also, Teresa noticed for the first time, pregnant. The cat reacted instantly to Grove, and scrambled away from her, raising weals on Debra's thin forearm which rapidly produced welling spots of blood.

Grove raised the rifle, while the skinny, wretched girl tried to back away, pressing her legs against an open tea-chest behind her.

Teresa thought, No! This didn't happen! Why didn't he go to the ExEx building?

The girl stumbled backwards, scraping her legs on the metal lip of the chest, but dragged herself around it, trying to hide.

Grove suddenly lowered the rifle, turned away, and without saying anything to the girl walked back through the house. He opened the front door and strode back to the car. He lifted the lid of the luggage compartment and threw in the rifle, then retrieved the handgun from between the front seats and tossed that inside too. He banged the lid down.

Neighbours were watching. One woman pushed her children back into the house, and followed them inside and closed the door with a terrific slam.

Teresa thought, Is this right? Did I prevent him from shooting Debra? Or was he not going to do it anyway?

She eased forward in Grove's mind, bracing herself for the onslaught of his crazed thoughts, but a sudden placidity had taken over. He was thinking about the best way to drive to

Welton Road. Should he drive to the bottom of the road, and turn back up to the Ridge along Holman Road, or turn round here and go back the way he had come?

The sheer normality of his thoughts was almost more repulsive than the hatred she had experienced before. He had murdered two people in the last half-hour, and threatened two other people with death, yet he could sit calmly behind the wheel of a car and worry about which direction to drive.

Once more Teresa retreated to the back of his mind. She was confused by the way these events were turning out and growing increasingly aware of the sensitivity of a scenario's development.

Grove's case was different from every other scenario she had entered. The details of all or most of the others were unknown to her when she entered the action. But when she first arrived in Bulverton from the US she was already broadly familiar with what Grove had done, and since then she had researched many more details. She had talked to witnesses, watched videos of newscasts and read dozens of different accounts and official reports. She suspected that material similar to this had been used by the ExEx programmers to develop the very scenario in which she was participating.

The other witnesses would have contributed too: those boys playing pool when Grove went to the Bulver Arms, Fraser Johnson, who had witnessed the drugs deal on the seafront, Steve Ripon, who gave Grove a lift in his van and who saw him again later in Battle Road, Margaret Lee, who was terrorized by Grove at the Texaco station, maybe the police who had driven past on their way to the filling station; maybe even the people who lived in the houses she was driving past at this moment!

And the others, the people she had spoken to only briefly, or those who had left town and perhaps had been traced and been paid by the GunHo people for their stories. All those who had witnessed something of Grove's disastrous adventure, many of whom she hadn't met, nor ever would, some who were still recovering from their injuries, those who would not speak to her because they thought she was a journalist, or for some other reason, those she had never even heard about because what they had witnessed was in non-ExEx terms only a confirmation of what others had said they'd seen; those who had fled Bulverton before she arrived in town.

She was trapped in Grove's vile mind, while he drove the car violently through the congested streets of the lower Ridge, and she was able to think out, think back to the real world, where she existed and had listened and taken notes, had accumulated other people's memories of these events in a way not unlike the building of this scenario.

She was tempted then to abort herself out of the scenario, to leave the virtual Grove suspended for ever in the action of driving the car.

The extreme reality she had entered was one she already knew. The physical surroundings were identical to the Bulverton in which she had been living. This was how Nick, Amy, Dave Hartland, the Mercers, all the other witnesses, knew and remembered the relevant parts of the town. And it was how she too remembered them: no surprises for her, except the now familiar simulated veracity, still almost shocking in its details.

Using Grove's eyes, she glanced about as he drove, and she saw graffiti daubed or sprayed on walls, litter left untidily on the ground, dents on the bodywork of parked cars, individual curtains hanging at the windows of individual houses; everything different, everything incredibly detailed.

No one could *remember* such fanatical details when providing their memories to the ExEx software; no one would say, even to themselves, that in this particular road there were so many houses, so many different colours of house paint, so many different ways of cultivating the small patch of garden in front of every house, so many different ways of letting it grow wild, so many irregularities and patches on the surface of the road, so many parked cars, of such different types and ages, in such different states of physical condition, no one would think to recall that a cat had dashed across the road in front of Grove's car, that through the trees at the top of the hill it was possible to glimpse the traffic moving along the Ridge: a red Norbert Dentressangle truck with its vivid and familiar logo, a white Stagecoach double-decker bus with an advertising placard for a local computer retail outlet, an orange and white Sainsbury's delivery truck, the glinting roofs of cars of different colours imperfectly seen because of the angle and the bright light from the sky. People saw such details only subliminally, recording them on an unconscious level of the mind, and so the details went somehow into the scenario, not as facts but as adumbrations for the participants to see and notice and react to, and, in a certain way, to create for themselves as ad hoc necessities.

Details are expected, by instinct or habit: no residential road in modern Britain, or indeed in any developed country, lacked cars parked at the sides of the road. No one would therefore specifically recall them when reliving their memories for the ExEx software, but the cars would nevertheless be included as outlines, and the scenario participants, seeing them because they expected to see them, filled in the details from their own memories, from their own take on the collective unconsciousness, or from their own knowledge of the world.

In this way the participant was more than a passive observer. The scenario responded to and was reshaped by the will, experience, thoughts or imagination of the participant.

Extreme reality was a temporary consensus, subject to the changing whims of all involved.

The limits of the imagination were the only absolutes: in a scenario one could turn a car round and drive away from the main action, out into the open country beyond city limits, and follow the highway to the horizon, and it would usually be as unconsciously expected, filled with convincing detail, awash with impressions of temperature and sounds and objects, and the sensory experiences of being in a car.

But in the end a limit would inevitably be reached, because one could imagine only so much: the road would turn out to roll for ever, you would never reach the shore to watch the sea, the stairs to an Underground station were blocked by a brick wall.

The restriction on the extreme reality of any scenario was the failure to imagine what might lie beyond its edge.

Grove had driven out of the housing estate, and without slowing he barged his way into the traffic moving along the Ridge. Teresa had lost all curiosity about what might be going through his mind, and she remained as far back in his consciousness as possible.

Through his eyes she peered ahead, looking for the road that led down to the ExEx building. It was coming up, two hundred yards or more on the left.

Grove began to reduce speed for the turn, just as she would if she were driving. She was interceding again.

On an impulse, Teresa used Grove's left hand to reach up to the base of his neck. Touching him initially surprised and slightly repelled her: his neck was thick and covered in stubbly hairs. It was sticky with sweat. She groped around, and quickly found the ExEx valve.

Had it been in place before? Had she found it only because she had expected to?

While she thought about that, Grove took control of the car once more, and threw it around the corner too quickly. The rear wheels swung out, and with an irritated gesture and a muttered obscenity Grove snatched his left hand back to the steering wheel and recovered from the skid. Teresa decided to let him drive in his own way.

Moments later he pulled up in the road opposite the entrance to the ExEx building, and turned off the engine.

Chapter 33

Teresa was not sure what Grove was about to do, and her uncertainty had an immediate effect on him.

He reached forward and began to fiddle with the volume and tuning knobs on the car's radio. They were held on only by spring or clip pressure; when he had pulled them off, the retaining bracket quickly came free, and a few seconds later Grove had managed to release the whole instrument from its mount. The manufacturers had attached a label to the inner case, warning that the radio was protected against theft by an electronic coding system. As soon as Grove saw this he pushed the radio aside in disgust. It swung beneath the dash on its extruded cables.

He climbed out of the car and walked round to the back. Teresa, realizing that they had come to the pivotal moment in the scenario, watched to see what he would do. This would be when he either took the handgun and the rifle from the car, or left them concealed inside.

As she thought this Grove went past the compartment lid, tapped his fingertips on it in a single gesture of annoyance, and walked across the road towards the entrance to the ExEx building.

She made him glance back once.

It was for her almost a final gulp of reality, like the last deep breath taken by a diver.

From here, the view of the town was distant, and today the haze made the panorama indefinite without concealing it. The softness of detail frustrated her; she wanted to devour the view.

Was the blurring of heat haze the way this scenario defined the edge of its own virtual reality?

Grove kicked irritably at a clod of earth, so Teresa let him turn and continue on his way. He pushed open the glass door of the ExEx building, and went across to the reception desk. Paula Willson was on duty.

Grove took the stolen money from his pocket, and tossed it on the desk.

'I want to use the stuff you have here,' he said. 'That's forty quid . . . should be enough.'

Paula said, regarding the loose notes on her desk, 'Are you a member, sir?'

No, he wouldn't be, Teresa thought. Grove would have failed the psychological profiling with the first three questions on the form. She wondered how he would lie his way out of this.

'Not here. Maidstone, I usually go to Maidstone.' Grove reached into the back pocket of his pants, felt around until he found what he was looking for, then pulled out the stiff plastic ID card. He held it up for her to see. It blurred in front of his eyes, so Teresa could not check it for authenticity; she knew that if he held it there a little longer it would swim into focus.

Paula took it from him. She appeared to see it in focus, and recognized it. She placed the four ten-pound notes in a drawer of her desk, then typed the serial number of the card into her terminal. After a short pause she swiped its magnetic strip through the reader, and passed the card back to him, together with the usual information pack for users of the ExEx equipment.

'That's in order, Mr Grove. Thank you. A technician will assist you when you have made your selection.'

Grove took the card and pushed it back into his pocket, then walked through the inner door. He, or Teresa, knew exactly where to go. A few moments later he had located an unused computer terminal, and was running the index software, seeming to be every bit as familiar with it as she was.

Her visits to ExEx were all so recent and commonplace that to Teresa it was a continuing shock to accept that she was still inhabiting Grove's body, that what was going on was merely a scenario. While Grove peeled his way through the introductory screens of information, Patricia walked past the desk, and Teresa made Grove glance up at her.

'Hi,' she/Grove said to Patricia.

'Hello, again.'

Was that Patricia's reply to her, defined from the adumbration of her expectations? Or was it actually to Grove, a known customer and member of the ExEx facilities, perhaps someone Patricia had seen several times before?

Teresa forced herself forward in Grove's mind, to try to minimize any more influence on his decisions. Every thought she had, back there in the recess of his mind, every tiny detail she noticed, became translated into a decision or action taken by Grove. In crossover, she actually became Grove himself. Never before, in any scenario, had she experienced such active response.

She tried to assume a state of mental passivity, and watched the screens of options scrolling by. She wondered what he was looking for; then she wondered if wondering would also influence him. It made him pause, at least.

She recalled the ease with which she had been able to talk to Shandy, that day in virtual London.

'Gerry?' she said.

'Who's that?'

'What exactly are you looking for?'

'Shut the fuck up!'

This was accompanied by a mental strike against her, a bludgeoning rejection, full of fear and hatred and bullying. Again, what felt like his hot breath welled around her.

She backed away, into the depths of crossover. He hunched defensively and began jabbing at the keyboard with movements that were so quick she could not see what he was doing. On the screen, the various menus and lists appeared and disappeared at dizzying speed.

Once again it occurred to her that her presence in the scenario was becoming unsustainable, that it was time to withdraw. To do that, though, would mean having to retreat from the Grove scenario now, at a point where it was becoming of real interest to her. What Grove had done inside the ExEx building clearly had an influence on the violent events that were soon to follow.

She didn't want to have to start over. Gerry Grove's movements on this day, recorded in such detail inside the scenario, were proving to be time-consuming and traumatic.

Teresa had never known such a long and exhausting scenario, nor felt so appalled by what she found. She did not want to have to cope again with the banal evil of his mind. Mostly, though, she could not face having to go back to the beginning and experience his murders again, to witness them and either by inaction appear to condone them, or by intervention appear to influence them.

She had come as far as this; now she wanted to see it through and find out what he had done.

His helter-skelter progress through the index listings continued; Teresa thought that because he was moving so quickly he could only be choosing selection boxes at random, almost on autopilot, simply clicking on one option after another, uninterested in where it might take him.

Suddenly he stopped, and Teresa felt his body relax slightly. He seemed to lean forward slightly, as if the tension of searching through the screens had been supporting his torso.

The top of the screen said:

Interactive/Police/Murder/Guns/1950/William Cook/Elsa Jane Durdle.

Next to Elsa's name was a video frame; a tiny static glimpse of bright sunlight and windswept palm trees, a row of diagonally parked cars glinting in the sun.

The chances of Grove selecting this scenario at random were too immense to calculate. She had always presumed that Elsa was uniquely hers! Teresa felt protest rising in her, but almost at once Grove responded to it and went back into action.

He continued to move swiftly through the hierarchy of options, the computer screen flickering as he somehow anticipated each new menu. Once again, he quit abruptly.

Participatory/Victim-enabled/Interactive/State or County PD/ State PD/Virginia/Fugitive/Multiple Murder/Spree/Guns/Sam Wilkins McLeod.

The video showed a group of people against a brightly lit and highly coloured background. For a moment it meant nothing to Teresa, but she made Grove lean forward and look closely at the image, and used the mouse to click on it; at once it expanded to occupy the lower half of the screen.

She was in Al's Happy Burgabar with her husband Rick, in a small town called Oak Springs along Highway 64 between Richmond and Charlottesville. The video frame had frozen on them as the family passed the main course self-selection counter, the vivid colours of Al's unmistakable logo dominating the room.

The shock of recognizing this, which was buried under layers of extreme experience deep down, long ago, away somewhere in her virtual life story, produced another automatistic response from Grove. The computer images on the monitor began to flicker brightly as he moved swiftly through the lists. Teresa watched the computer display again, feeling helpless.

Her own virtual past was fast-forwarding, fast-rewinding, while she stared through the eyes of a man she knew was on his way to a massacre.

He paused again, and the computer image steadied.

Participatory/Interactive/United Kingdom/England/National or County/County Police/Sussex Police/Multiple Murder/Spree/ Guns/Handgun/Semi-automatic Rifle/ Gerald Dean Grove/Part I.

Immediately underneath it said:

Participatory/Interactive/United Kingdom/England/National or County/County Police/Sussex Police/Multiple Murder/Spree/ Guns/Handgun/Semi-automatic Rifle/Gerald Dean Grove/Part II.

Grove stared at the screen, with the mouse pointer resting on the frozen video image of Part I, ready to start it running. The image was of Grove himself, sitting in a car on the seafront at Bulverton, leaning forward to tighten the hot-wired connections beneath the dash.

Deep in the recesses of Grove's mind Teresa thought, He's playing with me. Or I'm playing with him.

She knew she should abort the scenario. She had been completely unprepared for this.

The thought was sufficient to move him. Fatalistically, Teresa watched the screen to see what he would do.

Grove's next choice frame showed a western saloon, where a young woman was waiting to start performing in a pornographic movie. The video frame had caught Shandy in her off-guard moment before the filming began, when she was reaching behind her back, pinching at the material of her shirt, to try to ease the tightness of her half-cup bra.

Grove, of his own accord, enlarged the frame, and with a concupiscence Teresa was forced to share, ogled the tantalizing glimpse of the voluptuous young woman.

Grove's mind, his brain, whatever corrupt organ it was that Teresa occupied, was full of predatory lust and physical greed. He moved energetically, against Teresa's resistance, and slid the pointer to the ExEx box, glinting invitingly at the top of the image.

He stood up, and waited while the nanochips were processed by the equipment.

'No!' Teresa said, to herself, to Grove, out loud, or directly across, or however it was done. 'Not Shandy!'

'Shut the fuck up.' Grove had the phial of nanochips now, delivered at the dispensing peripheral built into the top of the desk, and swung himself out of the seat, out of the booth. 'Whoever the fuck you are, shut the fuck up.'

Teresa had grown up in a world of swearwords, but she had always loathed that expression and the kind of man who used it. It was invariably a man; women were capable of a lot of swearing, but they rarely used that phrase. She had been trained by the Bureau not to react to abuse from suspects and perpetrators, but that ill-tempered phrase had always got under her skin, once or twice to her jeopardy.

'Tough shit, lady!' Grove replied to the thought. 'Shut the fuck up.'

'Not Shandy, you bastard!'

'I told you to shut the—'

Teresa backed off, back as far as she could go, mortified by what was happening, and now unable to control events, except inadvertently.

She glimpsed an understanding at last of how a man like Grove operated. Everything she had experienced of him until now had been, for him, an unconscious blind, a shutting off of his true self. The muttered hatreds, the confusion, the vindictiveness, the banality; none of these represented the real Grove. They were instinctive moves, inadequate responses of an immature mind to a complex and subtle world. Now though, without warning, his true nature had moved in and taken command.

Grove was an obsessive, a monomaniac, capable of focusing on one thing only at any time. With the inviting view of Shandy getting ready for action, his psychopathic mind had become dominated by the frozen image of her. She had her shoulders turned away as she tried to deal with her momentary discomfort, twisting her body so that her backside and breasts were exaggerated, posed in almost a parody of the traditional cheesecake stance. The video snapshot had obviously been selected for that reason, a visual shorthand of the contents of the scenario. Grove could not know that, but could and did react on a gut level to what he thought he would find.

In his singlemindedness, Grove could no longer be influenced or diverted away. Teresa, a passenger in his mind, could only reside in a well of apprehension, disgust and concern as Grove took over.

This was what it must have been like in Bulverton Old Town on the day of the massacre. She had heard many accounts from different people: Grove seemed invulnerable as he strode through the streets with his guns. His victims were paralysed by their terror of him, or by disbelief at what they saw. No one challenged him until it was too late; only a few people were able to run away or hide. Grove had been impelled not by hatred, or by passion, or even by madness, but by singleminded determination.

Only at the end, when his obsession began to fade, did he become less fixated; then he was quickly encircled by the police, and his murderous spree was ended.

Now, though, in a terrible prelude to what would be happening later, he was in full thrall to his psychopathy.

She realized that she was also in his thrall. Grove was using her. He had already learned from her how a handgun should be held, aimed and fired; he had already found his way to Elsa Durdle, to one of the old FBI training scenarios, then to the scenario about himself, and now he had arrived at the innocent obscenities of Shandy and Willem.

He made her feel as if he was penetrating her cover, crashing in on her life, but the reality was that she was exposing it to him. Her unconscious mind was guiding him, educating him.

Yet she was helpless. While all this coursed through her mind, Grove had walked through to the simulator area of the building and handed over the phial of nanochips to one of the technicians. As the injection apparatus was quickly set up, and connected to the valve on his neck, Teresa braced herself for the shift into the scenario, knowing that aborting herself out of it was the last option she had.

Grove/Teresa became aware of heat, bright lights and clothes that were too tight. He blinked, and tried to see what was going on around him, but his eyes had not yet adjusted. There were people standing further back, beyond the ring of lights, and they were talking and working, paying no attention to him.

A woman came up to him, and brusquely patted his forehead and nose with powder. 'Hold still a while longer, Shan,' she said impersonally, then moved back into the ring of lights.

Teresa thought, I can't take this any more.

Grove said, 'What? Who the fuck is that?'

And Teresa, at last, much later than she should have done, decided to abort. She recalled the LIVER mnemonic, rattled through the words held within the acronym, focused on the system of closure they produced, and withdrew from the scenario.

  * * *   **You have been flying SENSH Y'ALL**   * * *
  * * *   **Fantasys from the Old West**   * * *
  * * * **Copyroody everywhere – doan even THINK about it!!** * * *

Before she remembered how to cut it off, the mindless electronic music jangled interminably around her.

CHAPTER 34

Teresa returned from the scenario and found herself in the familiar surroundings of one of the ExEx recovery booths. Waking up in reality after the sensory overload of a scenario always involved a profound readjustment, a feeling of disbelief in what she found around her. No return had yet been as concerning as this.

Teresa sat on the bench, legs dangling, staring at the carpeted floor, thinking of Grove, appalled by the thought of what trouble her entry into his mind might have caused.

A technician called Sharon appeared, and removed and validated the nanochips. At once Teresa was caught up in the practical routines of the business that was ExEx. Sharon led her through to the billing office and they waited for the paperwork to be churned out by the machine. Instead of the fairly prompt appearance of the receipt confirming the return of the chips, together with a credit card charge slip, this time a message of some kind appeared on the LCD display, invisible to Teresa from where she was standing.

Sharon picked up the desk telephone, and keyed in several numbers. There was a pause, and then she recited a code number. Finally, she said with a glance at Teresa, 'Thanks – I'll check that.'

'What's the problem?' Teresa said.

'There's something about the expiry date on your card,' Sharon said. She pressed one of the studs on the desktop, and a piece of paper wound out of the slot. She tore it off. 'Do you happen to have the card with you?'

'It's the one I've always used,' Teresa said, but looked through her bag for it. 'The girl on the desk outside validated it, and it's gone through OK until now.'

She found her Baltimore First National Visa card, and handed it over.

Sharon looked closely at it. 'Yes, this is what they told me,' she said. 'It's not the expiry date. That's OK. It's the "Valid from" date.' She held the card out for Teresa to see. 'You've started using the card too soon. It doesn't become valid for another couple of months. Do you have the old one with you?'

'What? Let me look at that.'

Teresa took the card. As usual, both validating dates were embossed on it. They looked OK to her; she had been using the card for several months without problem. She thought for a moment. It had been made valid from August the previous year; now they were in February. Not valid for two more months?

She slipped the card into her bag.

'I'll give you another,' she said, not looking at Sharon. She searched through her wallet and found her GM MasterCard. Before handing it over she checked both validating dates; she was securely in the middle of the period.

'That's fine,' Sharon said, after a close examination of her own. The transaction then went through normally.

Before leaving the building Teresa went to the Ladies' restroom and leaned against a washbasin, staring down blankly into the pale-yellow plastic bowl. She felt drained. Today's ExEx session had been a long one, and because of the awfulness of Grove's mental state it had also been stressful and alarming. She could still hardly bear to think of the consequences of what she had done.

She shrank from this, and other thoughts came at her in an onrush of trivial detail, a reaction against the tensions of the last few hours.

There were many practical things she had to sort out. Flight confirmation was one of them; she had made only a provisional booking and needed to hear back from the travel agents. Then she had to pack her stuff, and check out of the hotel. Get across to Gatwick Airport with enough time to turn in the rental car, check in, go through security, hang around in the departure lounge, buy books and magazines she didn't want, and all that. Flying always took time, but presumably never as much as it saved, otherwise no one would do it. Before she left England she should also check in with her section chief, or at least leave a message in his office. She still had a hunch trouble was waiting for her there; would

Ken Mitchell's one hour of effective passion compensate for that? Teresa combed her hair, peered closely at her eyes in the mirror. Gifts, she should buy some souvenirs to take back with her. She wondered if she would have time to go round the Old Town shops before they closed.

She glanced at her wristwatch.

Something was not right. How long had she been in Grove's scenario? What had changed?

The washroom was grey-painted, clean, cool. The sound of air-conditioning was loud around her, emanating from a grille high in the wall by the door. Bright sunlight glared into the room through a square window set in the sloping half-roof above her.

A memory of Grove came to her, but she thrust the thought away in panic. All this time in England, circling around the Grove issue, and now she had at last confronted it she shrank away from it.

She wanted only to get home, try again to restart her life without Andy. Out there: she wondered what was out there, in the confusing world made by Grove. She had taught him to shoot. That child, that woman, they might be alive now if she hadn't shown Grove how to hold his weapon correctly.

No! she thought. No, that's not true! Rosalind Williams and her little boy were shot and killed by Grove eight months before. On the day it happened she was in Richmond, Virginia, thousands of miles away. It was a historical certainty. What she had seen was only a scenario, a re-creation of the event which by close observation she had seemed to influence.

She had taught Grove how to handle his gun. Some influence.

In reaction to these unwelcome thoughts, another flood of personal concerns coursed through her: whether she should sell the house in Woodbridge, move into an apartment in Baltimore or Washington, or relocate right away from the area. She had good friends who lived in Eugene, Oregon; maybe she should make a break with everything, and move to the Pacific North West. In the meantime, should she stay with the Bureau, transfer to another section or station? Or maybe she should think about – what did they call it? – OCERS. The Optional Corporate Early Retirement Scheme. The Bureau management had been talking up OCERS, as if it was the answer to their many woes of funding, deployment, overmanning, and all the other administrative problems they regularly memo'd to the sections.

Closing her bag she looked up again and caught an off-guard glimpse of herself. She should have been ready for it, because she had been staring at the mirror off and on for the last five minutes, but for that instant she saw the reflection of a rather bulky middle-aged woman, her dark-brown hair starting to turn grey, her face not one she remembered or wanted to remember. Standing there in her warm quilted anorak, bundled up against the wintry weather outside, she thought, How did it happen so quickly? How have the years of my life vanished?

She walked through the reception area, looking ahead, zipping up her anorak and wondering if she should pull on the hood.

'Goodbye, Paula,' she said to the receptionist. 'See you again.'

'Cheerio, Mrs . . . Has it started to rain out there?'

'Rain? I'm not sure.' Teresa pushed through the glass doors, and walked across the hard-standing outside.

Heat from the sun-whitened concrete rose around her. The sun was high in a brilliant sky. Teresa stared around her in amazement: the trees were in full leaf, the distant sea was shining so brightly it seemed silver, the houses of the lower town were softened by a gentle heat haze. The only clouds visible were on the horizon far away to the south, somewhere over the French coast. Two young women, walking along the road, were dressed in shorts and T-shirts.

Teresa unzipped her anorak, and slipped it off. When she drove up to the ExEx building this morning there had been a cold easterly wind, spotted with ice and freezing rain. She remembered hurrying from her car, keeping her head down against the wind, then, in the reception area, flapping her anorak to try to shed some of the water from it, and mopping her face with a tissue. Now it was midsummer.

She looked around for her car. That morning, the cold morning, she had had to park it against the kerb, a short distance away. She walked towards where she had left it, but a dark-red Montego was parked in its place. The two nearside wheels had mounted the kerb and were resting on the grassy verge.

Her own car, the rented Ford Escort, was nowhere around.

Teresa went to the Montego. On its left side was a long paint smear across both doors, and a deep dent, where the car had hit something solid and white-painted. When she peered in the front window on the driver's side she saw a car radio, pulled from its mount but still connected by wires, discarded, hanging down under the dashboard.

Teresa tried the handle, and the unlocked door opened. Feeling a chill of fear, in spite of the stifling heat of the day, Teresa reached down to the release of the luggage compartment lid. She heard and felt the lock click open behind her. She went back, raised the lid.

A semi-automatic rifle and a handgun lay on the carpeted floor. Several boxes of ammunition were also there; one had broken open and a handful of rounds lay spilled about. She recognized the handgun as a Colt, the one Grove, and she, had used to kill Mrs Williams and her child in the woods. She had not been able to get a good look at the rifle while Grove was handling it, but now she recognized it as an M16 carbine.

Teresa slammed down the lid then stood there, staring at the car's polished paintwork, trying to think. The sun beat down on her neck. The temptation again swept over her to shrink mentally from the consequences of all this.

She had been in the scenario with Grove. It was a standard ExEx scenario. In this standard ExEx scenario she had shown Grove how to use the weapons; maybe he would have shot the people anyway, maybe he simply missed the first time, maybe he wasn't as incompetent as she'd thought, maybe he would have gone on and shot at them until they were dead.

Maybe she was making excuses.

All right, in the real world Grove had definitely shot those two: Rosalind Williams and her four-year-old child, Tommy. She had seen their names on the town memorial. She had seen video footage of the scene of the crime. She had seen the newspaper files. She had talked to Mrs Williams' bereaved husband, and to other people who had known them.

But until she had shown Grove how to shoot, he had been incompetent. He held the heavy, sophisticated gun like a boy playing with a toy pistol. Inside the scenario.

Had she not done so, what would have happened to his two victims? Inside the scenario.

Teresa turned away from the Montego, leaned her backside against it and stared down the hill towards the distant sea. Although the town shimmered under haze she could see it well enough: the line of low surrounding hills to left and right, making up the rest of the Ridge, the dull modern houses in their stultifying ranks; lower down, the more attractively arranged and time-weathered buildings of the Old Town, then the sea, a glistening silver-blue, the distant clouds over France. It all stretched out before her, endless and inviting.

The rest of England, the seas and the endless sky, the world, spread around her. A short drive to Dover or Newhaven and she could be on a ferry across that sea to France, thence to the rest of Europe. A slightly longer drive to the north and she would be at Gatwick Airport, ready for her flight home. There were no extremes to limit her.

But this was not the reality she had left. This was summer; in the streets of the town below people would be driving their cars with the windows down, the sun-roofs open and the ineffective cold-air blowers roaring. Pedestrians would be strolling in shorts and flimsy tops. Shops and houses would have their doors and windows open to the heat. No sun shone like this in Britain's winter, which she had woken up to, driven in, hurried through, shaken from her coat, only that morning.

It had been a standard ExEx scenario, written by the company that owned the ExEx building. The standard ExEx scenario had undoubtedly been Grove's, set on the day. Standard extremes, the corporate reality. GunHo scenarios were industry standard.

But Grove had gone on, using other software. Sick of the naked impact of Grove's mind Teresa had withdrawn, leaving him in the unlikely embodiment of Shandy in her porno rôle. Presumably he was still there, enjoying what must be for any man a novel sexual experience.

She remembered walking down Coventry Street in Shandy's mind, learning about the girl and the world she inhabited. The flashing logo, SENSH, was coming at them every half-minute or so. 'Doesn't that drive you crazy, Shan?' she had said. No, Shandy replied, you get used to it in the end.

It had been run as a closing message just now, when she left the scenario.

The scenario she had entered, the industry-standard GunHo scenario about Grove, was not the one she had left: she had been in Vic's homemade software, complete with bolted-on bits of London and Arizona, and terrible puns and spelling mistakes.

When she withdrew from that she had returned to the ExEx facility in Bulverton. But it was to a hot sunny day, like the one when Grove went berserk.

It made rough sense, of course. When Grove entered the Shandy scenario, taking her with him, her only way out was to the reality he had left.

The credit card that was too new to be valid; the cold winter's day that had turned to a heatwave; the Montego parked in place of her car.

She was still in the Grove scenario.

The implications were shocking, and impossible to comprehend fully, but at least she knew how to cope. With a desperate urgency to escape, unlike any she had previously known, Teresa recalled the LIVER mnemonic, and waited for the GunHo logo to appear as the scenario was aborted.

Teresa remained in Welton Road, outside the ExEx building, with Grove's stolen car gleaming in the midsummer sun. Nothing changed.

She had never known the mnemonic to fail before, although Dan Kazinsky had warned all the trainees that it was not infallible.

Standing there, in shock, but focused on what had happened, Teresa remembered a day during training at the Academy, when they had been given a long and technical lecture by a professor of psychology from Johns Hopkins University. This woman had drily explained the theory of mental override within an imaginary world. Several of the trainees afterwards admitted privately that their attention had wandered, but Teresa had taken it all in.

The psychological principle was that there was a normal inner requirement that reality should be firmly based. Human sensory equipment constantly tested the veracity of the world, and silently reported to the consciousness. Normal life functioned. An ExEx

269

scenario could therefore only function as a plausible-seeming alternative to reality by simulating the sensual information, and this continued so long as the participant gave or implied consent. Reality was suspended while the scenario continued. This meant that recognizing, isolating and consciously rejecting one of the simulated sensory inputs was the only way to escape from the extreme experience.

There were questions and answers, and a short break for refreshments. Later, when the professor had left, Dan Kazinsky said, 'You ought to know that sometimes you'll get stuck in there. The mnemonic won't always work. There's another way out. You got to know what it is.'

He explained about the manual override built into the valve itself.

Teresa reached behind her, located the ExEx valve and felt around the rim of it for the minute trip-switch, concealed within a specially stiffened fold of the plastic integument. When she found it she gingerly eased the plastic apart with a fingernail, trying to avoid straining the sensitive area of her skin.

She had never done this before, except in a dry run in Quantico under the instruction of Agent Kazinsky. She found that the switch was more difficult to flick over than she had imagined it would be, and it took her two attempts to do it. As the tiny plastic device closed with a tangible pressure, Teresa braced herself for the traumatic disruption of an emergency withdrawal.

Teresa remained in Welton Road, outside the ExEx building, with Grove's stolen car gleaming in the midsummer sun. Nothing changed.

She reached behind her, located the ExEx valve and felt around the rim of it for the minute trip-switch, concealed within its specially stiffened fold of the plastic integument. When she found it she gingerly eased the plastic apart with a fingernail, and returned the switch to its former position.

Once, years before, Teresa had been driving her car at night in downtown Baltimore, in the area north of Franklin Street, a part of the city she knew well. Not paying attention she had taken a wrong turn. Thinking she knew where she was she drove straight to what she thought was her friend's address, found a parking space, and got out of her car. As soon as she did, paying attention at last to her surroundings, she knew instantly she was in the wrong place, but she was still none the less convinced that it could not be so. She had driven there many times before, and knew the location well. Yet there were two small stores where the entrance to her friend's apartment block should have been, the streetlights were wrong, the buildings opposite were too tall, too decrepit. For a few seconds, Teresa had been convinced of two conflicting facts, knowing they were in conflict, but no less disturbed for knowing it: that she was in the wrong place, and simultaneously that she was not.

Now, as the hot summer's afternoon lay around her, the brilliant sunlight dazzled her, the rolling heat from the ground smothered her, Teresa experienced the same conflict. Her inability to abort the scenario meant that she was really here, on the day of Grove's mass murders.

But that was eight months ago; it couldn't possibly be so.

Perspiration was beginning to trickle from her hairline, down the sides of her face, so she undid the top two buttons of her blouse, and lightly raised and fanned the material, to try to cool herself. She found a tissue and mopped her face ineffectually. (The tissue was already damp: was it the same one she had used to dry her face when she staggered in from the arctic blast this morning?) Standing here in the street she could hardly start removing the warmest of the garments she was wearing: her snugly fitting jeans, and the thick tights beneath. She did have cooler clothes with her, but they were already packed in one of her suitcases at the hotel, ready for the flight home.

Staring at Grove's abandoned car, perplexed by what had happened, Teresa gave it a hard look, then went back across the street to the ExEx building.

CHAPTER 35

Paula Willson was still sitting at her desk, with a fan swivelling slowly to and fro across her. Pieces of paper on the desktop lifted fractionally as the draught swept by.

'Hi,' Teresa said as she walked in and closed the door. After the blazing sunshine outside the building felt cool.

'How may I help you?' said Paula.

'Well, I hope you can help me a lot. I want to ask you if you know who I am?'

'You were here a few minutes ago, weren't you?'

'I was leaving, and you asked me if it had started raining.'

'That's right,' said Paula.

'Can you remember why you asked me that?'

'I was surprised to see you, the way you were dressed. You'd put a coat on.'

'OK,' Teresa said. 'Had you seen me in here before then?'

'I don't think so. I think you'd been using the simulators. I assumed you must have come in before my shift began. You are one of our customers, aren't you?'

'Yeah, that's right. Look, I'm trying to locate—'

'May I have your name?'

'I've brought my customer ID with me.'

Teresa wanted to say that she and this young woman had been saying hello to each other most mornings for the last three weeks, but there was no point at all in that. She was no longer certain of anything. She groped in the pocket where she normally kept the plastic card, but it was not there. She tried her other pockets. Then she remembered: Grove had had a similar conversation with Paula, earlier that day, when he had arrived at this building. To cut short the formalities, Teresa had helped him find an ID card, which he had immediately reached for in the back pocket of his pants, exactly as she had done now. Grove had found an ID card; she could not find hers.

'I'm somewhere in your computer records,' Teresa said. 'Teresa Simons, Teresa Ann Simons. No E on Ann.'

'I won't keep you a moment,' said Paula, already typing at her keyboard and glancing at the screen. 'No, I'm afraid we don't have you, but we are recruiting new members at the moment, and there's a discount scheme with air-mile bonuses if you sign up now. If you would fill in this application form, and can supply a major credit card, we will grant you temporary membership straight away.'

She slid the sheet of paper across to Teresa.

Teresa said, 'I'm simply trying to find someone I know, who I think is here. I came in with him earlier. Could you at least tell me if he's still in here?'

The expression on the young woman's face remained one of professional reticence.

'I'm sorry. I'm not able to give out information on our customers.'

'Yeah, I understand the problem. This is slightly different, I think. I arrived with him.'

'I'm sorry,' Paula said again.

'Couldn't you even confirm he's still here? It's Mr Grove, Mr Gerry Grove.'

'I'm not allowed to,' Paula said with an embarrassed look, and a glance towards the inner sanctum. For an instant Teresa glimpsed the friendly and at times informal young woman she had often paused for a chat with on her way in or out of this building.

'Are you allowed to hand out that sort of information to fellow members?' she said. 'You know, if I fill out this form?'

'I'll see what I can do.' A quick smile of relief flickered across Paula's eyes.

Teresa moved away to one of the seats in the waiting area, and rapidly filled out the relevant details about herself. The form was the same one she had completed when she became a member the first time, but it looked subtly different: the print was larger, laid out a little differently, an earlier version of the form she had already handed in.

When Paula saw Teresa signing the form, she picked up the internal telephone and pressed a couple of buttons. As Teresa walked back to her desk, she was saying, 'Hi, this is Paula, on the front desk. I'm trying to trace one of the users. Mr Grove.'

'Gerry Grove,' Teresa said.

'Yes, that's right. OK, would Sharon know? It's a Mr Gerry Grove, apparently. Gerry with a G?' She looked up at Teresa, who nodded. Paula confirmed this, then made an expression towards Teresa with her eyes. 'They're trying to find out. Yes, I'm still here. OK. Thanks.'

She put down the phone and scribbled a long number on a scrap of paper.

'They say they know who you mean.'

'Good! I need to see him.'

'Now hold on, because they say I have to determine his status. They've given me his ID,' Paula said. She typed at the keyboard, glancing to and from the long number she had written down. 'All right, Mr Grove did check in here earlier.' She looked at the clock on the wall to one side. 'About an hour ago, I think.'

'That's about right. Is he still using the simulator?'

'No, it doesn't look as if he is. He didn't log much machine time. He paid cash upfront, but—'

'May I see?'

'Well . . .'

But Teresa had moved round so that she was alongside Paula and able to read her screen. It displayed fairly straightforward text information, showing Grove's name and a scenario reference number that Teresa instantly recognized: it was of course the porno video-shoot, with Shandy and Willem.

'You can see here,' Paula said, tapping the end of her ballpoint against the screen. 'It looks as if the scenario terminated after a few seconds. You'd have to ask one of the technical people exactly what that means. I don't have anything to do with the scenarios. But they can be stopped, can't they? The customer can decide to leave? I think that must be what happened here.'

'But after a few seconds?'

'It says eleven seconds.'

Teresa thought for a moment. She remembered arriving in the scenario, the awareness of heat and bright lights, the half-cup bra that was too tight, blinking against the lights, people standing beyond the circle of lights, a woman patting her forehead and nose with powder, then saying, 'Hold still a while longer, Shan,' and moving behind the lights again. She had thought, I can't take this any more, and then she had aborted the scenario. Was that eleven seconds?

'You say he isn't using the simulator now. But is he still in the building?'

'I can phone through for you, and find out.'

'Yes. Please do.'

Again, Paula used the internal phone. She asked if Mr Grove was in the recovery area, and listened to the reply.

She said to Teresa, 'No, they think he must have checked straight out. He's nowhere in the facility.'

Teresa felt a bleak desperation growing in her.

'Did you see him leave?' she said.

'People pass through here all the time.'

'You must know what he looked like. He was wearing . . .' Teresa paused, remembering. 'Dark-green pants with buttoned pockets everywhere, like army fatigues. A green muscle-shirt, with oily smears on the front. He came in here and had forty pounds in cash. He tossed it on the desk in front of you. You asked if he was a member, and he said he usually used the Maidstone facility. He gave you an ID card, and after that you let him through.'

'Gingery hair, dirty hands?'

'That's him! Did you see him leave?'

'No.'

'Are you certain? You haven't taken any breaks?'

'Now I know who you mean, I'd know if he'd gone.'

'Then he must still be here in the building.'

All through this Teresa had been holding her new membership application form, and now she gave it to Paula. For good measure she threw down her GM MasterCard beside it.

'That makes me a member, right?'

'Yes, I suppose—'

'You'll find the credit card has already been recorded. I'll pick it up in a moment.'

She pushed through the door before Paula could answer, and went into the main part of the building. It took her only a minute or two to establish that Grove was indeed no longer there. Few members of the staff had been aware of his presence while he was using the equipment; no one had seen him leave.

Teresa hurried outside into the bright sunshine, and went across to where his stolen car was parked.

She stood next to it for a while, staring at the view, the blue-and-silver sea, the distant roofs, the quiet streets, the weather in France. Her identity had crossed over into Grove's; she had entered the building with him, and he had left when she did. Where was he now?

A few moments later, she heard the sound of police sirens, in the distance among the houses, down in the quiet streets of Bulverton's Old Town.

CHAPTER 36

She picked up her MasterCard from the reception desk, together with her ExEx membership start-up pack, an introductory pamphlet, her air-mile certificate, discount vouchers for the first ten hours of ExEx run-time use, a free pen and a complimentary canvas tote bag emblazoned with the GunHo corporate logo. She gave a smile of acknowledgement to Paula and walked into the main part of the building to find a terminal she could use.

The computers looked slightly different from the ones she was used to, but they displayed the familiar GunHo logo. Of the three machines currently not in use she chose the one furthest from the corridor that ran through the open-plan office. She sat down and entered the new membership number she found in the promotional material Paula had given to her. No use entering her old number, the one she had learned by heart, so often had she typed it in.

After a perceptible pause, the program went into its start-up routine.

Teresa watched the display screens flick from one to the next, and she realized that between this day and the time some eight months in the future when she had been regularly using this system, there must have been a round of upgrades. The software looked much the same as the program she was used to, but it was obviously running at about half the speed. The keyboard and monitor also looked slightly different from the ones she remembered. She had always felt intimidated by the ferocious speed with which the software responded, and this earlier version actually suited her rather better.

The program paused, displaying the principal menu of options. Teresa glanced over it, and felt, without being able to be certain, that there were not as many options as she was used to. No matter.

Now then. She had to think.

She was faced with two explanations of her present dilemma, both based on impossibility.

All the evidence was that she was now living eight months in the past. Even as she stared blankly at the monitor, yet another piece of evidence for this swam into her awareness: the program always displayed the day's date in a tiny box at the bottom right of the display, and according to this the date now was June 3. The day of Grove's massacre.

To accept this would mean accepting that she had moved back through time. There were the dates on her credit card, the change in weather, the many small differences at the ExEx building. In the February of her real life, Paula Willson had told her that membership of the Bulverton ExEx facility was almost at capacity, and that they were planning to close the place to new members. A few minutes ago, the same Paula had pressed on her all the paraphernalia of a sales or membership drive.

But the whole concept of travelling back through time was, for Teresa, almost impossible to accept. She had never understood it on a philosophical level, and anyway she felt that all around her was practical disproof.

If entering the Grove scenario, then leaving it, had taken her eight months into the past via the medium of Gerry Grove's disgusting consciousness, how come she had turned up here in the same clothes she was wearing when she left the hotel this morning? How come she had the same shoulder-bag? Carried the same credit cards? Had the same tissue in her pocket when she needed to mop her face, the first time to wipe away the rain of a freezing day, the second time the perspiration of a heatwave?

More to the point, how had she lost her ExEx identification card, if Grove had not taken it when he needed to?

That wasn't consistent, though. The cards were electronically coded: when Grove gave his (or hers) to Paula, the receptionist had found records of Grove on her computer.

Teresa gave up that line of thought.

Her rental car had also disappeared, and she gave up on that too. All scenarios had inconsistencies, brick walls where you expected an Underground station to be.

It must mean she was in extreme experience, not living this as part of her own life. But it was no longer the scenario of Grove's day of murder: that was the scenario she had consciously entered, the one that had placed her within his mind, behind his eyes, as a witness to his crimes. She was herself, not Grove in any form.

Although the hyperreality of a scenario no longer surprised her, she had never been able to take for granted the sheer wealth of detail, the tiny plausible details, the irrelevancies, the unexpected and the accidental. All these underlined the sense of a heightened reality.

She could feel it now: looking around, she sought evidence of unexpected detail, and instantly found it.

The nail of her left index finger was broken: she had snagged it the night before when opening a drawer in her bedroom at the White Dragon, and had only had time to smooth down the break with an emery board. It was the same now as it had been this morning. Outside the cubicle in which she was sitting was a Swiss cheese plant in a pot, and it clearly needed watering or a spell in direct daylight. Three of the leaves were turning yellow, and about to fall off. On the far side of the open-plan office, barely visible above the partition walls, was a fluorescent light with a strip that needed replacing: at odd moments it flickered quickly, a constant minor distraction at the edge of vision. A dropped or discarded ballpoint pen lay on the floor behind her chair; she had not dropped it, it was not hers, and until this moment she had not even noticed it.

(But moments later she realized that the complimentary pen Paula had given her was no longer where she had placed it, that she must have knocked it off the desk, that the pen was after all hers. Details were maddening.)

Of course, such evidence would also underline the condition of reality, but Teresa had advanced beyond that.

Wherever she was, it was no longer the objectively real world.

But if it was a scenario, why had she been unable to abort it?

'Do you need a hand with running the software?'

A technician, a young man Teresa had never seen before, had paused while he passed the cubicle.

'No . . . I'm just trying to make up my mind what I'd like to do.'

'I'm here to help you, if you require it,' he said. 'You looked as if you were having trouble running the program.'

'It's fine. Thanks.' He could have no conception of the trouble she was having.

She waited until he had gone, then narrowed her eyes and again tried to think.

The rules had changed. When Grove entered the Shandy scenario, all the standard procedures for going into and out of extreme experience had been left behind. This, presumably, was what Ken Mitchell had meant by crossover: he described it as false memory syndrome, *post hoc* invention, interpretative spin. When she aborted the scenario she had imagined herself into existence here: there had been no corporeal body called Teresa Simons in a simulation cubicle, here, in the ExEx facility, on June 3. Yet she had returned from the Shandy scenario, and still was here.

The logic of the scenarios had been destroyed by Grove. The linearity Ken Mitchell held to be so essential had been given a third dimension, made matrical.

She began to browse as she had done so often before, but whereas previously she had been impelled mostly by curiosity now she had a purpose. She was looking for the area of the database called Memorative Principals, and recalled that when she had been searching for the extra information about Shandy it had not been accessible from any of the main option menus. She tried to remember how she had done it then, but saw nothing that reminded her. Back at the main screen of options, she finally noticed a small box in the bottom corner: **Run Macro**. She clicked on this, and to her relief saw yet another huge menu of options. One of these was **Connect Memorative Principals**.

She typed in 'Teresa Ann Simons', added 'Woodbridge' and 'Bulverton' as defining physical locations, and clicked to see what would happen. Nothing happened. Not even the first scenario she had ever used, the target practice, was on file. But that, of course, was then. Back then, some time in the future, next February.

She typed in 'Gerry Grove', added 'Bulverton' as a location, and then as an afterthought put in 'Gerald Dean Grove' as an alternative name. After a perceptible pause, the computer said that Grove appeared in three scenarios. Teresa ran the list of them. Two were shown as having no hyperlinks; there was a similarity to their code numbers that made them look as if they were the same kind of thing. The third looked different, and Teresa clicked on the video icon.

It was in a car, parked on the seafront at Bulverton. Sunlight poured in from the direction of the sea. Hands were tightening a hot-wire connection beneath the dash. A figure stopped beside the car, shading the flood of sunlight.

The video preview ended.

A familiar sensation rose in Teresa: that of imminent overload, constantly diverting her to new matters. The program was showing her more information than she could take in. The sequence she had just watched was the opening of the scenario she experienced with Grove: the drug deal, the theft of the car, the taking of the guns from his house . . .

This was the scenario she had been in, and had eventually aborted, the one that had trapped her within its time frame. Yet this scenario could not possibly exist today, the day on which the events actually occurred!

Meanwhile, what of the other two scenarios? She hadn't seen them in connection with Grove, in earlier searches of the program.

She clicked on one, and immediately recognized it. Grove had used the range for target practice; the video preview reminded her of the one occasion she had used the same facility. She let the preview run to its end, then clicked on the other and watched that as well. It was much the same. She looked at the back view of Grove's stocky figure with dislike.

The range itself did look slightly different, though, from the one where she had recorded her own target practice. Noticing an information button marked **Location Code**, she clicked on it and saw a narrative breakdown of part of the reference number. This identified the range in use as being the GunHo Licensed Extreme Experience facility, in Whitechapel Street, Maidstone, Kent.

She thought, I'm losing my grip on this. There's too much information coming at me.

Grove had said to Paula, as he checked into this ExEx facility, inside the scenario, folded back somewhere in her memory, Grove had said to Paula that he had used the Maidstone range, presumably implying that he did not normally come to this place.

Why had he said Maidstone? During her researches Teresa had read every available scrap of information about Grove, and she didn't recall a single mention of that Kentish town in his context.

She knew he had said Maidstone because she had prompted him to. She had been wondering how he was going to lie his way past Paula. He had reached into his back pocket and found a plastic ID card that had satisfied the girl, and whose identifying number was acceptable to the computer. Teresa must have inspired the off-the-cuff reference to Maidstone herself, perhaps dredging it up from the memory of Paula telling her about the waiting period for membership.

She looked away from the screen, with its burden of unexpected information. She stared at the keyboard, lightly running her fingers round the edge of the plastic case, trying to clear her mind. She thought, Any more of this and I really will be lost.

In the end, the information about Maidstone was irrelevant. It led up a blind alley, or at least into an alley into which she didn't want to venture.

She clicked back through the screens, to the one where she could search for links between principals. Once again she entered her own name and the defining locations, and the two versions of Grove's name, and waited to see what would happen.

There are 4 hyperlink(s) connecting 'Teresa Ann Simons' to 'Gerry/Gerald Dean Grove'. Display? Yes/No.

Four links had come into being, where none had existed a few moments earlier. Again with the feeling that her ability to understand was slipping away from her, Teresa clicked on **Yes**.

The first new link between her and Grove neither surprised nor worried her: it was to Shandy and Willem in their lustful clinch under the glare of the film lights. Neither did the second: this was Grove's deadly ramble around Bulverton.

It was the last two links that frightened her.

She now appeared to be connected with his target practice sessions in the Maidstone range. The list gave the dates and the code identified the location; the tiny video frames repeated what she had watched for herself only a few minutes earlier.

Had the act of briefly previewing those two scenarios somehow activated them, and linked her to them? But she had not actually entered the scenarios; she had merely viewed the video clips! In earlier sessions with the program she had previewed videos, without creating a hyperlink. It was only a computer program, a glorified card index system.

She clicked on the video icon of the Shandy scenario, saw the young woman go yet again through her awkward movements as she tried to ease her uncomfortable clothes. When it finished, a new message was on the screen:

There are 72 hyperlink(s) connecting 'Teresa Ann Simons' to 'Gerry/Gerald Dean Grove'. Display? Yes/No.

Seventy-two, when only a few moments ago there had been four? Dreading what might be happening, while still not comprehending it, Teresa again clicked on **Yes**.

The list unfolded slowly before her: she was hyperlinked to Grove's target practice sessions in Maidstone, and he to hers in Bulverton. In addition they were both hyperlinked to Shandy and Willem, Elsa Jane Durdle, William Cook . . .

She moved the mouse pointer rapidly to **Cancel**, and clicked. The listing ceased at once and the screen cleared. A feeling gripped her that Grove was insinuating himself into her life. She had a bleak, vivid impression of his consciousness, somewhere in virtual reality, moving through every experience she had ever had, linking himself with her, crossing over from his blighted life to hers.

After a long pause, the screen once again showed the message in which the links were declared. It now said:

There are 658 hyperlink(s) connecting 'Teresa Ann Simons' to 'Gerry/Gerald Dean Grove'. Display? Yes/No.

Where would this end? With every minute, more links were being added and at what felt like an exponential rate of growth. Once again, she clicked on **Yes**, and stared at the screen with dread.

The list scrolled sedately up the screen, with some of the items taking longer to appear than others.

Many of them were familiar: Grove's two target practice recordings in Maidstone, and the one of herself in Bulverton. Shandy and Willem were there again (five in total, but freshly linked to another one hundred and sixty-five unlisted scenarios). Some scenarios were new, but unsurprising: the Mercer family had thirteen scenarios linked to the shooting of Shelly. Others did surprise her. Who for instance was Katherine Denise Devore (ten links), and what was her connection either with Teresa or with Grove? Dave Hartland's name unexpectedly appeared (twenty-seven times), and there were sixteen others, in which Amy Lorraine Hartland, née Colwyn, and Nicholas Anthony Surtees were named as memorative principals. Rosalind Williams appeared on the list (four), then Elsa Jane Durdle (fifteen; why had some been added since she was last here?).

To Teresa it seemed as if a patchwork version of her life was being assembled inside the computer.

She clicked on the first of Elsa Durdle's video icons, and saw the swaying palm trees, the glowing sunlight, the shining parked cars. So much had that simple scenario meant to her, because it had first given her the idea that she was free to explore, that like a child returning to an old toy for comfort she was tempted to select it once again. She wanted to drive through Southern California in Elsa's big comfortable car, listening to Duke Ellington and Artie Shaw on the radio, watching the town move away and re-form around her as she travelled the endless highways of memory and mind.

Continue with 658 hyperlink(s) connecting 'Teresa Ann Simons' to 'Gerry/Gerald Dean Grove'? Yes/No.

Teresa clicked on **No**. She scrolled back through the list, and paused on the name Katherine Denise Devore. Who the hell was this woman, that she was suddenly significant to her?

She thought hard: Katherine, Kath, Kathy, Kathie, Kate, Katie? Had she ever known anyone with these names? Or Denise? Anyone at school, for instance? Teresa had repeatedly changed schools as her father was moved around from base to base. Most people grow up with a few old friends from their schooldays, but Teresa had hundreds of acquaintances and almost none she remembered as friends. Surely, somewhere, there would be a Katherine? Or maybe at one of her early jobs, at university, or at the Bureau? There had been a trainee on the ExEx course with her at the Quantico Academy, called Cathy Grenidge, whose full name was presumably Catherine . . . but now she thought about it she had never seen her name written down. She might easily have been Katherine or Kathy. What had happened to her? Something shadowed the memory of Cathy Grenidge. Teresa thought hard, consciously using a memory technique she had been taught long ago. Federal agents have to be able to retain a lot of names and faces out of the hundreds they encounter, and there were ways of recalling them. What was the mnemonic for doing that? She cleared her mind, concentrated on the face, and then she had it. Agent Grenidge; she had graduated at the same time as Teresa, then was posted to Delaware, someplace like that? They'd lost contact, swept away to their own careers in the Bureau. No, Cathy married, then left the Bureau after a few years? No, she hadn't quit. Teresa remembered that she and Cathy had married at about the same time, but Cathy was posted to somewhere in the Midwest soon afterwards. What had happened to her? She'd died in an accident, hadn't she? Or was it on an assignment? Who married her? Somewhere far away, a mental glimpse: Cathy and the guy she married, another agent, a practical joke at the wedding, something to do with a pack of cards and a trick, a brilliant piece of card manipulation that made everyone roar with laughter; a guy with large hands and a heavy body. Cal! Calvin Devore; Andy's friend Cal, the big guy with the large hands and the dainty movements that always amused and impressed her. Oh Jesus, Cal! His wife had been shot, trying to arrest a suspect in Dubuque, Iowa, hit in the head by a bullet, lay in a coma for a week, then died. Kathy Devore.

Continue with 658 hyperlink(s) connecting 'Teresa Ann Simons' to 'Gerry/Gerald Dean Grove'? Yes/No.

Teresa clicked on **No**, irritated with the program for seeming irritated with her.

Was she involved in Kathy's death? Was Grove? What was the link? She tried to think, clear her thoughts of all the sidetracks, all the extra information.

If she let this go on, if she went back again, there would be even more hyperlinks, hundreds more connections. How many more could there be? The sidetracks were endless. The crossover with

Grove was growing as if alive: it was spreading through virtuality, dragging in more connections between them, perhaps creating them.

It was that endlessness again, the lack of an edge or a boundary, only extremes.

She thought, It's enough. I don't want to know about Kathy Devore. Not now. It's too late for that. I have to concentrate on one thing. What I want, what I need. Hyperreality has broken down, and I can go to the extremes.

Continue with 658 hyperlink(s) connecting 'Teresa Ann Simons' to 'Gerry/Gerald Dean Grove'? Yes/No.

Teresa clicked on **Yes**. The seemingly endless listing resumed.

William Cook (one hundred and eleven main items, but with hundreds of others hyperlinked elsewhere), Charles Whitman (two hundred and twenty-seven main items, but with thousands of others adjacent), James and Michaela Surtees (two), Jason Hartland (thirty-three items), Sam Wilkins McLeod (fifteen), Deke Cannigan (who? – anyway thirty), Charles Dayton Hunter (eighty-one items), Joseph L. McLaughlin (twenty-four), José Porteiro (eighteen) . . .

After the six hundred and thirty-fourth numbered scenario, the program paused, but Teresa could sense it working, searching the database, assembling, sorting. Then the screen shifted one more time, and the last twenty-four scenarios were listed.

They were all for Andy/Andrew Wellman Simons.

The video frame of the first scenario of the twenty-four showed Andy's bulky figure standing alert beside a car. He was holding a gun in both hands, looking back over one shoulder into the distance. He had on his FBI bulletproof vest, the Bureau's famous initials clearly inscribed.

The hierarchical information for this item was:

Participatory/Operative-enabled/Non-interactive/State or County PD/State PD/Texas/Kingwood City/Multiple Murder/ Spree/Guns/John Luther Aronwitz/Federal Agent Andrew Wellman Simons.

Andy was what she wanted, all she wanted.

Tears were welling in her eyes as Teresa moved the pointer to the **ExEx** box. She clicked on it, and a few seconds later the equipment delivered her phial of nanochips.

Holding in her hand the life and death of her husband, Teresa walked through to the simulator area of the building, and found a technician to set the scenario in motion.

CHAPTER 37

Federal Agent Andy Simons parked his car outside police lines, pulled on his bulletproof vest with the FBI initials displayed prominently at front and back, jerked his cap down over his forehead and went to find Captain Jack Tremmins, officer in charge. According to protocol, Andy offered any assistance that might be required.

Teresa had forgotten how hot a Texas summer afternoon could be: a sticky, spreading heat, which made everything seem to burn around you, whether in shade or not. The concrete of the parking lot scorched through the soles of Andy's shoes, and the almost vertical sunlight battered down on the crown of his head through the thin plastic of his cap. There was a smell of rag-weed, stinging his sinuses.

Andy had always suffered pollen allergies.

Teresa stared through Andy's eyes around the immense parking lot, trying to orient herself. She had been in Britain long enough to forget the scale on which Texan shopping malls were built. Most of Bulverton's Old Town would fit into this lot and she knew there would be further acres of parking spaces on the other sides of the massive mall. The great dome of the Texan sky stretched overhead, its vastness emphasized by the flat horizons in all directions. Only buildings stood up against the sky to lend a sense of scale.

Texas was a place of extremes, a place without limits.

Away beyond police lines the normal business of the North Cross shopping mall continued: the gunman had been cornered in the service bay in the rear of the building, and after hurried consultations with the mall administrator, the police had allowed the stores inside the building to resume trading normally. The only restraint on movement was in this area, around the loading and unloading bays. Although the gunman had already killed several people, he was thought to present no further danger to the public.

Andy found Captain Tremmins, who quickly and efficiently briefed him on all this. He took him over to meet Lieutenant Frank Hanson, in charge of the SWAT team. Andy said to Hanson he would like to go through and talk with the mall administration, but if he was required to render any assistance . . .

Andy had to walk round the long way, past the service bays, to get inside the huge building. As he stepped under the police tape, sweating in the terrible heat, Teresa said, 'Andy?'

There was no response.

'Andy, can you hear me? It's me, Tess.'

He kept striding on, looking from side to side watchfully. He rounded a corner and came to a huge entrance vestibule built of steel and glass: overhead there was a sign intended to be read from a mile away. It said: *NORTH CROSS CENTER – West Entrance.* A group of armed police let him through, and at once he was in the air-conditioned chill inside.

'Andy? Can you give me a sign you know I'm here?'

He walked on without responding. There was a doughnut counter, a book store, a furniture shop, a leather-goods store; they came into a broad atrium with mature trees, a series of rolling waterfalls, a fountain playing under coloured lights . . .

Teresa remembered how she had learned to shift position when she was in Grove's mind: while she stayed at the back of his mind she could not communicate with him, but she influenced his decisions and movements; when she moved forward she felt as if he had taken control of himself again but she was exposed to all his thoughts and instincts. She tried to shift position in Andy's mind, but either the scenario was written differently or Andy was of sterner mentality. She could make no impact on his thoughts or movements.

'Andy! Listen to me! This is Tess, your wife. Don't go on with this, get back to your car. Wait until Danny Schneider joins up with you, consult with him, don't do this alone, you're going to be killed if you go on.'

She stopped, thinking how English she sounded, how polite and reasonable. In the old days Andy had sometimes teased her when a Liverpool phrase or a bit of slang from childhood crept into her speech. She'd always been able to imitate Ringo Starr better than anyone else around them; Andy had liked that.

'I don't think you should be doing this, Andrew,' she said, trying to capture Ringo's nasal tones.

But Andy went on, disregarding everything she said. Three more uniformed police directed him to the admin block, and one of them travelled up in the elevator with him. Andy made polite small-talk with the cop: he had a family, lived in Abilene, his wife was expecting another baby. He had a rolling Texas accent, most words given an extra syllable, and he called Andy 'sir' with every reply.

What it was to hear Andy's voice again! Slightly gruff, with a trick in some of the sounds, like he needed to clear his throat, but it was always there, just the noise he made when he spoke.

'I love you, Andy!' she cried desperately. 'Stop this! Please . . . leave with me! You're not needed here! Let's wait in the car until the cops have caught the man!'

There followed a short interview between Andy and the mall administrator, a woman called Betty Nolanski. Mrs Nolanski's main concern was the fact that the mall had only been fully open for three months. Last year two of the major chains had cancelled their leases at the eleventh hour, and she thought this incident might scare away more. She told Andy there were still fourteen major units standing empty. She wanted the gunman removed immediately, and with no more publicity.

Andy and Mrs Nolanski walked down together to the main floor while this was being said.

Teresa said, 'Tell her she's in a boom town, Andy. She wants to see a place with economic problems, she should go to Bulverton.'

At ground level the news was that Aronwitz had still not been apprehended. Andy asked Mrs Nolanski if there were any utility ducts or tunnels by which the service bay could be reached, and at once a buildings manager was instructed to show him where the entrances were. Andy had to explain that his rôle here was advisory only, and that Lieutenant Hanson should be given the plans of the utility area of the building.

Teresa felt panic rising in her as time went on ticking by. She knew that this incident was approaching its bloody end, and that she could not influence it in any way.

Non-interactive, it had said in the index heading.

Trying again, she said urgently, 'Andy, can you hear me? Andy! Listen to me! You're going to get hurt! Leave this to the police. This is their problem, not yours!'

She thought about aborting from the scenario, trying one of the others that dealt with Aronwitz, but she knew from her training that interdiction scenarios were mastered only by repeated attempts to get them right.

Andy left the administrator, and headed back towards the police lines. Once outside, in the broiling heat once more, he went straight to Captain Tremmins to be given a status update.

Some of Hanson's men had entered the service area through utility tunnels under the bays, but Aronwitz had shot his second hostage a few minutes ago and then disappeared. Tremmins was presently out of contact not only with the SWAT team but also with his own men who were supposed to be keeping Aronwitz under surveillance.

Andy said, 'Then he's gone underground too. You think your SWAT guys can take him out? They done this kind of thing before?'

'Some,' said Tremmins.

'Let's get round to the utility area. If he's going to break out, that's where it will have to be.'

'Yes, Andy,' Teresa said fervently, in his mind. 'That's where he'll be. Stop doing this! My God! Stop doing this, Andy!'

It was an area beneath the shadow of the service area of the mall: a large concrete yard, with waste silos, batteries of extractor fans, an electricity sub-station, and several huge fuel tanks. Suddenly, word came through on the radio that the SWAT team had located Aronwitz, who had fired some shots, eluded them, and was heading this way.

Tremmins ordered his men to take cover, and around twenty police officers circled the area with their guns.

Aronwitz burst into view, gun in hand. When he saw the police he halted, almost overbalancing from the loading platform he was on.

'*Freeze, Aronwitz! Throw down your weapon!*'

Instead, Aronwitz stood erect, and made a circling motion with his gun, a deliberate, wide swinging of the arm. He cocked the weapon, the click audible in every part of the yard.

Teresa stared in disbelief. The gunman was Gerry Grove.

Andy stood up, reacting to her shocked realization. Grove/Aronwitz saw the movement and turned towards him. Teresa watched, frozen in terror, as Grove levelled the gun at Andy, steadied his hand by gripping his wrist, and slowly squeezed the trigger.

Just as she had shown him.

Teresa desperately recalled LIVER, and managed to withdraw an instant before Grove shot Andy in the head, smashing away most of the top of his skull.

Teresa stared in horror at the image of the GunHo corporate logo as she heard the roar of the bullets of Captain Tremmins' men blowing away the gunman. Darkness fell.

Sharon was still on duty in the simulators, and as soon as Teresa was sitting up the technician came into the recovery cubicle and removed the nanochips. Teresa's mind was swirling with images of Andy: his voice, his large strong body, his way of walking, the calm and professional manner in which he had set up the circumstances that led to his own death. Entering that scenario had been everything she had once dreaded such an experience would be: a terrible closeness to Andy, a more terrible distance, and a total inability to save his life. That she had at last learned how he died was small recompense. None, in fact. She sat in morbid silence, going through an echoing reminder of her distress of the previous year, trying to cope, trying not to be overwhelmed by her feelings.

Sharon seemed equally preoccupied, but the business with the credit card went ahead smoothly, and Teresa slipped the paperwork into a zipped pocket of her new tote bag. She checked the time: less than an hour had elapsed while she had been in the Aronwitz scenario. The date was still June 3.

Sharon was uncommunicative, and seemed anxious to move on to her next task. Teresa asked her what the matter was.

'There's something happening in the town,' Sharon said. 'It's been on the radio. The staff have been told we can't leave the building until the police say it's safe.'

'I thought I heard sirens earlier.'

'They say that someone's going around with a gun. There are police outside the building now. They think the gunman was seen up here earlier.'

Teresa nodded, but said nothing. Sharon left her, so Teresa walked back to the computer cubicles, and found a terminal that was not in use. She put down her bags on the chair, and went into the Ladies' restroom.

Alone, she sagged. She could not help herself: she locked herself in one of the toilet cubicles and gave way to the grief. The tears flooded out. Someone else came into the restroom, used another toilet, and left again. Teresa managed to stem her tears until she was alone, then once more allowed her feelings to pour out.

They were but a reminder of the real anguish, and after the flood she regained her composure with remarkable speed. Drying her eyes, she realized that what had upset her was nothing new, that she had been through all that.

She wondered if she was merely suppressing the grief again. But no, the situation was different now: she was in a position actually to do something. Grove had changed the rules.

Most of the natural light in the room came through the sloping window in the half-roof, but there was another small frosted window in the wall at the far end. Teresa eased this open, to find a restricted view. An extension of the main building was opposite the window, so it was possible to see only a narrow angle to one side. By leaning out and craning her neck, Teresa could see a short section of Welton Road.

A cordon of bright-orange police tape ran alongside the row of parked cars; one of these was Grove's stolen Montego. No one was close to the cars, and all the doors and windows of the Montego were closed. An armed policeman wearing a bulletproof vest was standing with his back to her, looking about him systematically. There was no other sign of activity. She knew the police here would act the same as federal agents in the same circumstances: don't touch a vehicle known or thought to carry arms or explosives.

Teresa closed the window, left the restroom and returned to the computer cubicle.

She entered her new membership number, and after a pause the program went into its start-up routine.

Teresa watched the display screens flick past, and come to a rest on the screenful of main options. She rested her hand on the mouse, stared blankly at the screen, and tried to decide what to do.

Teresa recalled that she had made one decision early on: she wanted to know as little as possible about Aronwitz. He had come out of obscurity to take from her the only person who truly mattered in her life, and it had seemed to her from the outset that obscurity was where he should properly stay. Her work in the Bureau had shown her how criminals often became minor celebrities, because of media attention: some of the perpetrators she had had to deal with herself, who she knew were equipped only with viciousness, meanness, cruelty and a stunning mediocrity, briefly became notorious or perversely celebrated when they were arrested or their cases came to court. Being on the Bureau's Ten Most Wanted list, still in permanent use, was seen by many criminals as a status symbol.

She wanted Aronwitz to have no such celebrity, even in death. Her way of trying to ensure that, or at least making a start, was to close him off from her. She made a point of not finding out anything about him, of not knowing more than the barest outline of his life, of not trying to understand or forgive what he had done. She even went to great lengths to avoid finding out what he had looked like.

For a few days, while the story ran, an old Arkansas State Police mugshot of Aronwitz appeared regularly on TV and in the newspapers. Teresa never looked. If she realized it was about to be shown, she would look away, and if she opened a newspaper or magazine to find his face pictured there, she instantly blurred her vision, shied away from looking at him.

Inevitably, she could not make him disappear, and soon she had half-glimpsed him often enough to have gained an impression of him. She knew he was young or youngish, that he had fair hair, a broad forehead, eyes that were too small. But she felt she would never recognize him, or be able to describe him.

Would she ever have known that he looked like Gerry Grove?

Or, worse, that he was Gerry Grove?

How could this be? Grove was in Bulverton on the day, this

day, of the shootings. Historical certainty again. It was a fact, beyond question, in a way a scenario could never be. Scenarios were constructs, artificial re-creations by programmers of events remembered or experienced or described by other people. They were full of flaws, designed to be reactive to the people who went in as participants, they were subject to crossover, had extra bits, sometimes illogical extra bits, bolted on. That Gerry Grove appeared in Andy's scenario, taking the place of Aronwitz, was a product of the scenarios, not a statement of what had really happened.

Teresa was sure of that. Completely sure.

She thought back, wishing she had not denied Aronwitz to herself. She wished she had kept a file on him, brought it with her, could now look at the face she had never seen properly.

On the **Connect Memorative Principals** screen, she typed in her own name and Gerry Grove's and waited to see what would happen. The computer took several minutes to produce its response. It said:

There are 16,794 hyperlink(s) connecting 'Teresa Ann Simons' to 'Gerry/Gerald Dean Grove'. Display? Yes/No.

Teresa found some Post-it notes in a desk-tidy behind the monitor. She scribbled on one of them, *This computer is in use – please do not touch*, and stuck it in the centre of the screen . . . over the words 'Gerald Dean Grove', and not entirely by accident.

She went through to the reception area, and found Paula standing by the glass door, looking out into the road. There were now five police cars outside the building, and a cordon of officers in front of the main door.

Teresa told Paula what she would like to do, and with an air of preoccupation the young woman typed on her keyboard, and produced a credit-card slip and an access number. Teresa deliberately did not ask what was going on outside; the less she knew about Grove's movements, on this day of virtuality June 3, the better.

Paula had returned to staring through the glass door as Teresa walked through into Cyberville UK, next to reception.

The place was empty, the rows of computer screens all idle.

She went to sit at one of the terminals, and typed in the access code Paula had just given her. After a moment, a welcome screen appeared.

Teresa logged on to the website for the *Abilene Lone Star News*, and within a few seconds the newspaper's home page appeared. She glanced through it, then clicked on the icon for the archive.

She typed in the date: June 4, the day after this, the day after this one eight months ago. It was illogical: how could she look into the archived files of a newspaper that would not be published until the next day? It was another test of historical certainty against virtuality. If she was here, really here, time-travelled back to Bulverton on June 3, then of course what she was trying would not be allowed. But Teresa was certain that nothing any more was real, not real in the way she used to mean it. Just real enough.

Real-enough reality was confirmed: the facsimile front page of the *Abilene Lone Star News* of June 4 came into view, the graphic image scanning slowly from the top.

First came the title of the newspaper. Then the black headline, inch-high capitals, spreading over two lines: MASS SHOOTING AT KINGWOOD'S NORTH CROSS MALL. Text started appearing with three bylines: the terse, excited words put together by the team of reporters assigned to the story. A few inches down, set into the text in an outlined block, was the Arkansas mugshot of Aronwitz.

The image scanned quickly into view.

It was the face of Gerry Grove.

Back at the on-line database terminal, Teresa removed her Post-it note, clicked on **No** to the question about displaying the 16,794 hyperlinks, and cleared the screen. Then she connected her name with Grove's once more, interested to see how the exponential growth had proceeded. A few more minutes went by. Then it said:

There are 73,788 hyperlink(s) connecting 'Teresa Ann Simons' to 'Gerry/Gerald Dean Grove'. Display? Yes/No.

She clicked on **No**. She typed in her name and Andy's instead, and in almost instant response the computer said:

There are 1 hyperlink(s) connecting 'Teresa Ann Simons' to 'Andy/Andrew Wellman Simons'. Display? Yes/No.

She clicked on **Yes**, and the name of the scenario in Kingwood

City came into view. She cancelled it, knowing that that was not the one she wanted.

She now knew what she had to do. She typed in Andy's name again, and her own. This time, though, she called herself 'Teresa Ann Gravatt/Simons'. The computer said:

There are 23 hyperlink(s) connecting 'Teresa Ann Gravatt/ Simons' to 'Andy/Andrew Wellman Simons'. Display? Yes/No.

Teresa clicked on **Yes**, and with the list in front of her began constructing the remainder of her life.

CHAPTER 38

Teresa came in at night: she had always remembered it happening during the day. Her memories were exact, but apparently in error. The discovery frightened her because it made her think, inevitably, that what she was doing had gone wrong from the outset. She paused in the street, trying to decide whether to abort the scenario before it went any further, go back and check the preparations she had made, or to go on with it, and see what transpired.

While she stood there undecided, a door opened in the large building behind her, and a shaft of electric light played across the concrete. A young man stepped out, pulling a thick leather jacket round his shoulders. With his fists in his pockets, and his elbows sticking out, he strode past her.

'Good evening, ma'am,' he said, noncommittally, not really looking at her.

'Hi,' Teresa replied, then turned in shock and surprise to stare at him as he walked off into the night. It was her father, Bob Gravatt.

He passed under a streetlight, and she saw his close-shaved head, his round ears, his thickening neck, the roll of fleece visible at the neck of his jacket. He walked to a pickup truck, climbed in and drove away.

Teresa went into the barracks building, and climbed a flight of concrete steps. It was a communal staircase, with doors leading off landings to individual apartments. On the top floor she came to a brown-painted door that faced into the stairwell. A piece of card, inscribed in her father's square lettering, carried his name: *S/S R.D. Gravatt.* Cautiously, she pushed the door open. A short corridor ran towards the kitchen at the far end. Music from a radio could be heard from this, and the sound of kitchen utensils in use.

The temptation to walk down and see her mother was almost impossible to resist, but Teresa knew that it would lead necessarily to her aborting the scenario and having to start again. She had set up a chain of contiguity, and she was reluctant to break it so early. Instead, then, she turned into the first room on the right of the corridor, which she knew was her parents' bedroom.

A small girl stood there, next to a plain wooden chair in the centre of the room. An automatic handgun, instantly recognized by Teresa as a .32-calibre Smith & Wesson, lay on the chair. The child was facing a large mirror, the size of a door, attached to the wall opposite the double bed.

A mirror, a real mirror!

The little girl's reflection stared back at herself.

'Look what I've got,' said seven-year-old Teresa, and she picked up the handgun in both hands, straining to lift it.

Teresa gasped in horror at the speed with which this happened. She had no time to speak, only to make a futile grabbing action towards the gun. The movement distracted the little girl, who jerked around in surprise, and somehow those tiny hands managed to pull the sensitized trigger. Teresa ducked as the gun went off – a shattering explosion in the confines of the room – and saw the mirror on the wall smash into a dozen crazed pieces. The gun flew out of the child's hands, crashing on the floor. The pieces of broken mirror slid heavily to the floor, revealing the dirty wooden board that had been behind the glass.

'Tess?!'

From the other end of the apartment there came the sound of something heavy and metallic being dropped, then footsteps rushing down the corridor towards her.

Little Teresa was staring in disbelief at the shattered mirror, holding her hurting wrist, her face rigid with shock and fear and pain.

The door burst open, but before her mother appeared Teresa recalled the LIVER mnemonic.

She was in Cleveland, 1962. East 55th Street, outside a bank. She knew what was coming, and there was no need to allow it to happen. Six seconds went by, and the door she was standing next to began to open quickly. LIVER. Two hours' wait for Charles

Dayton Hunter in the dimly lit interior of a San Antonio bar had no more attraction. LIVER.

She was hiding behind a toll-booth at the northern end of a suspension bridge thrown high across a river. She was wearing a bulletproof vest, a hardened helmet and silvered shades. Around her were twenty or thirty other cops dressed identically. They were all carrying rifles of a make she could not identify. A helicopter was moving snappily overhead.

'Who we waitin' for?' Teresa gritted to the man next to her.

'It's Gerry Grove,' the man snarled, spitting a jet of orange tobacco juice. 'He's on the rampage in Bulverton, England, and we gotta stop him, and stop him *now*! There he is, boys! He's comin' our way!'

With several of the others, Teresa took up position in the narrow roadway that ran between two of the toll-booths. The other cops disposed themselves similarly. A man was running down the centre of the carriageway towards them. At intervals he loosed off a stream of bullets at passing vehicles, causing them to skid and crash. One caught fire, and rolled slowly backwards down the incline towards the booths, leaving a trail of burning oil.

From the helicopter came a loudly amplified voice, screeching down at the gunman from above:

'We know you're in there, Grove! Throw down your weapon or weapons, and come out with your hands up! Let the hostage—'

Gerry Grove rolled on his back, took aim, and pumped a dozen bullets into the belly of the helicopter. There was a mighty explosion, and shattered glass, engine housing and rotor blades flew in all directions.

'Let's get him, boys!' yelled the police captain.

With the others, Teresa raised her rifle and started to fire. A deafening fusillade roared out. Grove stood his ground with a calm expression on his face, firing back with deadly effect. In quick succession, policemen were thrown violently backwards by the impact of his bullets.

Teresa, staring at the man, said aloud, 'That's not Grove!'

She took off her shades to see better, then removed her helmet and shook out her long black tresses. She stepped forward. The man they had called Gerry Grove stared at her in amazement.

He was not Grove but Dave Hartland, Amy's brother-in-law. Shit, thought Teresa. I'm wasting a lot of time on this! LIVER.

'What?' said Teresa, as darkness abruptly fell.

She was in Bulverton Old Town on a cold winter's morning. It was her first full day in England, and she had gone for a walk to see the place. A frisson of recognition ran through her; recognition not from now, as she returned via the hyperlinked scenario, but from then. Why had she felt so at home here? It could hardly matter now. She was impatient to get on. LIVER.

She was in a hotel room, late one afternoon, daylight fading. A woman sat at a laptop computer that rested on a small working surface jutting out from one wall. She was typing slowly, and she looked tired. Her shoulders sagged. Teresa thought, This is how my life slipped away, trying to figure out the problems created by others, trying to investigate, detect, make sense of chaos. The woman stopped typing, pressed her hands down on the work surface, beginning to stand up; she looked ill and exhausted. She was about to turn, and would see herself there, so Teresa recalled the LIVER mnemonic and slipped away.

She was in Al's Happy Burgabar, standing by the brightly lit salad bar. The restaurant was full of families, and a cheerful noise filled the huge room. Teresa remembered the fruitless hours she had spent trying to thwart Sam Wilkins McLeod. She thought, And this is how the rest of my life slipped away, drifting in extreme reality. A movement in the parking lot, glimpsed through the plate-glass window, caught her eye, and she saw a pick-up truck parking in a row of cars. The driver took down a rifle from the gun rack. Teresa remembered the LIVER mnemonic.

She was in Bulverton, June 3, a hot day, brilliant sunshine. On the sidewalk outside the White Dragon. A car had collided with a bollard on the traffic island, while the driver slumped over his steering wheel with blood flooding out of a head wound. Gerry

Grove was on the other side of the road, carrying a rifle in both hands at chest height. He kept working the action, firing at anyone he saw. Teresa could see three people lying in the road. Grove saw her, turned the rifle towards her. Teresa stepped back in horror, but at that moment an elderly man rushed out of the door of the hotel, and yelled something at the gunman. Grove immediately fired several shots at the man, who fell back with blood spurting from his face. A stray bullet slammed into one of the large windows of the bar, shattering it and throwing the broken pieces inside. Again, Grove was turning towards her, so Teresa ducked away, hurrying towards the open door of the hotel. An elderly woman, covered in blood, was standing there, half blocking the way. 'Is Jim . . . ?' she said softly. Teresa pushed past her as Grove opened fire, throwing the woman to the floor, shrieking and dying. Teresa recalled LIVER.

A bank in Camden, New Jersey; a university campus in Austin, Texas. Both filled her with remembered horrors. São Paulo, Brazil, a knife fight in a salsa club; Sydney, Australia, a young drug addict running amok; Kansas City, Missouri, the McLaughlin siege . . . I should have realized that not all these would be relevant. My life is slipping away from me, as before it did, while I never saw how pointless it was. LIVER.

It was a blisteringly hot day, and the Duke Ellington Orchestra was on the radio playing 'Newport Up'. Teresa backed the Chevy station wagon away from the sidewalk, did a U-turn, and drove south along 30th Street. She eased herself more comfortably on the wide bench seat, and glanced up into the rear-view mirror, straining to see herself. Along the soft old bench seat, on the passenger side, was an elderly black woman. Her face was full of mild concern.

'Hi, Elsa!' Teresa said aloud, smiling across at her. 'What's doing?'

'I do what you want to do, honey.'

'Do you know where we're going?'

'I do what you want to do, honey.'

'Well, I want to tell you, I'm trying to find my husband. I've got to work towards him. I call it contiguity, where these stories overlap. It was you who showed me that, out there on the highway, when we drove towards the mountains and the landscape flattened out and we never reached the edge. Do you want to do that again, Elsa?'

'I do what you want to do, honey.'

'You don't know anything about this, do you, Elsa?'

'I do what . . .'

They rounded a corner between two hills, and as the road straightened out again they saw that a police roadblock lay ahead, with cops crouching down behind their cars. They were pointing their guns into the distance. Teresa said, 'It was along this road! Not the other! I've been going the wrong way!'

She slowed a little, and glanced again at the old lady sitting across from her. She was grinning, beating her fingers lightly against the dash in time with the music.

Teresa slowed even more, then steered carefully between the two police units. One of the cops shouted at them, and waved his arms. Ahead, a blue Pontiac had come into sight.

'You know what to do here, Elsa?'

'I do what you want to do, honey.'

'I'm going to leave you now. I love you, Elsa. Take care!'

She was in Eastbourne Road, Bulverton, June 3. Hot day of blood and broken glass, and Gerry Grove still on the loose. A kid screaming in a car, with his parents lying dead or wounded in the front seats. The engine was still running. The kid was pointing upwards, towards the roof of one of the buildings beside the road. There were scaffolding poles up there, surrounding the chimney stack and the tiles by the roof's ridge. A man's foot had been caught in a joint of the scaffolding as he tumbled backwards from his work. His leg was bare where his trouser-leg had ridden up towards his knee, but no more of him was visible. The child kept shouting, 'On the roof! *There's a man on the roof!*' A middle-aged woman with greying hair stood in the entrance to an enclosed alleyway that ran between two of the buildings, half shadowed. The child was screaming to her, imploring her to help, or at least just to look at the man on the roof. Grove was somewhere close at hand, firing at random. Teresa recalled the LIVER mnemonic.

She was following a gendarme on night patrol in the immigrant quarter of the city of Lyon; it was January 10, 1959. No time for this. LIVER. She was with Sergeant Geoffrey Verrick, a uniformed traffic policeman, passenger in a patrol car – LIVER. She was in the cramped rear seat of an open-top car, steering through the curves of Highway 2, north of Los Angeles, through the mountains . . . Teresa was impatient to get on, she should have researched this better, she had been in such a damned hurry to get to Andy—

LIVER.

She was standing in a long room, unused but for a small film set at one end. It had been made to look like a western saloon bar. A young woman, dressed as a cowgirl, wriggled uncomfortably in clothes that were obviously too tight.

A woman carrying a powder puff stepped through the ring of lights.

Teresa walked past the set and out through the door that led to the showers. At the far end of a narrow passageway was one of those emergency exits with a steel bar that had to be pushed down. Teresa pressed hard on the bar, but the door seemed to be stuck. She put her weight on it, and in a moment it grated open.

A small enclosed yard was outside, piled with black plastic garbage sacks, crates of brown bottles, and bales of paper bound up with wire. Traffic roared by somewhere close at hand, but out of sight.

Teresa retraced her steps along the passageway, opening every door that she passed, finding only small unused offices or closets. She saw a flight of steps leading down, and at the bottom there was another barred emergency exit. When she pushed this open, she emerged into the dry blazing heat of Arizona. The immense sky exploded into being.

* * * SENSH * * *

She looked back. Behind her was no trace of the door she had just walked through. She was in untamed scrubland, the gravelly ground littered with rocks of all sizes. A giant saguaro cactus stood a few feet away, looming over her; Teresa had never been so close to one before, and stared up at it in awe. The dry heat made her throat hurt, and the sun made the top of her head burn.

There was a paved road a short distance away, and parked on

304

the side was a white open-top Lincoln Continental. The driver was leaning across the front seat, waving and beckoning to her. Teresa walked quickly towards the car, wary of turning her ankle on the loose rocks.

'Hello!' said the driver, in a British accent. 'You want to go and look at Monument Valley with me?'

It was the young woman she had seen on the set, still dressed in her cowgirl costume.

'You're Shandy, aren't you?' Teresa said, realizing that they had never been face to face before.

'Yes. How do you know that?'

'I'm Teresa Simons, and I'm glad to meet you.'

* * * SENSH * * *

'Get in the car, Teresa. Let's get to know each other. Hey, isn't it hot? You want to loosen some of those clothes? Me, I'm just crazy about the heat. Phew!' She pulled at the top of her shirt, and with the sound of ripping velcro she opened it all the way down. Her barely restrained breasts popped into sight. 'Let's go somewhere, and—'

'Listen, this isn't going to work, Shandy,' Teresa said.

She looked ahead, and saw the road leading in a more or less straight line across the desert floor, the stunning, magnificent rocky buttes rising on each side.

'Is this your first time?'

'I got to go. I'm sorry.'

'I've got a friend called Luke. He'd love to meet you.'

'No, Shan. Maybe we can do this some other time.'

'Whatever you want,' Shandy said, pouting and looking straight ahead down the desert road.

'Yeah, I got to go,' said Teresa. She recalled the LIVER mnemonic.

* * *   You have been flying SENSH Y'ALL   * * *
* * *   Fantasys from the Old West   * * *
* * * Copyroody everywhere – doan even THINK about it!! * * *

She kept forgetting about that, but didn't have the energy to kill the music. She heard it through, until at last it faded.

A young woman was sitting at one of the tables in the picnic area, with plastic cups and plates, scraps of food, and several toys spread all about. She was laughing, and her child was running around on the grass, wrapped up in his game.

Teresa was standing at the edge of the clearing, but she stepped back quickly behind a tree. Gerry Grove lurched into view, the gun in his hand. He raised it with a deliberate, wide swinging motion of his hand, then cocked it, working the mechanism three or four more times, relishing the sound.

The noise made the woman turn towards him. She saw the gun levelled at her, and panicked. She shouted in terror to her child, trying to twist round on the heavy log, to get across to the little boy, but she seemed paralysed by her fear. The boy, thinking it was still a game, dashed away from her. The woman's voice became a hoarse roar, then, after she had sucked in her breath, she was incapable of further sound.

Teresa saw that Grove still didn't know how to hold or aim a gun. He held it at arm's length, pointing at the terrified woman, the weapon wavering slightly in his grasp.

This time, Teresa thought, I'm not going to show him how to do it properly.

Grove fired! The gun recoiled back in his hand, and Rosalind Williams screamed in terror. She ducked down, rushing across the clearing floor towards her child. Grove fired at her again. The gun bucked in his hand, this time apparently twisting his wrist. While Rosalind Williams scooped up her little boy in her arms, Grove held his gun arm against his stomach and leaned over it in pain. Crouching low, holding her screaming boy at an awkward angle, Mrs Williams scrambled past him, heading for the road.

Grove tried firing again, but his gun arm was obviously hurting and the weapon did not discharge. He transferred it to his left hand, took hurried aim at Mrs Williams, fired again. Once more, the recoil made the gun jerk in his hand. The woman escaped through the trees, clutching her child.

Giddy with relief, Teresa breathed in deeply, letting it out with a sob. Grove heard the noise and turned towards her. She was not making any more effort to hide.

'Who the fuck are you?' he said.

She began to laugh; she felt the madness of relief rising in her, and she spluttered and coughed, doubling up.

'I'll fucking kill you, you stupid bitch!' Grove shouted.

'You couldn't plug the side of a barn!' she yelled at him, thinking of a moment, centuries before, on a shooting trip with her dad, him yelling at her when for once she missed the target. Hi, she had said to her dad as he passed her on his way out of the living quarters. The last word she ever spoke to him? Hi Dad, you got me into all this, you gun-happy old bastard. She wished she'd said more while she'd had the chance. She was getting hysterical.

'Shut the fuck up!' Grove screamed at her, and let off a wild shot with his left hand.

'Don't ever say that to me, you creep,' she said, then recalled the LIVER mnemonic.

She was in a utility yard, in stifling heat, surrounded by cops. The tall side of the mall building loomed over them, casting little shade. One of the cops noticed her.

'Stand back, ma'am!' he said at once, raising his arms. 'You're in danger there! Please leave this area at once!'

'FBI,' Teresa said simply, and flicked her ID at him.

'Sorry, ma'am,' said the cop, evidently startled. 'But we have an armed suspect in there, and—'

'That's OK. Get back under cover. Is Agent Simons here with you?'

'You best speak with the Captain, ma'am.'

Teresa backed off quickly. She was trying to remember which way Andy had gone, after leaving the mall administrator. She hurried away, following the side of the building. Ahead of her, Andy let himself out of a small service door. He was carrying his gun. Before continuing he quickly cased all directions. He saw her at once, and raised his gun.

'Andy!' she shouted.

'Tess! What in hell are you doing here?'

'For God's sake, Andy!' She rushed towards him, wanting to hold him more than she had ever wanted anything in her life.

'I'm on a case, Tess,' he said, touching her arm with quick affection, but brushing her aside. 'You want to hang around here for a while, and we'll talk later?'

'Andy, you're in danger! Don't go on with this!'

He looked sharply at her. He said, 'Shit, how the devil you get down here to Texas?'

He strode on in sudden rage at her, heading back towards the utility yard.

Teresa said, 'Andy, this isn't your case. You're just liaising with the police. Let them finish it. That's their job.'

'I'm on assignment. Wait here!'

He thrust her back and away from him, and stepped round the corner into the yard. At that moment, someone shouted through a bullhorn:

'Freeze, Aronwitz! Throw down your weapon!'

Teresa darted round behind Andy, and collided with his back. He lurched slightly, and Aronwitz/Grove noticed the movement. He was standing on a slightly raised shelf of concrete, one of the outlet ducts where service trucks collected their loads. His gun hung loosely in his right hand. He saw the huge encirclement of armed police, crouching down, ready with their guns. Looking at Andy, he made a circling motion with his gun, a deliberate, wide swinging of the arm. He cocked the weapon, the click audible in every part of the yard.

Andy stood frozen. Teresa watched in terror as Grove levelled the gun at Andy, holding it one-handed at full extent.

He fired, and the gun bucked back in his hand. The bullet went past, missing Andy by several feet.

Grove died instantly in the explosion of police bullets that followed.

'Tess, don't you *ever* follow me on an assignment again. Why in hell did you do that? You know what we agreed. We never work together.'

'Andy, you were going to die.'

'No way! You saw how that hairball handled a gun. He was just a kid.'

'Just a kid who'd killed a lot of people.'

'He was no threat to me.'

Andy Andy Andy. How do I tell you? How will you ever know? What's the point?

She wanted to hold him, have him, roll him on the ground, but instead he was justifiably furious, this big angry man, humiliated by her presence, not knowing what he had missed, never ever going to know.

They got to his car and were about to drive off when Andy's partner, Danny Schneider, turned up in the parking lot.

''Scuse me, I gotta work,' Andy said grimly, and left the car to go over to talk with Danny. Danny, seeing her there, nodded politely to her. Andy stood with Danny a long time, over by the car, talking in the sun, pointing this way and that, a lot of nodding. Danny wrote something in his notebook.

Andy, I had to do this. Andy, how do I tell you? Fuck it, Andy! I saved your goddamn life!

But she loved to see him, loved his big old body and the way he held his funny head, resting a hand loosely against his side, sometimes making amusing gestures when he spoke. He and Danny had worked together for fifteen years, knew each other as well as any two straight men ever could. Andy and Teresa sometimes made jokes about Danny: he'd go and live with Danny and his wife, if Teresa ever left him.

Maybe he should do that now, Teresa thought, looking at the man she loved in the bleaching glare of the sun.

Andy Andy Andy . . . stop this. Come here!

In the end he did, and he climbed into the car and started the engine.

'I'll drop you off where you want to be,' he said, not looking at her. 'We'll talk about this tomorrow. I'm going back to Abilene, and I'll have to put in a report. Too many country cops saw what you did, and I've got a project to defend.'

'Andy, don't do this by the goddamn book. I saved your life.'

'Hell, you didn't.'

'Hell, I did. That wacko was going to kill you.'

'Get real, Tess.'

She laughed, a short sardonic noise. 'Get real, you say!'

'Yeah, we'll do all this later. I got to get back to Abilene, right now. This mess isn't over yet.'

'No it isn't.'

He swung the car round and drove off, squealing his tyres on the hot tarmac of the parking lot. The car bounced and bottomed out with a noisy underside scrape on the steep exit to the road, and as they headed down towards the freeway Teresa stared around, glorying in the endless detail of this boring Texas town: the supermarkets, the steak restaurants, the plazas, the multiplex movie houses, the office stationery warehouses, the malls, the car rental offices, the filling stations, the flower sellers at every main intersection, the shacklike houses, the bug exterminators, the hamburger joints, the thinning trees, the broken soil of plots cleared for development, the scrubby grassland, the unending road. Finally they hit Interstate 20 and joined the unknowing traffic, cruising sedately into the west, the sun beating down on them. They drove along through the unchanging scenery, Andy turned on the radio, and there was country music. All you can pick up around here, he said. He always said that when he was away from base. He liked country music, really. The first track finished; another segued in, a song about love and betrayal and men with guns; Andy muttered about country music all sounding alike, goddamn steel guitars, and switched to another station; Stevie Wonder came on with one of his old hits. Remembering a drive years ago, Andy and she when first in love, Philadelphia to Atlantic City, listening to Stevie singing in the night, Teresa reached across and gripped Andy's hand, wanting to cry, wanting to hold him.

Andy pulled his hand away.

'Where do you want me to drop you?' he said brusquely.

'Anywhere you like. I guess it doesn't matter.'

'You want me to leave you here? On the side of the highway?'

'As good a place as any.'

'Then what do you plan to do?'

Andy, you're going with me. None of this is real. I can't tell you that, and you'd never believe it, but we are at the edge, where reality ends. Where's Abilene? You're going to ask me that in a minute. We've been driving for half an hour, and those cars in front haven't changed, or those behind, and Abilene is no nearer. We'll never get there, because Abilene isn't in the scenario. Not even bolted on by a computer geek. The road goes on and on, to the edge, to where it runs out of memory. We can't go there, because at the edge there is nothing more.

He braked the car, still angry with her. It hauled over to the side of the road, swirling dust around them. The Stevie Wonder track died away; three quiet chords then silence. The rest of the traffic continued to sweep by on the interstate. There was no noise from the tyres or engines.

'This the place you want to be?' he said.

'No, Andy.'

'Then what? What do you want? Where do you want to be?'

Andy Andy Andy.

'Finland,' she said, and recalled the LIVER mnemonic.

She was naked, and Andy was on top of her. His strong hairy body touched and embraced her everywhere, leg sliding between hers, pressing gently into her cleft, caressing her with great weight and a wonderful deftness. His hand rested on her breast, and his fingers lovingly teased her nipple. His mouth lingered on hers, and their tongues played lightly against each other. She could smell his hair, his body. Stretched full-length they just about filled the row of three cushioned seats, but whenever they shifted position their elbows and hips and knees knocked roughly against the hard undersides of the arm-rests, which were raised erect to make this temporary couch.

As Andy slipped into her, pushing and thrusting, she craned back and started to turn, moving over so that Andy rolled to her side, facing her. She braced herself against the wall of the aircraft. The oval window was by her head, and she moved around, turning her face a little more with every thrust he made. Soon she could see through the strengthened glass, down towards the ground, where the trees and lakes were moving deliriously by. The great turbine engines roared, and the low evening sun glinted off the wing. The aircraft banked, turning to and fro, swooping low over the lakes, following the winding courses of rivers, its nose lifting to take them across the ridges of mountains, round and round, endlessly on, nothing but trees and water, green and silver, reflecting the light, soaring through the placid air, out to the extremes where all memory ends and life begins anew.

AFTERWORD BY JOHN CLUTE

Christopher Priest, for many years now, has made fools of critics. Possibly he meant to do so, though almost certainly he did not. But, wittingly or not, he has developed, over the thirty years of his career, into the kind of writer who cannot be fixed into place, which is the best way to discombobulate those whose jobs it is – as critics, academics, book page editors – to sort the world of literature into neat categories. Nothing makes one of these salaried savants more nervous than a writer – like the man who wrote *The Extremes*, which at one and the same time is a metaphysical thriller, a science fiction novel, and a very extreme non-genre study in the nature of stress – who will not sit still to be branded.

So there is something treacherous about Christopher Priest, a science fiction writer who is not one; a genre-hopper whose voice and concerns are absolutely distinctive, whatever the surface bent of the tale; a compulsive storyteller long obsessed by the unreliability of all stories and storytellers; a late modernist craftsman as artistically competent as (for example) his near contemporaries Martin Amis or Ian McEwan, but palpably more knowledgeable about the genres Amis and McEwan frequently invoke in their books than they are.

He does not fit.

He does not Make Beseech to Booker by writing tame sensitive mainstream tales in Oxbridge Pidgin about marital angst in the chattering classes, but he was selected as one of the 'Best of Young British Novelists' in 1983, 15 years after he began his career; he won the James Tait Black Memorial Prize for *The Prestige* (1995), the ninth of his eleven novels to date, but that intensely fine tale was conspicuously under-reviewed by the establishment press.

Christopher Priest's early years were unremarkable, as far as any record might depose. He was born in Cheadle, Cheshire, in 1943, slipping into the world just ahead of the first swell of boomers. He was educated at Warehousemen & Clerks. He had a dull job for a while. He became a professional writer in 1968, and has remained one. He has lived in London, Wiltshire, Devon, Essex; and lives now in Hastings, with his wife – writer Leigh Kennedy – and twin children.

What made him a ringer in the tower of establishment art was probably the company he kept in the early years. He consorted with science fiction fans – indeed, reader, he was one. And he first came to attention as a not-quite-fully-matriculated member of the writers associated with *New Worlds* magazine in the late 1960s, where a radical dismantling of science fiction from within had been engaged upon by Michael Moorcock and others. Priest still manifests a *New World*-ish dis-ease: with science fiction itself; and with the storylines of our official culture. This dis-ease, because it makes internal exiles out of those it inspires, is a proud legacy of those days; Christopher Priest, who does not suffer fools, and who does not trust the storylines of the world, is a true heir of the best place of the 1960s. But *New Worlds* soon suffered heat death; Christopher Priest continued to write science fiction, publishing his first novels, typically enough, with the eminently non-sf publishers, Faber and Faber. *Inverted World* (1974), *The Space Machine* (1976), *A Dream of Wessex* (1977) and *The Affirmation* (1981) are the best of these early books. *The Affirmation*, last of his Faber books, marked a deepening of Priest's central concern with the relationship between story and reality, between the teller of the tale and the story that tells the teller. Storytellers lie (but when?); stories lie (and are sometimes not even told by the teller who claims to be telling them); genres are packs of lies (but, like the tarot, can unpack truths previously unimagined): in the end, they all tell the only kind of truth that matters at all. They make meaning. Christopher Priest's tales may range widely in their plots and locations; but at heart, they are explorations in the generation of meaning.

All the novels after *The Affirmation* – *The Glamour* (1984), *The Quiet Woman* (1990), *The Prestige* and *The Extremes* – subject their readers to these increasingly artful lessons in epistemological seachange. *The Extremes* – which along with its immediate predecessor is one of the most ungovernably *readable* novels written in the past half century – plunges therefore into the same maelstrom, but a maelstrom with a new twist. The twist is Virtual Reality.

It is as though Christopher Priest had arranged his interests and constructed his career over half a lifetime just in case something like Virtual Reality came along. The problems that VR so crudely foregrounds – what is real, how do you tell, where does the story take over from the told, when is 'reality' less important than the tale that tells it – are problems he has been secreting solutions to for all these years. We arrived at the labyrinth of now and find Christopher Priest awaiting us, smiling. He hands us his new book.

The Extremes starts with mirrors and serial crimes, moves to twin cities oceans apart, incorporates police procedural riffs and *anti-roman* caesuras into a storyline which closes like a pincer on the just and unjust. There is hardly a shout in the book, it is quiet, or at any rate seems quiet till you go to bed and fall asleep and have your first dream; the quiet of *The Extremes* is the quiet of ice before the break.

John Clute